COLT

Previous Books by Georgina Gentry

Cheyenne Captive
Cheyenne Princess
Comanche Cowboy
Bandit's Embrace
Nevada Nights
Quicksilver Passion
Cheyenne Caress
Apache Caress
Christmas Rendezvous (anthology)
Sioux Slave
Half-Breed's Bride
Nevada Dawn
Cheyenne Splendor
Song of the Warrior
Timeless Warrior
Warrior's Prize
Cheyenne Song
Eternal Outlaw
Apache Tears
Warrior's Honor
Warrior's Heart
To Tame a Savage
To Tame a Texan
To Tame a Rebel
To Tempt a Texan
To Tease a Texan
My Heroes Have Always Been Cowboys (anthology)
To Love a Texan
To Wed a Texan
To Seduce a Texan
Diablo: The Texans
Rio: The Texans

COLT

The Texans

GEORGINA GENTRY

ZEBRA BOOKS
Kensington Publishing Corp.

ZEBRA BOOKS are published by

Kensington Publishing Corp.
119 West 40th Street
New York, NY 10018

ISBN-13: 978-1-61793-531-2

Printed in the United States of America

*This book is dedicated to Meredith Bernstein,
the world's best literary agent, who has handled
my business for over twenty-two years without a contract,
just a handshake deal. I have never regretted this
partnership because besides being beautiful,
she's a tough negotiator for her clients.*

*As our local cowboys would say,
"I'm much obliged, Meredith."*

Prologue

Summer 1852
The Texas plains

Abruptly Hannah felt something was wrong. She paused in dropping a sand plum in her basket and wiped at a drop of sweat that ran down her breasts under her faded blue gingham dress.

No one else seemed to sense anything. On the other side of the creek, the others continued to pick wild plums, the midsummer heat making dizzying waves in her vision as she watched them. It was just a smattering of people from the settlement out here picking today, mostly women, an elderly person or two, and half a dozen small children.

Hannah had crossed the creek because she was tall and there were a few bigger bushes with plump fruit that only she could reach. Now she smiled at the children and stood on tiptoe in her worn shoes to reach another plum. If they could buy a little sugar, these would make good jam for the winter.

Her smile turned to a frown as she watched her husband, Luther, leaning on his rifle. Guarding gave him an excuse not to help with the work, she thought. He glared at her and motioned to her to get back to work. Last night's bruises still ached and she felt old at the age of eighteen. Hannah gritted her teeth and returned to picking plums, hating Luther for the way he treated her. She had run away from an abusive stepfather at fifteen and had married Luther because he seemed to be so kind, and she had known little kindness in her life. How wrong she had been. Out here on the Texas plains, there was no place to run. It must be fifty miles to the nearest town and she had no money and could barely read and write.

Well, Luther might break her body, but he could not break her heart or her spirit, she vowed, thinking of their little son. Somehow she would survive and leave Luther. Right now, she brushed back a lock of blond hair and lifted her basket.

Then she realized what it was that had given her pause: the silence. The birds and all the insects had stopped their singing and it was deathly quiet. The other people didn't seem to notice; they all had their heads down, intent on the fruit in the straggly bushes.

Very slowly, Hannah turned to look over her shoulder and her heart almost stopped. On the nearby rise, a group of Comanche warriors sat on paint ponies watching the whites.

"Indians! Comanches!" Hannah shouted and started through the weeds, tripped over her basket, and fell, the ripe fruit crushed under her weight and staining the ragged blue of her dress.

Now the birds and insects exploded into a mass of noise as the Comanches galloped through the dry grass, coming down off the knoll. Already the other people were running for the safety of the settlement, little children crying, women screaming. Hannah heard the pounding of hooves behind her, but she didn't look back. She was only concerned with getting across the creek. The Indian war cries rang in her ears as they gained on her.

"Luther! The gun!" she shouted, but her cowardly husband had already dropped the rifle and was trampling over one child after another as he ran for the safety of the settlement. Had she expected any better from him? If she could reach that gun, she'd protect the retreat—she knew how to shoot. But then as she crossed the creek her foot caught the ragged hem of her dress and she tripped and went to her knees.

Now the mounted Indians surrounded her and she struck out at them with her bare hands. "Luther! Help me!" she screamed, but her husband only paused momentarily and then kept running, outracing the women and children to get to the safety of the cabins, where other men were now firing at the invading savages. If she could just make it to the cabins, she thought, but her way was blocked by screaming, painted warriors who rode around her, blocking her path.

She'd heard the horror stories about women captured by the Comanches and she'd go down fighting before she'd let them take her. Even as she thought that, the leader of the war party, an ugly, grinning devil, reached down and grabbed her arm, lifting her to his dancing paint horse. He smelled of grease and smoke and old sweat, and she fought him, while he grinned at her with yellow teeth. Then he struck her, hard.

She felt the pain, so familiar from a man's hands, and tasted blood as he hit her again. She must not pass out or she could not fight. Wasn't that what always enraged Luther? The fact that she fought back instead of taking his beating meekly like a proper wife should? Somewhere in the distance, she was vaguely aware that men still fired from the settlement and most of the plum pickers had made it to safety. Only one or two lay in the grass not moving.

Her captor shouted a command in a language she did not understand and then the group took off at a gallop, away from civilization, away from safety, one of the warriors brandishing Luther's dropped rifle.

She had to get away; this was her last chance or face terrible slavery or torture at the hands of the Comanche. Blood ran from her mouth as she struggled, but the ugly warrior hit her again and she could fight no longer as she hung from his saddle. The war party galloped away across the plains and she realized she was a captive.

Chapter 1

Spring 1856
Southwest Texas

Second Lieutenant Colton Prescott reined in his shaggy bay mustang and looked at the fort in the distance. "Well, Rascal," he muttered, "here's our new assignment, Camp Cooper and the Second Cavalry."

With that, he straightened his broad shoulders and urged his mount forward. He hadn't wanted this assignment, but the new fort on this outer limits of Texas civilization needed an officer who knew something about Comanches. Colt knew, all right—hadn't he spent ten years among them?

So he'd been sent to this post on the last fringes of civilization, which didn't look like much, just a few stone buildings, most still under construction. He urged Rascal forward. Lowly privates stared at him as he rode past, then returned to their stone laying.

This place couldn't take a major attack by Indians, Colt thought as he reined in before a stone building and dismounted. But then, Comanches weren't likely to attack a fort; they preferred surprise and small, lightly protected settlements where they could find food, weapons, and horses.

He tied his horse up at the hitching rail, returned the salute of the lean private on duty at the door, who seemed to be staring at Colt's ragged, dusty uniform. In return, Colt eyed the other's bright blue uniform with yellow stripes down the legs. *What a dandy,* he thought. *Must be new issue.* "Is the officer in charge inside?"

The private nodded. "Yes, sir. Major Murphy."

"Private, get my horse some water and feed. We've come a long way."

"Yes, sir." The private opened the door for him, and Colt bent his head to get his lanky frame through the door.

Inside, a lean older man with gray hair and a new uniform looked up. "Yes?"

"Second Lieutenant Colt Prescott reporting for duty." Colt saluted and drew his big frame to attention.

"Oh, yes, we've been expecting you. Sit down, sit down. I'm not much on formality. Would you like a drink?" The superior officer had a slight Irish accent.

"Yes, sir." Colt sank gratefully into a chair and slapped at the dust on his uniform. "Trail dust mighty thick out there and it's a long way from San Antonio."

The major continued to pour drinks, then paused to look out the window. "Saint Mary's blood, is that beast what you rode in on?" He grinned.

"Mustang, sir, great mount for the Texas plains."

The other handed him a tumbler and returned to his desk chair. "Wait 'til you see what we're riding here at Camp Cooper," the major said proudly. "Best thoroughbreds the United States could buy, and all matched. Each company of horses is a different color."

"Hmm." Colt sipped his whiskey. This was the good stuff from back East, not the rotgut he was used to. "Thoroughbred might be all the go back East, but they won't do out here on the plains, sir. They need corn and lots of care. Mustangs can get by on a little grass and a heavy dew."

"Nonsense." The major sipped his whiskey and wiped his mouth. "The Second Cav is the nation's best and newest Cavalry regiment; Secretary of War Davis has seen to that. We've got the latest weapons, too, including those five-shot Colt revolvers."

Colt raised his eyebrows. "Really? I've never seen one, but I've heard about them."

The major reached to hand his weapon across to Colt. "These Texans have been raising a howl about the Indians attacking their farms and ranches."

"Can't blame 'em, sir." Colt examined the pistol with curiosity. "Have you ever seen what's left after an Indian raid?" Colt's mind went back to sights he'd seen: burned buildings, tortured bodies, livestock lying dead with arrows sticking out all over like big pincushions, women carried off. That made him remember a long time ago, a pretty girl on a wagon train. He'd been a small boy then, and the Cheyenne had surrounded them. The girl's name had been Texanna. . . .

"Yes, Lieutenant, the Second Cav has the best of everything: handpicked men, the best new weapons, the latest uniforms. Half of us are here, the rest of the Second Cav is occupying Fort Mason." The major didn't seem to notice that Colt's attention had drifted.

Now Colt came back to the major abruptly and handed over the gun, very aware of how faded and dusty his uniform was. "I see the new yellow stripes down the legs."

The major nodded. "I hope we've got a uniform big enough to fit you and we'll get you a better horse."

"If you don't mind, sir, I like Rascal. We've been through a lot together and I'd just soon ride him."

"Your choice." The major leaned back in his chair and looked Colt over. "You look a little old to still be a second lieutenant. When were you at West Point?"

"I'm thirty-two," Colt said, "and it's a field promotion. I've never been to West Point. Rank has been hard to come by since the Mexican War."

"Don't I know it." Major Murphy snorted. "My wife's very disappointed I haven't made it to general by now."

"You fought in the war?"

"No, I had a desk job so my wife could stay in Philadelphia, which is where she still is." The major looked relieved. "Texas was too wild and uncivilized for her. My daughter came out with me."

"Beggin' your pardon, sir, west Texas is no place for a woman, especially one from back East."

The major chuckled. "Tell that to Olivia. She's headstrong and does what she pleases; we've spoiled her no doubt. I dare say she'll find you intriguing. I hope you dance, Lieutenant?"

"A little," Colt said. "Don't get much time for dancin' out here on the frontier."

Just then, a beautiful, petite, dark-haired girl opened the inner door and peeked out. "Am I interrupting anything, Daddy?"

"Oh, come in, dear. I was just telling the new lieutenant about you."

Colt jumped to his feet, twisting his hat in his hands. She was the most beautiful girl Colt had ever seen and unlike any he'd ever met: petite, with an elaborate upswept hairdo. She wore a very expensive pink percale dress.

The major stood and hugged his daughter. "Lieutenant Prescott, may I introduce my daughter, Olivia?"

Colt's heart skipped a beat and he bowed as the girl curtsied. "How do you do, ma'am?"

"Very well, thank you." Her long eyelashes fluttered over dark eyes. "Goodness gracious, I love your Texas drawl, Lieutenant."

She had the palest, most delicate skin, Colt noted. Colt didn't know what to say to this elegant lady. Although he was well experienced with cheap frontier floozies, he found himself stuttering for an answer.

The major chuckled. "Well, I see you've had the same effect on this Texan you usually have on men, Olivia."

She blushed. "Oh, Daddy. Now you're going to have this young man thinking I'm just terrible."

"Oh no, ma'am, Miss Murphy, not at all." He couldn't stop staring at her.

"Well," the major said, "I guess that about wraps up this meeting, Lieutenant Prescott. We'll talk more later once you get settled. Olivia, would you mind showing the lieutenant to the officers' quarters?"

He found himself stuttering like a schoolboy. "Oh, I wouldn't want to trouble the lady—"

"Not at all. I'd be happy to." The dark eyelashes fluttered again. "Come along, Lieutenant."

Colt felt like a clumsy boy as he saluted the grinning officer and followed his daughter out onto the boardwalk. He picked up his knapsack and stumbled along behind her, trying to think of some brilliant thing to say. Nothing came.

"Cat got your tongue, Lieutenant Prescott?" She glanced back over her shoulder, smiling.

"No, ma'am, I just wasn't expectin' such a charmin' guide in a far outpost such as this."

"It was a long, miserable trip," she complained. "Over seven hundred miles from Jefferson Barracks in Missouri."

"Very brave of you to make it." Colt tried to match his long steps to her small ones.

"I thought Texas would be a bold, exciting adventure." She sounded miffed. "Instead, it's just hot, dirty, and dangerous. Why, Daddy won't even let me ride outside the fort walls without an escort."

"Your father is right," Colt said. "You don't want to be carried off by the Comanche."

They had reached a stone building still under construction, and she stopped and looked up at him. "Why, I've read *Last of the Mohicans* and *The Song of Hiawatha*."

He had no idea what she was talking about. "I don't read much, ma'am. I came up the hard way."

"I just meant I know all about our noble savages."

"I doubt you do, Miss Murphy." Colt frowned down at her. "Most white women carried off are never heard from again or are found scalped and . . ." He started to say "brutally raped," but then remembered he was talking to a lady.

"Goodness gracious, I think it would be an exciting adventure." She turned pouty. "Well, anyway, here's your room." She smiled up at him and he thought he had never seen such a dainty, feminine beauty.

"Thank you for escortin' me, Miss Murphy." He bowed low. "I do hope I'll see you again."

"It was an interesting change to a very dull day," she said. "Do you dance, Lieutenant?"

"Not very well, I'm afraid, and not like the polished gentlemen you're used to."

"Oh, all those boys back in Philadelphia are such prissy dandies, not like Texas men at all."

He didn't know what to say. He stood there feeling awkward. "Well, much obliged for the escort," he said again.

"I'll be happy to show you around the fort, such as there is to see. You'll escort me on a ride, won't you, Lieutenant?"

"Yes, ma'am. One thing I do well is ride. All Texans are almost born on horses."

"I ride well, too, much better than I play the spinet or embroider. I'll be looking forward to it." The petite beauty turned and walked away, Colt staring after her, completely enraptured. He'd never met a back-East lady before. He watched her lift her dainty pink skirt above the Texas dust swirling around her feet. Yes indeedy, he'd be happy to take her riding. Now Colt was happy he'd been sent to Camp Cooper. Olivia was so different from the saloon tarts he was used to.

The next morning, he was called into the major's office. "Well, Lieutenant, did you get settled in?"

"Yes, sir."

"At ease, young man." He poured them both a whiskey. It was a little early for Colt, but he accepted the tumbler. He was beginning to wonder if the major drank too much and why.

The major lit his pipe. "Sorry our accommodations are so sparse. We're still building here, you know."

"I've had much worse, sir. I'm not used to bein' coddled." He thought of the nights sleeping under the stars with one thin blanket, or his years among the Comanche, fighting the icy wind wrapped in a buffalo robe.

"I asked for someone who knew something about Comanche ways." The major gave him a piercing look. "Are you that man?"

"I lived among them as a captive ten years, sir." In fact, he had a scar on his arm from the blood-brother ceremony. Should he tell the officer he was blood brother to Spider, one of the most savage chieftains on the plains?

"Have you heard much about the Second Cav?" The major leaned back in his chair and studied him.

"No, sir."

"We're a new outfit, pride of the country. Secretary of War Jeff Davis has spared no expense in outfitting us with the pick of Cavalry men, the best horses and weapons, and new uniforms. You've looked around, Lieutenant. What do you think?"

"The men seem good enough." Colt shrugged and sipped his drink. He'd rather have a late-morning cup of coffee, but Easterners didn't know how to make coffee anyhow. Texans liked it strong enough to float a horseshoe. "You've got some of the finest thorough-breds I've ever seen."

The major nodded and puffed his pipe. "Best horse-flesh in the country. Big horses that can cover a lot of ground."

"Like I told you before, sir, you'd find mustangs would be better for the Texas plains."

The major snorted. "You mean like that scruffy little beast you rode in on? I was planning on giving you your choice of our fine stock."

"If you don't mind, I'll keep Rascal. After a few chases

across the plains, you see why those fine thoroughbreds won't do. They need too much feed and too much care."

The major laughed. "Saint Mary's blood. We'll see about that. Our assignment out here is to hold back the Comanche. They're playing havoc with these outlying ranches—murder, pillage. Our goal is to drive them farther west, make Texas safe for future settlement. Congress and President Pierce are getting too many complaints from voters in the Lone Star State."

"That's a big order," Colt drawled. "These Comanche live in small bands and can move fast. By the time you get word of an attack, they're already finished and a hundred miles away."

"Well, that's what we're going to try to change." The major sipped his drink. "We're modeled after the French Foreign Legion forces, ready to ride fast and attack, not just sit at forts and wait for the enemy to come to us."

"That might work, sir."

The major ran his hand through his gray hair. "Damned dangerous place, Texas. I really didn't want Olivia to come along, but she's stubborn and willful."

"She's also beautiful." Colt had a sudden vision of the Comanche attacking the camp and what would happen to the petite beauty if Spider or some of his warriors got hold of her. He grimaced.

"What's wrong, Lieutenant?"

"Nothin', sir." He didn't want to share that image with her father. "Miss Olivia is talkin' about going ridin'."

The major snorted. "She doesn't realize how dangerous it is out here, and there's not a man I'd trust to ride with her and protect her. Well, maybe you, Lieutenant."

Colt flushed. "Thank you for your confidence, sir."

"Speaking of women, I know several have been taken captive over the years, that Cynthia Ann Parker and a Mrs. Hannah Brownley about four years ago. What are the chances we'll find them? The back-East newspapers would love that."

Colt shook his head. "Not much, sir. The life in an Indian camp is very rough. They may not even be alive anymore."

"Well, it was just a thought. I keep thinking of anxious loved ones who are almost certainly hoping for a miracle." The major puffed his pipe thoughtfully. "I'll introduce you to Captain Van Smyth and let him take you around and show you the ropes and introduce you to the enlisted men."

"I met Captain Van Smyth at breakfast this mornin'." Colt hadn't liked the captain much; he was too much of a spit-and-polish West Pointer from Boston who didn't seem to know a damned thing about Texas or Indians. His curly yellow hair had been too carefully combed, his mustache was wispy, and his new boots looked polished enough to see your face in them.

"Fine." The major stood up. "Olivia informs me that Captain Van Smyth is an excellent dancer, won the Cotillion trophy back in Boston, I understand. He's younger than you, of course, and hasn't seen any action."

Colt winced. A young, inexperienced officer leading charges against bloodthirsty warriors. But Olivia said he was an excellent dancer. Colt wondered suddenly if he was jealous.

He left most of his whiskey in his tumbler as he walked out of the office. Too much whiskey could destroy a man. Wasn't his own father a prime example of that?

Colt reported to young Captain Van Smyth, who returned his salute. "Glad to have you aboard, Prescott.

We'll watch some of the men drilling on the parade ground, and I'll show you our barns and our camp." His clipped, Boston accent grated on Colt, who was used to the soft drawl of Texans.

"Beggin' your pardon, sir, the camp doesn't seem very well protected."

The young captain gave him a sardonic smile and raised one aristocratic eyebrow. "Oh, now, surely, Lieutenant, you don't think a handful of savages is a threat to an army outpost?"

"You never know what the Comanche will do," Colt snapped. "But one thing I've learned is never to underestimate them."

The pink-faced captain chuckled. "I've yet to see a Comanche, just the few Tonks that hang around camp and beg for scraps or scout for us."

"Don't judge Comanches by Tonkawas," Colt said. "Totally different type of Indian."

They were walking across the parade grounds, and he realized the slight Easterner's uniform had been tailored to fit his trim form. Colt tried not to smirk as they paused to watch the troops drilling.

The captain said, "You sound as if you admire those red savages."

"I respect them." Colt didn't smile. "Best light cavalry in the world."

The captain fingered his mustache and laughed. "We'll see about that. I'm hoping to see some action soon and win some medals. Most of the time, it's just dull and dusty around here, although I've been hoping to take Miss Olivia riding. Let me introduce you to our first sergeant." He turned toward the marching troops and called, "Mulvaney! Front and center!"

"Mulvaney?" Colt watched the wizened old sergeant striding toward them. "Why, I believe I know him."

Mulvaney came to attention and saluted, sporting a big grin.

Colt grinned back as the captain said, "At ease, Sergeant."

"I'll be a sonovagun!" Colt threw his arms around the old Irishman and hugged him. "Long time no see, amigo."

The sergeant grinned up at him. "Haven't seen you, boy, since we left Mexico and we went separate ways."

Colt nodded. "Those were the days. Glad to see our paths have crossed again." He turned to the coldly stern captain. "Mulvaney and I served together back in forty-six in the Mexican War."

"Is that a fact?" The captain looked down his nose at the sergeant. "I don't think it wise to get too familiar with the noncommissioned officers." He turned to go. "Well, good luck and I'll see you at dinner."

"Yes, sir." Colt and the older man saluted, and the captain walked away, leaving the two old friends to visit and remember old times. Finally they broke up. Sarge returned to the troops he was drilling, and Colt, greatly heartened to find an old friend, walked back to his quarters.

The Second Cavalry might be America's pride, Colt thought, but they had a lot of raw recruits led by officers fresh out of West Point. Their first run-in with the battle-hardened plains warriors certainly would be an eye-opening experience for them.

That evening, he sauntered over to the barn to pet Rascal and make sure the orderly was taking good care of the little mustang. "You're gettin' spoiled," he murmured to the scraggly bay horse and scratched its ears. "You're not used to a fine barn, lots of corn, and highfalutin pedigreed stablemates."

Rascal snorted.

Colt laughed. "I don't think much of 'em either, but the major does. We'll have to prove to him that thoroughbreds can't hold a candle to mustangs."

He sauntered slowly back over to his quarters, enjoying the warm night air. Bluebonnets and Indian paintbrush were in bloom in the grass on the outskirts of the camp. It was dusk now and as he rolled a cigarette, he saw a rider coming at full gallop into the camp, rein up before the major's quarters, and jump down, bang on the door, and run inside. *Indian scout*, Colt thought with interest. *Something's up.*

He hadn't had time to finish his smoke before the scout ran out again and the major came outside, shouting orders. The camp began to come alive. Captain Van Smyth ran out of his quarters and hurried over to the major. The two talked, and now the captain looked agitated and excited. He motioned a sentry, and in moments a bugle sounded.

Colt threw away his smoke and stood up. Something interesting was going to happen. Captain Van Smyth strode back to him. "Lieutenant, get Sergeant Mulvaney and form a patrol. The Tonk's spotted a Comanche camp a few miles out. We're finally going to see some action."

Colt's pulse speeded up. "Yes, sir." He took off at a run with mixed feelings. He had many friends among the Comanche, but he and his blood brother Spider were bitter enemies. Colt had not seen him in many years since he'd been banished from the clan for daring to question the young chieftain's brutality toward prisoners.

The night was as black as the devil's heart as the patrol

formed out on the parade ground, and the women and the few Tonks came out to watch the Cavalry leave. Olivia waved a hankie, and Colt started to nod to her, then realized the elegant captain from Boston was nodding and smiling at the beauty.

Oh, so that's the way it is, Colt thought. It was not smart to take a shine to the captain's sweetheart.

But it was Colt she ran up to. "Here, Lieutenant. Here's my hankie. Tuck it in your sleeve like a favor to a knight of old."

Colt took the bit of perfumed lace, aware that now Captain Van Smyth was scowling at him. Just what Colt needed, a superior officer who disliked him intensely, but Colt was so smitten with Miss Olivia, he didn't care. He smiled and nodded to the lady and tucked the hankie in his belt.

The major had come out and was conferring with both the Tonk scout and the snooty captain. Colt was close enough to overhear what was being said and frowned. None of these soldiers knew a damned thing about Indians. That was stuff you learned by hard, brutal experience, things they didn't teach you at West Point.

The captain passed the order to Colt, and he turned to his sergeant, the gruff old soldier, Mulvaney. "Have the men mount, Sergeant."

"Yes, sir." Mulvaney saluted and turned to the troops. "Prepare to mount. Mount and look smart about it, lads."

Colt had already swung up on Rascal. He noted the sideways stares of the troops and the captain smirked. "Lieutenant Prescott, surely you aren't serious."

"Sir?"

"I mean, with all the fine mounts the Second Cav owns, you're riding to battle on that—that donkey?"

Colt heard muted laughter from the men. "Rascal is a mustang, sir. I broke him myself and he'll still be goin' when these fancy thoroughbreds drop."

More muted laughter.

The captain gave Colt a superior snort. "All right, Lieutenant. It's your choice. Give the order to move out."

Colt gave the order to Mulvaney, and the small force started from the parade ground and out the front gate. In the darkness, Colt heard the cicadas beginning their rhythmic chirp and listened to the night birds call. He was always alert to night birds because sometimes they weren't birds at all, but warriors out in the brush passing signals for an ambush.

He rode up next to the captain and the Tonk scout. The Tonk said something in broken English.

"I can't understand half of what he says," Van Smyth complained. "You see if you can understand his gibberish."

Colt addressed the scout in a respectful tone, speaking the scout's own language.

The man looked at him a long moment, respect in his dark eyes, before answering.

The captain snapped, "So you understand their gibberish? I don't know why they don't learn to speak decent English."

"He says the camp is a couple of hours' ride away. We ought to get there when the Comanche are getting ready to bed down."

"Good," the captain grunted. "Then we'll give them a real surprise, split up and surround them."

"Uh, Captain, I'm not sure splittin' up is a good idea. We don't know how many of them there are yet."

"That's what we were taught at the Point." The captain glared at Colt in the moonlight and fingered his wispy light mustache. By the way, Lieutenant, what year did you graduate?"

Colt shook his head. "I've never been out of Texas, sir. Mine is a field commission for service in the Mexican War."

"Humph." Scorn played across the captain's handsome face. "Then let me make the decisions about battle plans, understand?"

Colt took a deep, determined breath. It wasn't wise to conflict with his superior officer, but for the safety of this patrol, he had to try. "Beggin' your pardon, sir, but it was my understandin' that Major Murphy requested me because I had experience against the Comanche."

"I'll have you know I had high marks at the Point, so I doubt he really needed you. By the way, I notice you've already met Miss Olivia Murphy." His tone was seething.

"Just barely," Colt said, then added, "But I intend to deepen my acquaintance."

He heard the captain blow out an angry breath and chided himself. *Don't you have enough conflict with this dandy without goading him? The enemy is the Comanche.*

The captain seemed to get control of himself. "So you know a lot about fighting Indians, do you?"

"Yes, sir. Actually, I wish we didn't have to fight them. They've roamed these plains for hundreds of years, and they aren't gonna give up without a long, bitter struggle."

"They're just savages after all," the captain snapped. "You sound as if you respect them."

"I do," Colt admitted. "After all, it's their land and we're tryin' to push them off of it, send them to reservations to do nothin' but sit around and eat government rations. No real man would do that without a fight."

"But we're going to win," the captain said.

"Eventually, yes." Colt nodded. "In the end, they can't win and maybe they know it, but they won't surrender and give up their way of life without a battle. I wish there was room enough for white ranchers and the Comanches in Texas, but their ways of life collide, so I'll help put them on reservations. It's my job as an officer in the United States Army, but I regret havin' to do it."

"Injun lover!" Captain Van Smyth spat the words out, then nudged his fine black thoroughbred out ahead so he wouldn't have to talk to Colt.

The moon came up then from behind the horizon, throwing weird shadows across the landscape of straggly buffalo grass and cactus.

"Damn it," Colt muttered. The big moon lit the column up so they were easy to see. He said in a terse whisper to the Tonk scout. "How far?"

The Tonk kept riding and nodded. "Maybe when the moon is high overhead."

"I don't like attackin' under a full moon," Colt grumbled. "We need the cover of darkness."

The Tonk scout shrugged. "We take what the gods give."

Colt fell silent, listening to the jingle of bridles and spurs behind him. Here and there a horse snorted or whinnied and they kept riding.

After a while the captain came back to ride beside Colt as the scout ranged out ahead. "Lieutenant, do you think the Tonk might be leading us into a trap?"

Colt made a sound of disgust. "Captain, if you knew anything about Indians, you'd know the Tonks and the Comanche are old enemies. The Comanche think the Tonks are cannibals, and the Tonks scorn the Comanche because they are so savage. If they were to capture our scout alive, they'd torture him for days before they'd kill him. Learn to trust your scouts, Captain, because they know the terrain and the tribes better than you do."

The breeze had picked up. Colt sniffed the air, and about the same time, the scout signaled them.

Captain Van Smyth said, "Lieutenant, give the order to halt."

"We don't need any commands breakin' the stillness, and lettin' the Comanche know we're here," Colt whispered and signaled Mulvaney to halt the troops behind them with a movement of his hand.

The scout rode back and said to Colt what Colt had already sensed from sniffing the wind; there was a camp somewhere just past the rise ahead. The smell of campfires drifted on the air.

Colt said, "Sir, if you'd like, the scout and I will ride ahead and look over the lay of the land."

The Boston captain looked a little nervous. There were beads of sweat on his pink face even though the spring night was cool. "All right."

He was losing his nerve, Colt thought in alarm, probably had never really fired a pistol or a rifle at a live man before. He motioned to the scout, and they dismounted, left their horses, and crept silently through the darkness and hid behind straggly bushes above the Indian camp.

It was late, a few fires still burning, one or two people walking around. Dogs lolled near fires with old men talking and smoking; horses were tied to a picket line on the outskirts of the camp. Thank God the wind was blowing toward the soldiers, Colt thought, or the dogs would have set up a barking alert that there was enemy nearby.

There was something wrong, Colt sensed. There

didn't seem to be many men in the camp, although he couldn't be sure. The younger warriors might be gone hunting or out raiding some luckless, lonely ranch. He signaled the scout and they crept back to the captain.

"Well?" Van Smyth's well-manicured hands were shaking.

"Camp's pretty quiet and there don't seem to be as many men around as there should be," Colt whispered. "If we can run off their horses, they'll be afoot and a Comanche fights best on horseback. We can do a surprise attack and scatter their horses, burn as much of their supplies and weapons as possible."

Captain Van Smyth looked uncertain. This was apparently not something he'd ever studied at West Point. "All right. Lieutenant, give the signal to mount up. We'll take them by surprise and kill as many as possible while we attack."

"They seem to be mostly women and old men," Colt said.

"They're Comanche, aren't they?" the captain challenged. "They kill our women and children on every ranch they attack."

Colt sighed and gave a hand signal to Mulvaney. Mulvaney nodded. The whole patrol was tense, unlike the people in the camp below, who seemed to be settling in for the night.

"Attack!" Captain Van Smyth pulled out his saber and brandished it.

Colt unholstered his pistol instead. A damned saber was no good unless it got down to hand-to-hand fighting.

The soldiers broke into a gallop. In that split second, the Cavalry came up over the rise and down into the Indian camp. Immediately, pandemonium reigned, people running and screaming, soldiers shouting, gunfire echoing, dogs barking, horses rearing and neighing as the patrol rode through the middle of the camp.

Colt took aim and killed a warrior who was about to throw a spear at a galloping soldier; then he rode to the picket line, paused a split second to cut the rope, and fired in the air, sending the paint ponies neighing and rearing, running pell-mell into the night.

Behind him, the patrol's pistols and rifles roared as they chased Indians down, pausing to set fire to teepees and piles of dried meat and supplies.

"Lieutenant!" the captain yelled over the din and acrid smoke of gunfire. "Get us a hostage who can tell us what we need to know!"

"We can torture a warrior to death and he won't tell us anything!" Colt protested.

"That's an order, Lieutenant!"

Of all the stupid—! What they ought to be doing now that the horses were scattered and the camp aflame was chase after the survivors who were still shooting at them, but Colt sighed and wheeled Rascal to chase down a hostage.

Ahead of him as he galloped was a tall warrior, wrapped in a blanket, and running in confusion. Colt reined Rascal that direction, knowing full well the man could be carrying a knife or a war club and could kill Colt even as he tried to capture the man. He leaned out of his saddle and grabbed up the slender, running figure.

Too light for a man, he thought in surprise, and then the blanket fell away and he saw the terrified white face and long yellow hair reflecting like gold in the flare of burning teepees.

"Good God, it's a woman! A white woman!"

Chapter 2

The girl in his arms screamed something at him. He recognized the garbled words as Comanche, but there was too much noise to understand her. Yet instead of being happy to see a white soldier, she was fighting to get away from him. He hung onto the wildcat even as he looked around and realized his troopers were splitting up and riding off in all directions after the warriors. Colt knew this was a common Comanche ploy that would get any single soldier ambushed and killed.

Fighting to hold onto the white girl, he yelled at his sergeant "Mulvaney, sound recall!"

"Yes, sir."

Now it took all Colt's strength to hold the woman, who was biting and scratching as Captain Van Smyth rode up on his lathered horse.

"I didn't order recall! The men are hunting down the scattered savages."

"I did!" Colt yelled back. "They'll get drawn out and ambushed. We've done what we came for, now let's get out of here."

The captain stared at the fighting captive. "Good Lord! What—?"

"I don't know. Let's vamoose and then we'll find out."

"Ma'am," Captain Van Smyth shouted to the struggling girl, "don't you understand? We're rescuing you."

The girl continued to fight and yell.

Colt hung onto her by sheer strength. "She may be a bit addled sir, if she's spent much time with the Comanche."

"Could that be Cynthia Ann Parker?" The captain reined in his blowing horse.

"How the hell should I know?" Colt lost his temper as the girl bit his hand again. "Let's get out of here!"

The patrol had reassembled amid the chaos and noise. In the light of the flaming teepees, Colt looked down into his captive's eyes and they reflected back the flames in their pale blue depths. He realized suddenly she was terrified. He wheeled his mustang as the patrol rode out of the burning Comanche camp, the Indians firing scattered shots behind them.

Colt pulled the girl's slender body close to him and realized she was trembling in her dirty deerskin shift, but she was still fighting. She was trying to tell him something, but he couldn't understand her garbled Comanche. She must be frightened because she shook and her eyes were wide with fear, but she didn't cry. There were no tears in the pale blue eyes.

They galloped a quarter of a mile before they reined in.

Captain Van Smyth looked around. "Is everyone accounted for?"

Colt glanced behind him and relayed the question at Sergeant Mulvaney.

"Aye, it's Irish luck, I say," the ruddy-faced Irishman

shouted back. "Dugan's got a slight arrow wound to the arm, but everyone else is fine."

"Then mission accomplished." The captain smiled. "Now let's get back to Camp Cooper."

The thoroughbreds were lathered and blowing, but Colt's mustang was still good. The girl trembled and fought to get away, and he tried to reassure her as they rode. "It's okay, ma'am. You're safe now. We'll take you back to the fort and find your kinfolk."

"Go back!" she managed to say in broken English almost as if it were a forgotten language. "Got to go back."

"No, no," Colt soothed her and hung onto her, though she fought like a wildcat.

"What's the trouble, Lieutenant?" Captain Van Smyth rode up next to him.

"Shock, I think, sir. If she's been with them long, her mind may not be . . . well, you know."

The captain nodded and stared at the girl wrapped in her dirty blanket, then spurred his mount and rode up on ahead.

"Got to go back," the girl gasped.

Colt shook his head. "No, you don't understand, we've saved you. We'll find your kin."

She shook her head violently. "No. No."

He looked down at her, wondering what sort of hellish life she'd been living. Her face was dirty and smudged, her yellow hair a tangle. There wasn't much water for bathing on the sparse Texas plains.

She was fighting him again and he hung onto her, gritting his teeth. He could hardly wait to get this crazed girl back to the fort and hope they could find some relative of hers. Looking down at her, he felt pity; she was such a contrast to the pale, delicate features of Olivia and her ladylike behavior. Well, Olivia hadn't been brutalized and surely raped by a bunch of warriors.

After a while, the girl seemed to grow quiet in his arms as if she understood or was simply tired of fighting him. He relaxed his grip as they covered the miles. The men riding with him were quiet, exhausted, and dirty, some of them half asleep in their saddles.

Abruptly the girl came alive and fought her way out of his arms, fell to the ground, got up, and started running back along the trail.

"I'll be goddamned!" Colt swore and reined in, dismounted, and ran after her. She was tall as well as slender and she wore a ragged deerskin dress that showed long slender legs as she ran. "Come back here!" he yelled, but she kept running.

Oh hell, he didn't need this aggravation. He had a mind to just let her go, but of course he couldn't do that. How would he explain losing the rescued white girl when he got back to the fort?

She was fast and he was tired. He cursed as he chased her with all the men in the patrol reining in and laughing as they watched. "Hey, I put a silver dollar on the girl!"

"No, I think the lieutenant will catch her."

"She must be loco to want to go back to the Injuns!"

"Order in the ranks!" Mulvaney shouted while Colt put on a burst of speed to catch up with her. Again he cursed his luck on being assigned to the Second Cav.

Colt tackled her and they both went down, she still fighting and clawing. The dirty deerskin had slipped up, showing darkly tanned thighs. He felt soft breasts and a small waist as he wrestled with her, and then she turned her head and sank her teeth into his arm. He couldn't help but yelp. "Damn, she's worse than a coyote bitch!"

He gathered her up, kicking and protesting, and

carried her back to his horse. She was light, probably not very well fed, he thought as he threw her up on his horse and mounted behind her. "Look, you're safe now. The Comanche can't get you. What's your name?"

The column was moving again.

"Muakatu," she said softly in Comanche.

Moonlight, Colt thought, a perfect name for a girl with golden hair. "No, what's your white name? Do you have family in Texas?"

She paused as if she couldn't remember, or maybe she'd been so brutalized, she'd lost her memory of the past and her language.

Colt looked down into her dirty face and guessed she must be in her early twenties. "Maybe you have a husband?"

"Puhu Retsi," she whispered and Colt's blood ran cold. Spider. No wonder the girl was in such shock. Spider could be brutal when it came to women.

Colt rode up next to the captain. "I think we've just bitten off a big hunk of trouble."

The captain looked over at him. "How so?"

"This girl is Spider's woman. He won't let us take her without a fight. He must have been out of the village with his braves or we might not have gotten away from there alive."

"So what's one Comanche brave?" the captain laughed.

Colt didn't laugh. "He'll come after her or set the whole countryside ablaze in retaliation."

"Good Lord, you exaggerate, Lieutenant."

Colt shook his head. "I don't think so. He may gather up half the warriors in Texas and hit our fort. You don't take anything that belongs to that young brave without him wreaking vengeance."

"Oh, pishposh." The captain dismissed him with an airy wave of his hand. "Besides, once we get back to the fort, we'll send out messengers and find her family. Then she's their problem."

Colt didn't say anything. Right now, she was his problem. She had dropped off to sleep from sheer exhaustion, and he cradled her closer and felt protective because he knew Spider so well. His blood brother. She was probably terrified that if she didn't go back, Spider would torture her when he finally recaptured her. Well, Colt didn't intend to let that happen. She had suffered enough. He looked down into her suntanned face and her dirty, tangled yellow hair. Moonlight. So unlike the dainty Olivia.

He thought about the perfumed lace hankie in his pocket. Beautiful Olivia, so civilized and sweet-smelling, not at all like this pitiful captive.

It was the middle of the night when the patrol got back to the fort, but still, many of the inhabitants turned out to hear what had happened. The wounded man was taken to the infirmary, and Colt carried the struggling girl in and sat her on a bed there, too.

The sleepy old doctor came in and the captain sent for Major Murphy. Colt stepped back and took a good look at the woman he had saved. She was deeply suntanned, but bruises and scratches showed up on her dirty skin. She was slender almost to the point of skinny, plus she was filthy and her yellow hair a tangle. She looked around at everyone, blinking in the unaccustomed light of the kerosene lamps. Colt felt pity for her and wondered if she could ever readjust to civilization again.

Just then, the major, still buttoning his uniform,

came in, along with the lovely Olivia, and the curious crowd melted back to let them stand by Colt.

"Saint Mary's blood," the major sighed. "Who is this?"

The girl only looked at him, blinking those pale blue eyes.

Colt shrugged. "Can't get much out of her, sir, except that she didn't want to come with us."

The major moved closer and peered into the girl's face. "Are you Cynthia Ann Parker?"

The girl stared back at him as if having a difficult time with the English. Finally, she shook her head.

"Oh, maybe you are Hannah Brownley. Is your name Hannah?"

After a moment, she nodded, then tried to get up off the bed where she sat. "Little boy. Must go back."

The whole crowd took a deep breath, and the major gasped. Olivia said, "Oh, the poor thing."

The major squatted and took one of her dirty hands in his. "My dear, don't you remember? We were told your little boy is dead. He died right after birth."

"No." She shook her head and pulled away from him. "No."

"You are married, right?" the major said.

She nodded. "Spider."

A gasp from the crowd.

"No," the major insisted, "your husband is Luther Brownley. You were captured while picking sand plums almost four years ago. Remember Luther?"

She scowled and shook her head, then looked toward the door. "Go," she murmured. "Must go. My little boy."

"Goodness gracious," Olivia whispered and the rest of the crowd sighed in pity.

"Let me try," Colt suggested and squatted, took the girl's hand in his. It was a hardworking hand with blisters and calluses, and long, shapely fingers that had seen a lot of toil. "Moonlight," he said softly in Comanche, "you are safe now. Spider can't get you."

A look of fear crossed her suntanned face. "He will come," she said in Comanche.

"No." Colt shook his head. "I will not let him take you. We will send for your husband and you can go back to your old life."

"No." Her voice was stubborn. "Not Luther."

Colt sighed and turned to the crowd, shook his head and said in English. "She may have been so brutalized, her mind has been affected."

"Oh, that's so sad." Olivia began to weep big tears.

The bald old doctor pushed in just then, having treated the soldier's arrow wound. "Dag nab it, we need to give her a few days," he said to the major. "There's no telling what she's been through. It may take her some time to readjust to civilization."

Now Olivia said in a mixture of scorn and annoyance, "You'd think she'd be pleased to be rescued."

Colt stood up and turned to the delicate beauty. "Miss Olivia, you can't even imagine what she's been through."

Olivia was immediately contrite. "Oh, the poor thing. I'm sure you're right, Lieutenant. Maybe I can give her a bath and one of my dresses might fit her, although it will be too short."

The chubby doctor nodded. "Yes, that sounds like a good idea, Miss Murphy. And then I'll give her a sleeping potion in some water and maybe some food. She's awfully thin."

Colt didn't say anything, remembering there was not

always enough food in a Comanche camp, especially with the white men spreading out across the plains and killing off all the game.

The major said, "Everyone, you heard Doc. Let's turn her over to my daughter and her servant to clean up, and in the meantime, I'll send a messenger and maybe in a few days, we can track down her husband."

Everyone left reluctantly except Colt, the major, the balding doc, and Olivia and her squat, scar-faced Tonkawa servant girl.

Colt said, "I'll have an orderly get some water boiling and, Doc, you've got a washtub?"

He nodded. "Miss Murphy, if you'd get her some underclothes and a dress, we'll see what we can do."

Colt paused at the door. "Olivia, I'm not sure you can handle her, she's strong and taller than you."

"Nonsense. We can't have men handling a naked girl. It's my Christian duty to help this poor thing. You see about getting some hot water." She gave Colt her most winsome smile.

"You're a wonderful, caring person." Colt's heart warmed toward the beauty. He went out the door to get the water heating.

In a few minutes, he was back. The girl still sat on the bed in her filthy deerskin shift with Doc and a soldier standing guard. Olivia came in the door just then with an old dress and some underwear. "I'll look through my shoes tomorrow. I don't think she'll need them tonight."

Doc pulled a big washtub out in the middle of the floor. "All right, Lieutenant, bring in the hot water. I've got some soap."

"Goodness gracious," Olivia scolded. "Don't use that

old lye soap. I've brought some of my perfumed, French soap for the poor thing."

Colt smiled. "Olivia, you've got a big heart. That fancy soap needs to be rationed. You aren't going to be able to find it here in Texas."

Olivia simpered and blinked her long eyelashes. "It's the least I can do. I feel so sorry for her."

In the meantime, the girl seemed to be resigned to sitting on the bed, watching the proceedings.

"Well," said Doc, "I guess we'd better leave, Lieutenant. I think the ladies can handle this." He nodded toward Olivia and her stoic maid. He went out the side door to his quarters.

Colt looked down at the girl. He didn't think Olivia and her maid could deal with her. He leaned over and whispered to Olivia. "She may be a bit loco. I'll be right outside the door if you need help."

He went out the door, closed it, and leaned against a post of the porch, rolling a cigarette. It had been a long night and he was bone tired. He was now wondering if he'd done the right thing in bringing the girl back. She wouldn't be the first one to be returned to civilization and mostly, the women didn't readjust well and white society didn't seem to know what to do with them anyway. Sometimes their husbands didn't want them because they'd been used by savages and no one else wanted them either. He felt pity for the tall, slender blonde. Knowing Spider's cruelty, the girl had withstood brutality and, yes, if he wanted her, he might try to come get her, even if he had to invade the fort. Colt remembered how she had fit into his arms, trembling and thin, needing his protection, but still defiant, spirited, and without a tear. *She must be a Texas girl, all right.*

* * *

Inside, Hannah watched the two women preparing the tub of steaming water. It had been a long time since she had had a good bath. The Comanche people swam in lakes and streams, but so often, there was not even enough water to drink on the arid plains, much less enough to bathe in. It looked so inviting, that tub, but these white people weren't going to let her leave and she had to leave, she had to get back or Spider would be furious to find her gone when he and the other warriors returned from their hunting trip.

The elegant, petite girl turned to her with a smile. "Look, we've fixed you a bath. Will you get in?"

The language took her a moment to understand because she hadn't heard English in almost four years. She stood up and pulled off the filthy deerskin garment and moccasins. Her blue gingham dress had dissolved in tatters long ago.

Hannah nodded, and stepped into the tub, reached out her hand for the soap. What was the word? "Please," she said.

The delicate lady smiled and handed it to her. "That's more like it. Maria, help wash her back."

Hannah frowned at the Tonkawa as the maid knelt stoically and began to wash her. Tonks and Comanches were enemies, and she wouldn't trust the Tonk not to try to drown her. Oh, but the hot water and soap felt good. Hannah closed her eyes as the pretty one named Olivia smiled with satisfaction and sat down in a chair to watch. Hannah didn't like this delicate beauty, but she wasn't sure why. She sensed the major's daughter was really shocked and disgusted by the captive, but wanted the men to think she was kind and thoughtful.

Hannah was clean now and wondering what to do about her hair. Just then, Olivia got up off her chair. "I'll help wash your hair."

Hannah decided to let her, but Olivia's dainty hands were not gentle. She soaped Hannah's head, pulling at her hair as if she really wanted to hurt her.

"I'll do it," Hannah said, but Olivia was now pushing Hannah's head under the water of the tub. "You dirty savage," Olivia whispered. "Stop splashing, you're getting my dress wet."

Hannah came up gasping and threw both hands full of water at Olivia. "Stop it! You're drowning me!"

Olivia tried to push her head under again, but this time, Hannah came up out of the tub and grabbed Olivia, dumping her into the tub of dirty water while the maid stood by, blinking in surprise.

Hannah had to get back to the Comanches. She grabbed up her filthy buckskin and ran for the outside door, dripping wet and soapy. Maybe all the men had gone to bed and she could steal a horse and get away.

Colt was smoking his cigarette and relaxing when he heard the commotion from inside and Olivia's scream of indignation. He tossed away his smoke just as the door flew open and a slender, naked wet girl came running out. "Oh, no, you don't!"

He grabbed the captive and she was so wet and soapy he had a difficult time hanging onto her while she bit and fought him. However, he was stronger than she was and he hung onto her, too aware of her slender waist, long legs, and big breasts.

Olivia came to the door and she was wet, angry, and weeping. "I was trying to wash her and she tried to drown me. That's all the thanks I get for trying to help this poor, unfortunate—"

"I'm so sorry," Colt said, hanging onto the fighting girl. "I reckon she's too much for a lady to handle."

Olivia's eyes widened with horror. "Goodness gracious. She's naked, Lieutenant, and you—"

"Get me something; a towel, anything to wrap her," he ordered.

With a fresh flood of tears, Olivia ran back inside as Colt carried the struggling girl into the infirmary. Now Olivia came forward with a towel and a dress. "She's just a savage, that's all, and I was trying to do my Christian duty—"

"It'll be all right, Miss Olivia," Colt soothed her. "Here, give me the towel." He plunked the girl down on a bed.

"No, this just isn't civilized," Olivia protested. "Let my maid dry her off and put this dress on her."

"You sure she's up to it?" Colt stared at the stout Indian woman, who looked doubtful.

"Well, maybe it'll take all three of us." Olivia blushed and the three of them tackled the task of drying and dressing the captive. "I'm so sorry, Lieutenant. I know this must be embarrassing for a gentleman."

"Not much embarrasses me, miss," he said through clenched teeth as they got the girl into the chemise and drawers, then into Olivia's cast-off blue dress. Her hair was still a soapy mess and she managed to hit Olivia in the face as she struggled.

The major's daughter burst into a fresh flood of tears. "Did you see what she did? She did that deliberately. Why, she's like a savage herself."

The girl stopped struggling and sat down on the edge of the bed.

Colt took out a handkerchief and offered it to the weeping girl. "I'm so sorry, Miss Olivia. She's just more than a lady like you can deal with." He turned to the now-wet maid. "Go get Doc. Maybe he can get some food and some medicine down her."

The girl looked up at him as the maid left. She was prettier now that her face was clean, but she'd never be a great beauty like the petite Olivia. "She tried to drown me," she said slowly, as if searching for the English words.

"I did not!" Olivia wailed. "I was trying to help her and she tried to jerk me into the tub."

Colt looked down into the honest blue eyes and wavered; then he went to Olivia's side. "There, there, ma'am. You tried to help. Maybe she just didn't understand. She's had a hard time."

The girl looked toward the door again. "I need to go back to my little boy."

Oh, God, he felt so sorry for her. He came back and squatted before her, took one of her work-worn hands in his. "I was told your baby is dead, Mrs. Brownley. Don't you remember? In a few days, maybe your husband will come for you."

She shook her head, dripping water. "No. No."

He didn't know what to do. He felt helpless and he was a man who had dealt with death and killing, rattlesnakes and tornados.

Doc came in just then, accompanied by the maid. He yawned and looked around. "Dag nab it! What in the name of goodness happened in here? It looks like Noah's flood."

Olivia sobbed again. "I was trying to wash her and she tried to drown me."

"*Tsk tsk.*" The doc shook his head, muttering something about savages.

Colt looked at the girl with soap dripping from her

hair. "If I get you a bucket of water, would you want to wash your own hair?"

The girl nodded.

"Watch out!" Olivia warned. "She'll try to get away again."

"I don't think so," Colt answered softly and got a bucket of water, put it on the nearby table, and offered the girl a bar of soap and a dry towel.

Hesitantly, she took those from him and went to the bucket and began to wash her own hair.

Everyone seemed to sigh in relief.

Doc said, "Would anyone like something to eat? I've got some cold roast beef and some pickles if the maid can make sandwiches and she can put on a pot of coffee."

"Sounds good," Colt said, thinking it had been a long time since he'd eaten.

The doctor and the maid went back into Doc's quarters and Colt could hear them moving around in there and the clatter of pans and dishes.

In the meantime, the girl had finished with her hair and was drying it. Colt thought it looked like spun gold in the dim light. Muakatu. Moonlight. It had been an apt name for the captive. He knelt in front of her. "Are you hungry? Would you like some food?"

She seemed to think about it, then nodded slowly. "Yes, but I must go back."

Olivia snorted. "She must be deaf or stupid."

Colt took both the girl's worn hands in his two hands. "You can't go back. Do you understand? Your husband will be coming to get you."

"Luther?" She frowned.

"Yes, I reckon that's his name," Colt said.

"No." Her lip trembled, but she did not cry.

"You don't want to go back to your husband?" Colt whispered.

She shook her head.

"Goodness gracious," Olivia exclaimed. "What kind of woman is she? He'll take her back to her old life, back to civilization, and she doesn't even appreciate all our efforts."

"We don't know all there is to know," he said. Then he looked deep into Hannah's eyes. "All right, if you don't want to go with Luther, I won't let him take you."

For the very first time, the girl smiled and Colt wondered then why he had thought her plain. When she smiled, there was a shy beauty about her.

Doc came in just then with a coffeepot, followed by the maid with a tray of sandwiches and some gingerbread. He put it all down on a table. "All right, everyone pull up a chair and we'll eat."

The maid put small plates around the table and poured coffee. Colt could smell it from here and it smelled wonderful. The girl seemed to smell it, too, because she brightened. Colt took her hand and led her to the table, where she sat down uncertainly. It had probably been years since she'd used a chair, Colt thought.

"Well?" Olivia said. "Lieutenant, aren't you going to pull out my chair for me?"

"Oh, I'm so sorry, Miss Olivia." Colt hurriedly pulled out her chair, and the dark beauty sat down with a rustle of fine petticoats.

The girl stared at the sandwiches. Colt saw Doc slip a pill into her cup of coffee as he poured. Then Hannah reached out and grabbed a sandwich off the tray and began to wolf it down.

"Well!" said Olivia. "What atrocious manners."

The girl continued to wolf her sandwich and gulp her coffee as the two men watched in pity.

Doc reached out and patted her hand. "There's plenty more, Mrs. Brownley."

Colt said, "Sometimes in a Comanche camp, the food gets pretty thin for the whole tribe."

Olivia looked around the table. "Oh, dear, are there no napkins?"

Doc said, "I'm so sorry, Miss Murphy, I forget about how ladies are." He turned to the maid. "There's some on the table by the stove."

The stout, silent girl went off to get them.

In the meantime, Hannah wiped her hands on her skirt and reached for another sandwich and gulped the last of her coffee.

In a moment, the maid was back with the napkins and the others started to eat. Colt tried not to wolf his food, suddenly very conscious of his manners in front of the genteel Olivia. No one had ever taught him how a gentleman dines, and he had a feeling Olivia was watching with disapproval.

Hannah was finished before the others. The doctor poured her another cup of coffee and put a piece of gingerbread on her plate. He offered her a fork, but she had already picked up the cake with her hands and tasted it. "Gingerbread." She smiled.

Colt found himself smiling back at her. "I'll wager you haven't had any gingerbread for a long time."

"She's eating it with her hands," Olivia gasped in a shocked whisper.

Hannah hesitated, looked embarrassed and uncertain.

Doc said, "Look, I eat mine with my hands, too." He picked up the gingerbread and took a bite. Colt followed suit while Olivia gasped and primly helped herself to the gingerbread and ate it with her fork.

Hannah finished her gingerbread and reached for the last sandwich. She wrapped it carefully in the cloth napkin.

Colt said, "There's plenty. You don't have to squirrel food away."

She looked at him. "I take it with me when I go."

Colt sighed and looked over at Doc.

Olivia said, "I do believe she's daft."

Hannah's eyes gradually closed, and then she jerked awake. Doc's medicine was beginning to work, Colt thought.

"Here, Miss Hannah, wouldn't you like to bring your sandwich and sit on this bed?" Colt asked, standing up.

"No, I'm going now." She yawned and tried to stand up, but her legs gave out from under her and Colt caught her as she fell, took the sandwich from her hand, and carried her over and laid her on a bed.

"Doc, I think I'd better tie one of her wrists to the bed, otherwise, she'll take off."

"Do that. It'll be dawn soon and then there'll be other people to deal with her."

"Well," Olivia said, "I think my maid and I will be retiring now. I've got to get into some dry clothes before I catch a chill. My delicate constitution can't take being wet."

"We all appreciate your help." Colt looked up from tying Hannah's wrist to the iron bedstead.

"Well, she certainly didn't appreciate it." Olivia glared at the sleeping girl. "And I was trying to do my Christian duty. Why, my mother would have gotten the vapors if she could have seen me on my knees by that tub, trying to scrub that pitiful thing."

"And I'm sure she appreciates it," Doc said. "Now you and your maid can return to your quarters."

Olivia and her maid left with a whirl of skirts and a door slam.

Colt sighed. Dealing with a real lady was more trouble than he'd bargained for. "Doc, I think I'll sit outside on the porch, just in case Mrs. Brownley gets loose again."

"Do you think that's likely?"

"She's survived almost four years in a Comanche camp. She's pretty plucky and tough for a girl."

Doc nodded and went back through the door to his quarters.

Colt looked down at Hannah. The lines in her sun-tanned face had smoothed out and she looked younger and without care. Her dress was too short and it showed her ankles and her bare feet. She had tiny feet, but they looked like they had carried her a long way, mostly without shoes or moccasins. The Comanches were a mobile people who moved often, following herds of buffalo.

Colt put the precious sandwich back in her palm and she clutched it to her in her sleep. Remembering his own time among the tribe, he knew food was precious. Life among the plains tribes was hard and getting worse because of the white man's encroachment on their lands. He wondered again why she wanted so badly to return to the Indian camp and how long it would take before Luther Brownley would show up to reclaim his reluctant wife.

Colt spread a blanket over the sleeping girl and went outside, sat down, and leaned against a post and smoked a cigarette, thinking about his own life among

the Comanche and whether he wanted to stay in the
army. His enlistment would be up in mid-June. Finally
he dropped off to sleep.

In the middle of the night, Hannah awoke with a
start, tried to remember where she was and what had
happened. Then she realized she was tied by one wrist.
She tucked her precious sandwich into her bodice and
began to chew on her bindings. It was almost dawn
when she had chewed through the ropes that bound
her. Now she could escape.

Chapter 3

By the time Hannah managed to chew through the rope and free herself, it was coming dawn. She looked through the window and saw that tall lieutenant who had captured her sitting asleep against a post on the porch.

The whole fort was starting to stir, men crossing the parade grounds, the bugle sounding, the flag raising. She wouldn't have a chance of getting away right now, but she had to get back to the Comanche camp.

What to do? Hannah thought a minute. If she could convince all these white people that she was trustworthy and grateful, they would begin to trust her. In a day or so, she would be able to escape under cover of darkness because they wouldn't be expecting it.

She heard stirring from Doc's quarters and she got up and went to sit at the table. Doc came in just then, yawning and scratching his bald head and the fringe of white hair surrounding it. "Oh, are you up, young lady? How did you—?"

"It was hurting." She looked down at her wrist, which still had shreds of rope on it. "I feel better now."

"Good. I'm glad you seem to have come to your

senses. I know you have been through a terrible ordeal." His accent was clipped and sounded strange to the Texas girl. He must have come from farther north.

She had to think a minute to come up with English words. She had spoken nothing but Comanche for so long. "I—I was afraid last night, not sure what had happened."

He nodded and smiled. "I'll start us some coffee and bacon."

"Thank you, but I have my sandwich from last night." She nodded toward the leftover she had laid on her bedside table.

"Never mind. I'll throw that away and get you some biscuits and gravy. I'm pretty good in the kitchen. My wife died years ago and I had to learn."

As he turned away, Hannah said, "The lieutenant is still sitting outside asleep."

"Oh? I'll invite him in to share." Doc went to the door and opened it. "Good morning, Lieutenant. We're starting some breakfast. Care to join us?"

Past Doc's shoulder, she saw the big, dark-haired officer come awake with a start, and he stood up, moving as if he was stiff and sore. "Oh, hell, Doc. How's our captive?"

"Completely different this morning. Come on in."

She smiled at the tall soldier as he blinked at her. He had black hair and green eyes and a deep tan. He came inside and shut the door behind him, stared at her. "How did you—?"

"It hurt my arm." She shrugged and rubbed her wrist.

Doc said, "Dag nab it, I'll go get some coffee going, you two can talk." He left the room and went back to his quarters.

She felt the awkward silence.

The lieutenant cleared his throat. "How are you?"

She paused a moment, fishing for the English words. "All right now. Last night, I was not sure what was happening. Thank you for rescuing me."

He seemed to sigh in relief. "That's all right. I lived with the Comanche myself for ten years and was adopted into the tribe. I know what you've been through."

She winced, remembering Spider's brutality. "I'd rather not talk about it."

"That's right." He nodded. "You've got to look forward, not behind you, now that you're back among your own people again."

She smelled coffee coming from Doc's quarters and heard him bustling around, banging pans. "What—what will happen to me now?"

He walked over and looked down at her with understanding and pity in those green eyes. "I reckon the major has already sent out messengers tryin' to locate your husband. Until he comes for you, I reckon you can just stay at the fort."

She turned away so he couldn't see her face. "I don't think my husband will want me back, since, well, you know."

He put a gentle hand on her shoulder. "He'll want you back." His voice was soft and compassionate, a Texas drawl. "No matter what happened to you, it wasn't your fault and he'll understand that."

"You don't know Luther." She turned around and looked up at him. She was tall, but she had to look up into his rugged, tanned face. If only she'd met a man like this one when she was desperate and running away from home.

"Then he's a fool—a damned fool." His face flushed

and he stepped away from her. "Maybe you'll think different when you see him. That is, if they find him. A lot of things may have happened in four years. He may have left Texas or even be dead."

"So then what will happen to me?" She looked at him.

"I don't know. You're free now. You can do whatever you want."

"But if he does come for me . . ." She couldn't keep the tension out of her voice, remembering her husband's cruelty and his vain attempts to break her spirit.

"If you don't want to go with him, you won't have to. I'll see to that."

"Thank you." She didn't intend to be here if Luther showed up. She'd be gone by then, back to the Comanche camp. Being Spider's woman was no worse than being Luther's. Anyway, she had no choice; she had to return to the camp. "I trust your word."

He flushed and looked awkward, a Texas man not used to dealing with women. "Let's see if Doc has that coffee ready, and maybe later, Olivia can find you some shoes."

"Olivia?" She couldn't remember who that was.

"You know, the real pretty dark-haired girl who helped you last night and gave you a dress."

"Oh, yes, her." Hannah remembered the short-tempered girl who had tried to duck her head under water. From the lieutenant's tone, he thought Olivia was wonderful. Of course the petite girl was beautiful and Hannah wasn't. Men set a lot of store by beauty.

Doc came into the room just then carrying a metal coffeepot and three cups. "Here we go. You two sit down and I'll get the food."

"Can I help?" Hannah asked. She liked Doc.

"No, thanks. I can manage, young lady. You just sit down."

Dutifully Hannah sat down at the table while the officer picked up the big pot and poured the steaming brew.

She took deep breaths of the bracing scent. "We didn't get much coffee in the camp."

"I know." He pushed the sugar bowl toward her. "Or sugar either."

Sugar. White sugar. She grabbed a spoon and heaped it into her cup, stirred and stirred. She picked up the cup and sipped it, closed her eyes, and smiled. "It's the little things you really miss."

When she opened her eyes, the officer was sipping his coffee and staring at her with compassion. "Mrs. Brownley, you'll finally get past all this and it will be just a painful memory that will gradually fade."

"Call me Hannah, please," she whispered. "I don't like being called Mrs. Brownley."

"All right. And I am Colton Prescott. Most folks call me Colt."

"It fits you," she thought aloud. "Anyway, I'm much obliged that you risked your life for me."

He blushed. "It's my job, ma'am. Most women would have been cryin' their eyes out, but not you."

She shook her head. "I haven't cried in many years, not since . . . I found it does no good." She didn't want to think about Luther's beatings and the loss of her little son. Life with Spider had been a nightmare of constant rape. Spider's other wife, jealous of Hannah, never missed a chance to mistreat her or pile work on her. Yet Hannah had to get back to the Comanche camp.

Doc came in just then with a big platter of biscuits and gravy, bacon and jam, put the platter on the table. "Here you go. Even got some sand plum jam as a special treat."

Lieutenant Prescott grinned. "Been a coon's age since I've seen sand plum jam. You want some, Mrs. . . . Hannah?"

She swallowed hard. She had been picking sand plums the day she was carried off by the Comanche while her cowardly husband dropped the rifle and ran over old women and small children, saving his own cowardly hide. "I—I don't think so, thank you."

"But why?" Doc began, looking puzzled. The lieutenant seemed to see the look on her face because he shook his head at Doc.

She looked down at her plate and began to eat. "It's good. I haven't had a biscuit in a long time."

Doc grinned. "You just enjoy those, ma'am."

"I want to work," she said to him. "I don't want to be a burden."

"Dag nab it, you're not a burden," Doc answered. "You're providing a little company for an old geezer who's mighty tired of looking at scruffy soldier boys all day."

"Then maybe I can help around the infirmary," she suggested.

"Now that would be good," Doc said.

They finished eating in silence, and then the front door opened and the beautiful Olivia, in a fine blue dress, entered. "So how is our patient today?"

Both men scrambled to their feet. Hannah kept her head down while Doc said, "She seems to be fine this morning. Would you like some coffee, Miss Murphy?"

"Not if I have to drink it out of a tin cup," Olivia

laughed. "Honestly, Doc, I need to bring you some of my china."

"Aw, the soldiers would just break it," Doc said.

"Do sit down." Olivia waved the men back to their chairs. Now she looked directly at Hannah. She smiled, but her eyes were not smiling. "I do hope you are enjoying my dress."

"Yes, thank you very much. It was kind of you," Hannah said, stroking the faded blue fabric.

The lieutenant looked at the pretty Olivia with adoration is his eyes. "Sit down, Miss Olivia." He jumped up and hurried to get her a chair.

The major's daughter took it like a princess sitting down on a regal throne. She smiled back at the officer, but to Hannah, the smile looked fake.

No one else seemed to notice. Instead, the lieutenant leaned toward her and said, "Miss Olivia, our rescued lady is still barefooted, except for worn-out moccasins. Maybe you have some extra shoes?"

"Of course. We don't want her barefooted when her husband comes for her. He will be coming, won't he?" It was almost a challenge.

Doc nodded. "I understand your father is sending out riders trying to find him."

"Good." Olivia purred and then she fastened all her attention on the officer. "Colton, are we still going horseback riding this afternoon?"

And now it dawned on Hannah. The lovely Olivia saw Hannah as a rival for the men's attention.

The lieutenant smiled at Olivia, evidently charmed by her beauty. "Of course, unless the major has duties for me to take care of."

"Oh, I think he'll give everyone on the patrol a day off. He's so pleased with the raid. I tell you what, I'll go get Mrs. Brownley a pair of shoes and then I'll pack a picnic for this afternoon."

"Thank you," Hannah said dutifully. She was beginning to dislike the major's beautiful daughter.

However, the lieutenant smiled at Olivia as if she were the only girl in the world. "That sounds wonderful, but we can't get too far from the fort."

"Goodness gracious, I'm not afraid when I have a big, strong man like you protecting me." Olivia stood up suddenly and both men knocked their chairs over standing up.

Such was the power of great beauty, Hannah thought.

Olivia gave both men a dazzling smile, turned in a swirl of blue skirts and petticoats, and went out the door.

The lieutenant looked after her with a sigh. "Isn't she the sweetest thing and the most beautiful girl in all Texas?"

Not plain like me, Hannah thought, but she didn't say anything except, "You seem to be quite taken with her, Lieutenant Prescott."

"From the first time I met her." He smiled. "She's so pretty, she takes my breath away. Reckon I'd better be seein' to my men." He stood up. "Thanks for the breakfast, Doc, and I'm glad you're fine this mornin', Miss Hannah."

He turned and went out the door.

Doc said, "Did I detect some tension between you and the major's daughter?"

"Not at all." Doc was too quick-witted, she thought, and noticed too much. "I am properly grateful for the clothes."

"I notice the dress she brought you was very faded, almost ragged," Doc said, "and she owns so many beautiful gowns."

Hannah didn't say anything. Doc could be a good friend, but she didn't intend to be here past tonight. When it turned dark, Hannah intended to steal a horse and escape the fort.

She got up and began to clear the table. "I'll wash up, Doc. I imagine you'll have patients coming in this morning."

"Oh yeah. Malingerers claiming bellyaches or something so they won't have to clean stables or sweep the parade grounds."

"You don't seem like regular army," Hannah said.

"Does it show?" Doc paused, looking thoughtful. "I was a very successful doctor in Connecticut and then my wife died." He gazed out the window as if remembering. "Then all I thought of was our only child, but Mark was killed in the Mexican War. For a while, I did nothing but drink."

"And then?" Hannah asked softly.

Doc shrugged. "Soldiers needed doctors, and because of Mark, I enlisted. It gave me a new reason to live."

She paused. "A son gives anyone a reason to live."

Just then Olivia popped back in the door, carrying a pair of shoes. "Here, Mrs. Brownley. I was planning on giving these to my maid, but you need my charity so much more."

"Thank you. You are so kind." Hannah forced a smile as she took the shoes. They looked worn-out.

Olivia nodded and smiled. "You poor thing, I'm just doing my Christian duty." And she turned with a whirl of expensive lace petticoats and went out the door.

Hannah sat down on a chair and tried on the old shoes. Olivia might be a petite beauty, but she had big feet. The shoes were way too big for Hannah. "Doc, have you got some rolls of bandage?"

"Sure." He walked to a cabinet and took out some, handed them to her.

She took off the shoes and stuffed the toes so the shoes would fit her, then put them back on. "Thanks, Doc. Now I'll clean up the dishes and you can get to work yourself."

He paused and grinned at her. "You know, Hannah, I really like you. You're genuine and honest, rare things in a woman. Too bad some younger men are blinded by window dressing."

"You mean Lieutenant Prescott?"

He winked. "You understand perfectly."

She began to clean the table, feeling guilty because she was fooling this nice old man. He'd be shocked and disappointed when he woke up in the morning and she was gone.

Olivia walked into to her father's office. "Hello, Daddy."

"My darling." He stood up and kissed her forehead. "What can I do for you today? I hope you're not going to complain about how dull this post is again."

She sniffed the whiskey scent and frowned. "So early?"

"You sound just like your mother," he snapped, reaching for his pipe.

It didn't do any good to lecture Daddy about his drinking, although she thought it was getting worse. She sat down in a chair. "I've been over to see our poor girl rescued from the Indians and take her some shoes."

"That's my good girl." He beamed at his only child. "You're the sweetest, most thoughtful girl ever."

She smiled her most winsome smile. "I was only doing what any other kind, civilized woman would do. You have sent for her husband, haven't you? I'm sure she's really eager to get off this post and back to her family."

"Of course. I've sent telegraphs all over Texas, and if he's alive and still in the state, we'll find him." He poured himself a drink.

"Oh, Daddy, must you? You drink too much."

"I do not. This is my first little toddy of the morning."

"I don't think so."

"Now, have you been counting like your mother used to?" He sounded defensive and angry.

She decided to drop the subject. The tension between her parents had grown worse over the years, which was why they kept so many miles between them. "Wasn't that an exciting raid? The men are saying Lieutenant Prescott was so heroic. They think he deserves a promotion."

The major chuckled and reached for his pipe. "I'm way ahead of you, Olivia. I'm going to give him a battlefield promotion, making him a first lieutenant. He's waited a long time."

"And then he's bound to become a captain, isn't he?"

"Eventually. You kind of like that Texan, don't you?" The major paused in filling his pipe.

"Oh, Daddy, he's so tall and handsome. I just almost swoon every time I see him."

"Now, Olivia, you should remember, he's not like the boys you're used to."

"I know. All those in Philadelphia were just boys. Colton is a man."

"You call him Colton?"

She felt herself blush. "Oh, Daddy, you may as well

know, I've set my cap for him. I know he's a little rough around the edges, just like you were when you met Mother, but he can be tamed."

The major lit his pipe and frowned. "You don't want to make the same mistake your mother did."

"Goodness gracious, you don't seem so Irish as Mother says."

"She certainly didn't want to live on some dusty army post. It hasn't been much of a marriage, Olivia."

"Oh, but this is going to be different." Olivia leaned toward him with an eager smile. "I'll turn Colton into a gentleman, correct his grammar and his manners."

"Like your mother tried to do to me?" The major snorted. "You need to accept a man for what he is, my dear, not try to turn him into a silk purse from a sow's ear."

Olivia didn't want to hear that; she was already making plans. "Then we'll move back to Philadelphia and Mother can give him a job in her family's company."

"Colt Prescott doesn't strike me as the type to sit in an office back East." The major puffed his pipe.

"Well, if he insists on staying in the army, you and Mama can use your influence to get him promoted. I think 'Colonel' would be nice. We could be posted to Washington, D.C., where there's lots of social life and fancy balls."

The major smoked and shook his head. "His enlistment is up in June, Olivia, and I guess he'll stay in the army, but he's not the kind of man who can be led around by the nose by a woman. He's a Texan and they have a tendency to be stubborn and independent."

"Oh, just watch me!" Olivia said smugly. "Lieutenant Prescott is mad for me. He'll do anything I want him to do, like a trained lapdog."

"By Saint Mary's blood, I think you underestimate the Texan." The major leaned back in his chair and smoked his pipe.

"Daddy, don't sound so—so Irish." She frowned.

"In the first place, you don't know how Texans feel about the Lone Star State. They say they've got the Texas red dirt flowing in their veins and they won't leave her."

"I think he likes me better than he likes Texas," Olivia said.

"My suggestion for you is Captain Van Smyth. He's got the same kind of background you have, educated and cultured, and I've seen the way he looks at you."

"Howard?" She made a dismissing motion. "He's amusing, but so prissy and civilized. Why, have you noticed that pitiful little mustache and the extra padding in the shoulders of that tailored uniform? Colton certainly doesn't need any padding."

"I'm sure he's all man," the major agreed.

"I've decided I want him, Daddy, so don't be surprised if we're engaged in a few weeks and planning the biggest wedding Philadelphia ever saw."

"Well, I wouldn't object to the lieutenant as a son-in-law. He's a man's man. But I don't think you can bring him to heel like some placid dog."

Olivia stood up. "Just watch me. Oh, Daddy, is it all right if Lieutenant Prescott takes me riding and on a picnic this afternoon?"

"Of course. If it were any other man, I'd say no, fearing for your safety, but the lieutenant is not only an honorable man, he can deal with any emergency from Indians to rattlesnakes. Have a good time."

"We will." She leaned over and kissed her father's gray head. "You're such an old dear."

"And you wrap me around your finger just like you do every other man. You're so pretty, no one can refuse you."

She winked at him. "I know." And then she walked to the door, turned. "Oh, don't forget there's a dance tonight for the officers."

"How could I? And of course, you'll be the belle of the ball."

"I intend to, and you stop drinking so much." She closed the door behind her, feeling cocky and special as she went to her quarters, thinking about what gown she would wear to the dance.

He must be the luckiest man in the world, Colt thought, as he strode to the barn for two horses. Sergeant Mulvaney was there, directing privates in cleaning stables and grooming horses.

"Ah, Lieutenant." He saluted, but Colt grinned and offered his hand.

"Let's not stand on ceremony, Mulvaney—we've known each other too long."

"Ah, now that's a fact. It don't seem almost eight years since the Mexican War ended, sir."

Colt frowned. "There's some of it I'd just as soon forget."

The wiry little sergeant nodded in understanding. They'd both been on that detail to hang the American mutineers, and neither had thought it just. "I've got a snort hidden behind the saddles, sir, if you'd like—"

"Some other time, Sergeant. I'm taking a lady for a ride and I don't want her to smell demon rum on me." He clapped Mulvaney on the back and the other grinned.

"The major's daughter, is it? Aye, she's a rare beauty, that one."

"She is the most beautiful girl I've ever seen," Colt admitted and then frowned because the face that came to his mind was the plain, honest face of Hannah Brownley. Moonlight. Long yellow hair. "Get me a couple of horses saddled, Mulvaney. Rascal and whatever Miss Olivia usually rides."

"Yes, sir." The sergeant grinned and saluted. "Me boys will do it double-quick."

Colt beamed at the thought of the elegant, dark beauty as he led the two horses up to the major's residence and tied up at the hitching rail. He knocked on the door, took off his hat, and bowed, and the beauty came outside wearing a pretty green riding outfit with a saucy hat and veil.

"You are prettier than a spotted pup in a red wagon," he said as he offered his hands so the booted Olivia could swing up to her sidesaddle.

"What?" The lady looked puzzled.

He grinned. "That's Texas talk. Means you couldn't be any prettier. Anyway I'm honored, ma'am, to take you ridin'."

"It's my pleasure." She smiled down at him from her fine bay thoroughbred mare. The expensive riding habit's skirt swept almost to the ground and a perky feathered hat sat on her dark curls. "I brought along a picnic."

"Life doesn't get any better than this." Colt grinned at the beauty as he tied the basket behind her saddle and mounted Rascal.

It was a breezy, comfortable day, the kind that made him feel lucky to live in Texas, Colt thought as the pair started off at a walk. "There's a shady place down by the river that would be perfect for a picnic." Then another thought. "Ma'am, you did ask your father's permission for me to take you ridin'?"

"Of course, Colton." She gave him a dazzling smile. "Daddy has a lot of confidence in you. So do I or I'd be worried about Indians."

He frowned. "That makes me wonder about Mrs. Brownley. She's suffered a lot."

Olivia shrugged. "Oh, her. Well, maybe her husband will come get her soon and she won't be our problem anymore."

"I didn't think of her as a problem." Colt gave her a searching look as they rode. "She's been through hell."

"I know, poor thing," Olivia said. "Since you're so worried about her state of mind, I'll invite her to the officers' dance tonight. Maybe that will brighten her outlook."

"I don't know if she's ready for all those people, the stares she'll get."

"Nonsense. It will be good for her. I'll lend her a nice dress."

He felt his heart melt. "Miss Olivia, you are a really good person."

She blushed and pulled a hankie out of her sleeve and wiped her eyes.

"I didn't mean to make you cry." Damn, this beauty spilled tears like a fountain.

"I was just so touched by your compliment." She dabbed at her eyes. "You're wonderful, Lieutenant."

He glanced over at her as they rode. "No, Miss Olivia, you're the one who's wonderful."

Her long eyelashes flickered downward modestly. "Why, Lieutenant, you say the nicest things."

"I hope I'm not bein' too forward, Miss Olivia, but I hope to get to know you a whole lot better."

"Oh, Colton, you make my heart flutter."

He hoped she wasn't going to cry again. They rode through the bluebonnets and scarlet Indian paint-brush as they crossed the prairie.

"Isn't this fine country?" he murmured. "Good grass belly-deep to a horse. A man could get a few acres and a few cows and in no time, become a rancher."

She looked around. There was nothing for miles except the fort behind them and the tree-lined Brazos River ahead. "It would be pretty lonely out here, no cotillions or ladies' luncheons to dress up for."

"Oh, Texas has a social life, ma'am," he assured her. "Why, there's barbecues and church socials and maybe a barn dance now and then."

"How exciting," she said, but she didn't smile.

"Here's the river up ahead." He nodded toward the slow-moving Brazos, whose banks were lined with live oak and cottonwood trees.

"Are you sure we won't be ambushed by Indians?" she asked as she reined in.

"I've got my rifle and my pistol, Miss Olivia," he reminded her, "and I'm the best shot in the outfit. You're safe with me." He reined in and dismounted, came around to help her.

Olivia looked down at him, giving him her most win-some smile. Yes indeed, she did feel safe with him. This big, broad-shouldered Texan was more man than any she'd ever met. She decided right then and there that she was going to marry Lieutenant Prescott. He was a little rough around the edges, but she would change all that when she got him back to Philadelphia or even Washington, D.C. As he held out his arms to lift her down, she decided this picnic was the perfect time to get him to propose to her.

Chapter 4

Olivia let Colt lift her down from her horse, and she looked up at him, pursing her lips in a way she knew men found irresistible. "You are so strong."

He flushed and looked uncomfortable as he stepped back. "You don't weigh as much as a newborn filly, Miss Olivia."

She reached up to get the picnic basket tied on the side of her horse, but the lieutenant was already there, untying it and taking her arm. "A little thing like you shouldn't carry anything heavy, ma'am."

"You're so gallant. I declare, I just feel so safe and protected around you."

He paused and smiled at her. "Texans expect to look after women. I'd always look after you, Miss Olivia. I never met such a dainty lady before."

She held onto his arm, feeling the muscle there. This was a stallion of a man. She might be playing with fire. "Tell me, Colton, have you never had a sweetheart?"

He flushed and they continued walking to the edge of the river. "No, ma'am. Oh, I know a lot of women, but not ladies like you. There's lots of girls in the saloons. . . ."

He paused and began spreading the blanket she had brought, set the picnic basket down. "Well, I shouldn't be talkin' about women like that with a lady."

Honestly she was very curious about whores and saloon girls but knew she shouldn't be. This Texan was probably very experienced with women, just not back-East ladies. She wondered what it would be like to have him make love to her.

She spread her green skirt and sat down on the blanket, began to open the basket. "I brought fried chicken, homemade bread, and pickles. Oh, I've even got a pound cake."

He grinned as he sat down across from her. "A good cook. I just knew you had everything it would take to make a wife."

"Of course." She gave him her brightest smile as she handed him a plate of food, making sure their hands touched. As a matter of fact, she had a maid and a cook back home in Philadelphia. Olivia didn't have the slightest idea how to cook even an egg and didn't see any reason to learn. Her Tonk maid, Maria, had fixed this basket.

"This looks larrupin'," he said as he took the plate.

"Is that Texan for delicious?" She giggled.

"Yes, ma'am." He began to eat and Olivia sighed. She would have to do something about his table manners or she could never take him to a formal dinner or an evening at the opera. Well, he was so handsome, she decided she could retrain this diamond in the rough. She could already imagine him in formal wear at the White House. All the other women would be so envious of her with this tall Texan as an escort.

"Would you like some lemonade, Colton?"

He looked up from his chicken. "I'm much obliged, ma'am. Reckon we should have saved some of this for Mrs. Brownley. I reckon she hasn't had fried chicken and pound cake in a long while."

Olivia gritted her teeth, but she smiled with a show of sympathy. "I'm sure she hasn't. Maybe tomorrow, I'll cook up a great meal and take it over to her and Doc."

He smiled at her. "You're so kind."

She ate very little. Ladies were supposed to have birdlike appetites. Besides, she could gorge herself on the leftovers when she got back to the fort.

The Texan was enjoying his food and she handed him a linen napkin, afraid he might wipe his greasy face on his sleeve. "This is really good, Miss Olivia. You should eat more. You haven't eaten enough to keep a sparrow alive."

"Ladies have such delicate constitutions," she sighed. "We need big, strong men to look after us."

"I'll sure do that, Miss Olivia. You'll come to no harm as long as I'm around. Why, if you were mine . . ."

"Yes?" She leaned forward, making her lips as pouty as possible.

"Never you mind." He set his plate down and wiped his mouth, looking embarrassed.

She leaned forward so that he could smell the sweet scent of her perfume. "I know we barely know each other, Colton, but you're so different from the boys I've known in the past. You're a man."

He looked awkward. "Most Texans are men by the time they're fifteen. There's a lot of responsibility and danger in this state that makes them grow up fast."

"I could see a life with you," she whispered and leaned toward him.

Colt looked down at her. Their faces were only inches apart and he could see her breasts move as she breathed and smell her delicate perfume. Her lips looked so soft and inviting and it had been a long time since he'd had a woman. His maleness came up hard and aching, and without thinking, he reached out one strong arm and pulled Olivia to him, crushing her lips under his. Her lips parted, urging him on, and he kissed her and then abruptly, he jerked back.

"Oh, Miss Olivia, a thousand apologies. I don't know what I was thinkin'. You a lady and me grabbin' you like you were some saloon tart—"

"Oh, but isn't that what people do when they decide they love each other?" She looked up at him, her dark eyes wide. "I mean, you are going to speak to Daddy about courting me and all that, aren't you?"

He hesitated only a split second. Why did Hannah Brownley's face come to his mind? Hannah was a married woman, and besides, Olivia was the most beautiful girl he'd ever met and she liked him, too. Well, of course he'd be a lucky hombre to marry the major's daughter. He brushed thoughts of Hannah aside. "Of course, Miss Olivia. I'll ask your father if it's okay with him if I court you."

"I'm sure it will be fine with Daddy." She smiled at him, leaned over, and gave him a quick peck on the lips. "We'll announce our engagement tonight at the officer's dance."

"So soon? I mean, shouldn't I court you awhile to make sure it's gonna work?"

"Don't you love me, Colton?" Big tears gathered in her beautiful brown eyes.

He couldn't stand to see her cry again. "I think I do, Miss Olivia. What man wouldn't? But you've got so many fellas to choose from and underneath, I'm just a Texas cowboy."

"I think you're wonderful, Colton, and I think I'd love being married to you."

Why was he hesitating when this highborn beauty wanted him? For a split second, the tall, blond captive crossed his mind. There was something about Hannah that called to him, but he reminded himself she was married and her husband would be coming for her any time now.

He took a deep breath. After all, he had compromised the lady by kissing her with abandon. Of course now she expected him to offer marriage, not like the whores at the saloons and hog ranches who would spread their legs for anyone. This was a pure, virginal lady, and he had broken a Texan's rule and kissed her without asking permission.

He brushed any regrets aside as he smiled down at her. "It's gettin' late. Maybe we'd better get back," he said and began to gather up the picnic things.

Olivia stood up as he folded the blanket. "Oh, Colton, I'm so happy. I can hardly wait for the rest of my family to meet you." She put her arms around him and hugged him.

He kissed the top of her head, still in awe of her beauty. "I haven't got any family left to meet you."

Why had he been so hesitant? This highborn beauty wanted to marry him and sleep in his arms at night. He took a deep, shuddering breath at the thought of making love to her. She'd get used to Texas whether he decided to reenlist or go into ranching.

He carried the picnic basket back to tie on her horse and then lifted her to her sidesaddle. She leaned over and gave him a quick peck. "I've been wanting you to kiss me since the first time I met you."

He felt himself flush. "And I've been wantin' to kiss you since the first time I saw you," he answered with a grin as he mounted up on his bay mustang. They took off at a canter back toward the fort. Somehow Colt had thought he'd feel more than lust when he met the right girl, but maybe that would come later. What man wouldn't be willing to give up saloon girls to have a beautiful lady in his bed every night? And their children would be true Texans, loving the Lone Star State as much as he did.

He escorted Olivia to her quarters and then felt drawn to go by the infirmary to see how Mrs. Brownley was doing. She was down on her hands and knees scrubbing the floor.

"Oh, hello." She looked up.

"You shouldn't be—"

"The place isn't as clean as it could be," she said and continued scrubbing. "I intend to pay for my keep."

Doc came in from his quarters just then and frowned at Colt. "Dag nab it, I tried to make her stop, but she insisted," he said apologetically. "I must say the place needed a woman's touch."

"Mrs. Brownley, I just wanted to tell you there's an officers' dinner and dance tonight. Miss Murphy will be coming by to invite you personally."

"How polite of the major's daughter." She paused and then stood up, wiping her hands on her apron. "No, I don't think I want to face people. They'll be so curious."

"I'd protect you," Doc said. "I haven't been to a

dance since my wife died. It might be good for both of us to be out among our own kind again."

She shook her head and Colt felt such pity for her. "Miss Olivia is going to lend you a dress and there'll be dancin'."

"I haven't danced in such a long time." She sounded wistful. "But no, I don't think I'd feel comfortable."

Colt put his hand on her shoulder. She was tall for a woman, but he was taller. Her skin was deeply tanned, so unlike a lady, and her skin and hair smelled like soap. Her hair was pulled back in a simple way and when the Texas sun shone through the window and touched it, it looked like . . . moonlight. "Would you come for me?"

She pulled away from him and looked at the floor. "I'll have to think about it. People will stare."

"So let them. You've dealt with Comanches—can't you deal with a few curious white people?"

She looked up at him. "I'll think about it."

"Fine. I'll see you there then. Doc will bring you."

Colt turned and went out the door. There was something about Mrs. Brownley that drew him to her. Maybe it was because they were both Texans or maybe because both had been captives of the Comanches. She's married, he reminded himself as he walked back to his quarters, and besides, you're now engaged to Miss Olivia. In fact, you ought to feel flattered that the beauty wants to keep company with a rough, poorly educated Texas hombre when she could certainly have her choice of all those rich dandies back East. Why, the elegant Captain Van Smyth always looked at her like a hound dog eying a ham bone.

Hannah certainly didn't want to attend the officers'

party, but she was afraid she would raise suspicions if she didn't, so she accepted another of Olivia Murphy's cast-off dresses, a yellow one this time, combed her hair and put it up in a French twist, and let Doc escort her over to the officers' mess hall.

Doc must have felt the tension in her arm as he took it, because he whispered, "Now, there's nothing to be afraid of, Mrs. Brownley. Some of these people will be curious because they've all heard about you, but you'll be fine."

She wished she had that kind of confidence, she thought as they entered and everyone stopped talking and turned to stare at her.

She saw Lieutenant Prescott and Olivia over by the refreshment table and managed to smile at them. The dark-haired beauty wore a white gown that emphasized her pale ivory skin and dark hair.

Immediately, the lieutenant took Olivia's arm and steered her over. Colt Prescott was so tall and handsome, she thought, and so different from the men she'd dealt with in her life. If only . . . no, she must not think about that. She must get back to the Comanche camp, maybe tonight after everyone was asleep.

"Mrs. Brownley," the lieutenant bowed slightly. "You look lovely tonight, so glad you could come."

Olivia's mouth smiled, but her eyes did not. "Yes, you do look lovely. I'm so glad my old dress fits you."

Colt frowned at Olivia, then looked at Hannah again. "I do hope you'll save me a dance later, Mrs. Brownley."

Olivia took the lieutenant's arm possessively. "Oh, Doc, I want you to be the first to know—Colton and I are engaged."

"Dag nab it, congratulations!" Doc pumped Colt's hand. "You're getting an awfully pretty girl there, Lieutenant."

"Don't I know it." Colt grinned, but Hannah thought he looked a little uncertain.

"Yes, congratulations," she whispered.

The two men began to talk about horses, and Hannah stood there awkwardly, looking around. People were talking again, but they were staring at her.

Olivia glared at her. "Oh, you must tell the ladies about your ordeal among the Comanche," she said. "They're all dying to hear the lurid details."

Hannah gave her a cold stare. "I'd rather not discuss that, thank you."

Doc must have caught part of the exchange because he stopped talking suddenly and took Hannah's arm. "I forget my manners, Mrs. Brownley. Would you like some punch?"

"Oh, yes, that would be lovely." Anything to get out of this situation. She had a sudden desire to slap the major's daughter, and that would never do. She let Doc lead her over to the refreshment table and get her a cup of punch.

Now a group of ladies who had been standing nearby nudged one of their older members and she came over to Hannah. She wore expensive dark blue lace with a fine cameo at the throat. "I'm Captain Van Smyth's aunt, Mrs. Maude Van Smyth, visiting from Boston. How do you do?"

"Very well, thank you," Hannah replied, "and I am—"

"Oh, we all know who you are. The ladies are wondering if you'd care to tell us about what it was like being a captive of the savages. Did they—?"

"I don't think I care to discuss it," Hannah said, gritting her teeth and forbidding herself to throw the cup of pink punch in the stern older woman's face.

"Well!" The lady humphed. "I was only trying to be sociable." At that point, she whirled and marched back to her group of ladies, and the murmuring and laughter started again.

Doc took a deep breath. "Danged old biddies don't have enough to occupy themselves," he muttered. "Oh, look, the band is about to start up. I'm sure lots of the men will want to dance with you."

"I don't think they will." What she'd really like to do was leave. She'd had enough of the stares and tittering, but she wasn't going to let them run her out of here. She was a survivor and she'd dealt with much worse than a bunch of curious people. She knew what the women wanted to know: Had she been raped by a lot of the savages and what was it like to be bedded by a Comanche warrior? She flinched, not even wanting to think about it. Both Luther and Spider had tried to break her spirit, and turn her into an obedient, spineless female, but she was as defiant as ever.

"You gonna let them win?" Doc asked as the band started a slow waltz and some of the couples took the floor.

"I—I can't stop them from gossiping." She swallowed hard, watching the young officers gathered around Olivia like bees around a honey tree, vying for her attention.

Doc asked, "Mrs. Brownley, would you care to dance?"

"I don't think—" But he was already taking the punch cup out of her hand and leading her toward the dance floor. Lieutenant Prescott and Olivia were on the floor now, with eager officers cutting in.

Could Hannah even remember the steps? She wasn't sure, but she raised her chin, pasted a frozen smile on her face, and let Doc lead her out on the floor.

Doc took her in his arms and whispered in her ear. "Now, it'll come back to you, just follow my lead. I wanted to get my dance in before all those young officers start asking you."

But of course they didn't. After that dance, she and Doc stood on the sidelines as song after song was played. While men looked at her and whispered, none asked her to dance. They probably didn't dare, not with their women glaring at Hannah.

"Doc, I think we should leave early. I'm getting a headache."

"You gonna turn tail and run?" Doc challenged. "Or are you gonna stand your ground like a real Texas girl?"

She was a Texas girl, all right. She took a deep breath and glared back at the people who were staring at her. Then the music stopped, and Lieutenant Prescott led a reluctant-looking Olivia to join them.

"Goodness gracious, isn't it a great dance?" Olivia laughed. "Why all these handsome soldier boys have about danced me breathless, even though I'm an engaged woman." She smiled at Hannah, but it was not a real smile.

Just then the major stepped up on the bandstand. "Well, before the band starts again, I'd like to make an announcement, something my daughter told me a few minutes ago. I'm announcing her engagement to Lieutenant Colton Prescott and I'll be very pleased to have him as my son-in-law."

The crowd applauded and then circled around the couple to shake Colt's hand and wish Olivia much happiness. The major opened several bottles of champagne and everyone took a glass and toasted the happy couple, including Hannah, but she couldn't swallow the wine. She didn't think Colt really knew what Miss Olivia was like, and the rich society girl would make married life miserable for him. Hannah wished she'd met a man like Colt before she married Luther, but now it was too late.

The music started again and the crowd scattered to the dance floor or the sidelines. Colt set down his glass and held out his hand to Hannah. "Mrs. Brownley, you look like a sunbeam in that yellow dress. Would you do me the honor? I've been waitin' to dance with you all evenin'."

Olivia snapped, "I don't think she wants to dance, do you, Mrs. Brownley?"

Hannah looked into the other's flashing eyes and then took Colt's hand defiantly. "Why, yes, Lieutenant, I think I'd enjoy waltzing with you."

She heard Olivia's gasp of dismay as Colt led Hannah out onto the floor. People began to whisper and gave way, leaving them plenty of room to waltz. Hannah closed her eyes and held onto the man's big hand, enjoying being in his arms. This was a real man, a true Texan, who could hold his own in a fight, or hold a woman protectively. For a long moment, they waltzed and she was aware of nothing else but the pleasure of his embrace. If only she had met this man long ago, but now he was engaged and she was heading back to the Comanche camp.

Then as she slowly opened her eyes, she became

aware that everyone else had left the dance floor and were watching the lone couple with horrified looks and scandalized whispers. When she looked over at the sidelines, Olivia looked like an angry shrew, her pretty face flushed and her fists clenched.

It occurred to Hannah that she might be ruining the lieutenant's chances for advancement, him dancing with a woman who had been in the bed of savages. She didn't want to do anything to cause him trouble.

"I—I think I need some air," she whispered, pulling out of his arms and walking rapidly out the door. She leaned on the porch railing, taking deep breaths. She had known it would be like this if she was ever rescued and had to return to white civilization. The public expected a virtuous white woman to kill herself before she'd let herself be used by a savage. Well, there hadn't been that much difference between Luther and Spider. Only her indomitable spirit had kept her alive all these years, and now there was another reason. . . .

She heard the door open behind her. Maybe it was Doc. Good, she'd like to go back to the infirmary now.

"Are you all right?" It was Colt's deep Texas drawl.

"I—I'm fine."

"You're not cryin', are you?"

She turned to look up at him, shook her head. "I haven't cried in a long, long time. It doesn't do any good." And besides, it made her look vulnerable and she would never be that again.

"I didn't mean to cause you pain by askin' you to dance." He put his hands on her shoulders and she tried not to tremble.

"I know you meant well, Lieutenant, but it wasn't good for your reputation and besides, your fiancée wasn't happy that you asked me." She turned and gazed out across the fort's grounds.

"Olivia? Oh, I'm sure that's not true. She's a wonderful girl."

He was warm against her back. She didn't say anything but pulled away from him. His nearness was too much for her. She wanted to go into his strong arms and have him hold her close and tenderly, tell her she was his and he would protect her from pain and misery and hurtful people from now on. No man had ever held her tenderly.

"I shouldn't have come," she said. "I knew that, but I hoped—"

"They just don't have much to talk about around here," Colt said. "And anyway, you'll be leavin' soon, when your husband hears we've found you and comes after you."

That would be even worse than going back to Spider, she thought with a shudder. However, she didn't intend to be here if and when Luther Brownley showed up.

"You go back to the dance." Hannah managed a smile as she turned to face him. "And I'll walk on back to the infirmary."

"I'll walk you back," he said.

"That would cause talk." She shook her head. "I'll be all right." She stepped off the porch as she heard the door open again and Olivia's voice.

"Darling, what are you doing out here?" Olivia sounded angry. "People are talking—"

And then Colt's annoyed voice. "Damn it, Olivia, are you cryin' again? I haven't done anything wrong."

"But you followed that—that woman outside and you danced with her and—"

"Let's go back inside, Olivia, and please stop cryin'!"

Hannah heard the door slam shut, and she paused, listening to the faint music and laughter from inside. For a long moment, she remembered dancing in Colt's arms and sighed. She had never met a man like him, powerful, protective, yet gentle. Olivia didn't appreciate him like she should.

Well, that didn't matter now. Hannah walked back to the infirmary. She would roll up a small bundle of clothes and a little food and hide it under her bed. After Doc came back and went to his quarters, she would wait until the whole camp was asleep, then sneak over to the stables and steal a horse. The Comanche camp had surely moved by now, but she could follow tracks and by this time tomorrow, she'd be back in Spider's teepee. She shuddered at the thought, but she had to do it.

Hannah got her stuff together and went to bed. When Doc came in, she pretended to be asleep and heard him go into his quarters and shut the door. It was all working out the way she had planned. She would wait another hour until she was certain everyone was asleep; then she would be fleeing this fort.

Chapter 5

Hannah waited until it was silent as a tomb outside before she gathered up her things, put on the dirty old hide dress and moccasins. Then, taking her small bundle, she sneaked out the door. Once outside, she paused, listening. The night was dark and moonless, which was good. It was so silent, not even a dog barked. She began creeping toward the barns.

There would be a sentry on guard at the fort gate, of course, but if she were lucky, he might be half asleep and wouldn't hear her riding away.

A slight breeze blew across the prairie, bringing the scent of bluebonnets and scarlet Indian paintbrush. The barn loomed large and silent in the night, but when she opened the creaking door, she smelled the pleasant aroma of fresh hay and the warm scent of horses. Several of them stamped restlessly in their stalls and one whinnied. She held her breath, worried the noise might disturb someone who would come to investigate, but the breeze was blowing in her favor.

Which horse should she take? She didn't have much faith in the army's fancy thoroughbreds; she'd been riding Comanche mustangs too long. Lieutenant Prescott rode a mustang, a scrubby, tough little bay horse. That's the one she needed, not a fancy grain-fed mount that would give out under her if the army pursued her. What did he call it? Oh, yes, Rascal. She went up and down the stalls, trying to find the horse in the darkness. "Rascal? Rascal, are you here?"

In answer, she heard a soft nicker down the row of stalls and felt her way down there. The moon came out from behind a cloud, and through a barn window, she could see the wiry little horse. The lieutenant would be furious, and she felt bad about it because he'd been so nice to her, but she needed the best horse for covering lots of plains country.

Quickly she got a saddle and bridle, led the little horse out of his stall. He nuzzled her and she patted his ears. "When we get there, I'll turn you loose and you can come back to Colt."

She saddled up, tied her small bundle on the back of the saddle, and mounted. Then they eased out of the barn as quietly as possible and started toward the gate. The moon had gone behind a cloud and she was grateful for that. Maybe she could get out of the fort without the sentry being aware of her. The little mustang's hooves seemed to echo in the silence as they rode across the parade grounds. There was no sound except the cicadas, and somewhere in the distance, a coyote howled faintly. At any moment, she expected to hear a sentry shout at her to halt, but it was silent in the warm Texas night. How would she get past the fort gate without being spotted?

Then she remembered she had seen a break in the low stone wall a few hundred yards from the gate. She reined the mustang that direction, still walking it and hoping for luck. The moon came out big and yellow, illuminating the whole scene and throwing shadows of her and the horse across the bare ground. Up ahead lay the break in the wall. She took a deep breath and headed for it. In the distance, she saw the sentry at his post by the gate.

"All right, little mustang, we've got to go fast now." She leaned down on Rascal's neck, making herself as small as possible as the horse stepped through the broken place in the stones. At the same time she dug her heels in Rascal's flanks and gave him his head, the sentry seemed to come alive.

"Halt! Who goes there?"

At that, she slapped Rascal with the reins and they took off at a gallop with the sentry yelling after them and then a shot echoing through the silence. Hannah thought she felt the bullet whizzing past her, but she didn't slow down. She kept the horse at a gallop for another quarter of a mile; then she paused the lathered mount for a long moment on a rise and looked behind her. Dim lights winked on here and there at the fort. It would take a while before they figured out what had happened and who was missing. Maybe they wouldn't bother to pursue her, she thought; then she grimaced. No, she had taken the lieutenant's favorite horse. He would come after her, no matter what.

She rode the mustang at a slow lope for a while, trying to decide which way to go. The Comanches would have moved their camp by now. She had to rein in and think. Where would they be? Maybe in the rough, untamed Llano Estacado. It was a long, difficult ride, but she had a good horse under her and a full canteen. If she were lucky, she could find the Comanche camp before the soldiers found her.

* * *

Back at the fort, Colt came awake to a pounding on his door. "Lieutenant! Lieutenant Prescott!"

He jumped out of bed and ran barefooted to the door, swung it open. "What the hell?"

Mulvaney stood there, breathless and nervous as he saluted. "Aye, sorry to wake you, sir, but the major said to get you."

"What's happened? Let me get my pants and boots on." Colt ran back into his room with the old sergeant following him. "I thought I heard a shot."

"That was me, sir," the little Irishman said. "I don't know who, someone stealing one of the horses. I fired at him but he kept riding. You think it's Injuns?"

"Not hardly." Colt had his pants on and grabbed his shirt and boots. "They wouldn't take just one horse. Reckon we got a deserter who's had enough of the Cavalry."

They walked outside and Colt sat down on the step and pulled his boots on. Other soldiers were milling around, awakened by the noise. "You men go back to your bunks," Colt ordered. "If it's a deserter, we can wait 'til mornin' to go after him. If he doesn't know the country, he won't get far; especially if he heads west. It's so desolated, hot, and flat out there, even jackrabbits and coyotes avoid the Staked Plains."

Sergeant Mulvaney said, "Beg pardon, sir, not tonight?"

Colt shook his head. "He'll be lucky if we find him before the Comanches do. They'll roast him alive. Tell the major I'll look into it and I'll go see which horse he took."

"Yes, sir." Mulvaney saluted and was gone.

Damn it all to hell, he hated being awakened like that. He always came up out of his bunk grabbing for his pistol. It was a reflex of all these years living on the Texas frontier. He lit a lantern and strode toward the barn. Inside the darkness, he was greeted by the scent of hay and warm horseflesh, and several horses nickered a greeting. Colt walked up and down the rows of stalls. These big thoroughbreds couldn't take the long haul. The deserter would find himself stranded out on the plains with a played-out horse and not enough water if he hadn't thought to take a canteen.

Everything seemed to be all right, he thought as he walked up and down the row of stalls. And then he came to Rascal's stall. It was empty. He held the lantern higher in disbelief, than began to curse. The deserter was smart enough to know which horse could take the heat and still keep running.

"Damn his eyes! When I get my hands on him, I'll beat him to a pulp before I toss him in the guardhouse."

Immediately, Colt forgot about waiting until morning. Some trooper had stolen Colt's own horse. That added insult to injury. Now who in this bunch of troopers would be smart enough to take the ugly mustang instead of one of the fine thoroughbreds? Then an idea crossed his mind. "No, she wouldn't dare."

But the captive was just the one who would know which horse was the best for a long ride. He'd better check first. Still carrying the lantern, he left the barn and with long strides, crossed the parade ground to the infirmary and banged on the door. "Doc? Doc? Damn it, open up!"

After a moment, Doc opened the door, still yawning and in his drawers, scratching his bald head. "Dag nab it! What in the—? Oh, it's you, Lieutenant. What—?"

Colt pushed past him, looking around. "Where's Mrs. Brownley?"

"Who?" Doc blinked in the lamplighter.

"Mrs. Brownley!" Colt shouted at him and then strode into the infirmary, his boots making loud sounds on the bare wood floor. "Ahah! Just as I thought!" Her bed was empty.

"What?" Doc scratched his head again. "What's going on?"

"Our damned captive has run off and she took my horse."

"Why, she came in from the dance and went to bed." Doc seemed half asleep and puzzled.

"She's smarter than we thought she was," Colt complained. "I should have left her with the Comanches."

"Now why would she want to go back?" Doc asked.

However, Colt was already whirling to leave. "How the hell should I know? She's probably not goin' back to the Indians, she's just runnin' away."

"But why—?"

"Tell the major I'm in pursuit." Colt took off toward the barn at a dead run.

Doc called after him. "Don't you think you'd better wait 'til morning and take a patrol with you?"

"She's stolen my horse," Colt yelled back and kept running. "Besides the major won't want a white woman goin' back to the Indians. It's unthinkable."

It *was* unthinkable, Colt thought. Hannah was either loco or . . . he couldn't think of any other reason. Surely she wasn't in love with Spider after the way he must have treated her? He shook his head. There was no figuring women. If she wanted to go back to the Comanche, he didn't give a damn, but the fact she'd stolen his favorite horse was an insult that set his blood boiling.

He went through the barn, looked over horses, and finally picked one, Olivia's blood bay. It looked better than the others, although he had no faith in the fancy-blooded horses. Obviously, neither did Hannah Brownley.

He made sure he had two canteens of water as he saddled up and mounted. With any luck, he might outsmart her because he, of all the soldiers, had an idea where the Comanches might be camping now. There was a small stream in the desolate area called Llano Estacado, better known as the Staked Plains, and he knew a shortcut. With any luck, he could intercept Hannah before she reached the Indian camp.

As he rode out onto the parade ground, Major Murphy strode out to meet him, still half dressed. "A deserter? Lieutenant, I think it can wait 'til—"

"It's Mrs. Brownley, sir." Colt saluted. "I think she may be tryin' to rejoin the Comanches."

"What? A white woman who's just been rescued? Why would she do that?"

Colt shrugged, still furious with her. "Loco, I reckon, sir."

"We can't allow her to become a captive again. Go after her, Lieutenant. That's an order. Maybe when you get back, Doc can do something to help the poor thing."

Colt saluted again and dug his heels into the big blood bay. He'd make her think twice before she took his horse again. After what he'd gone through to rescue her, she repaid him by stealing Rascal. As he rode through the gate, he imagined turning her across his knee and spanking her. No, he couldn't do that. She wasn't his to spank, and besides, her husband should be arriving soon to take her away. As much trouble as she was, Colt would be glad to see her gone.

As he rode through the night at a slow lope, Colt remembered the scent of her when he'd danced with her. She didn't wear fancy perfume like Olivia. She just smelled clean and warm, and her yellow hair had been soft as corn silk when he pressed his face against it. And she'd just fit into his arms like she belonged there. He gritted his teeth and swore. Yes, she'd pulled at his emotions at the dance, evidently plotting to sneak out, steal his horse, and ride away only a couple of hours later. So much for trusting women.

Colt rode a long time, stopping now and then to rest his horse, and once to pour water out of his canteen into his hat to give the horse a drink. He looked up at the dark sky, trying to guess the time of night. About a half mile up ahead was a pile of rocks that might intersect where she would come riding by. Since Colt had taken a shortcut, he could be there ahead of her. They were still miles from where the Comanche liked to camp. If he was lucky, he would be waiting for her when she came along.

He rode to the pile of rocks and dismounted, let the horse graze while he watched the trail. Maybe she hadn't come this way or maybe he had missed her. By now, she might be almost anywhere. He started to roll a cigarette, then remembered she had been among the Indians a long time. Hannah might be able to smell the scent of burning tobacco. Living among the Indians taught a person a lot.

He leaned against the boulder and listened for the sound of hoofbeats. What would he do if he missed her? Let her go back to the Comanche and be damned, he thought, but he wanted his horse back. After a while, he thought he heard the rhythmic pounding of a horse's hooves coming up the trail. He grabbed his mount's muzzle to keep it from nickering a welcome. Now as he peered around the boulders, he could see her coming, a small lean silhouette on a mustang, riding at an easy lope. He waited until she was almost to the boulders, and then he stepped out, pistol in hand. "Halt or I'll shoot!"

Any other woman would have reined in, but this damned feisty girl reined around him, dug her heels in Rascal's sides, and went around Colt, leaving him standing in the dust looking after her.

"Damn you!" Colt mounted up and took after her. "Stop or I'll shoot!"

Instead, she rode faster.

He'd never catch the mustang in the long run. Instead he yelled, "Rascal!" And whistled long and loud.

The mustang slid to a halt and the girl went over his head. Colt dismounted and ran to her. "Serves you right! Are you hurt?"

She came up fighting tooth and nail, clawing at him as he tried to help her up.

Any other woman would be nursing her bruises and weeping, but Hannah stood her ground and fought him as he helped her to her feet. "Let go of me! Let me go!"

"You little wench! You stole my favorite horse!"

He had his arms around her, but she wasn't giving up and it was like hanging onto a bobcat. Now they both went down, rolling in the dirt as they fought. She was slender, but big-breasted, and she kicked at him with those long legs as he managed to pin her against the ground. "Give up, Hannah. You can't win."

In answer, she reached over and bit his wrist hard.

"Damn!" He turned her loose and she tried to get out from under him, but his weight held her down. She lay there with her deerskin shift half torn open, gasping for air, but she wasn't crying. "Let me go! I've got to get back to the camp!"

He sat on her now, nursing his bite and staring down at her. Her half-naked breasts were clearly visible as the moon came out from behind clouds again. "Why have you got to go back? Do you love Spider?"

She shuddered and made a face. "God no, I hate him!"

"Then why—?"

"If—if I let you take me, will you let me go?" She looked up at him, still breathing hard, but not fighting anymore.

He realized abruptly how tempting her slender, warm body was, and he hadn't had a woman in a long time. "Why, you little tart. You're offerin' to have sex with me if I'll let you go? What kind of—?"

"Please," she whispered and her voice trembled. "I've got to get back to the camp."

God, he was suddenly tempted. And who would ever know? His manhood rose at the thought of taking her right here in the dirt. As much as he was aroused, it wouldn't take two minutes. But he was engaged, he remembered, engaged to Olivia and he was an honorable man.

Instead he stood up slowly and pulled her to her feet. She was dusty and her deerskin shift torn, but she still wasn't weeping. She was defiant, blue eyes blazing like cold fire. "All right," he said, "why is it you've got to get back to the Comanches if you don't love Spider and—"

"There's a child," she begged. "I've got a little boy in the camp."

"I thought your little boy died right after birth?" Colt asked, mystified.

"That was my husband's child. This is Spider's son."

And now it all came clear to Colt. She had left a half-breed son behind, and she would do anything to get back to him. Knowing Spider, he wouldn't let her take that child, so she had to return to her baby.

Colt nodded in understanding. "Tell me about it."

She sat down on a rock and brushed the yellow hair out of her eyes. "After he stole me, Spider made me his wife." She closed her eyes and winced as if remembering the events. "I have a son by him. He's a little over two years old."

Colt remembered what he knew about the tribe. "Doesn't he have other sons? Other wives?"

"Another wife, yes." Hannah nodded. "But she has given him no children, so she hates me for being his favorite. I'm afraid Tariito will mistreat my son if I don't get back to protect him."

Tariito, Colt thought. It meant "Claw" in Comanche, and the tribe tried to give everyone a name that fit their personality. The woman must be a terrible shrew.

"I know Spider. He is my blood brother." Colt held out his arm for her to see the scar. "You don't want to go back; he will continue to be cruel to you."

"I know," she said. "He tried to break my spirit, but I was as determined as I was against Luther and my stepfather. No man can make me vulnerable. Still I have to return to protect my son from Tariito."

"Why didn't you tell me that the night we captured you?" He sat down next to her with a sigh.

"I—I tried. No one would listen to me and there was so much confusion and I couldn't remember the words. It's been a long time since I spoke English."

"Where were all the warriors the night we hit the camp?"

"Gone on a hunt. Little Grasshopper was inside the teepee with Tariito. I was trying to reach them so you could take us both out of the camp."

"Oh God, I wish I had known that."

"So you see why I have to go back." She looked up at him with those wide blue eyes.

"Look"—he put his big hands on her small shoulders—"I can't let you return, knowing he'll beat you and rape you again."

"That doesn't matter. I've got to protect my son."

"If I promise to bring the troops to save him, will you go back with me?"

"I don't know if I can trust you." She looked deep into his eyes and she seemed so defenseless and vulnerable. He fought an urge to take her in his arms and hold her close, protect her from all the horrible things that this brave Texas girl had endured.

"Hannah, I promise. You know when a Texan gives his word, it's as good as gold."

"Yes, it is. I trust you, Colt, and I've never trusted a man before. My real father was killed in the Fannin Massacre and my stepfather drank and beat me. I ran away at fifteen and married a man I thought loved me, but he didn't."

"Luther Brownley?"

She swallowed hard and nodded.

"He'll be comin' to get you," Colt said.

She shook her head. "Maybe not. Would you want a woman who had been used as a plaything by a savage?"

"It wouldn't make any difference to me," he answered.

She gave him a rare smile, and he thought, in that

moment, that she was beautiful when she smiled. Why had he thought her plain?

"You're different than most men, Colt. All right, I have your word, so I'll go back with you."

"And you've got to promise me you won't try to take off again." He stood up and reached a hand down to her.

She took it with a strong, callused hand that had always worked and worked hard. "I promise."

"Come on then. Let's get back to the fort before it gets daylight. I don't want a stray Comanche scout to run across us. I left the tribe on bad terms with Spider."

He pulled her to her feet and they walked toward the horses. Rascal nickered and nuzzled Colt's shirt. Colt scratched his ears. "You're a good judge of horse-flesh, Hannah."

"I knew the mustang would get me there. How did you find me?"

"I lived among the Comanche, remember? I know about that spring in the Llano Estacado. There's almost no other water out on those dry Staked Plains." He looked over his fine thoroughbred, realized it was going lame. He bent and examined the blood bay's leg, shook his head. "I told the major these fancy horses were no good out here. I'll have to lead him back and we'll ride double."

He offered his cupped hand. She put a moccasined foot in it, and he lifted her to Rascal's back, then mounted up himself. He could appreciate a woman who would sacrifice everything, even her own freedom, to return for a small son. He would talk to the major about leading a raid into the Comanche camp again. He had made Hannah a promise and he intended to keep it.

She fit so naturally against him as they started back to the fort. He felt her shiver and, without thinking, he pulled her close against him and tried to remember that he was engaged to a beautiful lady. It was difficult with Hannah leaning back against his chest as they rode.

He could smell the sweet, clean scent of her yellow hair as he put his arms around her to guide the horse. Something about her made him want to hold and protect her. Then he reminded himself he must not have feelings for this girl. Her husband would be coming for her and besides, he was engaged to Olivia.

They got back to the fort just before dawn. Colt returned her to the infirmary and went about his duties. Hannah said she would begin a vegetable garden and help Doc with the few patients.

That evening at dusk, Colt stopped her out near the infirmary. "I've talked to the major. He's waitin' for new supplies to come in, but I reckon we'll head for the Comanche camp in a few days."

"Can't it happen any faster?" She was concerned for her son.

Colt shook his head. "Just be patient. You promised, remember?"

She nodded, trusting this man as she had never trusted another.

Finally darkness fell and one light after another winked out.

Hannah went to bed, but she could not sleep. She lay there, thinking about Colt and wishing things were different, but of course he was engaged to the major's daughter and she was uncertain what her future was after the army rescued little Grasshopper. She didn't think Luther would come for her and certainly she didn't intend to return with him and live as his wife. Finally, she dropped off to sleep.

She was awakened sometime in the middle of the night by a sound. For a moment, she wasn't sure what it was and wondered if she had imagined it. Then she realized it was the slight noise of a window sliding open and then light footsteps, no louder than a cat.

She froze, ready for anything, still not completely awake. And then a dark shadow loomed over her and she felt the sharp blade of a knife against her neck.

"Do not call out," the guttural voice snarled in Comanche, "or I will cut your throat."

She felt ice-cold terror, but she did not move. There was no mistaking that cruel voice. It was Spider.

Chapter 6

Colt was awakened just before dawn by fists pounding on his door and Doc's voice. "Lieutenant! Lieutenant! Wake up! Mrs. Brownley is gone!"

"What? Not again!" Colt came out of bed in his drawers and stumbled to the door, opened it to chubby Doc, his bald head shiny with sweat, the white fringe all disarrayed. "What happened?"

"I tell you, she's gone. Must have run away again in the middle of the night."

"Well, damn it all to hell!" Colt walked over to grab his pants and boots. "She promised me she'd stay until we could mount a patrol to get her little boy back."

"Dag nab it, I don't care what she promised, she's gone." Doc rushed into the room as Colt stepped into his trousers and sat down on his bunk to put on his boots.

Then Doc seemed to hear Colt's words for the first time. "Boy? What boy?"

"She's got a son in the Comanche camp." Colt was more than annoyed with the blonde; he was disappointed. He would have bet his life the girl would keep her promise.

"Ohh." Doc nodded in understanding as Colt pulled on his boots and the two walked out onto the porch. Outside there was noise of confusion from the gate, a bugle blowing, sleepy troopers running about.

"Now what?" Colt grumbled, running his hand through his tousled black hair. He yelled at a running soldier, "What's happenin'?"

The soldier slid to a halt and saluted. "With the changing of the guard, they just found the night sentry with his throat cut."

"As you were, soldier." Colt waved him on, his mind working. No, Hannah would not cut a man's throat.

"What the hell?" Doc asked. "You think she killed—?"

Colt shook his head. "There's only one man I know who could kill a guard, sneak inside a fort full of armed men and take a prisoner, sneak out again without wakin' anyone. It has to be Spider."

"You mean that Comanche—?"

"We'd better get to the major," Colt said and took off in long strides so fast Doc's short legs couldn't keep up.

The major was already up and in his office, still buttoning his shirt as Colt walked in and saluted. "I know, I know. We've had a guard killed."

"Also," Colt said, "Hannah—Mrs. Brownley is missin'."

Olivia came into the office just then in her pink satin dressing gown. "Goodness gracious. What on earth is happening?"

"Now, daughter, don't get upset." The major made calming motions. "We've had some sort of trouble."

"Mrs. Brownley is missin'," Colt said, "and a sentry's been killed." He decided to spare the delicate lady the gruesome details.

"You think she killed the guard?" Olivia's eyes grew wide.

"Certainly not!" Colt growled. "That's the most ridiculous—"

"Then what—?" Olivia asked.

"We had a warrior in the fort sometime during the night," Doc said, still puffing from the walk.

"Oh my! We could all have been murdered in our beds." Big tears welled up in Olivia's dark eyes.

"Now, now," the major said, "don't get hysterical, dear."

"How can I not?" Olivia shrieked. "What—?"

"He came to kidnap Mrs. Brownley," Colt said. "She's gone."

"Oh." Now Olivia didn't seem so concerned. "I mean, how terrible. Is there any chance she went with him willingly?"

Colt blinked, considering that possibility, then shook his head, decided not to mention the child. "I don't think so."

"Well, you might consider it," Olivia said and brushed her hair back. She looked all askew this early in the morning. "After all, she's been with the Comanches so long, she might be happier among them. Maybe she shouldn't have been brought back after all."

"Surely you can't mean that," Colt said.

"It's gotten one of our soldiers killed, hasn't it?"

Colt looked at Doc and sighed while the major patted his daughter's shoulder. "Dear, you're upset. Why don't you go have Maria make us a pot of coffee while we decide what action to take?"

"Upset? I could have been murdered in my bed; of course I'm upset." Olivia turned with a flip of her dressing gown and went back into her living quarters and slammed the door.

Colt was surprised at the beauty's actions. She didn't seem to have much sympathy for the missing woman, but then, she was probably upset and sad for the dead soldier.

The major gestured the two men to chairs while he finished buttoning his shirt.

It seemed to Colt they ought to be taking action right now, but after all, Major Murphy was the commanding officer. "The way I see it, sir, I think Spider decided he wanted her back, slipped into camp, killed the guard, and took her. We've got to mount an attack—"

"Lieutenant, we can't do that today," the major said. "Remember, we are awaiting fresh supplies."

"Well, I could take a small patrol and—"

"Lieutenant, calm down." The major walked over to his desk. "Now let's think rationally. And while we're waiting for Olivia to make us some coffee, let's all have a drink."

Doc smiled. "I'll wait for the coffee. Remember I'm on the wagon, but thanks."

Colt gritted his teeth in frustration. "How can we stand here talkin' about coffee and whiskey when there's no tellin' what's happenin' to Hannah right now?"

Olivia entered just then, carrying a silver tray holding a pot of coffee and three cups, which she set on her father's desk. "Colton, dear, it sounds as if your interest is personal."

"Of course it's personal. She's helpless and I know how cruel and vengeful Spider can be."

Olivia returned to her quarters, again slamming the door.

"Don't mind Olivia. She's upset," the major apologized.

"Or jealous," Doc suggested.

Colt hardly heard either of them. Of course she was upset. Probably every woman in the fort was, thinking about a savage invading the fort and no one sounding the alarm. Yet here they were standing around talking when every minute put more distance between Hannah and her rescuers.

"Let's have some coffee," the major said and poured three cups, adding a slug of whiskey to two of them.

Colt took his cup and drank it, but he hardly tasted the steaming brew as it went down. "If we have to wait for fresh supplies to mount an attack, there's no tellin' what might happen to her." In his mind, he saw her being beaten by the cruel warrior, maybe raped repeatedly. He winced at the thought. He had become so protective of the tall, slender girl who had led such a terrible life.

The major didn't say anything.

"Sir, I know the Comanche, I've lived with them for ten years. Maybe I could go alone and sneak into their camp, and—"

"By Saint Mary's blood, absolutely not!" the major snapped. "That's a suicide mission, Lieutenant. You're letting your concern for Mrs. Brownley override your good judgment as a soldier."

"But if we launch a full attack," Colt protested, "there'll be women and children killed, maybe including Hannah and her son."

"She has a son?" The major looked up from lighting his pipe.

Colt nodded. "By Spider."

"Hmm," mused the major, the pleasant scent from his pipe drifting around the room. "That's not going to sit well with her husband."

"Her husband?" Colt had forgotten about him.

"Yes, the army's managed to track him down." The major blew smoke in the air and sipped his coffee. "He should be here in a couple of weeks. I don't know how he's going to feel about a half-breed child."

Colt shook his head. "I'm certain she won't go with him without her little boy."

"Dag nab it, what a mess," Doc said.

"Anyway, to protect the fort, I'll issue an order to double the guards for the next several days," the major said.

Colt slammed one fist into the other in sheer frustration. "It won't matter. Spider's got what he came after. He won't be comin' back to the fort."

"Lieutenant, you just take a deep breath, stay calm, and when those supplies get in, we'll go after Mrs. Brownley." The major poured another cup of coffee, added more whiskey, and sipped it.

"Yes, sir. May I go now?" Colt saluted.

"Certainly." The major returned his salute.

Doc said, "I believe I'll stay for more coffee."

To hell with coffee, Colt thought as he turned and left the office. He had been a soldier for more than ten years and he usually obeyed orders, but in his mind, he saw Hannah being beaten and raped by his cruel blood brother and it made him furious. He had been the one to rescue her, and now he felt responsible for the brave but unfortunate girl. He was sure he had a better chance of getting Hannah and her child out of that camp all by himself. The major was right, it was a suicide mission. But if he waited until the fresh supplies arrived, she might be dead or badly beaten, before the army mounted its campaign.

He decided then that he was going to disobey the major's orders and slip out of the camp after dark. He would rescue Hannah or die trying.

Colt waited until the dead of night to sneak out of his quarters. Instead of boots, he put on his old Comanche moccasins so he could move as quiet as a cougar. He had his pistol, a rifle, and a big knife stuck in the top of his tall moccasins. For food, he took a little beef and hardtack. He could not be encumbered by a lot of heavy gear because he would have to travel fast.

He saddled Rascal and led him across the parade grounds, thanking God that the moon was down tonight so the darkness was as black as a tarantula's back. He knew where there was a break in the stone wall, far from the sentry. He led his little mustang through that place and mounted up. His experience told him where the Comanches might be camped and he started off that direction in a ground-eating lope, stopping to rest his horse now and then.

He hated Spider for all the cruel things he had done, the murders of innocent women and children. That was why Colt had left the Comanche and returned to white civilization. Yet he knew he could not kill Spider. One blood brother must not kill another; it was taboo and would bring the wrath of the four winds and the other gods down upon him. Maybe he was more Comanche than he had thought.

As he rode, Colt wasn't certain whether he should try to sneak into the camp and steal Hannah and her little son out or walk in boldly and announce that she was his woman and he wanted her back. The elders of the tribe would listen to that argument. He found to his surprise that he wished it were true; he wanted to have Hannah as his own, hold her, protect her, and make love to her.

Then he reminded himself that he was engaged to a classic beauty, much prettier than Hannah, wellborn and educated. He should consider himself lucky; there were others like Captain Van Smyth who would be thrilled to be engaged to the dark-haired beauty. And of course, Hannah had a husband who would be coming for her. He was saving the girl for Luther Brownley. At the moment, that didn't matter. He didn't even want to think what Hannah must be going through tonight in Spider's teepee.

It was almost dawn when he rode into the Comanche camp. Dogs began barking and people came running. A few young warriors who did not know him brandished spears.

"How dare a white man ride into our camp?"

Colt held up his hand in a peace sign and said in Comanche, "I am blood brother to Spider. I do not come to fight."

Others were gathering now—old leaders, women, and curious children. Colt dismounted as he recognized some of the elderly warriors including Spider's father, Many Scalps.

He held up his hands to show they held no weapons and said in the Comanche language, "Ho, Many Scalps, I come in peace."

Many Scalps nodded and stepped forward to shake

hands. "It has been a long time, Young Stallion. What brings you to our camp?" Then he frowned. "I see you wear the clothing of the yellow legs."

"I am indeed a soldier now," Colt acknowledged. "I would not fight my brother Comanches if they would but move farther west and stop attackin' the white man's ranches."

The other old warriors frowned, and Many Scalps said, "We will eat and smoke a pipe and talk."

Colt looked around. "Where is my brother Spider?"

Just as he asked, Spider came walking boldly from a teepee. "Why come you to this camp, white man?" He gave Colt a menacing look.

Many Scalps grabbed his son's arm. "Young Stallion comes in peace."

Spider glared at Colt and spat on the ground. "He comes for the woman."

Colt took a deep breath, and then Hannah and a small half-breed boy emerged from the teepee. Hannah looked bruised and exhausted, standing there holding her child's hand, but she did not speak and there were no tears in those big blue eyes.

"Come." Many Scalps gestured. "We will eat and smoke and talk."

"No, send him out of this camp," Spider snarled.

His father glared at him. "We will eat and talk. I am still leader of this band."

The other old men murmured agreement.

Colt knew Spider had always been rash and hotheaded. He nodded to the warriors, knowing most white men rushed to talk about why they had come while the Indians liked ceremony and a lot of discussion. White men lacked patience. Colt could wait, but he did not intend to leave without Hannah.

Soon the men had set up a big circle around a small fire, all sitting cross-legged and waiting solemnly while the women poured big tin cups of strong, sweet coffee and the pipe was brought out, filled, and solemnly passed from hand to hand.

Spider made a wry face. "I will not smoke the pipe with Young Stallion. I do not trust him."

His father looked at him. "He is your blood brother, my son, and you will join in the ceremony as the other warriors do."

There was going to be trouble before this was over, Colt thought as he accepted the pipe and took a deep puff of the fragrant tobacco. He could not fight his way out of this camp—there were too many warriors—but he had decided he would die fighting rather than leave Hannah here. She stood watching, holding onto her little son's hand. Her eyes begged for help, but she did not weep.

"Now," Many Scalps said as the pipe finished making the circle and the women started to serve food, "now we will talk."

Hannah was dutifully serving stewed meat in gourds around the circle of men and Colt noted her hand trembled as she put meat into his dish.

"So," asked Many Scalps, "what is happening at the fort?"

Colt took a deep breath. "It is hard for us to maintain peace with the Comanche when Spider slips in at night and cuts the throat of one of our soldiers."

The other men turned to look at Spider.

His father glared at him. "I gave you no leave to sneak into the fort."

Spider shrugged. "It was necessary; I wanted to get my woman back."

"She is my woman," Colt said before he thought. "She was my woman before she was yours and I want her back."

"Never!" Spider put his hand on the knife in his belt. "My other woman gives me no sons. The white woman will give me many more like Grasshopper."

"She is my woman and I want her back," Colt said sternly.

Murmuring around the circle.

"I have lived too long when blood brothers quarrel over a mere woman." Many Scalps sighed and abruptly looked very old. "When I was young, the buffalo were like grains of sand across the prairie and our women were fruitful. Life was good for the people and our allies."

A murmur of wistful agreement from all the old men.

"Now," Many Scalps continued, "the white men are killing all the game and plowing up Mother Earth to plant their crops."

"And putting up fences to keep us from roaming," Spider snarled.

"I know all this and it makes me sad for the people," Colt agreed, "but it will not change. The white men are more numerous than raindrops in a spring storm and they will slowly spread out across this place they call Texas and push the Comanche and the other tribes farther west."

"So how will it end?" another white-haired old warrior asked.

Colt hesitated. There was no answer that held any hope for the Comanche. They and the other plains tribes would be crowded farther and farther until there was no place for them at all and then they would be put on reservations and fed government rations. This would be a terrible end for the best horsemen of the plains, who had always roamed wild and free.

He cleared his throat. "There is no good answer except to try to make peace with the whites and stop attackin' their ranches because the Big Chief in Washington has sent more soldiers and supplies. They will come after you every time you go on the warpath."

"We have the best warriors and we will fight!" yelled a young brave and the other young ones took up the shout. "Fight! We will fight!"

Many Scalps held up his hand for silence. "What Young Stallion says is true, and I know that, finally, the white man must win."

The young warriors set up a chorus of denial.

"Hear me!" Many Scalps thundered. "What he says is true, but we cannot accept being penned up like a herd of tame sheep, so we will fight on until we can fight no more."

Colt sighed. "It is what I expected to hear, but I wanted to bring you the truth." He looked around. Hannah and her little boy had disappeared into a teepee.

Many Scalps looked at the sky. Storm clouds were gathering on the far horizon and an occasional blade of lightning split the darkness. "So, my adopted son, my old eyes are happy to see you once more. Will you stay?"

Colt shook his head and glared into Spider's dark eyes. "No, I have pledged my word to the leader of the white soldiers, but I mean the people no harm. I come only to get the white woman. My blood brother has had her warming his blankets for almost four years now and I want her back."

Spider jumped to his feet. "I will kill Young Stallion

before I let him take the yellow-haired captive. I want more sons from her."

"You have a first wife," Colt said. "And many Comanche maidens would be pleased to be your second woman."

"She is a prize I took in a raid," Spider snarled, "and I like showing the white girl off when other tribes gather."

Many Scalps motioned his son to sit back down. "You know you may not kill your blood brother, especially not over something so unimportant as a woman. We all have captured women and used them as slaves and wives—"

"But not one with yellow hair," Spider insisted.

"Does not Peta Nocona have one with yellow hair?" Many Scalps asked.

"Yes, but that is another band of our people. You know mine is the only white girl in our band."

Colt shrugged. "I want the yellow-haired one returned. She has warmed my blood brother's blankets long enough."

One of the old men suggested, "As blood brothers, you can share the woman."

Colt winced at the thought of the slender Hannah under Spider's hard-driving body. Colt knew he could be brutal. "That is true." He nodded. "And if I were to stay in the camp, we could share her, but I must return to the white soldier fort, so I come for her."

Spider again put his hand on his knife. "She gives me more pleasure than any woman I have ever lain with. I will not give her up."

He would do anything to protect Hannah, but of course, he could not kill his blood brother. He looked toward Many Scalps. "I will stand by the wisdom of the Council of Warriors."

Many Scalps's shoulders sagged. "All over a mere woman. She is not worth trouble between blood brothers."

Another old brave spoke up. "I have a beautiful daughter, Running Doe, who many young men have offered horses and gifts for. I say I will give her to either of these warriors if it will solve this conflict."

A murmur went around the circle and there was much nodding of heads at the wisdom of this compromise. Obviously, Running Doe was a beauty, but Colt shook his head. "I want only the yellow-haired woman."

"And I will not give her up!" Spider was on his feet, shouting and shaking his fist.

"Then there is only one way to settle this," Many Scalps sighed. "The two will have a wrestling match and the winner will get the girl."

"No!" shouted both Colt and Spider at once.

"Be silent!" Many Scalps thundered. "This is my decision: Spider and Young Stallion will wrestle for her this afternoon and neither will use a weapon."

Thunder rumbled across the camp as the other warriors murmured that this was just. The winner of the match would get the white girl, and then the tribal elders could move on to more important things than women.

Colt stood up. "I will do this thing you ask, Many Scalps." He began pulling off his shirt. "But it has been a long time since I have wrestled."

Spider scoffed. "Living among the white men has made you soft, Young Stallion. I will beat you easily, and tonight, as you ride back to the soldiers, I will be lying between the warm thighs of the yellow-haired woman, pumping my seed into her."

Colt ground his teeth at the thought. He had already chosen another woman for himself, and yet, the thought of Hannah in Spider's arms enraged him. He had to win to get Hannah out of the Comanche camp. He sat down and began unbuckling his belt.

Word quickly spread through the Comanche camp that two noted warriors would be wrestling this afternoon for possession of the yellow-haired slave and everyone began gathering. Each combatant went off to a solitary place to rest and pray for good medicine.

The time seemed long to Colt and he wished he could speak to Hannah, but she was hidden away in a teepee. Finally Colt and Spider stripped down to nothing but breechcloths and moccasins. Each had painted his face and prayed for good medicine as dozens of Comanche formed a circle.

The dark clouds overhead had thickened and the wind picked up suddenly as the two stepped into a ring made by hundreds of curious Comanches.

Many Scalps gestured. "Bring the prize out so she can watch and know that the victor has fought a great fight to possess her."

Two of the women went to drag Hannah out of her teepee, kicking and screaming. Colt fought a desire to rush to her aid, but he knew he must not. He ignored her as if she were nothing but a prize to be won. Her worn and tattered deerskin shift was almost falling from her shoulders, exposing her fine breasts. She tried to cover them in vain.

Many Scalps said, "Stake her where the two can see the prize."

And two warriors stepped forward and tied her

hands behind her back so that she could no longer hide those fine breasts that were now visible for all to see. They tied a rope around one of her slim ankles and drove a stake into the ground so that she was on a tether like a dog on a leash.

She looked at Colt, her mouth quivering, but she did not shed a tear.

"Now," said Many Scalps, "my two sons will move to the center of the ring and you will wrestle. The winner gets the girl and that will end the conflict between blood brothers."

Colt intended to take Hannah and her little son out of this camp or die trying. He stepped into the circle made by the hundreds of Comanches. Young girls giggled and looked envious as if they each wished two great warriors would fight to possess them. He gave Hannah an encouraging nod as she stood there tall and proud, seemingly oblivious to the other warriors staring at her smooth skin and fine breasts. Many of them would like to bed Yellow-Hair, Colt knew.

He gave her a nod of confidence, but he did not feel confident. He knew he could out-fight any of the soldiers at the fort, but he also knew this Comanche warrior was as tough as a cougar, his muscles rippled under his brown skin. He was not at all sure he could win against Spider, although he had often beaten him when they wrestled as boys. Yet when he thought of Hannah lying under Spider tonight as an object of his lust, he knew he could not lose because he would not let her be used as Spider's plaything anymore.

Many Scalps stepped into the circle and motioned for both men to come forward. He placed a wrinkled hand on the shoulder of each man and began a singsong chant of prayer and the hundreds of Comanche quieted reverently. After a moment, he finished and the gathering was so silent, Colt could hear his own heart beating.

"Now!" said Many Scalps and stepped back out of the ring.

For a long moment, the two adversaries crouched, glaring at each other and moving about carefully, and then Spider rushed in and tackled Colt around the knees and took him down to the ground.

The crowd set up a shout, urging on their favorites as Spider sank his teeth into Colt's thigh and Colt struggled to get out from under him.

God, that hurt! He felt the other's teeth go deep into his flesh as he twisted away and staggered to his feet, blood running down his leg.

Spider grinned at him without humor, blood on his mouth. Colt knew he faced the most formidable enemy on the plains now. To keep the yellow-haired captive, Spider would bite and claw and gouge and even break arms and legs to disable his opponent.

Each circled the other warily, respecting the other's fighting skills. Colt pretended to jab, then suddenly rushed Spider, slamming him across the ground and into the fire. Spider rolled out of the campfire, quick as his namesake. Colt could hear the whole silent crowd take a deep breath as they faced one another again, each breathing hard. Night was coming on and the clouds turned darker on the horizon. The air was as thick and warm as wool and both men were wet with sweat and covered with dust from the dry ground.

Spider feinted, then caught Colt off balance, knocking the breath from him as they rolled over and over in the dirt, the crowd giving way before them. His bitten leg ached as Colt fought to get out from under the skilled Comanche warrior, but Spider was going for the kill, Colt could see it in his angry eyes. He grabbed Colt's arm and twisted.

Biting his lip, Colt fought against the pain as Spider tried to break Colt's arm. It took all the strength he owned to throw Spider off him and stagger to his feet. He struggled to rotate that arm, getting the feeling back into it, but he was hurt and he could tell from the slight smirk on Spider's face that he knew it and he would have no mercy.

Before Colt could recover, Spider dived at him again, caught him around the waist, and quick-jabbed Colt's kidneys as he struggled to escape. Then Spider moved his iron grip up to Colt's chest and began to squeeze until Colt thought he would pass out as he fought for air. He was losing; he could tell from the triumphant gleam in Spider's dark eyes and the agonized expression on Hannah's face. He could smell both sweat and blood as he struggled to escape the iron grip.

Spider put his face close to Colt's ear as he squeezed him tighter. "Tonight, I will take the yellow-haired one again and again until she gives me another son!"

The thought of the slender Hannah helpless under the cruel Comanche enraged Colt and gave him super-human strength. He reached back and caught Spider's head in his grasp even as Spider squeezed him almost into unconsciousness. It took all the energy he had left, but Colt managed to toss Spider over his shoulder and flat on his back onto the ground with a resounding loud thump.

The crowd gasped and then murmured as Spider groaned and then lay still. Colt, sweating and gasping for air, stepped back.

Many Scalps stepped forward and looked. "Spider's head has hit a rock. He will not awaken for a while. Young Stallion is the winner of this match and the woman."

The crowd cheered as Colt leaned against his knees with both hands, still gasping for air. Obviously Spider was not that popular with the other Comanche.

Now Many Scalps approached him as thunder rumbled again in the distance. "You have fought fair, my adopted son, but the storm comes soon and you cannot leave tonight."

Colt looked at the sky, gulping great breaths of air, knowing the old warrior was right, there was a bad storm coming fast. He wanted to take Hannah and her child and ride out of there, but the lightning now flashing across the sky might be more dangerous to them than the Indians.

"All right, my adopted father, I will stay the night, but I fear Spider will not take his defeat well."

Everyone looked toward Spider. He now lay groaning and moving ever so slightly.

Many Scalps put his withered hand on Colt's shoulder. "You have won fairly and the right to reclaim the white slave. We will give you a special teepee for the night so that you may enjoy her, and I will deal with my angry son."

He led Colt over and ceremoniously handed him the rope that tied Hannah. Colt took the rope and stood looking down at her, half naked and vulnerable. Did she understand enough to know that she was being given to Colt for his night's pleasure before the Comanche would allow them to leave the camp?

Chapter 7

Several of the women pushed forward, giggling and one said in Comanche, "Ho, Young Stallion! You have waited a long time to bed your woman again. Tonight we will prepare her for you."

Colt nodded and let them lead Hannah away, his mind already wondering how he was going to handle this. He was an honorable man, engaged to the major's beautiful daughter, and Hannah was a married woman, her husband even now probably making the trip to the fort to get her. And yet the maleness of him was tempted, so tempted, by the slender beauty. It had been a long time since Colt had had a woman and tonight, he could have Hannah; the Comanche had ordered it. He could enjoy her tonight, and tomorrow he could take her back to the fort, turn her over to her husband, who would never know nor would anyone. Hannah would be too proud to tell anyone that her lithe body had been the prize in a fight between blood brothers. As his body grew excited at the thought, he realized that maybe he was more savage than civilized. He had won the right to this woman's body, and as warrior Young Stallion, he was expected to take it.

Colt spent the next hour wandering about the camp, visiting with old friends. He knew many of these people personally and they had been good to him. It troubled him that someday soon he might have to attack them.

Spider had been carried off to his own teepee and did not reappear as the storm built and rumbled toward them. Soon there would be a terrible rainstorm and maybe a tornado sweeping across the bare plains.

Colt went down to the creek with some soap made from yucca and washed himself thoroughly and then stood naked in the warm air to dry. His bitten leg ached and his twisted arm seemed sprained. He stood there naked by the water and flexed his muscles, thinking about Hannah and what she must be thinking right now. More than that, what about Spider? He didn't think the warrior would give Hannah up without another confrontation, and when they attempted to ride out, Spider might do something desperate. Even tonight, when Spider thought of Colt in the arms of the slender blonde, he might try to kill Colt to take Hannah back.

Colt heard giggling and looked around. Several Comanche girls were watching him from the shadowy bushes, their hands over their mouths. He grabbed for his pants, but it was too late. He heard muffled mumblings of "big stallion" as the girls fled. He looked down at himself. He might be bigger than most men, all right, or maybe it was just the thought of sleeping with Hannah that had engorged his manhood. All he could think of was mating with her, and she would have no choice in the matter. Yet he was an honorable

Texan and engaged to another woman. God, how was he going to handle this?

In the darkness, He strode back to the camp where Indians were doing chores and cooking food, feeding horses. Women smiled at him as he passed, letting him know that if he would prefer a Comanche maiden, many of them would be happy to provide him with pleasure.

A pretty maiden led him to a special teepee that had been prepared for him, complete with soft buffalo robes to lie on and a set of new buckskin clothes. There were also big dishes of stewed meat, fried bread, and the fruit of cactus.

Clad in only his blue trousers, he sat down before the small fire cross-legged. After a time, he heard women laughing and he looked out to see them leading Hannah toward the teepee.

Colt caught his breath at her beauty. She had been washed and perfumed with wildflowers in her long, yellow hair. She wore a fine, beaded white deerskin and walked with dignity toward the teepee as if accepting her fate. The women thrust her into the teepee and then scattered into the night. Outside, it thundered again and then the rain began, light at first and then a downpour.

Colt closed the opening of the teepee and they were alone before a small fire with rain beating down outside. "Are you all right?" he asked.

She nodded and did not smile. "You have won me and I thank you for saving me from Spider. Would you like food now?"

He shook his head, mystified. She was acting like a typical captive as she settled back on her knees with her hands in her lap.

"Have you had anything to eat?"

"Does Young Stallion give me permission to share his food?"

"What's the matter with you, Hannah? Of course I do. I've come here to rescue you. Where is your little boy?"

"Many Scalps's wife is watching him tonight while I do my duty to pleasure you."

"Is that what you think I fought Spider for? The chance to bed you?"

She shrugged, blue eyes sparking fire. She had a fiery spirit and that would never be broken by any man. "The Comanche expect it and the whites back at the fort would never know. You must know I would not tell anyone."

"I would not want you that way." He remembered now that what he had been attracted to was Hannah's defiant spirit. A man might take Hannah by force, but he would never break her. To make her come to him willingly would be any man's challenge and a very sweet victory.

Instead he dished meat into a gourd and handed it to her. "Here, eat. Remember I am engaged to Olivia and I have honor."

She shrugged. "Honor sometimes fails when a man has a chance to bed a woman, even if she is not as pretty as the major's daughter—or is it that you want a virgin?"

He stared at her, wishing he could have been Hannah's first man. He could have made the experience so wonderful for them both because he was skilled and because he knew how to be gentle. His manhood swelled at the thought and he wanted to forget about Olivia and take this girl in his arms, make her his completely. "Shut up and eat."

"At least servicing you would be better than the hateful Spider."

He noticed bruises on her face as she took the gourd and began to eat and he wanted to kill the warrior, wanted to choke the life from him for hurting this slender girl. She was not his to protect, he reminded himself again. He watched her eat as the thunder rolled and the rain pounded outside. "Look, Hannah, we both know you are married and I am engaged to Olivia."

"And she is much more beautiful than I am."

"I reckon most people would think she is, but when you smile, I think you are the most beautiful woman I have ever seen."

She looked up from her food and smiled, ever so slowly, and he wondered again why he had ever thought her plain.

He said, "In all that today, I never saw you shed a tear, not when you were being used as a prize, not when you were standing there bound and half naked before that crowd."

She tossed back her long golden hair, which gleamed in the firelight. "Remember I never cry. I learned long ago, it does no good. Many men have hurt me and mistreated me, and I decided long ago that no man would ever make me vulnerable and dependent enough to weep again."

Colt thought of Olivia, who seemed to weep tears like a fountain at the slightest opportunity. "Finish your food. It's going to be a long night."

She set her gourd aside and studied him. "You know Spider as well as I do. Do you really think he is going to let me spend the night in your arms and then let us ride away in the morning without ambushing and killing us both?"

"I don't know. He is obsessed with you." He didn't look at her, but he knew she was right. They probably weren't going to get out of this alive because of Spider's treachery. At least Colt wouldn't. The evil warrior wanted Hannah back in his blankets and if Colt couldn't get her out of the camp, she faced years of Spider rutting on her slender body, filling her belly with his seed so that she would give him more sons.

Hannah leaned forward to add twigs to the fire and he saw the rise of her full breasts under the delicate doeskin. He could not stop staring at them despite himself.

She gave a scornful laugh, then stood up and grasped the hem of her doeskin shift. "In spite of what you say, Young Stallion, I know what you are thinking."

He held up a hand to stop her from pulling off the shift. "I'm sorry, Hannah. You must know I wouldn't take you by force. You've had enough of that in your life." He sat cross-legged, his maleness swollen and throbbing with need as he looked up at her. Her skin was pale as milk with long, slender legs and big breasts. Colt had a terrible need to pull her down on the soft buffalo robes and make passionate, frenzied love to the girl, pulling her almost inside him as he coupled with her and stroked that delicate skin.

"Are you sure?" She stared at him with those soft blue eyes.

Colt took a deep breath and clenched his fists, fighting his own need. "I told you you could trust me and I meant it."

She looked down at him a moment longer. He could smell the scent of the flowers in her hair and the warm, womanly scent of her, and he had never lusted for a woman like he lusted for this one. It was taking all his strength not to grab her hand, pull her down beside him, and taste those full breasts.

"Thank you." She seemed to be trembling as she sat down across from him again.

It was going to be a long night, he thought. While the Comanches thought he was taking the girl over and over in a frenzy of lust, he was going to have to control himself not to do just that.

He said it without thinking. "You have no idea how much I want to take you, make you my own at this moment."

There was only a pained expression in those wide blue eyes. "I know, but I—I trust you."

Somehow that was more important, more satisfying to him than taking her. "And have you never wanted a man, wanted him inside you, wantin' him kissin' and pleasurin' you?"

She shook her head. "I have been used, but I never found any pleasure in it. It was painful and cruel."

For a minute, he thought she might actually weep, but instead, she took a deep breath and swallowed hard. "What happens now?"

He noticed she was trembling and realized the rain outside had caused the teepee to grow cool. "We have a long night ahead. We will try to leave before dawn. Spider may not be expecting that and we may be able to get away."

"I will not leave without my little son," she said. "That is what brought me back to this camp and Spider's blankets in the first place."

"I will rescue him, too," Colt promised softly, but even he was not sure how he could accomplish that.

"Thank you." She nodded. "I'm beginning to think you are different from the other men I have known."

If only she realized how much he lusted for her at this moment, she would not say that, he thought. However, he only gestured toward the soft buffalo robes. "You are cold. Take the robes."

He saw the suspicion in her face.

"Don't worry," he assured her softly, "I promise I will not touch you."

She hesitated, and he hated the two men who had hurt her and put that fear in her eyes.

"Hannah." He took her hand and pulled her over next to him, threw the soft buffalo robe over her. "Lie down and go to sleep. I will keep watch."

She lay down next to him, still shivering. He was cold, too, but he only stared into the fire and listened to it rain outside. He did not want to look at her, she was too tempting. Besides he was in love with the beautiful Olivia. He imagined the dark-haired beauty naked in their wedding bed and still she did not arouse him like the thought of Hannah did.

"You are cold," Hannah noticed.

He shrugged. "I am a soldier and before that, a warrior. I am used to hardship."

"I will share the buffalo robe with you," she whispered.

"Aren't you afraid?" He looked down at her in the dying firelight.

She seemed to consider his question. "No, for the first time with a man, I am not afraid."

He grinned at her and slid under the robe. Her lithe body put out heat like a stove, and he realized how cold he really had been. Taking a deep breath, he put his arm under her head and pulled her closer, warming his half-naked body with hers. She stiffened and then relaxed, letting him cuddle her up against his chest so that she was protected from the cold and anyone who would hurt her.

He looked down at her small face as her eyes flickered closed. He had never felt so protective and tender toward a woman before. He had lain in many a woman's arms, but this one was special somehow. She fit up against him as if she had been born to be his. He reached down and gently pushed the yellow hair away from her face and without thinking, brushed his lips against her temple. Again his manhood rose against her warmth and he needed her, desired her as he had never needed a woman. *She's married,* he reminded himself, *and her husband will be coming for her. You cannot send her back to him with your child in her belly, no matter how great your need.*

Think of the beautiful Olivia, he chided himself. *The dark beauty was much prettier than Hannah and an innocent virgin. If you marry Olivia, you will be proud to display her on your arm and teach her how to make love, and she will give you fine sons.*

Hannah would give a man fine sons, too, Texas-born-and-bred sons, tough cowboys and Rangers and sheriffs, not the delicate, back-East civilized men who dipped snuff and wore silk cravats.

He must stop thinking like that, but as he held Hannah, close, he could think of nothing else. She radiated warmth like a small kitten, and he held her even closer as the rain poured and he lay there. Finally he dropped off into a restless sleep in which he dreamed of a small ranch and him riding up to the house and Hannah, in a blue gingham dress and a white apron, running to meet him. He took her in his arms and kissed her deeply, thoroughly, running his hand down the lace of her bodice to cup her breast.

He awoke, sweating and breathing hard. His hand was cupping her breast and he did not move it for a while, liking the feel of it in his palm. Her slender thighs were pressed against him and his manhood was so hard, it was painful. All he had to do was push up the doeskin shift because she wore nothing under it and he could relieve his body of this terrible need. But he had promised her and she trusted him.

With a sigh, he pulled away from her and sat up. The rain had stopped and he wondered what time it was. Silently he slipped out the teepee opening and looked around. The camp was quiet, a few campfires still shone with glowing embers. It must be near dawn. Now would come the hard part, getting out of this camp. He was sure Spider didn't care who won the wrestling match, he wouldn't let Colt take Hannah without a fight. He stepped out into the brush to relieve himself, then quickly took in the landscape. The horses were tied to a picket line a few hundred feet away. Rascal raised his head and nickered, and Colt took a deep breath, froze in place, afraid his horse might have awakened someone. No one moved.

He sighed and crawled back into the teepee, lay down next to Hannah. She seemed to smile in her sleep and cuddled up close to his warmth. God, he could lay here all day, holding Hannah close. That would be enough for him, just to hold her. Right now, he must forget about what he'd like to do. He had to get them out alive.

"Wake up, sleepyhead," he whispered against her ear and stroked the yellow hair.

Her eyes flickered open and she started, then seemed to recognize him and lay still. "What time is it?"

"Not far from dawn. If I can get Rascal saddled and

gather up some food, can you get Grasshopper without wakin' up the camp?"

She nodded and sat up. "He's a good baby. He knows not to cry."

Colt was doubtful about that. He thought of the chubby half-breed toddler. They had a much better chance of escaping the camp without trying to take the boy, but of course, it was unthinkable to leave him behind.

She looked at his blue pants with the yellow stripe. "The Comanche can see that color a long way."

Colt nodded. "You're right. I'll put on these new buckskins I was given. That white doeskin can be seen a long way, too."

She shrugged. "I can't help that. I can't get other clothing without taking a chance of waking everyone."

Colt pulled on the buckskin shirt, then reached for the pants and hesitated.

"This is no time for modesty." She frowned.

"All right then." He stripped off the blue trousers, stood naked before her while he pulled on the buckskin pants and moccasins. "All right, let's go then."

She crawled over to the teepee opening and then paused and looked back. "Colt, however this turns out, I want to thank you for risking your life to try to rescue us."

He made a dismissing gesture to hide his nervousness. "Part of my job as a soldier."

"Nobody else came," she reminded him.

He was embarrassed and awkward. "Will you stop yammerin' and get Grasshopper? I'll meet you at the horses."

She nodded and slipped out into the darkness and he followed, taking some of the dried meat and parched corn from inside the teepee and striding toward the picket line. As he saddled Rascal in the darkness, he knew they hadn't a prayer of getting out of this camp. He, by himself, might have a chance of escaping. All he had to do was mount up and ride out, leaving the burden of the woman and child behind.

It was tempting, but then he saw a picture in his mind of Hannah's blue eyes, so trusting, and the cruel Spider, raping her tonight, running his dirty hands over her pale body. Colt grimaced and knew he could not betray her, even though it would have helped his chances of escaping.

Time seemed to tick by in agonizing heartbeats, and then he saw her hurrying toward him, holding a sleeping child close to her body. He wished that were his son, he thought, and then was surprised at himself.

She ran to him in the darkness, the sleepy toddler moving slightly while she shushed him.

Maybe luck was with them, Colt thought with disbelief. He lifted Hannah and her little son up on Rascal's back and untied the mustang and a pinto horse from the picket line. Taking a deep breath, he led the horses away from the sleeping camp into the thicket of wild cedars near the creek. They might be lucky after all. Colt could hardly believe it himself as he led the horses away. Behind him, there was no hue and cry, no shouts of alarm, no dogs barking to wake everyone. They were several hundred yards away from the camp now and he looked up at Hannah and she smiled at him. They were going to escape after all.

And then Spider stepped out from behind a tree. The dim dawn light reflected off the big knife in his hand.

Colt slid to a halt, unbelieving. He heard Hannah clap her hand over her mouth to muffle a scream.

Spider stepped toward them, brandishing the knife. "So, my blood brother," he hissed, "did you think I would actually let you ride out of here with my woman?"

"I won her fair and square," Colt reminded him.

"And I'm sure you have enjoyed her all night." Spider ground his teeth. "Did you plunge over and over into Moonlight's hot depths? Did you taste her breasts and bite those soft lips as I have done?"

"No, I am a man of honor," Colt reminded him.

"Then you are more than a fool." Spider spat to one side and brandished the knife. "You should have enjoyed her because she would be the last woman you ever took."

"Spider, let us go." Colt tried to keep his voice strong. "I am taking her away as Many Scalps promised."

"No, you won't take her," Spider promised, crouching, the knife gleaming in the coming light. "And I intend to geld you, white soldier, so that you will never sire sons."

"Spider, we are blood brothers—" Colt began.

"I know I may not kill you." Spider grinned with yellow teeth. "But I will geld you," he promised. "You will no longer be Young Stallion."

Colt knew he had to do something quickly. They could not get past Spider without a fight. "If we must fight, let me put the woman in a safe place so the spooked horse won't run away."

Spider nodded and grinned at Hannah as Colt lifted her and her sleeping child, set them up against the base of a tree, and tied Rascal and the pinto to a limb.

"You," Spider hissed at Hannah. "Tonight, the white

man will no longer be a man and I will remind you what a real man feels like."

Hannah shuddered. "I haven't forgotten your cruelty."

Colt tried to think. How was he going to deal with this? He stepped toward Spider, holding out his empty hands. "I have no weapons."

Spider snorted. "You expect me to be fair? I will give no more thought to this than I would if I were gelding a horse. Before sunup, you will no longer be Young Stallion—you will be known as White Gelding."

He must take him by surprise if he was to have a chance at all, Colt thought and dived toward Spider. The Comanche stepped backward and dodged as Colt tackled him, stabbed Colt's arm and ripped downward.

Colt managed to muffle his own scream of agony as he felt the steel blade rip through the muscle and the blood spurted. He heard Hannah gasp and looked toward her. She had laid her sleeping child down and was watching from the sidelines, but there was nothing she could do to help.

He staggered from the pain and felt the warm blood running down his arm. He could smell the coppery scent of it as it dripped onto the dirt. If he didn't disarm Spider quickly, he would soon bleed to death before he could finish this fight.

He must not kill a blood brother, his honor told him that and he must obey, even if this Comanche wasn't willing to. He dove in, grabbed Spider's knife hand, and they struggled for the weapon. Colt used all his strength to push Spider up against a tree trunk and slam his arm against the bark. He slammed the arm hard, trying to dislodge the knife from Spider's grip.

They locked and rolled across the ground, Spider now smeared with Colt's blood.

Spider's mouth was near Colt's ear and he swore, "By the four gods of the winds, I will hang your manhood over my blankets tonight as I take the yellow-haired girl and remind her she is mine and only mine to enjoy!"

"Not if I die!" Colt promised as they meshed. He threw Spider against the tree again and the warrior dropped the knife and it clattered to the ground. Before he could retrieve it, Colt charged him again and they fought, both slippery with Colt's scarlet blood.

Colt tripped and went down, and now Spider was on top of him, reaching for a large, jagged stone. "Now!" Spider seethed. "Now your brains spill on the ground!"

He was trying to fend the warrior off, but in his weakened condition, he was not going to be able to stop Spider from crushing his skull. Then past Spider's shoulder, he saw a flash of white doeskin and yellow hair as Hannah bent to pick up the knife and then she loomed over Spider's back and plunged the blade deep, again and again.

Spider made a surprised, gurgling sound and then the rock fell from his nerveless fingers. He fell and Colt scrambled out from under him. The warrior now lay jerking on the ground, the knife up to its hilt in his back, scarlet blood running everywhere.

Hannah stepped away, her mouth wide with horror. "Oh my God! I didn't—"

"It's okay, you saved my life." Colt grabbed a sleeve of his shirt and tore it off. "Quick, tie my arm up before I bleed to death."

Hannah seemed to come out of her stupor, although

she was still shaking, and began tying a tourniquet around Colt's arm. "I—I couldn't let him kill you."

I know." Colt took her in his arms. "But the Comanche will think I broke a taboo and did it. If they catch us, they'll torture me to death and maybe bury you alive in Spider's grave."

"My child." She ran over and picked up the sleeping toddler.

"Here," Colt ordered, "get mounted and let's clear out of here before the camp awakes and they find the body."

She just stood there seemingly hypnotized as she stared down at the bloody corpse.

Colt grabbed her and the child, carried them both, and put them on Rascal. "Here, you ride on ahead of me. I'll stay back in case they start after us. If they catch me, you can still get away and follow the tracks back to the fort."

"No, I can't let you do that," she protested, "not after you saved me—"

"Hannah, you do as I say," he ordered in a no-nonsense tone. "Now get!" He slapped Rascal across the rump hard and the little mustang took off running down the trail.

He watched them disappear over the rise, and then he looked down at Spider. They had been boys together and had shared many adventures. Many Scalps had taught Colt to hunt and track, and he would feel betrayed, thinking Young Stallion had murdered his son. He wished he could explain, but the tribe would not give him a chance. They would kill him slowly for breaking the taboo and killing his blood brother. He must get away, if for no other reason than to make sure Hannah made it safely back to the fort.

He mounted the Comanche pinto mustang and took off at a gallop, listening to the sounds of the camp coming awake behind him. It wouldn't be long before they found Spider's body and then an agonizing death awaited Colt, but he didn't intend to be caught.

Chapter 8

Colt caught up with Hannah and her son and they rode hard, knowing the Comanches would soon be looking for them.

Finally Colt yelled to her, "These horses are about tuckered out. We're gonna have to give them a break."

He dismounted and helped her down, reached to take the little boy from her arms. The child jabbered at him in Comanche and smiled with dark eyes and big dimples.

"Come on, little buddy." He grinned and put Grasshopper on the ground.

The horses were lathered and blowing as the couple began to walk to cool them off. Grasshopper toddled along beside his mother.

Colt looked at her. "If they catch us, I'll tell them I killed Spider."

She stared at him in horror. "They'll torture you to death for breaking the taboo."

"But Grasshopper needs a mother, so if need be, I'll try to delay them so you can get away."

She shuddered. "I can't go back. I'd rather die."

He smiled down at the little boy. "I don't intend we should be caught. I know a place, a small cave along a bluff on the river, if we can get that far."

"I'm worried about you," she said. "You look bad."

"I'm fine," he lied. In truth, he had lost a lot of blood from the knife wound and feared it might become infected. He knew lockjaw was a common threat on the frontier.

Soon they mounted again and kept riding.

"I'm not usin' the usual Comanche trails," Colt explained, "and they'll expect me to."

At almost noon, they came to the river and Colt pointed out low brush under the edge of the bank. "There's a cave behind that and the brush is thick enough to hide the horses."

"Won't they be tracking us?"

Colt looked up at the sky. It had turned dark with cool winds and ominous thunder. "If we're lucky, we'll get another rain that'll wash out the tracks. Indians don't like to ride in the rain. They may camp and wait for the storm to pass before they take up the chase again."

Little Grasshopper began to whimper for food.

"Be quiet, baby," Hannah whispered in Comanche. "I'll give you a few bites of bread."

"There's some dried meat in my knapsack," Colt said, "and here's my canteen."

"You look like you could use some water and some food yourself," she answered as she dismounted and took the canteen, then dug in his saddlebags for food.

"I'm just fine," he lied again and licked his dry lips. He needed some food bad to give him strength, but he wanted the toddler fed worse. Grasshopper was a handsome and sturdy little boy and someday, he would grow into a fine man, a Texan.

They rode down a trail to the brush just as the rain pattered a little, making small splats in the dry dust. Colt tied up the horses under the lee of the cliff, in the brush where they wouldn't be spotted, and took the gear and blankets into the small cave.

She looked at him as he swayed unsteadily. "Colt, you stay here with Grasshopper. I'll go down to the river and fill the canteens."

"Let me do it," he protested, but she jerked the canteens from his hand.

"You look like you might faint, and then how would I get you back up the rise and into the cave as big as you are?"

"You're right," he said, but he didn't like a woman having to look after him. He took Grasshopper by the hand and led him into the small cave, then held his breath, watching Hannah crouch down and move along the treacherous narrow ledges down to the water. In minutes she was back inside the cave just as the rain came down in torrents. It smelled good, he thought in a daze. Fresh rain on a dusty day always smelled so good.

She handed him a canteen. "Here, you lean back against this wall and drink some of this."

Colt tasted it. It might be a little muddy, but it was cool and he was parched. He drank and drank.

The temperature slowly dropped and he began to shiver. Little Grasshopper watched him curiously.

"I was afraid of this," Hannah said and reached for a blanket to wrap around Colt. Her hand went to his forehead. "You've got a fever."

Her hand felt cool and gentle on his sweating face.

Colt couldn't stop his teeth from chattering, and she took a second blanket and wrapped it around him. Outside, the rain poured and the river became a white-foamed torrent as it rose and raged through the arroyo.

"Hannah, I want to tell you how to reach the fort if I get so bad you have to leave me."

"I'm not leaving you," she said.

"If I get too sick, you'll have to," he whispered. "You can't stay here long. We don't have that many supplies. Besides the longer you stay here, the better the chance the Comanches will find you."

"You're not in command anymore, Lieutenant," she snapped, "and I'm not leaving you; not after what you went through to get me out."

He was too weak and tired to argue with her. "I'll just rest a minute," he murmured, "and then we'll ride on."

"Okay," she said, "now just hush and sleep."

When he opened his eyes, she had torn off a piece of his shirt, soaked it in cold water from the canteen and wiped his hot face.

"That feels so good," he whispered, loving the gentle touch of her hand on his fevered brow.

"I'm sorry I can't light a fire," she said, leaning over to brush his dark hair from his eyes. "Then I could get some coffee or broth going."

He enjoyed the touch of her hand stroking back his hair. "I know. The Comanche would smell the smoke for miles. We can't chance it."

"What are the odds we'll make it back to the fort?"

"Oh, good," he lied. "The Comanches will probably give up huntin' us and go back to their camp."

"After I've killed a major warrior? Not likely."

"Then why did you ask?" He sighed.

She turned and watched the little boy playing happily with a couple of sticks at the back of the cave. "They will want Grasshopper, and I don't want him raised as a Comanche."

"We'll get him back to the fort," Colt promised, but he was not at all sure he could keep that vow. He slipped off to sleep in spite of himself and awoke late in the afternoon to find Hannah washing and dressing his arm wound. It looked swollen and discolored. Outside the rain had stopped.

She noticed he had awoken. "It doesn't look so bad." Her voice was more cheerful than her face.

"Your blue eyes don't lie," he said. "I've seen wounds like this before. That redness and discolorin' will gradually spread all over the arm and I'll get delirious and out of my head."

"Maybe not." She cleaned the wound and poured a little whiskey over it.

He winced and had to grit his teeth to keep from screaming in pain.

"I'm sorry, Colt. I don't want to hurt you."

"I know. You're a brave girl, Hannah, a real Texas girl." He looked down at his arm. "I've seen doctors in the war saw off an arm not much worse than mine."

"I'm not sure I could do that."

"You're a Texan. You could do anything you had to, but I'd rather be dead than lose my right arm. A soldier or a cowboy without an arm is useless."

"Don't say that."

He managed to turn his head and saw the toddler now asleep on a blanket at the back of the cave. "He's a good kid, a brave one; any man would be proud to have him for a son."

She shook her head. "He's a half-breed bastard. No white man would accept him."

"I would," Colt said impulsively, "If only . . ." He let the words drop. What the hell was he saying? He was engaged and she was married with a husband due to come for her anytime.

"I've got a little dried meat and hardtack," she said and dug in the saddlebags.

"Save it for Grasshopper."

"But you need to keep up your strength," she protested.

"I can manage until we get back to the fort." He almost added, *if we get back to the fort,* but stopped himself. "We'll wait for dark and then we'll ride out again. Hannah, I want you to promise me one thing."

"Anything, Colt." She took his hand between her two and looked deep into his eyes.

"If I get too delirious and out of my head, I want you to abandon me and ride on. The fort is about ten miles to the northeast."

"No." She shook her head. "After what you've done for me, I couldn't leave you out here to die."

"You listen to me." His voice became stern and he was once again a commanding officer. "It's important to me that you and your son get out of this alive. I didn't go to all this trouble to have you die out here on the plains because I fell out of my saddle or couldn't remember my directions. Now you promise me."

He was clinging to her hand, his green eyes so intense with fever that she nodded. "Of course I promise. Now you just take it easy and maybe we can all get out alive."

He relaxed and settled back against the cave wall, shivering.

About dusk, as little Grasshopper was awakening,

she heard the distant thunder of hoofbeats. She took a deep breath, trembling. What were the chances it was the Cavalry looking for them?

Then she heard a shout in Comanche and knew it was a war party searching along the river. Colt's eyes opened wide, and she made a shushing sound to him, then grabbed for her child.

Grasshopper began saying, "Mama, Mama," in Comanche, and she put her hand over his mouth and held him close, praying that the Comanche wouldn't find them.

Her heart seemed to be beating so hard, she thought everyone must surely hear it. It was almost dark, so that was in the fugitives' favor. She held her child close and prayed for the darkness to come faster. From the mouth of the cave, she saw the silhouettes of the war party on their painted ponies, spears and shields in hand, searching along the riverbank below, looking for where the fugitives might have crossed.

She understood some Comanche language, but not enough to understand what they were shouting to each other. She turned questioning eyes toward Colt.

He whispered, "They are lookin' for tracks and promisin' they will roast us both alive if they find us."

"Oh, God," she gulped, but she did not cry and she did not get hysterical like most women would have.

Colt found himself admiring her even more. "Listen, Hannah, if they capture us, I'm gonna tell them I killed Spider and carried you off against your will. That way, you and your child will be taken safely back to their camp."

"I'd rather die than become a Comanche slave again. And what would they do to you?"

He shook his head, closed his eyes. "You don't want to know, but it doesn't matter. I want you and Grasshopper to be safe." He had ridden with the tribe for ten years and although he had never participated in the torture, he knew the Comanche could keep a man alive for days, screaming in agony, hurting him enough that he prayed for death. Well, he didn't intend to be captured; he had to get this woman and her child to safety.

They watched the warriors hunting along the stream for tracks, crossing the river, looking about, then riding farther downstream, until they were lost in the blackness of the coming night.

Colt heaved a sigh of relief. "That was close. We'll wait a while until we're sure they're gone."

Hannah trembled now; he could see her outline in the mouth of the cave. "I didn't intend they should take us alive," she whispered. "I've got your pistol. I was going to get as many of them as I could, then save the last bullets for us."

"You're a brave woman, Hannah," he said with admiration. "Give Grasshopper some of that dried meat and some water, and then we'll try to get out of here."

"I don't think you're fit to ride," she protested.

"We've got to," he said, struggling to get up. "They'll be back at daylight, rechecking all along the river."

He was sicker and weaker than he had realized, he thought as he stumbled to the mouth of the cave. "You gather up our stuff and I'll saddle the horses."

"All right."

His fever was raging and he had to fight to keep his teeth from chattering, but he managed to get the two horses saddled. "You ready?"

She came out of the cave carrying a bundle of gear and leading Grasshopper by the hand. "I'm ready."

He helped her on Rascal, then handed up the toddler. "Now, Grasshopper," he said in Comanche, "you must be a brave warrior because we have a long ride ahead of us."

"Brave warrior," the child said proudly.

Colt swung up on the Comanche pinto horse and the mustang snorted a welcome. He had put Hannah on Rascal because his little horse could be depended on to get her back to the fort, no matter what. "Okay, Hannah, follow the stars. The fort is right under the Dog Star, remember that."

"I'll remember." She nodded as they started down the steep ravine at a walk.

He felt himself sway in the saddle and forced himself to sit upright. "If something happens, if I should go unconscious and fall, you must keep riding. You promised."

She was not going to argue with him. "All right." But she knew she could never leave him to die.

"You must be a strong Texas woman and save your child. Anyway if I should fall off, you're not big enough to get me back up on my horse."

She nodded agreement, but she thought if he collapsed, she would try to fashion a travois and drag him back to the fort. She would not leave him for the Comanche to torture.

They rode mostly at a walk, sometimes at a slow lope.

"We've got to spare the horses," Hannah explained.

However, he knew that if they broke into a gallop, he would not manage to stay on his horse, and that was why she was riding slowly. "With any luck, we ought to be there by daylight."

"Suppose the Comanche are between us and the fort?"

She heard him sigh. "Then we ride like hell and hope they don't ride us down. Remember, you must say I took you and your son against your will."

"All right," she said to placate him, but she knew she wouldn't. She would go down fighting and clawing, killing as many warriors as she could and save the last bullet for Colt because she would not let him be tortured.

Sometime during the long night, Grasshopper nodded off to sleep in her arms. When she looked over at Colt, he appeared to be unconscious, but still in the saddle. "Whoa." She reined in and the pinto stopped, too. She dismounted and lay the sleeping child on the soft buffalo grass and looked up at Colt. "Colt? Are you all right?"

He didn't answer. She reached up and touched his hand, and it was sweaty with fever. He was so sick, and only his strong will was keeping him in the saddle. She got a length of rope, ran it around his hands, and tied them to the saddle horn. He was right about one thing: if he fell off, he was too big for her to lift back on his horse. She looked around the dark prairie. There was nothing but grass moving like a dark sea for miles, nothing she could use to fashion a travois.

"Now, mustang," she whispered to the pinto, "don't you step into any holes or shy from anything. He's got to stay on your back."

Rascal nuzzled her as if urging her to move on.

God, it was late and she was bone tired, but they must reach the fort by daylight because they were so visible out here on the flat plains. It was a good thing it was a moonless night.

Hannah picked up her sleeping child and remounted. *Follow the Dog Star, the fort is under it*, she remembered and started off that direction, leading Colt's horse. They were either both going to make it or neither, because she would not sacrifice him after everything he had done for her. If worse came to worse, she would tie Grasshopper onto Rascal, give the little horse his head and let the savvy mustang find his own way back to the fort. She at least wanted her child to grow up to be a Texan, not a Comanche.

It was such a long night, Hannah thought it would never end, and yet she prayed it wouldn't because she was not certain how far they had come and how much farther it would be. She must not be caught in broad daylight out on the open prairie, where the pair could be seen for miles.

Colt had not spoken for hours except to mumble now and again, and she knew he was delirious and out of his head. She prayed he did not start screaming or shouting. Grasshopper was awake now, but she whispered to him in Comanche to be quiet and he obeyed. Every muscle and bone in her body ached, and she was exhausted and hungry. She stopped a few times and managed to get some water into Colt, but he spilled a lot of it. The rest she gave to her child. Now the canteens were empty and she could see a pale glow in the eastern sky that promised that soon the first gray light of dawn would creep across the prairie and then the golden sun would loom large over the far horizon and expose the pair riding across the vast Texas plains.

She was defeated, she knew. It was almost daybreak and she had not made it to the fort. The horses were so tired, they were stumbling and Colt was reeling in his saddle. At any moment, he might fall to the ground.

She was distraught, but she did not weep. Weeping would not solve anything. Anyway, that was for weak women and she was strong. Circumstances had forced her to be. If she didn't make it to safety, at least she had tried her damnedest.

The sky slowly turned pink and lavender in the east and in a few minutes, the sun would come up over that far rise. Already gray light spread across the vast plains.

She heard a triumphant shout and looked behind her.

"Oh, my God! Colt, wake up!" The war party, a dozen painted warriors on pinto ponies, had appeared on the rise behind her, and they had spotted her, although they were at least a half mile away.

Colt must not have been conscious, because he did not answer. For a minute, she wavered, staring at the triumphant brown faces marked with scarlet and yellow paint as they galloped toward her. Colt was right; she could save herself by telling the furious Indians that she and her child had been kidnapped.

No, she wasn't going to do that. She wouldn't go down without a fight. "Colt, damn it, wake up! Colt!"

He seemed to rouse at the same time Grasshopper began to whimper as she kicked her horse hard in the flanks and started loping. She glanced back at Colt. He was awake now, but looked uncertain as to where he was. "Ride, Colt! Ride! The Comanches have spotted us!"

She pushed Rascal into a gallop, dragging the pinto along as Colt seemed to stir into semiconsciousness.

She must win this race. Colt seemed to rouse and hung onto the saddle horn as she pushed both horses into a gallop. The mustangs were exhausted from traveling all night, but they broke into a run.

Behind her, she heard the Comanches' triumphant shrieks as they gained on the fugitives and kicked their horses into a gallop. They would overtake the pair, she knew that, but she wasn't a weakling to surrender. The two horses were blowing and lathered, but she urged them on, hearing the hooves behind gaining on her. Her heart was in her throat as she rode. If they'd only had another hour, if it had kept raining, if . . . then she topped a rise and there lay the fort ahead of her, with a Cavalry patrol riding maneuvers on the prairie just outside the gates.

"Help!" she shouted. "Comanches!" And she took off at an even faster pace toward the patrol. Colt was awake now, but weaving in his saddle and struggling to stay on his horse as they galloped toward the Cavalry.

She saw a glint of brass as a bugle went to a soldier's lips and a charge sounded out in the coming dawn. Hannah thought she had never heard such beautiful music. Then the Cavalry thundered toward them.

Behind her, she heard the shrieks of surprise as the Indians spotted the patrol, realized they were outnumbered, and reined in their rearing, neighing horses. She didn't look back, intent on reaching the blue uniforms galloping toward her, stirring up dust as the bugle sounded again. She heard the shouts of the Comanches turning and racing away behind her as the soldiers now surrounded her, firing at the enemy.

At that moment, Colt slid from his lathered horse and lay in the dirt, unconscious. Hannah reined in, handed her child to a surprised bugler, and dismounted, running to Colt's side. He lay in the dirt, his injured arm bright with fresh blood. His green eyes flickered open as she struggled to protect him from the dust the churning Cavalry horses kicked up as they reined in.

"Did we—did we make it?"

"Yes, we made it! Give me a canteen!" She ordered

a soldier as he dismounted beside her. She pulled Colt into her lap and splashed water on his fevered face and then gave him a long drink. "We're all right! The Cavalry is here!"

The elegant Captain Van Smyth, who led the patrol, dismounted and walked over to her. "Good Lord! Who is this?"

She realized then that Colt still wore the disguise of buckskin and moccasins. "It's Lieutenant Colt Prescott. He's a hero; he rescued me and my child."

"Wrong!" snapped the elegant young officer. "He's a deserter and out of uniform. He'll probably be shot!"

Chapter 9

In his fevered mind, Colt was a small boy again, traveling with a wagon train through north Texas. The trip had been uneventful until the morning they woke up and discovered they were surrounded by a large war party of Cheyenne warriors.

The wagons were circled, but the settlers saw the size of the war party and the leaders knew they would have to negotiate with the Indians because the whites were outnumbered. Colt's father offered to walk out and find out what the Cheyenne wanted.

Colt remembered being very much afraid for his dad as the man took the long, lonely walk out to meet with the chief, a handsome big fellow on a fine black horse and wearing bright face paint and a luxurious eagle-feather war bonnet.

The two men talked for a while and then his father walked back to the circled wagons.

The curious settlers gathered around him. "Well, what does he want? Food? Weapons?"

Colt remembered now the look of worry on his father's tanned face. He was, after all, a farmer from

Indiana. "No, that's not what he wants, but if we don't give him what he wants, they'll attack our train and wipe us out."

The older Prescott turned and looked toward a young, yellow-haired beauty traveling with the train, Texanna. "He wants her."

"What?" A gasp ran through the whole crowd.

The preacher drew himself up. "Why, we can't do that, turn a white girl over to a savage for who knows what."

But all the men knew what; young Colt saw it in their faces.

"That's what I told him, but he wants Texanna and if we don't give her up, his war party will attack us."

And then the whites began to argue. Some wanted to fight the Cheyenne, although they had no chance against them. Some wanted to give up the girl to save the train. The arguing went on most of the day, with friend turning against friend, women crying and fussing and everyone staring at the beautiful Texanna with her long yellow hair streaming down her back. She looked terrified, and young Colt felt so sorry for her because he knew she did not want to be the sacrifice.

The argument had turned ugly, men yelling and swearing, a few blows exchanged. The women looked furious with Texanna because her beauty had brought this trouble down on them. Half the pioneers wanted to tie her up and give her to the chief; the other half wanted to fight to defend her.

In the end, Texanna, without a word, walked out between the wagons and toward the warriors. She was gone before the arguing white people even realized she had sacrificed herself. Colt saw her leaving and called after her to come back, but she did not heed and she did not stop. She walked up to the chief, who reached down and lifted her up before him on his fine black stallion, and the whole war party galloped away.

Colt would never forget how her golden hair had glittered in the last rays of sun as she rode off. The next morning, the wagon train continued on its way and no one ever spoke of Texanna again. The men must have been ashamed of their cowardice and the women were ashamed too, that they had been willing to sacrifice the young, innocent virgin to save themselves.

The Prescotts settled in east Texas and began to grow cotton. Colt hated the poor subsistence and the grubbing in the dirt. He was still a boy when he ran away from home, was captured by the Comanche, and later, joined the army.

Now in his fevered mind, he once again saw Texanna of the golden hair as his eyes flickered open. "Come back," he whispered. "Come back."

The blond girl leaning over him put a cold rag on his forehead. "Are you all right? Doc and I have been worried about you."

Texanna. No, it was not Texanna. It was . . . it was Hannah. The events of the last several days came flooding back to him and he remembered he and Hannah and her little boy were being chased by Comanches when, suddenly, a blue-coated troop of soldiers had sounded the charge.

He tried to sit up, wondering where he was.

"Take it easy," she said, and he realized how tired she looked. "You're going to be all right. Doc says."

He looked around and realized he was in the infirmary, then relaxed. Whatever happened now, at least he and the girl and her little boy were safe from torture.

"I've got to go see about Grasshopper," she said and smiled as she stood up.

Why had he ever thought her plain? When she smiled with those big, blue eyes, she was the most beautiful woman he had ever met.

No, the most beautiful woman was Olivia and he was engaged to her. Even as he tried to speak, Hannah said, "I'll be back later," and left.

Doc came in just then with a bowl of stew. "Dag nab it, I'm glad to hear you're awake. You've been out several days."

"I don't remember much," Colt admitted as Doc piled pillows behind him and handed him the stew. He took a bite. "This is really good."

"Hannah made it from some of the vegetables in her garden." Doc sat down in a chair by his bed. "She's hardly left your side."

"Oh? What's going to happen to her?"

"We found her an empty shack down on Suds Row. I think she can make a living like some of the other women by washing and ironing for the soldiers."

"Has anyone heard from her husband?"

Doc shook his head. "I don't know. She hasn't mentioned him, so I haven't either."

"She won't want to go with him," Colt murmured as he gulped the hot stew.

Doc wiped his handkerchief across his balding head. "Dag nab it, Colt, let an old man give you some advice. She's married and you're engaged, and that makes for a mess if you don't back off."

"I know." He looked out the window, not meeting Doc's gaze.

"You'd better be thinking about yourself," Doc cautioned. "You went over the hill, deserting. You could be shot or court-martialed. Right now, you're confined to the infirmary and probably then to your quarters 'til some action is decided."

"I'd forgotten about that." Colt laughed without mirth. "What is this? The middle of May? I'm due to leave the Cavalry June fifteenth unless I decide to reenlist."

"But right now, you're still a Cavalry officer and you could be shot or thrown in prison for desertion," Doc reminded him. "Frankly I think they ought to give you a medal for rescuing Hannah and her child, but then that would be common sense and the army ain't long on common sense."

Colt finished the stew. He heard the door open and both men turned to look. The elegant Olivia came through the door, her dark hair up in ringlets around her beautiful face. She wore a fine pink dress that would look more at home on a street in New York City than at this frontier fort.

"Oh, darling, you're awake." She rushed to his side, big tears in her dark eyes. She pulled out a lace hankie and wiped them. "Goodness gracious, I've been so worried about you!"

Doc stood up and took the soup bowl, frowning. "I think I have work to do in my office, so I'll leave you two alone."

Colt heard his footsteps and the door closing as Olivia knelt by his bed.

"I'm all right," he said.

She kissed his forehead. "That loose woman, the one that slept with the savage, has been hovering around you for days. Why I could hardly get in to see you."

"Hannah? She couldn't help it that she had a child by that Comanche. It wasn't as if she was given a choice."

"That's not what all the women around the fort think." Olivia sniffed disdainfully.

He didn't want to talk about Hannah. He had come to admire her. She had all those rare qualities of a true Texas woman. But she was married and her husband would be coming to get her. And Colt was engaged to the beautiful Olivia and facing court-martial.

"You know, Olivia, I'm in trouble now and maybe you might want to rethink being engaged to me—"

"Oh, but I've already decided," she said. "You don't think I would desert you now in your hour of need? Besides you are what I've always wanted: tall, handsome, gallant. Now, Colton, you've been at death's door for a few days and you aren't thinking straight, so we won't discuss this anymore right now."

He was suddenly very tired and not wanting to argue with her. He only wanted her to leave. "I reckon you are right," he admitted. "We'll talk later when I'm up and around."

"That's my dear boy. Why goodness gracious, I've already been planning the biggest society wedding Philadelphia ever saw. You'll be so handsome in your uniform."

"Olivia, I'm not sure I'm gonna reenlist."

"Well, that's all right, too." She smiled at him and patted his arm. "You'd make a successful businessman, and I'd have a fine home and the best carriage in town. All the women would envy me."

He was too weary to deal with her anymore. "I'm tired, Olivia. I think I want to sleep."

"Of course." She kissed his forehead and he smelled the scent of expensive perfume. "Now my brave little soldier just needs to rest and I'll be back to see you later."

He sighed with relief as he heard the rustle of her fine dress going out the door. She was beautiful, he reminded himself, and she was his. Half the young officers in the country would envy him. Then why was he having such doubts?

Olivia headed for her father's office. It was up to her to save Colt from his desertion charge, and her parents always gave her everything she wanted.

Captain Van Smyth was just coming out the door as she entered, and he took off his hat and bowed low, his beautiful curls so carefully combed.

"Good afternoon, Miss Olivia. You're looking lovely as usual today."

He was a dandy, she thought as he fingered his wispy little mustache. Funny, she used to think he was so grand until she met a real man, Colton Prescott. "Thank you, Howard. Is my father in?"

"Yes, ma'am. Miss Olivia, if I'm not being too bold, perhaps we might go riding some afternoon."

"Why, Captain, you shock me. I thought you knew I was engaged to Colton Prescott."

"Well, but there's no ring yet and after all"—he fingered his mustache again—"we are more from the same class than he is. Why, he'd probably drink out of a finger bowl and have no idea what to do with a shrimp fork."

She flushed because that was probably true. She doubted if Colton had ever seen a shrimp fork or a finger bowl, but she could turn Colton into a polished gentleman. "I'm in a hurry, sir, and I do not want to discuss my fiancé."

"You do realize he's facing a court hearing?"

"I'm sure Colton will come out of this just fine. We'll be announcing our wedding date soon."

"All right." He smiled at her. "But I don't know what you see in that rough-hewn country lout. You and I are from the same background, Miss Olivia, and we would make a splendid couple. If you change your mind, I'd love to take you riding."

"I'll remember that." She curtsied and pushed past him and into her father's office.

Daddy was sitting at his desk doing paperwork as she entered, went behind him, and draped both arms around his neck. As usual, he smelled of whiskey.

He patted her hands absently. "Oh, hello, dear. What brings you in here?"

"Goodness gracious, do I have to have a reason to come in and see my own dear daddy?" She kissed his gray hair, went around the desk, and settled herself into a chair.

"Well, you usually do." He smiled at her. "How's the lieutenant doing?"

At this she began to cry, pulled a lace hankie from her sleeve and dabbed at her beautiful eyes. "He's conscious, finally. Oh, Daddy, I was so afraid he wouldn't make it." She began to sob.

He frowned and reached for his pipe. "Maybe he'd have been lucky not to. You know he's probably facing court-martial for deserting."

Now a flood of tears. "After the brave thing he did, rescuing that—that woman and her half-breed brat? Why half the people at the fort think he should get a medal."

He leaned back in his chair and put tobacco in the

bowl of his pipe. "I'm afraid that's not how the system works, dear."

More tears. "I love him so much, Daddy, and how can I marry him if he's disgraced and shot or sent to prison?"

"Saint Mary's blood, why is this my problem?" he murmured and then lit his pipe. "I hate to make you so unhappy, dear, but—"

"Just suppose he hadn't deserted?" She looked up, dabbing at her dark eyes. "Just suppose you had really sent him on a secret mission to rescue Mrs. Brownley and no one else knew about it?"

He frowned and reached into his desk drawer for a bottle of whiskey. "Now, dear, you know I can't do that. Why, my whole career—"

"But you're the officer in charge, aren't you? You're not Irish trash like Mama's family says you are. Why, you're a major in the elite Second Cavalry, and you can do anything you want to do."

"I wish I could," he muttered and poured a slug of whiskey into a smudged tumbler, thought it over, and filled it up. "Olivia, you're asking me to go against everything I believe in and if I got caught—"

"But you're the officer in command and you know Colton doesn't deserve to go to prison." She let loose a wave of tears like Noah's flood.

He took a big gulp of whiskey as she sobbed and sobbed. "Please, dear, don't cry."

"How can I stop when I love him so and we were planning a big wedding?"

He sighed. "I'll have to think about this awhile, Olivia." He gulped his drink.

She jumped to her feet, ran around the desk, and hugged his neck. Daddy was spineless compared to

Mama. "Oh, thank you, Daddy. I just know you'll find that secret order in your desk that you didn't tell the other officers about, in case the mission was a failure."

He waved her away and smoked his pipe and smiled. "You know, I may remember that I did order Lieutenant Prescott to go after Mrs. Brownley. He's the only man in this fort brave enough to send on a mission like that."

She wiped her eyes. "Oh, Daddy, I knew he didn't desert. He's a hero after all."

"Now go along with you, I've got work to do."

"I love you, Daddy."

"I love you too, pumpkin." He nodded to her as she went out the door.

She had known she could do it. She started across the parade grounds toward the infirmary. Men, especially Daddy, were putty in her hands. Why that Captain Van Smyth would crawl on his knees for her if she asked him to.

Now should she convince Colton to remain in the army? He would look so good in a colonel's uniform, or maybe even a general's, and Mama's family had so much influence in Washington. Too bad Daddy wanted to rise on his own merits and was stuck as a major. If he'd just ask Mama's brother for help, Daddy could be a general by now. After all, Uncle Ernest was a congressman. On the other hand, if she persuaded Colton not to reenlist when his term was up in a few weeks, Uncle Ned would find a place in one of the De Ville family businesses in Philadelphia.

Olivia could already imagine their life together. She and Colton would own a big mansion near the center of the city and she would have a fine carriage with a matched pair of black horses—no, maybe she'd rather have white. She pictured Colton, handsome and tall,

dressed in the latest style, escorting her to the opera
with all the women swooning with jealousy.

Olivia stopped short when she saw Mrs. Brownley
disappearing into the infirmary. That woman. How
dare she go out in polite society after sleeping with a
dirty savage? Of course she had. Everyone's tongue was
wagging over that half-breed little redskin she had
brought back with her. And Mrs. Brownley was carrying a dish of something that smelled very good from
here. Olivia's mood was immediately ruined.

She turned and went stomping off to her quarters
behind the major's office. "You, Maria," she said to the
Tonkawa maid. "I want you to cook up something
scrumptious for me to take to my sick fiancé—maybe
a good vegetable soup."

The maid shook her head. "Have no vegetables,
missy."

Who had vegetables? Mrs. Brownley had planted a
garden behind the infirmary. "Then go steal some out
of that white slut's garden and hurry up. I want to take
my fiancé something delicious."

The maid hurried out to obey. Humming "Beautiful
Dreamer" and smiling, Olivia went in to put on her
best dress, recomb her hair, and spray on some expensive perfume. If that plain Mrs. Brownley thought she
could steal a man from a society belle like Olivia De
Ville Murphy, she had another think coming.

Hannah had paused at the door of the infirmary,
seeing the major's daughter walking toward her. She
knew the girl did not like her and would not appreciate the fact that Hannah was bringing venison stew in

to the lieutenant. Then the girl saw her, frowned, turned, and walked away.

Hannah sighed with relief as she went into the infirmary. "Hello, Doc. How's our patient?"

Doc stood up, smiling and sniffing. "He's better, as are the other two patients, one kicked by a horse, the other down with some kind of fever."

"I think I brought enough for all of you," she said and put the big bowl on the table.

"Good." Doc's bald head nodded. "I'll dish it up, and you go in and see Lieutenant Prescott."

She felt her heart beat faster. "Are you sure he's awake? I don't want to disturb—"

"If he's not, he'll wake up. Now go along with you."

Hannah brushed back a wisp of yellow hair that had escaped her bun and tiptoed in to stand by Colt's bed. He was asleep, and she stood a long moment, looking down at him. She was beginning to have feelings for this man, and she had never had feelings, except hatred and fear, for any man. Every one she had known before had mistreated her, but this one was so kind and gentle.

Don't be a fool, Hannah, she scolded herself. *He's pledged to the major's daughter and she can offer so much more than you can. And yet* . . .

As she stood there, wondering whether to leave, Colt's green eyes opened very slowly and he smiled. "I thought I was dreamin' you were here."

She half turned apologetically. "I didn't mean to disturb you."

He reached out and caught her hand. "Don't go. I haven't thanked you enough for your hours of tireless nursin' and all the good food you have brought."

She liked the feel of his big, strong hand. Hers seemed to fit into it so naturally. "How did you know?"

"Doc told me." He pulled her down on her knees by his bedside so their faces were close.

Oh, she had an urge she had never had before, to reach out and touch his face, but of course she did not. She averted her eyes. "It's me who should be thanking you," she whispered. "After all, you saved us from the Comanche and nearly lost your life doing so."

He brushed her hair back, such an intimate gesture. "How are you gettin' along? How's the boy?"

"I've moved into one of the cabins on Suds Row." She pulled away from him to break the spell, but he did not let go of her hand. "Soldiers can always use more women to wash and iron their clothes. I think I can manage financially so you don't have to worry about me."

"Good," he said, "but I wasn't worried. You're a Texas girl and Texans are always strong and independent."

She flushed at the compliment and pulled away from the grip of his hand. "I reckon Grasshopper and I could live here indefinitely if the soldiers' dirty laundry holds out," she laughed.

He smiled up at her, liking to watch her laugh. She seemed to laugh so rarely and when she did, her plain face lit up and became beautiful, with little crinkles in the tanned skin at the corners of those huge blue eyes.

He had never felt this way about a woman before. Oh, he had lusted after pretty saloon girls and had seen Olivia as a perfect, beautiful wife upon a pedestal, but there was something different about Hannah, brave and independent, yet sad and vulnerable. Olivia. What was he thinking? Hannah was married and her husband would be coming for her soon, and he had pledged his troth to Olivia. His troth, maybe, but he knew at that moment, his heart belonged to this shy, work-worn prairie girl.

Doc broke the spell just then, coming in with bowls of stew. "Hey, Colt, you're gonna like this. This gal can cook."

Hannah flushed and stepped back, wiping her hands on the faded blue gingham dress that was one of Olivia's castoffs. "Oh, Doc, it's nothing special."

"It's the best venison stew I ever tasted. Gal, if you wasn't already married, I'd try to marry you myself."

Colt saw immediately that Doc had said the wrong thing.

Hannah's face fell and she stuttered, "I—I have to go. I've got a child to tend to and ironing to do."

She turned and fled out the door.

Doc handed Colt a bowl and sat down in the chair. "What'd I say?"

Colt sighed, sat up, and took the bowl. "I think she hasn't got good feelings toward her husband."

"That's too bad," Doc muttered, "especially since the major tells me Brownley's due here soon."

Colt paused, his mouth full of stew. It had been delicious, but now it tasted bitter and cold. He swallowed it. "How soon?"

Doc shook his head.

"Has anyone told her?"

Doc chewed his lip. "I don't think so."

"It isn't good to surprise her like that."

"Well, maybe things have changed and he'll be thrilled to see her. I think they lost a little boy. Maybe he'll really want Grasshopper. That's a cute child."

"Yes, that would be nice, wouldn't it?" Somehow, Colt didn't think that was going to happen. Anyway it wasn't his business, he reminded himself as he ate. He was set to marry the major's daughter if he didn't go to prison or get shot for desertion. Hannah would have to make her own decisions.

Doc scratched his bald head. "You look like you're feelin' fit as a hound dog."

Colt nodded. "I am. How soon can I get out of here?"

"Maybe tomorrow or the next day, depending on what the major says about whether he wants you confined to quarters."

"Good," Colt said, his mind busy. He wanted to be there when Luther Brownley rode in. It might not be Colt's business, but he intended to make sure Hannah really wanted to go with her husband. Otherwise, Colt would face him down and not allow him to take her away.

Chapter 10

It was the next day, late in the morning. Colt had spent the night in the infirmary. His arm, under the bandage, was still sore, but he was up and almost dressed when Olivia came in in a swirl of blue silk. "Surprise, darling, I've brought your dinner."

He smiled at her, wishing he had shaved. "So soon? Why, it must not be later than eleven o'clock."

She sat down in a chair near his bed and uncovered the small bowl. "It's vegetable soup, my best."

"Oh, that's nice. You should have brought enough for Doc and the other patients." He sat down on the bed across from her.

"Oh, I'm so sorry, dear. I didn't think of it. Now you just eat this like my brave little soldier and get well and strong."

"I wish you wouldn't talk to me like that, Olivia." He didn't like being talked to like a child with that condescending tone, but he took the soup from her although he wasn't hungry because Hannah had brought him a good breakfast. Of course he knew better than tell Olivia that.

"Like what? Why you are my brave soldier." She smiled and showed her pretty white teeth. She was so beautiful, it was hard to be annoyed with her. "Now eat your soup."

He tasted it, but it wasn't very good. "Mmm, delicious." He forced himself to eat a few bites.

"I wanted to get here before that woman brought you in something. Honestly, Colton, everyone in the fort is talking."

He blinked and paused, the spoon halfway to his lips. "About what?"

"About what? Goodness gracious, darling, you are so naive." She laughed. "About you bringing that woman back, about what might be going on."

"There is nothin' going on. I rescued her; any man, at least a Texan, would do the same."

"I didn't mean to sound jealous, my love. You're right," she soothed and patted his arm. "You're so gallant."

She was so beautiful, and she leaned closer, her soft lips so tempting. He tried to remember that he was once so bewitched by her. "Mrs. Brownley means no harm. She brings food for Doc and all the other patients, too."

Olivia sniffed disdainfully. "But everyone says she's really bringing it for you. People are gossiping."

"Then tell them to stop," he snapped and set the bowl on the bedside table. "Mrs. Brownley is just an unfortunate woman who is grateful for my help."

"Mmm," Olivia said and reached out and patted his face with her manicured, soft hand. "Oh, speaking of which, I think you can forget about the charges."

He tried not to think of Hannah's work-worn hand that was so much gentler than Olivia's touch. "Why?"

"Why? Well, Daddy suddenly remembered that he had given you a secret order to go rescue her and you did, almost at the cost of your life, so you're a hero, not a deserter."

"I see. And what did you have to do with this?" He kept his voice cold.

"Well, goodness gracious, I couldn't marry a convict, could I?" She avoided his eyes. "Why, Mama and her family—"

"Olivia, I'm a man and I'm used to dealin' with my own responsibilities. A Texan would never hide behind a woman's skirts, and—"

"Well!" She stood up and glared down at him, the very epitome of righteous indignation. "I don't understand your ingratitude. Why, you're a whole lot like my father, never appreciating everything Mama's family's influence could have—"

"Olivia, I think we need to have a long talk." He stood up, towering over her diminutive form.

"After you calm down, darling, and realize that I'm only trying to help you." She reached up and caught his hand again, but he yanked away from her. "My," she simpered. "My soldier boy is really in a bad mood."

"Please don't talk to me like I'm a dim-witted child," Colt almost shouted at her. "Hannah never—"

"Hannah! Hannah! Hannah!" she screeched back at him. "That slut is causing people to titter behind my back, and I won't have it, you hear?"

He wanted to strike her, but he had never struck a woman, no Texan would, so he gritted his teeth and controlled his temper. "Don't call her a slut."

"Well, everyone knows half those women on Suds Row do more for soldiers than just wash and iron their shirts." She stepped back, seemingly nervous at his anger. "Now Colton, dear, you've been very sick, so I'll overlook your unseemly outburst because after all, we're to be married and you owe Daddy and me a great deal of gratitude."

"And I suppose you will remind me of that every time we have a disagreement over the next fifty years?"

"You're such a growly bear." She came to him, stood on tiptoe, and gave him a quick kiss on the lips. "Why don't we go riding tomorrow if you're up to it and talk about our wedding plans?"

"Olivia, about that. I've been rethinking and I'm not sure—"

"Oh, darling, this isn't the time to discuss our marriage, not when you're still upset with little old me. Let's go riding tomorrow. I'll pack a little picnic, all right?"

Before he could protest, she had fled out the door in a swirl of blue silk.

"Well, damn it all to hell!" he grumbled and flopped down on the bed.

Doc came in just then. "I saw Olivia fleeing out of here like the devil rode her coattails. What happened?"

"I'd rather not talk about it," Colt snapped. He might be angry with Olivia, but he was still a chivalrous gentleman.

"I see she brought you some soup." Doc picked up the spoon and tasted it. "Okay, I reckon, but not as good as Mrs. Brownley's."

Colt snorted. "Don't let Olivia hear you say that. She made it especially for me."

"From vegetables stolen from Hannah's garden," Doc said.

"What?"

Doc laughed. "From my window, I saw her maid,

Maria, out there picking vegetables. I reckon Maria made the soup, too. Well-born ladies don't cook much."

"Well, that was a cheap trick," Colt complained. "How soon can I get out of here, Doc?"

"Dag nab it, Colt, you're as touchy as a boil. You can leave anytime. Just take it easy for a few days. I don't want that wound opening up."

Colt sighed and rolled a cigarette. "I reckon the major will put me under house arrest."

"No, I don't think so. Here, have a drink." Doc went over to a cabinet and poured him some liquor. "It seems you had secret orders to go rescue the damsel in distress."

Colt swore under his breath and lit the smoke. "Now, Doc, you know that ain't true."

"Everyone now thinks it is, my boy." He winked and handed Colt the tumbler of whiskey. "And if you're smart, you'll smile and nod when everyone congratulates you."

"How can I? Why, it's like hidin' behind a woman's skirts."

"Would you rather do a long stretch in the federal pen after a court-martial or maybe face a firing squad?"

"No, but I knew what I was riskin' when I set out after Hannah."

"Then you were morally right, even though you didn't have official orders."

Colt sipped his drink. "I don't think the army sees it that way."

"They do now, so let sleepin' dogs lie, my boy."

"But Hannah—"

"And another thing." Doc leaned against the wall and lowered his voice. "If I were you, I'd call her Mrs. Brownley and forget about her. You don't think the major's daughter saved you for any other reason than she wants a bridegroom, do you?"

"I won't be her pet like some prissy little poodle."

"Get used to it, Lieutenant. I think she's already bought the collar and leash. All she needs now is the license."

"Dammit to hell!" Colt swore and took a long drag on his smoke. Then he drained his whiskey and stood up. "Thanks for the advice, Doc, but you know Texans are pretty damned independent." He gathered up his gear and started toward the door, turned. "I feel like a rattlesnake caught in a gigantic spiderweb."

Doc grinned. "Just remember what they say in Texas, 'dance with the one what brung you' and forget about Mrs. Brownley. She'll be gone in a few days anyway."

"That's right and then everything will be back to normal." Colt almost felt a sense of relief as he went out the door and over to his own quarters.

He managed to stall Olivia for three days, telling her he still didn't feel like riding. He found himself passing close to the infirmary or dropping by to visit Doc, but Hannah seemed to be avoiding him. To pass the time, Colt whittled a little toy horse out of a branch of Osage Orange wood. Finally Colt took some of his shirts down to her cabin to get them washed and ironed. He tucked the little horse in his pocket.

She came to the door when he knocked.

"I haven't seen much of you lately." He smiled.

"As you can see, I'm busy." She wiped perspiration from her forehead and reached to get an iron off the stove.

"This is awfully hard work for you."

"Not as hard as farm work or skinning a buffalo." She kept her eyes on the shirt she was ironing. "Besides, I'm content; I've got a roof over my head and I'm making enough to buy food. I do wish the children would treat Grasshopper better, though."

The toddler stuck his head around the corner, grinning at Colt, then ran to him.

Colt picked him up. "Hey, look what I've got for you." He pulled the toy horse out of his pocket.

Grasshopper giggled and grinned as he took it. "Rascal," he said in English.

Hannah seemed to try to hold back a smile. "He does like you a lot, Colt."

"And I'm crazy about him." Colt tickled the toddler, then put him on the floor, and Grasshopper played with the little wooden horse. "He needs a white name if he's gonna fit into white society."

She paused. "I've thought about that, but I didn't come up with a good one."

Colt watched the little boy playing on the floor. "What about namin' him for a real Texas hero, like one of the defenders of the Alamo? Give him something to live up to."

She nodded. "You've got a point there. Bowie? Crockett?"

"I was thinkin' more like their leader, Colonel Travis."

"Travis." Hannah seemed to roll the name around on her tongue. "Yes, that's a good, strong Texas name. All right, Grasshopper is now Travis."

The toddler said, "Travis?"

Colt grinned down at him. "Yes, you are now Travis, and you are a Texan like your mother."

"Like Colt and Rascal?" The toddler returned to playing with his toy and crawling around on the floor.

"Yes, like Colt and Rascal." Hannah smiled and Colt found her smile so enchanting.

Colt watched Hannah laboring over her ironing board. "Don't you want more than this, Hannah? Ironin' and washin' all day long at the fort?"

She shrugged. "I don't expect much out of life, and what man would want me now that I've been with a redskin?"

Colt almost said, *I would*, then stopped himself. "A lot of men wouldn't give a damn."

She looked at him with those spirited blue eyes. "You know better than that. I can hardly walk over to the commissary without seeing women turn away and whisper, and men laugh and make crude jokes when I pass."

"Who are they? I'll—"

"It's not your concern, Lieutenant. And you'd better not be seen coming here too much."

"What? To pick up my laundry?"

She kept ironing. "The major's daughter won't like it."

"To hell with the major's daughter," he said.

"That's a fine way to talk about your fiancée."

He shook his head. "I'm havin' second thoughts about that."

"You'll wreck your career."

"I'm havin' second thoughts about that, too. I've only got a couple more weeks, and then I might not reenlist."

She looked up from her ironing. "Hasn't the army been your life? What else would you do?"

Colt shook his dark head. "The army has always been everything to me, but I don't know. Lately, I'm not sure. I've got a little money saved. I might buy a ranch, raise some good cattle and horses. If the war comes, the Rangers will need men to hold back the Comanches once the U.S. forces leave Texas."

Hannah shuddered. "You're right. If the army should leave, the Comanches will run amok and ranches all along the Western frontier will be burned, people murdered, women—"

"I reckon you're right. I promised Olivia I'd take her ridin' this afternoon." He stood up. He started to ask about her husband, decided not to.

"Your shirts will be ready tomorrow," she said, "but I'll leave them on your doorstep."

"Why? I can come by and—"

"Colt," she said softly and put the iron down, came around the ironing board to face him. "Don't come here anymore."

He was looking down into her face, and while her tone was spirited as ever, her eyes were tragic and vulnerable. He fought an urge to pull her to him and kiss her.

She must have felt the electricity, too, because her full, soft lips opened slightly and her eyes half closed. Even as he reached for her, she took a deep breath and stepped away, straightening her small shoulders. "We both know why, don't we?"

"Yes." *She's a married woman,* he reminded himself, *and you are engaged to the most beautiful and cultured woman on the frontier. Do you want to start tongues wagging?* For himself, he didn't care, but Hannah had had enough trouble in her life without him adding to it. He took a deep breath. "Of course you're right."

He turned without a word and strode out her door and across to the stable.

"There you are." Olivia stood just inside the stable

door with a small picnic basket. "I was beginning to think you had forgotten, darling."

"I—I was delayed," he said, not looking into her dark eyes. Was he loco? This girl was the most beautiful woman he had ever met and she was certainly a virgin. He could think of a million reasons why he was a lucky man to be engaged to Olivia and not one good reason to get involved with Hannah. He was an honorable man, and to a Texan, his honor meant everything.

A private walked up leading two saddled horses and saluted. "Here's your mounts, sir, just as Miss Murphy requested."

Colt returned the salute. "Honestly, Olivia, I would have preferred Rascal."

"But he's not very pretty, and we have these fine thoroughbreds here at the fort."

The private was watching and listening, Colt decided, so he wouldn't take that fuss any further. He was annoyed the horses had been saddled. He didn't like treating his men like servants. "Olivia, I was capable of saddling horses."

"Goodness gracious, I was just trying to be helpful, since you're just getting out of the hospital, and anyway, that's what enlisted men are for, to look after officers."

He hadn't realized Olivia was so snobbish. Colt dismissed the private and helped Olivia mount up, then tied her picnic basket behind her saddle.

He wasn't looking forward to this ride at all, and now he realized the reason why. He was falling in love with Hannah, a married woman whose husband should be coming for her any day now. He must wipe the blonde from his mind.

"Darling, you're awfully quiet," Olivia said as he mounted up.

"Am I? Just have a lot on my mind, I reckon. Let's ride to the river."

"That will be nice. I brought cold roast beef, some chocolate cake, and homemade bread and pickles. Oh, and I tucked in a cold bottle of wine."

"That will be wonderful." He forced himself to turn in his saddle and smile at her as they nudged their horses into a walk.

Olivia prattled on and on about getting the latest fashion magazine in the post from New York City, how one just couldn't find good fabric or a dressmaker here, and on and on and on.

Had she always talked so much? She didn't seem to even be taking a breath, and he wondered if he could ever get a word in edgewise if he wanted to. She had a high-pitched voice that scraped across his nerves, but her constant prattle kept him from having to keep up a conversation.

In his mind, he heard Hannah's soft, low voice telling him not to come again and they both knew why. He realized that she had felt the same breathless attraction he had felt, and he knew somehow that he could have swung her up in his arms, carried her into her bedroom, and taken her with all the lust and need he felt. Yes, he must stay away from Hannah.

"So what do you think?" Olivia looked over at him as they rode.

He managed a smile. "About what, dear?"

"About the wedding. Should we have it in Washington, D.C., or Philadelphia?"

He blinked. "Does it matter?"

"Of course it matters." She looked annoyed. "Now it all depends on whether you stay in the army or not, as to whether you wear a dress uniform or I have Uncle Walt's tailor make you a fine broadcloth suit."

"I haven't given it much thought." He sighed and looked ahead toward the river. This was going to be a long afternoon.

"Goodness gracious, Mama will want to know soon. Putting on a giant wedding takes almost a year of planning, you know."

He looked at her, puzzled. "Why would it take a year? Most folks just step up in front of a parson and it's done. Then there's maybe a little cake and punch—"

"You aren't serious?" She looked at him as if she didn't know whether to laugh or burst into tears.

He didn't want to fuss with her so he just shrugged. "I don't know anything about plannin' weddin's, Olivia. Most men don't. I reckon I'll just leave that up to you."

She smiled triumphantly. "Good. I've been looking at all the copies I have of Godey's *Lady's Book*, but of course they are old, and probably out of style and who knows where one can buy real French lace around here, so I'll have Mama send to Paris and—"

Colt disappeared back into his own thoughts. In his mind, he had stepped forward in that little shack and taken Hannah into his arms and kissed her, really kissed her.

"We're here," Olivia announced, taking a breath from prattling on and on about French lace and wedding cakes.

Colt came out of his thoughts with a start. "Of course." He reined in, stepped down, and came around to help Olivia from her horse. She looked up at him as if she expected him to steal a kiss, but he had no desire to kiss that perfect mouth. Instead, he began to untie the picnic basket.

"I brought a blanket, too," she said and walked ahead of him to the placid river under the shade of the big live oak trees.

"I've got it." He followed her with the blanket and the basket as she picked a spot. He spread the blanket and sat down while she dug into the basket.

"Darling, would you like some wine?"

He nodded. He needed a little courage for what he was about to do. He must be out of his mind. Every officer on the post considered the major's daughter a catch, and they all wanted to marry her, she was so beautiful.

"Now," she said and handed him a glass of wine. "The reason I need to know whether you are staying in the service or not is I thought a military wedding would be lovely, and if we had it in Washington, Mama could invite all sorts of important people—why, maybe even the president."

"The president?" Colt sipped the wine. It was a dark red burgundy and delicious.

"Of course, silly." She smiled at him. "You know, if there is a war, and everyone says there will be, you'll be right there, knowing all the best people, and you'll get promoted fast, not like Daddy, who insists on staying out on the frontier where the upper echelon has forgotten all about him and he'll never get past major."

He was beginning to understand why the major drank, he thought, if Olivia's mother was anything like her daughter.

"Washington? You'd want to live in Washington?" Such a thing had never entered his mind.

"If you stay in the service"—she nodded—"you'd

rise fast, maybe even to general and there'd be all sorts of cotillions and balls to attend. You'd be so handsome with all that gold braid and medals on your chest."

He looked at her, thinking she was more shallow and petty than he had realized. "Olivia, if there's a war, it will be horrible—men killed, towns sacked and burned, children left fatherless—"

"Oh, but we'll be in Washington and you won't have to take part in any of that." She laid out tiny beef sandwiches on pretty flowered plates.

"Suppose I don't want to reenlist?" he asked and poured himself another glass of wine.

"Oh, that's all right, too, darling." She handed him a plate with a hand that was so perfectly manicured.

"Olivia, do you know how to iron?" He said it without thinking.

"Iron? Iron what?" She looked baffled.

"Clothes. Have you ever ironed a shirt in your life?" In his mind, he saw Hannah, perspiration on her tanned forehead as she labored over a shirt.

"Are you joking, Colton, dear? Of course I don't know how to iron or do laundry or any of those mundane things. I have servants to do things like that. Now, I can speak French and do watercolor paintings and play the spinet."

"None of those seem too practical on the Texas frontier," he said and picked up a sandwich.

"Texas?" She wrinkled her nose. "Goodness gracious, I can hardly wait to leave here. I thought it would be interesting, but it's just a big prairie with wild horses and hostile Indians."

"Texans love the Lone Star State," he said and poured himself another glass of wine. "They wouldn't live any place else."

She laughed. "I love it when you joke, Colton, dear. I thought if you didn't reenlist, Uncle Ned, Mama's brother, would find a good spot for you in one of the family businesses. We could live in the best part of town and you'd work in an office and go to the club with Mama's brothers. Just think how business will boom if a war starts. We manufacture iron and steel, you know."

"For cannons and guns?" He looked at her. She was so beautiful, such pale skin that had never been out toiling in the hot sun, such soft hands that had never done a minute's work in her whole life. He saw her as she really was: a doll, a beautiful fashion doll with no brains and no interests except clothes and high society.

"It's too bad you didn't go to West Point," Olivia sighed, "but no one needs to know that. You know, Mama's father got Daddy into West Point, but he never really fit into their family."

"I'm afraid I won't either," Colt said and ate his sandwich, understanding now why the major stayed out on the frontier.

"Oh, but of course you will, silly. When we go back East, I'll hire someone to teach you etiquette and how to dress and we'll join the best clubs. Uncle Ned can use his influence to—"

"You got this all thought out without ever once consultin' me?" He was growing angry.

"Well, it never occurred to me that you wouldn't go along with—"

"Olivia." He tried to keep his voice from rising. "Texas men are used to making decisions. You should have asked me what I thought. Whether I stay in the army or not, I never intend to leave Texas. I love it here."

"What? Why? Why would you even consider staying

in a rough, uncivilized state?" Her big brown eyes had turned an angry dark.

"Because maybe I'm a rough, uncivilized Texan," he fired back. "You know, Olivia, I think maybe we need to end this engagement. Maybe we aren't right for each other."

She was huffing with indignation. "How dare you? Why, everyone wants to marry me, and I chose you—"

"I'm sorry, Olivia, but I've changed my mind. I don't think we're suited to each other at all."

Out came the lace hankie and the big tears. "Boo hooo, what will people say? I'll be humiliated."

"I will be a gentleman," he assured her. "I will tell everyone you broke the engagement because you decided I was an uncivilized lout and not up to your high standards."

She was sobbing into her hankie. Colt felt like a terrible villain for breaking her heart, and yet he had a sudden feeling of freedom and relief. Sometimes a man ought to look beyond a beautiful face.

Abruptly he heard the sound of a galloping horse and grabbed for his pistol. But it was a blue uniform in a light buggy rattling over the horizon from the direction of the fort.

The private reined in, got down, and saluted. "Sir. Miss Murphy. Sorry to disturb your picnic, Lieutenant, but Major Murphy wants you back at the fort."

Colt stood up and saluted, feeling relief. Any excuse was a good one to leave this awkward scene. "What is it, Private?"

"There's a man in the major's office, and the major thinks you need to come right now."

Olivia was already gathering up the picnic stuff and blanket.

Colt was mystified. "A man? Who—?"

"His name is Luther Brownley and he's here about his wife."

Colt's heart fell. Somehow he'd hoped Hannah's husband would never show up. "Private, would you help Miss Murphy gather up our picnic things so I can get back right away?"

"Yes, sir."

And with that, Colt mounted up, lashed his horse into a gallop, and headed for the fort.

Chapter 11

Colt galloped back to the fort. He wasn't quite sure what he expected to do when he got there. Maybe he was only curious to see the man Hannah had married, or maybe he wanted to stop Luther from taking her, which, of course, was not his business. He only knew he wanted to be there for Hannah when she faced her husband again.

He rode up to the major's office, dismounted, and handed the horse's reins to a private. "I don't think I'll be here long," he said as he paused at the major's door.

There was a fancy buggy tied up at the hitching rail. Strange, he'd thought the man would be some poor farmer. He squared his shoulders and walked in.

The major looked relieved. "Oh, there you are, Lieutenant. This is Luther Brownley."

The lanky man stood up. He was well dressed, but looked like a farmer, red neck and tanned face. His beard was straggly and gray-streaked. He offered his hand, nodded, and said, "Howdy do?" and Colt could see his teeth were stained with chewing tobacco.

Colt shook his callused hand. "Good to meet you."

But he wasn't glad to meet him at all. This well-dressed cracker was coming to take Hannah away.

The major motioned Colt to a chair. "I was just telling Mr. Brownley that you were the man who rescued his wife."

"Well, thank you kindly," Brownley said with no show of emotion. "She's been gone most four years now."

"Drink, gentlemen?" The major got out the bottle and tumblers.

"Don't mind if I do." Brownley grinned and took a glass, settled down in his chair.

Colt took a glass, but didn't taste it. What was wrong with this man? If Hannah had been Colt's long-lost wife, he would have wanted to see her immediately.

They drank, but the atmosphere seemed strained.

"So you've come to take Hannah home?" Colt asked finally, trying to understand this man.

"Not prezactly," the other man said and drank his whiskey. "I was real surprised when the message came; I gave her up for dead a few months after she was carried off."

"The major said it was hard to track you down, Mr. Brownley, being as how you had moved to another county," Colt said.

Brownley grinned with his uneven, brown teeth. "Got a new, big farm now and a fancy house."

Colt fiddled with his whiskey tumbler in the strained atmosphere. Finally he couldn't stand the man's lack of interest anymore. "Aren't you wantin' to know how she's doin' and what happened and see her?"

The other man frowned and reached in his jacket for a twist of chewing tobacco. "I reckon she's all right, alive, at least, and I can guess what them savages did to her." He frowned and Colt didn't know what to say.

The major twisted in his chair. "Lieutenant, would you take Mr. Brownley down to her cabin so they can talk?"

Colt frowned. "Does she know he's here?"

The major shook his head and didn't meet Colt's gaze. "I thought it might be a shock since they haven't seen each other in so long. I thought maybe you'd show him the way."

"Certainly." Colt put down his untasted drink and stood up. There were a million things he'd rather do than take Luther Brownley down to be reunited with Hannah, but he reminded himself that, after all, she was married to this man, and he had every right to claim her.

The lanky man put down his empty glass and stood up. "Well, much obliged, Major Murphy. I thank you for whatever you've done for her."

The major shrugged. "All we did was rescue her. She's been through quite an ordeal, Mr. Brownley. You may have to be patient with her until she gets back to normal."

For the first time, the farmer looked a little disturbed. "She ain't loco, is she?"

"No," Colt said, "she's fine, but she needs gentle treatment for a long time."

"Humph," said Brownley and he followed Colt out the door.

Colt already didn't like the man. It wasn't just because he'd come to take Hannah away; it was his uncaring attitude.

Brownley gestured toward the fancy rig as he untied the horse. "Hop in and I'll drive us."

"Very nice," Colt complimented as he got in and Brownley got up on the seat beside him.

"Ain't it though? Emma bought it for me, new clothes, too."

Colt didn't have any idea who "Emma" might be, but he didn't ask. "Just drive down the length of these buildings and we'll be at Suds Row."

Brownley looked sideways at him as they pulled away, the fine gray horse stepping smartly. "Where?"

"Suds Row. It's where the ladies who do laundry for the soldiers live. Hannah has been there, makin' her way ironin' and washin' for the troops. Before that, she was helpin' around the infirmary."

"She always was a hardworkin' gal," Brownley said with no show of emotion. "Good cook, too, but stubborn and too high-spirited to be a good wife."

"High spirits is good in a woman," Colt defended her.

"Maybe in a horse, but not in a wife." Luther spat tobacco juice to one side as he drove.

Colt didn't reply, wondering if Brownley knew about little Travis. He had a sinking feeling that the major hadn't had the courage to tell Brownley about the half-breed child.

"Stop right in front of that third one," Colt instructed.

People were coming out of their quarters to watch, staring at the fine buggy as it went by. Evidently word had spread quickly that the Comanche captive's husband had finally come to retrieve her. Colt wished they'd all go back inside, but there wasn't that much daily excitement around the fort and this promised to be an interesting little drama for the curious.

Brownley reined in and said, "Wal, I'll just get down and go in. Has anyone told her I was comin'?"

Colt shook his head, wishing now he had a chance to tell her. She needed time to comb her hair and fix up some, put on her best dress that Olivia had given her. Come to think of it, she hadn't seemed very enthused when she'd first been rescued and he had told her they would try to find her husband. Maybe she thought he was killed in that Comanche raid.

He had a sudden feeling that he needed to be there. "I'll come in," he said abruptly and got out of the buggy as Brownley tied up the horse.

"No need." The lanky farmer frowned at him. "I don't aim to be here long."

"She'll have to have time to pack her few things," Colt answered and followed him up on the porch.

It was a warm day and the door was open.

Colt knocked on the doorjamb. "Mrs. Brownley? Are you home?"

"Colt?" He heard her call from deeper inside the house. "Come on in. I'm trying to get some shirts finished."

Brownley looked at him and grinned knowingly. "So that's how it is."

"No." Colt gritted his teeth. He wanted to punch that tobacco-stained mouth. "She's a very moral woman and she's been through a lot. You're a lucky man, Mr. Brownley."

The other man didn't answer as they went into the tiny front room. Colt was relieved not to see Travis. The toddler must be in the back room with his mother. He didn't know what Brownley would think about the child. After all, it hadn't been Hannah's fault that she'd been raped by Spider.

Suddenly Colt would rather have been anyplace but here. He heard Hannah's small feet coming from the back. "Hello, Colt, I hope you didn't come for your shirts—"

And then she skidded to a halt and just stood there, staring at both men, her mouth open.

"Hello, Hannah." The farmer stood with his straw hat in hand, staring at her awkwardly.

She stood there and stared back, her face going pale.

Colt cleared his throat in the deathly silence. "I—I'll wait out on the porch. If you need me, Hannah—"

"She don't need you," the other man snapped and gestured Colt out the door. He went out reluctantly.

Hannah stared at the man facing her. He was familiar, and yet not so in the fine new clothes. They'd always been so poor and he'd always worn beat-up overalls.

"Hello, Luther," she managed to say after a few deep breaths.

"Well, you don't seemed thrilled to see me," Luther said.

She didn't know what to say. She wasn't thrilled to see him; in fact she had hoped to never see him again. She wiped her wet hands on her apron.

"What are you doing here?" she managed finally.

"Now ain't that a helluva thing to say to your husband after not seeing him for almost four years?"

She squared her shoulders, deciding at that moment that she would not go with him, no matter what he said. She could see the blue of Colt's uniform outside on the porch, and that gave her courage.

"Frankly, Luther, I'm not glad to see you. I reckon you never expected to see me alive again."

"No, I really didn't," he admitted. "I figured after them Comanche bucks got through with you, they'd torture you to death or you'd kill yourself like any respectable white woman would do."

She raised her chin, always determined and defiant. "They didn't treat me any worse than you did, didn't beat me as much, as I remember."

He glared at her, tobacco juice stains on his thin lips. "You was never an obedient wife, Hannah. You always was too sassy and didn't obey me like the Good Book says a woman should do."

"I never respected you," she seethed. "You were always a coward. You think I don't remember you deserting me out there on the prairie, running past the women and kids to get back to the safety of the settlement? You had a rifle and you didn't even try to use it. I was trying to get to your gun to shoot them myself when they overran me."

"That's no way to talk to me, you sassy piece." He advanced on her.

She reached over and picked up one of the heavy irons off the stove. "You'll never hit me again, you mean bastard. You come one step closer and you'll get this hot iron in the face."

Looking past his stooped shoulder, she saw Colt standing in the doorway, ready to come in, and shook her head at him. She could protect herself this time.

"You tart, you're as ornery as ever. You always was too spirited for a decent woman."

About that time, she heard small footsteps behind her and Travis toddled into the room carrying the small wooden horse Colt had carved for him.

"Mama?" he said in Comanche.

Luther's face went white with shock. "You got a kid? You got a bastard pup by some Comanche buck? And you gave me a weakling son that died."

"Because he was born early." Hannah remembered that horrible day as she put down the iron and picked up Travis. "Because you knocked me down a flight of steps, or don't you remember that?"

"You was sassin' me," Luther snapped.

"I'm not going with you." She faced him, ready to fight.

"I didn't ask you to. And if I'd planned to, I wouldn't want some half-breed redskin kid in the deal. You should have killed yourself like a decent woman would."

She would not cry. It never did any good. It only made her seem more vulnerable, and she could not trust any man not to exploit that weakness.

Behind Luther, Colt stepped into the room, his face stern and angry. "I think you'd better leave, Brownley, before I throw you out."

She shook her head at Colt as Luther snarled, "This ain't your business, soldier boy. I only come to get her to sign a paper, that's all, and then I'm gone."

Hannah sighed with relief. "What kind of paper?"

Luther brought out a folded paper from his pocket. "You got a pen?"

She put Travis down on the floor, and he clung to her blue skirt as she searched around on the table for pen and ink. "What's the paper?"

"It's a divorce," he said, and laid the rumpled paper on the table. "I thought you was dead, so three months after you went missing, I married Mrs. Mailey."

Hannah blinked. "The fat, rich widow with the big farm?"

"Emma is a wonderful, God-fearing, obedient wife," he answered. "Now just sign this and I'll be gone."

Hannah smiled a rare smile. "So if I don't sign, you're not legally married and have committed bigamy."

"I don't want to lose Emma," he said. "Just sign it."

"You mean, you don't want to lose all that money and farm land?" Hannah picked up the pen.

Luther raised his fist. "Just sign it, damn you, so I can get you and your Injun bastard out of my life—"

Before she could protest, Colt grabbed him from behind, whirled Luther around, and hit him in the mouth. The two went tumbling out onto the porch.

Colt couldn't remember much of anything except the red rage that enveloped him when he saw the farmer raise his fist as if to strike Hannah. He had saved her from the Comanches and he sure as hell didn't mean to have some white man to hurt her now, even if he was her husband.

They tumbled out onto the porch, where Colt grabbed him again and threw Brownley off into the dust in front of the tiny cabin. Then Colt landed on top of him, hitting him in the mouth until blood mingled with the brown tobacco juice that ran down his beet-red face.

Behind him, he heard Travis crying and Hannah yelling, "Stop, Colt! Stop! You'll get in trouble!"

"I don't give a damn! It's worth it!" Colt stumbled to his feet, hauling Brownley to his, noting the fine coat was now covered with dust and chicken droppings.

Brownley came at him, cursing, but Colt dodged the blow easily. In the background, he saw people gathering to watch, soldiers running and even Olivia and the messenger driving up in the light buggy. She looked horrified.

They were fighting in front of Brownley's fine rig now, and Colt hit the farmer again, knocking him down and under the fine gray horse's legs. It reared, startled, as the two men rolled around in the dirt under its hooves.

He took Brownley by the coat collar and dragged

him to his feet. "You mean bastard! Get out of here and don't ever come back!"

Then he grabbed him like a sack of potatoes and threw him up on the buggy seat.

"I'll get the law on you!" Brownley waved his fist from the fancy rig. Colt started up into the buggy after him, but one of the other officers grabbed his arm.

Olivia was suddenly on his other side, pulling at his coat sleeve. "Darling, are you out of your mind? You can get court-martialed for this!"

"I don't give a damn!" Colt shook free of her and tried to shake free of the other officer. He realized then that his arm wound was throbbing and probably bleeding again.

There was a large crowd gathered in a circle to watch and more coming all the time, but Colt didn't care. He wanted to kill the farmer for the way he had treated Hannah.

Hannah ran up just then, grabbed Colt's arm. "Don't hit him again, Colt. Let him go." She turned to Brownley. "Here's your paper. I signed it and good riddance to you."

"Now I can go back to my respectable wife," Brownley snarled, wiping the blood from his mouth, and clutching the paper, "and be glad I ain't still hitched to a Comanche buck's whore!"

A gasp from the crowd as Colt went after him again, trying to drag him down from the buggy, but Brownley, clutching the crumpled paper, backed his rig away from the hitching post and took off down the dusty road toward the front gate.

Colt tried to go after him. "I'll kill the son of a bitch!" But two officers held him back and now Olivia was holding onto his sleeve again. "Colton, have you lost your mind? This is no way for an officer to behave."

Behind him, he heard Hannah's soft voice. "Let him go, Colt. There's been enough trouble."

There was a murmur through the crowd as he took a deep breath and looked past Olivia's beautiful face to Hannah's blue eyes. "Are you all right?"

She nodded and picked up her toddler. Any other woman would have been weeping and hysterical by now, he thought, but she only had a small muscle near her mouth twitching and he saw her fist clench.

It was Olivia who was crying like a fountain. "Oh, Colton, dear. You're going to be in trouble for this. Couldn't you just have let him go?"

"No, I couldn't." Colt took a deep breath and the officers let go of his arms. He stood there, brushing the dust off his uniform. His wounded arm throbbed hard.

The officers shooed the curious crowd away. "All right, there's nothing more to see, folks. Everyone should go home."

Hannah started to say something to Colt, then turned and carried her toddler back into her cabin.

Olivia looked up at him, wiping her eyes. "Colton, sometimes I think I don't know you at all. What got into you, meddling in someone's personal business like this?"

"You wouldn't understand, Olivia," he sighed and dusted his coat off, strode back to his quarters, leaving her standing there by the messenger's buggy, looking humiliated. He was in trouble all right, maybe facing court-martial or at least discipline from the major. He didn't give a damn. Seeing that blood smeared on Brownley's face and the chicken shit all over his fine coat had made whatever punishment he got worth it.

It wasn't long in coming.

Colt was ordered to report to the major's office. When he got there, the major looked up and sighed. "At ease, Lieutenant."

Colt obeyed, realizing for the first time that he still had dust on his coat and his sleeve was torn.

Major Murphy said, "By Saint Mary's blood, what am I to do with you? You attacked a civilian?"

"He was mistreatin' Hannah," Colt said.

"And as a lieutenant in the U.S. Second Cavalry, that was your business why?"

Colt felt the flush creeping up his face. "Because she's a helpless woman, and since I rescued her, I feel responsible for her."

"And nothing more?" The major leaned back in his chair and surveyed Colt.

What could he say? The major probably thought Colt was still engaged to his daughter. "Well, sir, it's this way—"

"Never mind. I don't want to hear it." The major gave him a dismissing wave of his hand. "You created a public scene, brawling like a hooligan in the dirt with a civilian with half the post watching."

Colt didn't answer.

"I'll have to punish you as an example to the others," the major said, "so you're confined to quarters for a week. I'd do more, but you're one of my favorite officers, Lieutenant. You almost remind me of myself before . . . never mind. Now get out of here, and next time, I'll break you in rank."

"Yes, sir." Colt saluted and left the office. Now what

was he to do? There would be patrols going out against the Comanches and they really needed his expertise. This trouble was his own fault, but he would do it over again. No man was going to mistreat a woman while Colt Prescott was around.

The grounds were quiet now, and he decided to stop by Hannah's cabin on the way back to his quarters.

"Hannah? Are you here?"

She came out of the back room. "I just put Travis down for a nap. Thank you for what you did. Are you in trouble over it?"

"A little bit," he admitted. "Confined to quarters for a week. Are you okay?"

She bit her lip and didn't look at him. "I'm embarrassed over the ruckus it caused, but I'm relieved not to be married to Luther anymore."

"I hate the way he talked to you."

"I'm used to it." She shrugged. "At least this time, he didn't hit me, thanks to you."

He stepped closer and she looked up at him. She looked so slender and vulnerable. Without thinking, he took her small face between his two big hands. Her skin was so warm and tender and her eyes as blue as Texas bluebonnets in the springtime. Her lips were slightly parted, and he leaned down and kissed her very gently.

Her soft lips trembled under his and for a moment, he thought she would come into his arms so he could hold her close against him and protect her forever from anyone or anything that might harm her, but Hannah pulled away from him. "Did you think fighting for me gives you the right to bed me?"

"No, Hannah, I'm sorry." He stepped back and realized she was trembling, whether from emotion or rage, he couldn't be sure. "I kissed you without thinkin'."

"I think you'd better leave now." Her voice was cold. "Your fiancée might not like the idea of your being here."

He started to apologize again, then realized it would do no good. He started out the door, turned, and looked back at her. "Hannah, I promise I meant no insult."

She didn't say anything, only looked at him, disappointment in those blue eyes.

"Oh, hell," he muttered and strode off her porch and toward his own quarters. So Hannah thought he was trying to claim her body as a prize. To the victor go the spoils. He'd made a mess of things. "What else can go wrong?" he whispered and then realized Olivia stood near the major's office, and judging by her angry face, she had seen him come out of Hannah's cabin.

Chapter 12

He merely touched the tips of his fingers against the brim of his hat by way of greeting and kept on walking toward his quarters, which meant he would have to pass her.

However, he could see in her angry face that Olivia didn't intend to let him get past her without conflict. She caught his sleeve. "How dare you!"

"Miss Olivia," he said softly, "I don't think we should make a public scene."

"A public scene?" Her voice rose to an unladylike screech. "A public scene? After you behaved like a common soldier while half the people at this fort saw you brawling and rolling around in the dirt? What are you trying to do? Humiliate me?"

He tried to placate her. "Olivia, it had nothin' to do with you. You are so much more refined than I am and you deserve better. I'll tell everyone you broke up with me."

"Don't you dare! I haven't even told my father yet.

As far as everyone at this fort is concerned, we are still engaged."

"You don't want a man who is often in as much trouble as I am, Olivia. I'm sorry if I've hurt you, but I'm afraid I can't be the man you want."

She burst into tears and was still weeping loudly as he brushed past her and strode to his quarters. He slammed the door and flopped down on his bunk. Damn it. He'd made a mess of things with two women. He was an officer, but he was still behaving like some wild cowboy. Maybe he needed to give up on relationships and go back to whores on a drunken Saturday night. But that's not what he wanted. He wanted a love that he could call his own waking up beside him every morning for the rest of his life. He wanted kids and a life in Texas. It dawned on him then that what he really wanted was Hannah. But she didn't seem to believe he wanted anything but a roll in the hay. He shouldn't have kissed her, knowing her past with men. He should have waited.

Hannah had straightened the overturned furniture, given Travis a sandwich, and put him in the back room to play when she heard a knock on her front screen. She took a deep breath as she realized when she went around to open it, that it was Miss Murphy. "Yes?"

"We need to talk." The major's daughter opened the screen and without an invitation, came inside.

Hannah caught the other girl's mood and stiffened. "About what?"

"Oh, you know about what." The pretty brunette bristled. "You just caused a public scene and got Lieutenant Prescott in trouble."

"I didn't mean to," Hannah said. "It all just happened."

"And somehow, my Colton just came running to get in a fight like some knight of old?"

Hannah shrugged. "He was out on the porch, and I guess he could tell things weren't going well."

"Well, now he's in trouble for the second time over you," Olivia snapped. "Mrs. Brownley, you have brought a lot of conflict to this army post. What are your plans for the future?"

"I don't know. I don't see how I can leave." Hannah decided she must control her temper. "I have little money and as you know by now, my husband only came here to get my signature on divorce papers."

"You shouldn't set your sights on my fiancé," Olivia said. "Everyone is talking and it may keep him from getting promoted."

"I have not set my sights on the lieutenant," Hannah said, "and I wouldn't do anything to harm his career. Now, Miss Murphy, if you're leaving, I've got more laundry to do."

"Are you dismissing me?" Olivia's patrician nostrils flared.

She must not slap her; that would only bring more trouble. "I thought you had said everything you needed to say." Hannah tried to keep her voice even, while gritting her teeth.

"Did I make myself clear?" Olivia snapped.

"Yes, you did." Hannah stepped around her and went to the screen, held it open. "Good-bye, Miss Murphy."

"I am engaged to marry Colton and don't you forget it!" Olivia turned on her heel and marched out the door.

Hannah slammed it behind her. It had been all she could do not to slap the snooty socialite. That would only make things worse for her and Travis, she realized as she returned to her ironing. She had to add more money to her small stash, or she could never leave the fort. Either that or marry someone who would take her away.

Marry. Yes, that would solve her problem. But who? Although there was a shortage of women in Texas, there was no one at the fort that she could even imagine sharing a life and a bed with. In fact, the thought made her shudder. No one but Colt Prescott, and he was engaged. Plus he was already in trouble since he had come to Hannah's defense. She thought about it while she ironed and decided there was no man available who could take her away from here. It was up to her to solve her own problem.

When Travis tired of playing with the toy horse Colt had carved, she took her little boy out to her garden, picked some fresh tomatoes and lettuce, and walked over to the sutler's store. On the way, she passed several white women. She spoke to each politely, but they turned their heads and ignored her.

The sutler's store smelled like tobacco, spices, and pickles. "Mr. Hutton?"

The owner came out of the back room. Hutton always needed a haircut and shave and his shirt was usually soiled. She gave him her warmest smile. "I brought some of the produce from my garden. Do you want to buy it?"

The look he gave her made her want to button up the neck of her frayed dress even more. "Vegetables, huh? Yeah, I think I could sell them. Most of these settlers are too busy or don't have the knack for growing their own."

She laid the vegetables on the counter. "I might also be willing to wash and iron your shirts in trade for a few things like coffee and some of that peppermint candy you have in the counter there."

"Hmm, might be a good idea." He scratched himself and leaned over to peer down at her son. "Little redskin likes candy, huh?"

"His name is Travis," she said firmly.

Mr. Hutton laughed. "Looks like a redskin to me. All right, Mrs. Brownley, I'll buy your vegetables and you can do my shirts." He looked at her closely. "I heard there was some trouble at your place a couple of hours ago."

Hannah felt her face burn. The whole fort must be talking about it. "It was a personal matter."

"Well, now you got no man, is that right?"

She nodded and then spoke, keeping her voice cold. "I don't need a man, Mr. Hutton. Travis and I are managing fine, thank you. I'll take my money for the vegetables now."

He went over to the small cash register and opened it, handed her a few coins. "That enough?"

She looked at the money in her hand and stared at him. "Now you know it isn't."

He laughed and handed her another dollar. "Gotta hand it to you, you stand your ground better'n most women. Comes from dealin' with the Comanche, I reckon."

She didn't answer, but took the money, grasped her son's hand, and went outside. Sooner or later, she might have trouble with Mr. Hutton, as with dozens of other men at this fort who thought any woman who had belonged to a Comanche buck was no better than a whore. At least she had found a way to build up her small stash of coins. What else could she do to earn money so she could leave? When she would leave or where she would go, she had no idea, but she had to have money to do anything.

After dark, she put Travis to bed and changed into an old nightgown of Olivia's. It was faded and too short for Hannah, but of the softest embroidered lawn. It was a warm night and she opened the windows, but she locked the front and back doors in case some drunken soldier tried to get in.

She had barely blown out her lamp and climbed into bed when she heard a noise outside her window and froze, reaching for the butcher knife she kept on the bedside table.

"Who's there?"

"Hannah, it's me, Colt."

"What do you want?"

"That's a fine way to thank me for steppin' in and helpin' you today."

She was immediately chagrined. "I'm sorry. What is it you want?"

"I was just checkin' to make sure you're all right."

"Aren't you supposed to be confined to quarters?"

"Yes, but the guard went to sleep and I sneaked out the window. Let me in before someone sees me and reports it."

She wanted to let him in, wanted him to kiss her again, but she remembered Olivia's beautiful, angry face. "Go away. You're engaged to the major's daughter."

"I broke up with her."

"That's not what she says."

He cleared his throat and she could imagine him weighing his words. "Believe me, Hannah, I broke the engagement."

She wanted to believe him; but she was still suspicious of men. "What is it you want?"

"I—I don't know, but I wanted to apologize for kissin' you this afternoon."

She relived it for a moment—the warmth of his big hands on her face, the taste of his mouth. "It's all right."

"No, it isn't. I should have asked your permission."

She was abruptly angry with him. "That's okay. You're like the other soldiers; you figure I've been a redskin's woman, I might as well let any white man have me now that my husband doesn't want me back."

"You know me better than that."

She took a deep breath, thinking the kiss had been sweet and gentle.

"Hannah, let me in so we can talk. I'd hate it if that's what you really believed about me."

She was torn between what Colt was saying and what Olivia had said. And yet she owed this man for saving her from her ex-husband. "Come around and I'll open the door, but you really should go back to your quarters before someone finds out you're missing."

"Speakin' of findin' out, the sentry is walking this way."

"Quick, come around." She flew through the darkened cabin and unlocked the door. The big Texan slipped in and closed it behind him.

Why had she let him in? She knew this could only mean trouble for them both, and she wasn't some cheap tart to slip around with some other woman's man.

Colt stood there, all tall and muscular in the moonlight that filtered through the window. Hannah was abruptly aware that she wore nothing except a sheer lawn nightgown that was certainly almost transparent. "Colt, you need to leave. I don't know why I let you in."

"You know as well as I do, Hannah. I've thought of nothin' else but you since I rescued you." He took a step forward.

"What about Olivia?"

"I swear to you that I don't care for her."

She wanted to believe that, wanted to believe that he really cared about her and wasn't just needing a woman to slake his lust. "I—I think you need to go."

"If you want me to." He half turned toward the door and she took a step forward, put her hand on his arm.

"I—I haven't thanked you for what you did this afternoon. I think Luther would have hit me."

"No man beats a woman while I'm around."

"Well, thank you anyway. I'm afraid I've gotten you in serious trouble."

"It's not your fault," he insisted. "Hannah, you deserve better than that. You deserve a man who will really love you—"

"And which one could forget I've been a redskin's whore for the past four years?" she asked, her voice bitter.

At that, he turned and took her in his arms very gently. "You're brave and beautiful and strong," he whispered. "A Texas woman, that's what you are." And he kissed her very gently, his mouth soft and warm on hers.

Her heart hammered and she clung to him, wanting him, wanting to belong, wanting the security of a strong man's arms—wanting Colt. She pressed her body close to his, knowing he could feel every inch of her through the sheer lawn nightgown. Hannah let her mouth open and he kissed the inside of her lips, touching her tongue lightly with his own. She felt his manhood rise up hard and throbbing against her belly. She wanted him in a way she had never wanted a man before. Hannah had been used by two different men, but neither had cared about her feelings or her needs as she hoped this one did. At this moment, she didn't care if Colt took her here on the floor like some slut in a saloon as long as he held her close and kissed her lips and whispered soft words.

His hand went to her breast and she didn't protest, wanting his big, callused palm on her nipple, wanting him to stroke her body, wanting him to take her.

She heard a slight whimper and jerked away to see a sleepy Travis standing in the doorway. "Mama?"

Colt froze and she turned toward her child. "What—what is it, honey?"

"Drink of water," he mumbled. "I'm thirsty."

"All right, I'll get you a drink. Go back to bed." She stepped away from Colt, realized she was shaking. She had come so close to coupling with this soldier, wanting him, wanting him to want her. "You've got to go," she whispered to Colt.

"Can I come back later?"

"No." She shook her head and backed away from him, scared at how close she'd come to letting this man make love to her. That would only cause more problems for everyone. "Just leave, please."

He nodded and slipped out the front door. She closed and locked it behind him, listened to his big boots leave her porch. How could she believe or trust him when half the men on the post were trying to get between her thighs? Olivia could have Hannah and her child thrown off the post if she slept with Olivia's fiancé, and the beauty was vengeful enough to do so. Hannah realized she must keep away from Colt, make plans to leave the fort as soon as possible. She drew a troubled sigh and went to get her son a dipperful of water.

Once back in bed, she lay there sleepless a long time, still tasting Colt's hot mouth and feeling his virile body pressed against hers. The officer had aroused feelings in her that no man ever had before. Yes, she had to get away before she ruined both their lives.

Just after dawn, Hannah awakened and decided the cool of the morning would be a good time to pick vegetables to take over to the sutler's. When she looked in on her little boy, he was still asleep. She dressed in one of Olivia's castoffs, got her basket, and walked out behind the commissary. In less than an hour, the fort would be coming awake, but she was enjoying the peace and tranquility of her garden. She hadn't slept well, thinking about Colt.

Hannah heard a sound as she picked tomatoes and looked up. Captain Van Smyth leaned against a corner of the building, stroking his wispy mustache. "Good morning, Mrs. Brownley." He touched his hat politely.

"Good morning, Captain." She didn't like the way he was staring at her.

"You look like you're working hard. Would you like some help?" He walked toward her.

She stood her ground. "No, thank you. I can manage. Isn't it about time for roll call, Captain?"

"Not yet." He grinned and moved closer. "I saw you come out your back door and thought I could help you pick all that stuff."

"Thank you, but I can manage." She kept her voice cold.

"Oh, don't tell me you couldn't use some help?" He paused near her and pulled a tomato. "These really look good. You've got a green thumb."

She managed a wan smile. "So they tell me."

He walked up and put the tomato in her basket. "Pish-posh, this is too much work for a pretty thing like you."

"I think you ought to be going," she said, "before your commanding officer comes looking for you."

"I've got a minute." His voice lowered. "And you can be nice and give me a minute or two, can't you?"

"No, I can't." She glared at him, standing her ground.

He faced her, staring at her. "You can give some filthy Injun buck some time but none for a white man? Come now, you white whore, I only want a quick—"

"Captain, if you don't leave, I'll scream."

He advanced on her. "I don't think you will. You're too proud. All I want is for you to lay down here and give me a quick ride—"

She backed away, and he reached out and grabbed her sleeve. It tore away and she stumbled over a plant and they both went down between the rows of vegetables, with him on top of her. He was right, she was too proud to scream. Instead, she clawed at his face, and he cursed and ripped the front of her bodice. "Good Lord, you got nice tits! Now you just lay still and I'll be through—"

Instead, she fought him with her nails and teeth, struggling to get out from under him. She managed to reach her basket and grabbed the small hand shovel and hit him across the face. He cursed and slapped her while she swung at him with the little shovel; then she rolled out from under him and ran toward her cabin, leaving him bloody and cursing behind her. The whole bodice of her dress was torn and her cheek stung where he had slapped her. Hannah locked the door behind her and was pinning her bodice closed when Travis came stumbling out of bed and into the kitchen.

"Mama, what's wrong?"

"Nothing, honey." She turned her back on her son so he wouldn't see the marks on her face and body.

"I—I'll fix you some oatmeal, okay? Now you go put your clothes on."

The toddler turned and left the kitchen and Hannah took a deep breath of relief and leaned against the cabinet. She'd have to be more careful in the future now that word had gotten out around the fort she was a divorced woman and so, available. She must not let Colt find out what had just happened or there would be more trouble. Hannah was surrounded by men who needed women and they thought with her past, she should welcome any white man into her embrace.

Yes, she was going to have to leave this fort, but it would take time to get a little money. Hannah tried to calm her shaking hands while she made oatmeal and put on a pot of coffee for herself.

Over at his quarters, Colt had spent a sleepless night. After a while, a scrawny private brought him a breakfast tray, saluted, and was gone. Colt tasted it without much appetite. It wasn't nearly as good as Hannah's cooking. He went to the window and peered out.

The bugle sounded and the flag went up as soldiers stood at attention. A patrol rode out through the gate, headed for who knew where. He ought to be leading that patrol or at least advising them, but here he was confined to quarters.

He flopped down on his bunk and stared at the ceiling. Eventually he dropped off to sleep, and in his dreams, Hannah came into his arms willingly and her lips were as soft and tender as before, only this time, she kissed him back with all the passion that he could only hope for. It was last night again and she stood there in that sheer nightdress, pressed against him.

He'd been a fool to go to her cabin. He could only cause trouble for them both.

There was a knock at the door that awakened him. Colt mumbled, "Come in, Private."

Instead, Olivia poked her pretty head around the door. "I've brought you a lunch tray, you naughty boy."

He sat up, blinking in surprise. "I thought you were furious with me."

"I've decided to forgive you," she announced grandly and came into the room, her fine pink skirts swishing as she put the tray down on his desk. "Daddy said you were just a wild young man feeling your oats."

Colt sighed. "You haven't told your father we have broken up?"

She shook her head and smiled up at him. "I'm giving you time to reconsider. After all, I have so much more to offer you than any other woman you'll ever meet."

"I reckon that's true, but—"

"Don't say another word, dear." She tiptoed to the door. "I want to let you think. In the meantime, maybe I can get Daddy to lessen your sentence."

He stood up, not wanting to be beholden to the girl, but knowing his men needed him. It was a form of blackmail, he knew, but he had duties to perform. "I'd be much obliged for that, Olivia. I need to be leadin' my men, not cooped up here like some tame chicken."

"I'll talk to Daddy." She winked at him as she went out the door.

What was he to do about this girl? Well, that wasn't today's problem. He was hungry because he hadn't eaten much last night or this morning. He sat down at his desk and picked up a fork. He was sure Olivia hadn't cooked this, but maybe her maid had sent something he could eat.

No such luck. He ate it slowly, but nothing was good. The vegetables were overcooked, the meat was tough, and the biscuits like cannonballs. Even the coffee was tepid and too weak.

He spent the rest of the day pacing and staring out the window, getting restless with no activity. Even the troopers marching on the parade ground looked more interesting than what he was stuck with.

That evening, there was a knock at the door and Colt sighed. Neither Olivia nor the post food was something he was looking forward to. "Come in."

The door opened and it was Hannah holding a tray. She stood there awkwardly, wearing a faded blue dress. "May I come in?"

"What are you doin' here?" He motioned her in.

"I thought you might be hungry and so I made a chicken pot pie and a wild plum cobbler."

He could smell the food from here and it smelled delicious. "That's kind of you. Where'd you get the chicken?"

"I traded some laundry for it."

That meant she had worked hard all morning for his benefit and he was touched. "You didn't have to do that, Hannah. The army feeds me."

She shrugged, brought the tray in, and set it on his desk. "I owe you something for your help yesterday and I always pay my debts."

"Oh." So that's all it was. "Hannah"—he turned toward her—"about yesterday and last night. I'm sorry I took advantage—"

"No need to apologize, I understand." Her blue eyes were cold. "You thought I owed you that, and I understand men—"

"No, it was more than that."

She looked at him as if she wished she could believe him, then made a dismissing gesture. "Let's not talk anymore. Your food will get cold."

"But I want to explain—"

"You don't owe me anything. I'll always be grateful to you, Lieutenant, for rescuing me from the Comanche and then again yesterday. I can never really repay you."

"Damn it, I don't want repayment." He strode over and caught her arm. For just a moment, they looked into each other's eyes and he wanted to kiss her again, kiss her and hold her close and never let her go. Then he noticed the bruise on her cheek. "What happened to you?"

"Oh?" She reached up to touch the spot, winced, and turned away. "I—I fell, that's all."

He didn't believe her. "Did someone try to—?"

"Colt, you're in enough trouble already because of me. In fact, I imagine Olivia saw me come in here—"

"Don't change the subject," he thundered and held onto both her arms. "Who was it?"

She tried not to look at him. "I fell, I tell you."

"Hannah, you're a poor liar. Now tell me who the bastard was and I'll—"

"You'll only get you and the captain in trouble and it wasn't anything important."

"Did he—?"

"No, I hit him with my little hand shovel."

Colt cursed. "I'll kill him!"

"No, you won't." She pulled away from him and went to the door, turned. "Forget it, Colt. You're already in enough trouble. I don't want you dishonorably discharged or shot for fighting with a superior officer."

He hesitated, wondering how he could make her

believe he really cared for her and would do anything for her. In that split second as he hesitated, the opportunity was lost. She fled out the door with him calling after her, "Hannah! Hannah, wait!"

What a mess he had made. His good sense told him to forget about the girl with her sad past and fear of men. He could marry a society beauty and have wealth, advancement, and everything else beautiful Olivia offered.

With a sigh, he sat down at his desk and tasted the chicken pot pie. It was delicious, as he had known it would be—light, crispy crust and a filling of tender chicken and vegetables. There were hot rolls, too. He finished it off with a cup of strong coffee and the tart wild plum cobbler. Then he leaned back in his chair with a smile. Hannah could cook, there was no doubt about it.

Just then there was a knock at the door. Probably a private with his dinner. Colt stood up. "Come in."

However, it wasn't the private; it was Olivia with a tray. "Hello, soldier boy." She smiled coyly. "I brought you some dinner."

"Oh, thank you," he answered politely.

Then she spotted the dishes on his desk. "Oh, you've already eaten."

Now what should he do? "Yes, someone brought me something."

She put her own tray down on the desk with a bang and surveyed the empty dishes. "That doesn't look like regular army fare." She looked up at him, suspicion in those pretty dark eyes.

"Uh." He didn't know what to say. He didn't want to get Hannah in trouble.

He could see Olivia beginning to boil. "It's that

tramp, that Comanche captive. She's got a lot of nerve, bringing food to my fiancé. Why, everyone on the post will be talking."

"Olivia," he said gently, "why not just drop it? It's only food, after all, and it doesn't mean anything."

"Humph!" Olivia stuck her nose in the air and went sailing out the door, slamming it behind her.

Well, now what? He didn't like being caught between two women. Once he got out of confinement, he was going to volunteer for every patrol and stay as far away as he could from this fort. He went over and took a look at Olivia's tray. It was some kind of stew, but it didn't look appetizing, and a bowl of pudding that was runny. Thank God he had already eaten.

Now he rolled a cigarette and thought about the captain. He ground his teeth with rage. What was he to do about that bastard? Hannah was right. Colt could get in big trouble attacking a superior officer, but if he didn't stop the man, he'd try it again and Hannah was too proud to let Colt know. In fact, he would never have learned about what had happened this morning if he hadn't noticed the bruise on her face.

No matter what she said and no matter that Captain Van Smyth was a superior officer, Colt was going to see that he never tried to touch Hannah again, even if Colt had to kill him.

Chapter 13

Three days later, Colt was finally back on duty. The first thing he did was report to the major.

As he entered, Colt saluted, then winced. His injured arm still pained him.

The major leaned back in his chair. "At ease, Lieutenant."

"Yes, sir."

"Sit down and have a drink."

Colt stood there, fidgeting. "If you don't mind, sir, I have work—"

"By Saint Mary's blood, sit down. That's an order," the major snapped.

"Yes, sir." Reluctantly, Colt sat down.

"I don't generally delve into my men's private lives." The major poured them each a drink and stared into Colt's eyes. "But when the man is my daughter's intended, I think maybe I do need to give him a little advice."

Colt started to say something, thought better of it, and accepted the drink. "Sir?"

"I know you've got until the middle of June to

decide whether to reenlist, Prescott, but you strike me as a man who'd make a great career soldier."

"That was what I'd always planned on, sir."

"You've got the talent and the drive to end up as a general if we go to war with the South, and that's a strong possibility." He gulped his drink.

"Yes, sir." Colt sipped his drink.

"Or if you decide against this hard life, my wife's family is rich and has important connections. You could live a life of luxury and ease back East, and all you would have to do is keep my darling daughter happy."

Colt started to ask why the major hadn't chosen that same road, decided it was impertinent. "Yes, sir."

"I just want to warn you to stop causing fights and problems. You need a clean record, no matter which you choose."

"Yes, sir."

"That's all." The major sighed and poured himself another drink and reached for his pipe. "Dismissed."

Colt stood up, snapped the major a salute, and left his office. He could either tell everyone on the post he was no longer engaged to Olivia and embarrass her, which wasn't good for his career, or insist Olivia do so and she didn't seem so inclined. Hell, what a mess.

But first on his mind was dealing with Captain Van Smyth. He sought him out, saluted. "Captain Van Smyth?"

"Yes?"

"Will you take off your jacket and give me satisfaction?"

The captain looked annoyed. "Over what?"

Colt was barely able to contain his rage. "Sir, you know over what. Hannah Brownley."

The captain smirked. "Pishposh. For an officer engaged to the most beautiful girl on the post, it seems odd, Lieutenant, that you want to protect the honor of some slutty trollop—"

"Sir, I'm warnin' you not to use those words."

"Are you threatening me, Lieutenant?"

"No, I'm promisin' you, sir."

Out of the corner of his eye, Colt could see enlisted men turning to catch the exchange as they passed.

"Very well," the captain snapped. "I will give you satisfaction out behind the barn about sundown tonight."

"Thank you, sir."

"Dismissed," the captain said curtly and, as Colt turned to go, the superior officer added, "Oh, by the way, Lieutenant, maybe no one told you I was the middleweight boxing champion at West Point a few years ago."

Colt turned. "I was not aware of that, sir."

"Then would you like to apologize and withdraw your challenge?"

"No, sir, I wouldn't."

The captain smiled. "It's your funeral, Lieutenant. I'm looking forward to beating you bloody, unofficially, of course."

"And, sir, I'm lookin' forward to wipin' up the dirt with you because of those scratches on your face and the bruise on hers, unofficially, of course."

The handsome captain scowled and fingered his wispy mustache as if to make sure it was still there. "Dismissed. I'll see you behind the barn tonight, and if you want my opinion, you're a damned fool. I hope the fair Olivia realizes that."

"I wish she did, sir." Colt snapped him a salute and strode away. He went down to the stable to inspect horses and soon, Sergeant Mulvaney came in.

"Oh, hello, Sergeant."

The older man snapped a salute. "Permission to speak, sir?"

"Oh, don't stand on ceremony, Bill. We've known each other too long for that."

"Well, then I'll speak to you like a son." The old man put his hand on Colt's broad shoulder. "'Tis all over the camp in minutes that you and Captain Van Smyth are squaring off tonight behind the barn."

"Nothing travels faster than gossip around an army camp, does it?" Colt grinned.

"So it's true, lad?"

"You know it is."

The grizzled sergeant groaned aloud. "Holy Saint Patrick. Don't ye know the captain was a boxing champion?"

"So he told me."

"Then are you out of your mind? Has this Texas heat drove you loco?"

"Maybe so," Colt mused.

"He outreaches you," Mulvaney pointed out.

"Then he'll probably wipe up the dirt with me." Colt walked outside with the sergeant right behind him.

"And wait 'til it gets back to the major."

"I expect he'll hear about it in less than twenty-four hours." Colt rolled a cigarette. "Fort gossip travels faster than the telegraph."

"Do ye not fear Miss Olivia will hear about it?"

That made Colt sigh. "I'm sure she will."

"Then, for God's sake, man—"

"Sergeant, I know you mean well, but I had to challenge him."

"Why? It's not as if the gal was a lady who hadn't been pawed at before—"

"Mulvaney, shut your mouth before I forget we're friends, okay?"

"Yes, sir."

"Now I reckon you have chores to do?"

"Yes, sir. By the by, there's post gossip about a raid against the Comanches soon. Of course that could be just gossip."

"Hmm. In that case, I'd double-check all the equipment anyway, just in case."

"Yes, sir." He snapped a salute.

"You're dismissed, Sergeant. I expect most of the men will be out behind the barn tonight?"

The old Irishman grinned. "I might as well tell you the majority are bettin' on the captain, but I put down a fiver on you, sir."

"I hope you don't lose your money," Colt growled. "But I'll do my damnedest to bust the captain's head open."

"Yes, sir. That would make most of the enlisted men very happy." The sergeant saluted again and left.

Colt sighed and looked up at the sun. It was late afternoon. He walked out on the parade ground and saw Hannah and her little boy leaving the sutler's and heading for her cabin. He waited a minute and looked around. The fort was quiet in the warm sun, the lull just before supper. He walked around to Hannah's back door and knocked softly.

"Who is it?"

"It's me, Colt."

Now her voice was guarded. "What do you want?"

"I just wanted you to know I'm callin' Captain Van Smyth out for what he did to you."

She came to the back door. "I've already heard. It

was all over the fort in a few minutes. Come in before someone sees you on my back porch and the gossip starts again."

He came in, glanced around. "Where's Travis?"

"Playing in his room with the toy horse you carved him."

He looked down at her, wanting to stroke that yellow hair. "Doesn't he ever play with the other children?"

For a moment, he thought she might cry, but she didn't. Instead she shook her head. "You should know the other women don't want their kids playing with a half-breed."

"Damn it, why are people so cruel?" He put his hands on her shoulders. "You need to leave this place."

"I know, and I plan to." She looked up at him. "Just as soon as I can. Mr. Hutton offered me a part-time job working at the store, and I'm doing a lot of ironing. I figure in a few weeks, I might have enough money to leave."

The thought of her leaving, never seeing her again, made him wince. "Where would you go?"

She turned away from him. "It doesn't matter, just as long as it's away from here. Maybe someplace where no one knows my past and I can make a fresh start."

He had no right to offer her anything; his life was muddled enough already. "I just came to tell you about the fight in case you hadn't heard. After I beat him up, other men will think twice about botherin' you again."

"Oh, Colt, you don't need the trouble that'll bring you."

"Listen, I'd do this for any woman. No Texan would let a man take liberties with a helpless girl and not call him out over it."

She looked up at him. "You're a fool."

"Maybe, but that's just the way I am."

She hesitated, and then her small arms slipped around his neck and she turned her face up to him.

He looked down at the bruises there and touched her cheek with one finger. "I ought to kill him for that, much less beat him up."

"Oh, Colt," she whispered and then she kissed him. He pulled her to him so tightly she could scarcely breathe, and the kiss deepened, her tongue going into his mouth as both their breaths quickened.

He held her close. "If only things were different," he whispered against her hair.

"Can't I talk you out of this silly fight?" She kissed his face. "It's noble of you, but it's not as if I've got any honor left to protect."

"Don't say that!" he snapped and almost shook her. "As far as I'm concerned, you are the most innocent lady I know, and I'd kill any man who tried to take advantage of you." He pulled away from her, and neither said anything for a long moment.

"I'll see you later." He turned and left before he did what he wanted to do, which was sweep her up in his arms, carry her to her bed, and make passionate love to her.

Colt strode across the parade grounds toward the barn. The sun was low on the western horizon as he walked. Hannah was right of course and he knew it. He had a great career ahead of him and could marry the beautiful virgin from Philadelphia. Olivia would love him and give him children. And maybe in bed at night, he could make love to her and pretend she was Hannah, the poor Texas girl he had rescued from the Indians and who hadn't a thing to offer him—not great beauty or wealth or even her virginity. Somehow, that didn't matter. And yet, he knew she was right. He was a damned fool.

Hannah tried to keep her mind busy by scrubbing her kitchen floor, yet her mind was on the coming fight. Everyone said the captain was a skilled boxer and would flatten the Texan. All because of her. What could she do about it? Nothing. Men and their damned pride. She'd rather have let the snooty captain rape her than get Colt hurt.

There was a knock at her door and she got to her feet, smiling. Maybe it was Colt coming to tell her the fight had been called off. She hurried to open it.

Instead it was Olivia.

"Yes?"

"You might invite me in," the beauty snapped.

Hannah hesitated. It was probably about the fight, and she didn't want to cause Colt any more trouble. "I'm sorry. Come in, Miss Murphy."

The girl entered, looking down her nose at the small cabin. "I'm having a going-away tea for the captain's aunt. Remember her? You met her at the dance."

"Oh, yes." Hannah swallowed in surprise. "I—I'm not sure I have anything to wear—"

"Oh, I'm not here to issue an invitation." Olivia laughed cruelly. "If that's what you thought."

"Of course I knew that," Hannah lied, but felt her face flush with humiliation.

"Doc tells me you are an excellent cook and my Maria is none too good."

"I'm not sure that's true." Hannah spoke up loyally for the squat Indian woman.

"Anyway, the tea is tomorrow afternoon as she's catching a stage out tomorrow night. I thought perhaps you could bake some fancy little cookies and tea cakes?"

Hannah blinked. "Oh, yes, of course." Her mind was busy, thinking about adding to her small stash of money. "And of course you intend to pay me?"

"Certainly." Olivia turned back toward the door. "Will a dollar be enough?"

"Not hardly," Hannah snapped. "I want five dollars."

Olivia gasped. "Five dollars. Why, that's highway robbery."

Hannah shrugged and opened the door as if to dismiss her. "Then let Maria bake the cookies and tea cakes."

Olivia gasped and her face turned angry. Evidently she was not used to anyone opposing her. "You drive a hard bargain."

"I'm trying to gather enough money to leave the fort," Hannah said.

Olivia smirked. "For that, I will pay five dollars. Very well, the tea is at three o'clock tomorrow afternoon and all the officers' wives will be there. See that the sweets arrive on time." She turned and started out the door with a grand sweep of skirts.

Hannah held out her hand. "I'd like to be paid in advance, please."

"You don't trust me? Do you know who I am?" The patrician nose went up in the air.

"I'd still like to be paid in advance, please," Hannah said again.

"Of all the nerve! Very well, I'll send Maria down with the money as soon as I get back to my quarters." She stepped out on the porch. "Odd. It's dusk and there doesn't seem to be anyone around. Where do you suppose all the soldiers are?"

So Olivia hadn't heard. Hannah wasn't going to be the one to tell her.

"Don't forget the money," she said and closed the door behind the woman.

Hannah leaned against the door and sighed. Even now, the fight was probably starting and there was nothing she could do to help Colt. Damn men for their pride.

As Colt walked over to the barns in the growing dusk, Captain Van Smyth was waiting for him behind the barn with a group of his friends. Colt nodded to him and looked around. Soldiers were coming from every direction. The camp gossip had traveled faster than the telegraph. A clandestine fight between officers was a rare and noteworthy experience and not to be missed.

Grizzled old Mulvaney walked up just then.

Colt said to him, "Since you've got a fiver on this fight, will you be my second?"

The other rubbed his lined jaw and nodded. "You know I will, boy."

The men gathered in a large circle behind the barn, the late-afternoon sun throwing long shadows around them.

Captain Van Smyth said to Colt. "Captain Dever will be my second."

Colt flexed his hands and then pulled off his jacket and shirt. "Any time you're ready."

The other nodded and turned to the crowd. "This

is a fight between men, not officers. No matter who wins, this fight never happened; you understand?"

He peeled off his own tailored jacket and shirt as a murmur ran through the crowd, which made a close circle. They could all be in trouble if Major Murphy got wind of this.

Captain Van Smyth sneered at Colt as he adopted a fighter's stance, fists doubled. "I suggest the Marquis of Queensbury rules."

"I never went to West Point," Colt growled, "so I don't know what you're talkin' about. I learned to fight in the corrals and saloons of Texas."

"I expect you to fight like a gentleman," the captain snapped as he crouched in boxing position.

"Let's get one thing straight; I'm no gentleman and you aren't either or you wouldn't have tried to take advantage of a lady," Colt said and moved in closer as the ring of men around them yelled encouragement.

"Pishposh. She's no lady." Captain Van Smyth sneered. "She's just some savage buck's—"

Colt hit him then, coming in under the captain's fists and slugging him hard in the face, sending him stumbling backward into the weathered barn door. "Watch your mouth!"

"No fair! You gave me no warning!" And the captain struck a boxing pose again.

"I told you I learned to fight in saloons, not gentlemen's clubs," Colt yelled and charged the other man, grabbing him around the waist and taking him down into a pile of horse manure.

The crowd roared and crowded even closer as money exchanged hands, and Sergeant Mulvaney shouted, "Get him, lad! That's it, rub him in the horse shit like he deserves!"

It was a warm day, even though the two were stripped to their waists and the sun would soon sink beyond the far horizon. They were both sweating now as they fought and the other men shouted and cheered them on. The captain's body was muscled, with no scars. Colt's body had dozens of scars from old fights and battle wounds. Otherwise, he thought they were fairly evenly matched. And then he realized his arm wound was starting to throb. He'd have to ignore it.

The captain was light on his feet, too, dancing in a circle now, his hands clenched in classic boxing mode.

Colt knew nothing of fancy footwork and boxing. When he saw a weakness, he dived in, caught the other around the waist, and they went down, rolling and tumbling in the grass.

"You low-class bastard!" the captain snarled, but Colt came out on top and hit the other in the mouth. Blood ran down the perfect, handsome face and into the wispy mustache.

Colt stumbled to his feet as the other stood up and went into boxing stance again. The soldiers were all shouting and waving their fists, urging their favorites on. Colt could feel sweat breaking out on his big body, and his arm ached.

Blood trickled down Captain Van Smyth's face and dripped onto his chest as he stood up and faced Colt. "All right then, we'll fight like your Texas barroom brawlers, if that's what you want!"

He was angry, Colt could tell by his distorted red face, and with his anger, his reason and caution disappeared. He charged Colt, swinging wildly, and Colt stepped aside deftly and caught him with a right jab to the ear as the captain lunged past.

The captain swore and staggered, then moved in

close, swinging hard. This time he caught Colt above the eye.

Colt gritted his teeth to hold back a cry of pain. He knew from the feel that the captain must have opened a cut above his left eyebrow, and then blood trickled into his eye, blinding him. He heard a low moan around him as he stepped back and shook his head, throwing blood on the men nearest him.

Sergeant Mulvaney stepped up. "I say we stop this fight now, Lieutenant, you can't even see—"

"Not a chance!" Colt cursed and slung his head to clear his vision.

The captain grinned. "Now, you Texas tramp, I'll show you how a gentleman fights!" He stepped in and hit two punches, hard and fast, to Colt's ribs. Colt, half-blinded by blood, staggered and grabbed onto the other man, stalling for time, but the captain punched him hard in the kidneys.

The pain was unbelievable, worse than his throbbing arm wound. Sweat and blood ran down Colt's face and dripped on his chest. He could smell his own rank sweat and the copper scent of blood as he backed away, stalling for time so he could recover from the blows.

The captain charged, and in a daze, Colt saw that grinning face, the wispy mustache, coming in for the knockout. In Colt's mind, he saw Hannah's terrified eyes and knew if he didn't whip him, the captain would go back later and attack her again. Colt had to make a believer out of the arrogant officer.

"Don't you ever touch her again," Colt gasped between cut lips.

"Hell of a thing, to be fighting over an Injun's whore." The captain grinned, his light curls now hanging across his forehead. "Why, she ought to be happy to take on any white man now."

Colt had never felt such fury. She was not his to love and protect, but his anger boiled up inside him like a volcano as he charged in, forgetting pain and blood. All he could think of was Hannah. "You snooty sonova-bitch! You ever touch her again, I'll kill you and anyone else who tries!"

He struck the captain with a right cross, then a left. The captain staggered backward, blood spurting from his mouth as Colt hammered him. But Colt showed him no mercy, not even when the captain threw his hands up in front of his face, backing away until he staggered and went down, Colt on top of him, pum-meling him again and again. He wanted to kill the man for daring to touch Hannah, and that was all he could think of, pounding the man's sneering face.

Now two soldiers were pulling him off even as he fought to keep slugging the superior officer. Sergeant Mulvaney was one of those attempting to hold him back as Colt struggled to return to the fray.

"Lieutenant, the man's out cold!" the old man shouted in his ear.

Colt ceased swinging and took a deep breath, stepped back. He felt both blood and sweat streaming down his own battered face, but the captain looked in worse condition. The arrogant Easterner lay battered and bruised, his face almost unrecognizable.

"Someone get some water," Colt gasped, leaning against his knees, breathing in gasps.

The captain's friends poured water over him and after a few minutes, he sat up, but there was no fight left in him. He sat there on the ground, one eye swollen shut, looking up at Colt.

"Want some more?" Colt stepped forward, his fists clinched, but the other shook his head, holding his hands up to protect his face.

His friends stood him slowly on his feet.

It was dusk dark now. One of the other captains made a dismissing gesture. "All right, everyone, show's over. Break it up, and everyone keep your mouth shut."

Men nodded, and Colt saw money exchange hands and heard losers grumble. It was turning dark and Colt hurt all over. His injured arm felt as if it were on fire.

The old Irish sergeant grinned and handed him his shirt and jacket. "Good show, Lieutenant. I'll buy you a beer."

Colt only grunted. He felt like one mass of pain and bruises, and he knew from the way the captain limped that Van Smyth felt the same as he gingerly slipped on his clothes.

Sergeant Mulvaney put Colt's arm over his shoulder to help him walk. "Ye hurt bad, Lieutenant?"

"Not as bad as he is." Colt leaned on him as they limped away. "He won't be botherin' Hannah again."

Behind him, he heard the men still talking as they broke into smaller groups and drifted away.

"Where to now, lad?" The old sergeant looked up at him, concern on his grizzled face. "The infirmary?"

"Oh, hell, no," Colt swore. "Doc would feel duty bound to report this and the major would explode. He's got enough trouble without his officers tryin' to kill each other. Take me to my quarters."

"That eye looks like you need some help," the sergeant protested.

"I'll manage somehow," Colt gasped as he gritted his teeth and hobbled across the parade grounds.

It was dark so maybe no one had noticed the men

coming from behind the barn, two of them limping. Colt could only hope. Every step was painful, every muscle seemed bruised. He could only imagine what his face looked like. He grinned in spite of himself. He doubted Captain Van Smyth, or anyone else, would bother Hannah again; they'd be afraid to. At least he could stop worrying about her while he was out on patrol.

It was dark inside his quarters as the sergeant helped him to his bed and lit a lamp. Colt collapsed on the edge of his bunk and tried to suppress a groan.

The other man turned around and looked at him, frowned. "Holy mother of God," he said, "you look like the dogs have been draggin' you around under the porch. Here, let me get some of that blood off."

"I'll be all right," Colt mumbled and fell back on his bunk. He felt the other yanking off his boots and putting his feet on the bed, then bending over him.

"I can wash the blood off a little, lad, but I think you need more than that, maybe some stitches."

"Don't get Doc," Colt closed his eyes. "I don't want the major to know about this."

"All right."

Then Colt heard footsteps and a door closing.

Colt opened his good eye. He was alone. Good, Sergeant Mulvaney had gone to his own quarters. Well, he couldn't blame him. Anyone who might have a connection with this fight could face big trouble if the major found out about it.

Colt stifled a groan and closed his eyes again. His mouth felt like dirty cotton and his split lip stung. He'd give a front seat in hell for a drink of water, but he wasn't sure he had the energy to get up and stumble across the room to the pitcher. Perhaps in a little while he would try. In the meantime, every muscle and bone in his body was hurting. Maybe if he could sleep a little while, he'd wake up feeling better.

He heard a door open.

"Colt? Oh, my God, Colt?"

A woman's voice. He opened his eyes slowly to see a dim form standing by his bunk.

And then a small, cool hand touched his forehead and he heaved a sigh of relief. "Hannah? You don't belong here."

"The sergeant came for my help," she whispered. "And it's a good thing he did. Now you lay still and let me see what I can do."

Colt smiled and relaxed. He didn't care how mangled he was. If Hannah was here, everything was going to be all right.

Chapter 14

Hannah surveyed the injured man and shook her head. Men. They were always fighting about something. This time, she knew it was about her. That had been silly of Colt; she didn't have any honor left to protect.

His eyes were closed and he had probably drifted off to sleep. Just as well, she might hurt him cleaning those wounds. She put Travis on the floor to play, cautioned him to be quiet. Then she got a washbowl of warm water and some clean rags, began to wash Colt's body. Most of the injuries were bruises, but that cut over his eye was going to have to be stitched.

He stirred and moaned.

"This is going to hurt some," she warned him.

"Probably no more than it did when I got it," he murmured.

"I'll have to stitch it closed and I don't have anything but plain thread and needle." She bit her lip, not wanting to hurt him.

"Stitch away. I'll pretend I'm a torn shirt." His green eyes opened and he grinned at her.

She got a needle and thread and used whiskey to

disinfect the cut, then gave him a drink from the bottle. "This is no joke," she scolded. "You'll probably always have a scar there."

"The captain has some, too."

"It wasn't worth it," she said as she bent over him.

"It was to me. I couldn't let him get away with that. If I did, every man on this post would try to grab you."

She couldn't help but sigh and smile down at him. "You've got an old-fashioned sense of honor."

"I'm a Texan," he muttered. "We take care of women."

"All right, grit your teeth and pretend to be an old shirt." She had her needle poised.

"I'm ready." He closed his eyes and winced as she pulled both sides of the wound together and began to stitch.

"I'm so sorry I'm hurting you," she whispered as she sewed the wound up.

"I've been hurt worse," he said between gritted teeth.

After a few minutes, she stepped back and took a deep breath. "There, I've finished and I've got most of your wounds bandaged. Would you like something to eat?"

He reached out and caught her hand. "I'm not sure I can handle a fork."

She pulled away from him, busied herself putting things away. "How about some soup?"

"That'd be nice."

"I've got a big pot at home and some fresh baked bread to float in it. I'll be back in a minute."

He didn't answer, his eyes closed.

She thought he looked like a hurt little boy lying there, his face swollen and bruised, his lip cut. Without thinking, she leaned over and brushed her lips across his. He didn't stir. "Come on, Travis. Let's go get some soup." She picked up her child and went out the door.

It was pitch dark when she returned with the soup and put Travis on the floor to play.

"Colt?" she whispered as she leaned over him. "Wake up, I've got some food."

His green eyes barely opened and he moved about. "Huh? Oh, I'm stiff and sore."

"I'll wager the captain is, too. Here, let me prop you up on pillows and feed you some of this. If you're lucky, you can make sick call and take it easy for a few days."

She sat down on the edge of his bunk and put a pillow behind him. "I've put some of that fresh bread in the soup, should make it easy to eat." She put a spoonful between his lips.

"Hey, that's good." He smiled up at her despite his sore mouth. "You're a good cook, Hannah."

"I've been running a house since my mother died when I was nine."

"You deserve a better life that you've had," he said as she put another spoonful in his mouth.

"I'm not complaining," she answered. "I take life as it comes."

"You're a fighter," he said as she fed him. "You're a Texas girl to the core."

"Here, eat the rest of this and go to sleep," she commanded and gave him the last of the soup. Then she leaned over him and pulled the pillow out from behind his head.

He felt her long hair brush across him as she leaned close and he smelled the warm, clean scent of her. Had he imagined that she had kissed him before? Maybe he had. "I'm much obliged to you," he whispered as she fluffed his pillow.

"It's okay, Colt," she said. "I've got to go; I've got cookies and tea cakes to bake."

"I like cookies—cold milk and cookies," he murmured, smiling as he closed his eyes and sighed. "Mama used to bake me cookies." Everything seemed to be hurting, but his stomach was full and this woman had looked after him. No one had really looked after him in all these years. His mother had died on the trip out from Indiana. He heard the door close softly and he drifted off to sleep, imagining that Hannah was in his bed, snuggled up close to him, her blond head in the crook of his shoulder so that he could turn and kiss her forehead. His dreams were pleasant that night and he fell into a deep sleep.

A sound brought him straight up in his bed, a loud sound that interrupted his sleep. What the—?

Then he recognized a brash bugle call even as his body complained about the sudden movement. It was barely dawn in his little room, and for a moment, he blinked, wondering why he hurt and what the hell was going on.

Then he heard the sound of confusion outside, running feet, and the bugle blew even shriller. He swung his legs over the side of his bed and groaned at his pain and stiffness.

Now a loud rap at his door. "Lieutenant, there's a patrol this morning." Sergeant Mulvaney's Irish accent.

"What?"

The grizzled old man opened the door and saluted. "Texas Ranger just brought word. Big party of Comanches movin' west, sir. We're going to try to intercept them."

"At ease, Mulvaney. All right. See that Rascal is saddled. Who's in charge of the patrol?"

"Captain Van Smyth, sir."

"Oh hell," Colt grumbled. "This will be one helluva day. Go on, Sergeant. I'll be out as soon as I pull my clothes on."

"Yes, sir." The sergeant slammed the door and was gone.

Colt stumbled to the window and looked out. Men were running everywhere; horses galloped to the parade ground, rearing and lining up. "Just what I need to start my day off right: a patrol with Captain Snooty chasin' Comanches in the June heat." He grabbed for his boots.

It took him only a moment to dress, every bone and muscle in his body aching and complaining. He was hungry as hell and what he wanted was biscuits, bacon, and eggs, but he'd be lucky to get a cup of coffee.

The only thing that cheered him was the fact that the captain would be as pained and hurting this morning as Colt was. And the two of them faced a long, hot dusty day chasing after Comanches.

He strode outside and found the grizzled sergeant holding Rascal's reins. "By Saint Patrick's bones, you look like death warmed over, lad."

"Thanks, Mulvaney. Good mornin' to you, too."

"Here, I got you a canteen of coffee, sir."

Colt nodded his appreciation and took a big swig. It was hot and had a good slug of whiskey in it. That seemed to revive him and he looked around. Captain Van Smyth was already mounted, and his face, all swollen and discolored, looked worse than Colt felt. Around them, horses whinnied and reared as troopers mounted and lined into formation. Word about the patrol must have gotten around the post fast because a lot of people were outside to watch the Cavalry ride out. He spotted Hannah in the crowd, holding her sleepy little boy, and he nodded to her. She nodded back, looking anxious.

The major strode out of his office just then, Olivia by his side. The captain saluted him and then the major turned toward Colt and Colt saluted. The crowd quieted.

The major looked over the two officers and frowned. "It seems some men are so eager for a fight, they can't wait for the Comanches."

Neither officer said anything. Colt knew they both looked like they had been stomped on by a runaway horse.

"By Saint Mary's blood, you'll get your fill of fighting today," the major shouted. "A Texas Ranger has brought news of a big war party moving west from here, gentlemen. If we can surprise them, maybe we can save a few ranches from being pillaged and burned."

Colt shifted uneasily in his saddle, avoiding Olivia's curious gaze. He could only imagine what she had heard about the fight.

The captain snapped the major a salute. "Your orders, sir?"

"You are to intercept the enemy and do as much damage as you can. That's why the Second Cav was sent to Texas."

"Yes, sir." The captain snapped another salute and the little army band struck up an old army marching tune.

Olivia ran to Colt's side and reached up a perfumed hankie to him, her eyes full of tears. "What happened to your face?"

He looked over at the captain. "Uh, I fell gettin' into bed."

"Me, too, Miss Olivia," Van Smyth said.

She looked baffled, but turned back to Colt as he took the hankie. "For luck, my brave soldier!" And she blew him kisses.

Colt felt very conspicuous as he tucked her lace hankie in his shirt pocket and nodded to her. Out of the corner of his eye, he saw Hannah and knew she had seen the whole thing. How could he ever convince her he and Olivia were through when Olivia insisted on melodramatic scenes like this?

Captain Van Smyth gave the order and the troops mounted and swung into line, the fine horses stepping smartly to the music as they rode out of the fort with the crowd behind them waving and shouting encouragement.

Colt turned in his saddle and looked back. Olivia was still blowing kisses, but Hannah only stood there holding her child, staring after him.

It was going to be a long, hot day, he thought, riding up beside the captain. It was dusty and they were headed west where water was scarce and the forage for horses thin. His mustang would eat almost any grass, no matter how dry and tasteless it was, but they'd had to bring along a supply wagon to haul grain for the fancy thoroughbreds.

Worse yet, every bone in his body ached as his horse moved, and Captain Van Smyth looked like he felt as bad as he appeared, his face all purple and bruised. This wasn't good, Colt thought, out on a patrol with a superior officer he had no confidence in, a man from back East who didn't know the Texas terrain.

He glanced back at the grizzled old sergeant and

saw the set, grim face. Mulvaney didn't have any confidence in the fancy West Point officer either and with two officers who hated each other, the day would probably not go well.

They reached a point in another hour where the unshod pony tracks gradually disappeared on the rocky terrain. The captain looked confused. "Lieutenant, see what you make of it."

"Yes, sir." Colt dismounted and studied the ground. "They're tryin' to lose us all right. Permission to ride up ahead and see if I can pick up the trail, sir?"

"Permission granted. Take the sergeant with you."

Colt and Mulvaney rode up a quarter of a mile and dismounted, studied the ground. It was hotter than hell with the lid off, Colt thought as he took off his hat and wiped his face. There wasn't a breath of air stirring and his horse was lathered. Sweat ran down his tanned face and he winced when it hit a raw cut and stung. His blue shirt was plastered to his body and his mouth tasted like dry straw.

"God, if we don't find some water soon, our horses will begin to suffer."

"You see anything, Lieutenant?"

Colt blinked against the blinding sun and knelt down. He saw a broken wisp of grass where something had passed by. He took three more steps and saw just the slightest imprint of an unshod horse. All the army horses were shod. "They came this way, all right. I'll bet they've got scouts out that already know we're on their trail."

"The red devils may try to ambush us," the older man muttered.

"If they knew how green our captain was, I reckon they might," Colt agreed. "And that supply wagon loaded with food, corn, and ammunition will draw Indians like flies to a honey tree." He swung up into the saddle, and he and the sergeant rode back to the captain, saluted. "Sir, they passed this way, all right."

"Good, we'll just keep hot on their heels." The captain nodded.

"Begging your pardon, sir," Mulvaney said, "our mounts need to be cooled out a little. We've been riding hard now for a couple of hours."

The captain glared at him. "I didn't give you permission to speak, Sergeant."

Colt sighed. "Sir, he's right."

"Nonsense, we're not going to let them get away," the captain barked. "I'd like to have a medal out of this patrol."

"Yes, sir."

Colt and the sergeant exchanged glances and returned to their positions.

The patrol kept riding another hour. By now, all the horses were lathered and the men were drinking up the last of their canteens. The sun hung like a fried egg in a hot blue sky and there was no view of anything for miles around but rough country and an endless sea of prairie grass.

"Permission to speak, sir." Colt saluted.

The other frowned. "Granted."

"Beggin' your pardon, sir," Colt said, "I think I recognize this country. There's a little tank off to the right a few miles with a few trees."

"Tank?"

"It's what Texans call a water hole, sir. We ought to stop and give the men and horses a chance to fill up."

The captain glared at him. "Are you trying to give me orders, Lieutenant?"

"No, sir, but I thought you might—"

"We'll keep riding. I don't want to detour out of the way, we'll lose some time."

Colt took a deep breath. He was stuck with a glory-hunting commanding officer who didn't know much about Texas or horses. He was going to ride everyone into the ground in this heat. If horses started dying or going lame, the patrol would be in big trouble.

"Yes, sir."

They rode another three hours in the relentless heat. Colt's cut lip was now cracked and his canteen was almost empty. He dismounted once and poured a little of the precious water into his hat and gave Rascal a drink.

The captain scowled at him. "You better save your water, Lieutenant. We'll be running short."

"Yes, sir," Colt snapped back, "but if I have a dead horse, I'm stuck out here on the prairie and that's worse yet."

He glanced over at the grizzled sergeant and caught his eye. The old soldier looked worried and he had a right to be, Colt thought. Two feuding superior officers and one of them green as grass. Here they were out on the vast western plains of Texas with a blistering sun beating down on them.

The terrain ahead grew rougher, with more hills. As the afternoon wore on, up ahead lay an arroyo, a deep one with banks twice as high as a man's head.

The captain said, "We'll ride through there."

"Beggin' your pardon, sir," Colt said, "that's a good spot for an ambush. I think we'd be better off to go around."

"Then we'd lose time," the captain snapped. "You wanting those Injuns to get away, Lieutenant?"

"No, sir, but they may have scouts out, know we are followin' them and that'd be a good place for them to trap us."

"Good Lord, Lieutenant Prescott, I didn't know Texans were so cautious." The captain grinned with sarcasm. "You afraid of a few Injuns? We've got a pretty good-size patrol here."

"Sir, I didn't go to West Point, but I know even a small force can keep a big force pinned down if they get above them and surround them."

"Nonsense. My training tells me those ragged Injuns are fleeing as hard and fast as they can, knowing the army is after them."

"Beggin' your pardon, sir, but I know Comanches. I lived among them for ten years. They're the best light cavalry in the world and they haven't survived all these centuries without being smart. They may not have been to West Point, but they can teach you a thing or two about battle tactics."

"Enough, Lieutenant!" the captain roared. "Now if you're afraid, I can send you back—"

"Are you callin' me a coward?" Colt's free hand rested on the butt of his pistol.

"Sirs," the sergeant interrupted, "begging your pardon, but can we continue our patrol and you two finish your disagreements back at the fort?"

Colt felt suddenly ashamed. He had a lot of men with him and they were depending on their officers to follow orders, attack the Comanches, and get them safely home.

"He's right, sir. We'll finish our argument back at the fort. Duty comes first."

"You're right," the captain agreed and peered ahead. "How long is this arroyo anyway?"

Colt took off his hat and scratched his head. "I've forgotten, maybe a quarter of a mile or less. It bends here and there like a snake."

"Then there's no way it could hide a hundred warriors," the captain scoffed. "We'll ride ahead through it so as not to lose time going around."

Colt started to argue, remembered the West Pointer was his superior. Instead he sighed. "Yes, sir. Alert the men, Sergeant Mulvaney."

The old Irishman rode back along the line. "Look lively, men. We're riding into the arroyo."

Colt heard grumbling behind him. Some of these men were native Texans and they knew the lay of the land. This crooked wash through the hills was a perfect place for an ambush and they knew it. Nevertheless, they followed orders and the troops rode slowly into the canyon, the supply wagon lagging behind.

Colt was as edgy as a cat. He rode forward, but he kept his gaze on the rim of the little canyon. There was a lot of dry brush and some cactus growing along the edge, and brush and low willows in the arroyo ahead of them that stretched like a jagged scar across the Texas plains, chewed out by rushing water in rare rains over eons of time.

"Captain, if you want my advice—"

"I don't." The officer's voice was curt.

Colt tried again. "Sir, that supply wagon should be moved up. That arroyo is a perfect place for an ambush—"

"We've already discussed this, Lieutenant," the captain snapped. "Now just do your duty. I'm in charge of this patrol."

"Yes, sir." Colt kept his eyes on the rim of the canyon

as he rode. The sun was so blinding, he had to squint. The captain might not see anything, but the hairs on the back of Colt's neck rose up and he was sure he felt sinister eyes watching them.

They were halfway down the arroyo now, the sun blistering, the afternoon so quiet, there was no sound save their horses' hooves on the dry clay and gravel and an occasional snort or a light buzz as dragonflies rose up off weeds ahead of them.

And then Colt saw a metallic glint reflected from the sun along the rim of the canyon. "Look out! Indians!"

"Where? Where?" The captain's horse reared as he jerked the reins, but the men were already dismounting without orders and scurrying behind boulders.

"Lieutenant!" the captain shouted. "I don't see any Indians! Have you gone crazy?" And his horse reared again even as a shot ricocheted off a rock near him and he came sliding off in a near panic. "Good Lord! How many of them are there?"

"There's no way to know." Colt crouched down behind a boulder, shouting orders to his sergeant to get all the men dismounted and under cover. He began to curse at the lack of knowledge that had gotten them into this mess. "Save your ammo, men!" he shouted. "Don't shoot unless you're sure."

Back along the route, he heard shrieks and shots and then silence. "Damn it, they've taken our supply wagon. I told you to move it up!"

The captain's face was already discolored from last night's fight; now it turned pasty white. "There's extra ammo on that wagon."

"Yes, sir." Colt nodded. "And now the Comanches have it."

Along the rim of the canyon, dark heads with lurid painted faces popped up now and then, fired, and then sank out of sight.

The captain's face turned as pale as milk with sweat beading on it and running down his blue collar. The bruises stood out all green and purple on his handsome features. "Maybe we should try to break out."

"We'd be like ducks in a small pond," Colt shouted back. "We need to wait 'til dark and maybe we can figure out something."

"We could be here for days then," the captain whispered.

"Yeah, we could." Colt didn't look at him; he was so furious with the novice officer that he wanted to grab him and shake him until his teeth rattled.

The grizzled old sergeant scurried up to him. "Sir, we've got one dead and two wounded, and whoever was with the supply wagon."

"Figure those troopers are dead," Colt snapped.

The captain seemed to have given up all interest in command. He just blinked and pulled at his mustache, staring into space.

Colt took over. "Make the wounded as comfortable as possible, Sergeant, and tell the men to save their water. We may be here for a while."

"Yes, sir." The old man saluted and crawled away.

The captain wiped his pale face as bullets hit rocks around them with a zinging sound and glanced off. "Are they liable to shoot our horses and leave us afoot?"

"Normally, yes." Colt took off his hat and wiped his sweating face. "But these are fine horses. They'd like to take them as prizes, trade them to the Comancheros."

"What—what's a Comanchero?"

Colt sighed. "Mexicans and renegade whites who trade with the Injuns. Fine horses will bring a good price in places like Mexico City."

No one spoke then, and the canyon got quiet—too quiet.

The captain whispered. "Maybe they've left?"

Colt laughed without mirth. "Just stick your head up and you'll find out. There's no reason for them to leave. Time is on their side, and now they've got fresh supplies, thanks to our slow-movin' wagon."

Just then a new recruit stuck his head up to look around. A shot echoed off the rim of the canyon, and he went over backward, blood spurting from his head.

Colt swore. "Got your answer now?"

The captain groaned and reached for his canteen.

Colt frowned at him. "You'd better hang on to whatever water you've got. We'll need every drop."

Reluctantly, it seemed, the captain put away his canteen without opening it. "Isn't there anything that will get them to leave?"

"Reinforcements," Colt muttered, "but those we don't have."

"Anything else?"

"If we managed to kill one of their leaders, they might take it as bad medicine and withdraw," Colt suggested, "but that's a long shot."

They settled down for the afternoon, and Colt watched the long shadows creep across the arroyo. No one spoke or smoked because Colt had sent out orders that the tiny bit of flame might draw gunfire.

The captain sighed. "This is the longest day I've ever spent."

"Wait 'til night comes and you can't be sure if every

shadow is a bit of brush or a warrior sneakin' up on you to cut your throat," Colt replied. "Then you'll know how slow time really moves."

"They aren't that brave, are they?" In the shadows, the captain looked panicked. "I mean, to sneak up on us?"

"Yes." Colt nodded. "They can cut a man's throat before he makes any sound but the gurgling of blood rushing out of his neck."

"Oh, dear God," the captain murmured. "Oh, dear God."

The sergeant crawled over to them again. "Sir, it'll be dark soon. Any orders?"

The captain tried to say something, finally shook his head.

Colt said, "Sergeant, tell the men to eat a little hardtack and stay alert. They may try to rush us in the dark when they think we've dropped off to sleep."

"Yes, sir." The sergeant crawled away.

The moon came up, big and round and yellow as a pumpkin. The night felt as hot as a dark wool blanket.

Colt cursed. "This is what we Texans call a Comanche moon. They can see as good as owls in this moonlight. I was hopin' for clouds so it might be dark enough for us to slip out of this canyon and get away."

"No chance?" the captain asked.

"Captain, look out there. You can see the shadow of a rabbit big as a steer if it tried to cross that bare prairie."

Drums started in the distance and then the chanting.

"Jesus!" The captain sounded frightened. "What in the hell is that?"

Colt shrugged. "They know they've got us trapped. They're gonna enjoy the night with a little dancin' and feastin', figurin' they finish us off at dawn."

The captain's hands shook on his rifle. "It's getting on my nerves. I don't know if I can take that all night." His voice rose and he started to stand up, but Colt grabbed him by the shoulder and pulled him back down.

"That's what they want, for us to panic and start runnin'."

"You're right." The captain's voice shook.

"They'll leave a warrior or two guardin' this arroyo while the rest of them celebrate. The man who tries to ride out of here for help is a dead man or worse."

"What could be worse?" The captain wiped his sweating face.

"You don't want to know," Colt said and moved a little, trying to make his muscles stop aching.

"What do you suggest? That we wait and let them pick us off at dawn?"

"Sir, you got us into this. What would the West Point rule book say?"

"That's insubordination, Lieutenant. I'll have you court-martialed for that!"

"Captain, if we get out of this alive, I'll be glad to face a court-martial. Anyway I'm due to reenlist or get out next week, so it looks like I'm not gonna have to make that choice."

"Send a man to the fort for help," the captain said.

"Is that an order, sir?" Colt asked.

"Yes."

"Then let me try it. Rascal is a mustang and he's got a better chance, and I know the trails. I might make it."

"No." The captain's voice shook. "If something happens to you, I've got this on my own, and I'm not sure I—I know what to do." He hesitated.

In the background, the Indians sang and the drums

echoed. "Sergeant!" the captain yelled. "Sergeant Mulvaney!"

"No, don't make him do it," Colt argued. "He's near retirement."

Mulvaney crawled over to them. "Sir?"

"Sergeant," the captain whispered, "do you think you could sneak out of here and ride to the fort for reinforcements?"

The old soldier hesitated. "Sir, I reckon I could if anyone can."

"Let me do it," Colt protested.

"Begging your pardon, sir, but no." The old Irishman shook his head, "Lieutenant, if something happens to the captain, you'll be the only officer left. The men will be leaderless."

That was true, Colt thought, and the men had no confidence in the green West Pointer.

The captain said, "Sergeant, ride to the fort and get us some help."

"Yes, sir." The old man saluted.

Colt frowned. "Mulvaney, at least take my horse. Rascal will have a better chance of gettin' through than these fancy grain-fed show horses."

"I'll do that, sir."

"Wait 'til you're sure no one's watchin' you," Colt cautioned. "There's bound to be sentries posted to keep us from escapin'."

The sergeant grinned. "I been in Texas a long time, sir. I can smell a Comanche a mile away."

"Don't try to fight your way out," Colt warned. "Just ride like the devil is on your tail."

"I can do that, sir."

Colt hesitated. "You know what's at stake here, and you know what your chances are."

"None too good, I reckon." The old man winked at him, and then Colt grabbed his arm and shook his hand. "Good luck, Sarge."

"Thank you, sir. I've already prayed to the Blessed Mother. I know I need a miracle." Mulvaney crossed himself, then crept away into the darkness.

Colt swallowed the lump in his throat. "Captain, you've just sent one of my best men on a suicide mission."

"I didn't know what else to do. Isn't he the man you'd recommend?"

"I would have been glad to try it myself," Colt said.

"I need you here."

Colt said a silent prayer for the old man and mentally cursed green officers. The night grew silent again, and a breeze picked up, carrying the sound of the drums and the chanting. Somewhere in the arroyo, a wounded soldier moaned softly.

"Poor devil." Colt took his canteen and crawled through the brush to where the man lay. The full moon lit up his tortured features. Hey there, soldier, how are you doin'?"

The man tried to smile. "Fine, sir. But I've seen better days."

"Ain't we all?" Colt joked. "Here, I've got some water."

The man shook his head. "There's others need it worse than me, sir."

"This is an extra canteen," Colt lied, although it was his own. "You don't need to feel guilty about drinkin' some."

The man drank gratefully and Colt licked his own cracked lips. God, what he wouldn't give for a cold, fresh spring to dive in right now. He imagined swimming naked in it, splashing and diving and drinking gallons of it.

"Thank you, sir."

"Jones, you think you can ride if we get a chance to get out of here?"

"I'll do my damnedest, sir." the man promised.

"No one can ask more than that, soldier." He looked at the man's wounds. His side was blood-soaked. The chances of him riding were nonexistent.

"Hang in there, soldier. Remember, we're Texans."

"Yes, sir." The man managed a weak grin.

Colt crawled on to the next wounded man. He could see the dirty bandage in the moonlight. "Soldier?"

No answer.

"Soldier, it's Lieutenant Prescott. How are you doin'?"

No answer.

Colt crawled up to him. The man looked peacefully asleep. Colt reached out and touched his face. Stone cold.

Colt gritted his teeth. Here was a soldier who had died in the line of duty without complaint, without whining. By midmorning tomorrow, they all might be in the same condition. He crawled back to the captain.

"What's going on?" the captain asked.

"One wounded man still alive, the other dead."

The captain sighed. "Somehow this isn't the way I imagined it at West Point."

Colt felt sudden pity for him. "Fightin' Comanches isn't like fightin' any other enemy. They will die bravely and they expect you to do the same."

"What do you mean by that?"

"Never mind. Just save the last bullet in your Colt for yourself."

"Good Lord, are you joking?"

"I wish I was."

The captain's blue eyes were wide in the moonlight. "You suppose the sergeant's got a chance?"

"I don't know. He's smart enough to wait until the moon goes behind a drift of clouds, but still, Comanches have eyes like hawks. My mustang will outrun most Indian ponies because Rascal is better fed, and Mulvaney has the advantage of surprise. All we can do is wait."

Minutes dragged by and Colt leaned back against the rocks, thinking this was going to be the longest night ever. The incessant drumming and chanting kept up until it was pounding in his head. It would drive any man insane. He wondered again if the sergeant had managed to get away and go for help. As if by answer; in the distance, he heard shots echoing and reechoing.

The captain looked at him. "You think that's the sergeant?"

Colt nodded. "I just hope he outrode them."

"When will we know?"

"That's a stupid question," Colt snapped. "Towards morning, if reinforcements come chargin' in, he made it."

"Otherwise?"

Colt didn't want to think about it. "Otherwise, he didn't."

The wind picked up and changed direction, blowing toward the Indian camp now. It made the sound of the drumming fainter, which was as big a relief as the cool breeze. Colt looked up and down the arroyo at his men. They were sprawled behind rocks, rifles at the ready. Some appeared to be dozing. They might as well sleep, Colt thought. Unless Sergeant Mulvaney made it back to the fort, they'd all be picked off one at a time when the sun rose.

After a few minutes, he heard a new sound, a high-pitched shriek that sounded like an animal in mortal pain.

The captain sat up. "What the hell—?"

Colt's heart sank as he heard the scream again and again. "They got Sarge. He didn't make it after all."

Chapter 15

"Oh, good Lord!" The captain's hands shook as he held his rifle. "Are they killing him?"

Colt swore. "I wish they were. They'll keep him alive as long as possible, knowing it will spook the rest of us to hear his screams."

Sergeant Mulvaney shrieked again and the sound drifted on the air over the drumming.

In the dark shadows of the arroyo, Colt saw the men stirring uneasily. He crawled out from behind the boulder and went to the first bunch of men. "It's okay, soldiers. There's nothin' we can do about it."

"Oh, God, Lieutenant, is that gonna happen to us?"

Colt shook his head with more confidence than he felt. "We'll figure out something."

He crawled down the crooked canyon, stopping to pat each man on the shoulder. "Buck up, fellas. We're the crack Second Cav, we'll get through this all right."

Mulvaney still shrieked in agony as Colt turned and crawled back to the captain, who was vomiting. "I can't stand it! I can't stand to hear that man scream!"

"Shut up, man! If you get hysterical, what do you

think the men will do?" Colt was furious with the captain. After all, he was the one who had sent Sarge out on this impossible mission, but there was no point in mentioning that. The captain was falling apart and Colt needed him now.

Sarge screamed again and Colt swore long and loud. "He doesn't deserve to die like this. I've got to do something." He checked his rifle.

"What—what are you going to do?" The captain sobbed in terror.

"I'm gonna do what I have to do." Colt's voice was grim. "Sarge and I have been friends since we served together in Mexico. I'm gonna crawl up there and put him out of his misery."

"You can't do that! Shoot one of our men? You can't do that!"

Sarge cried out again.

Colt winced and swore under his breath, looked at the blubbering captain. "Then you do something."

"I—I don't know what to do," the other officer confessed. "They didn't cover this at West Point."

Colt grabbed his rifle and crawled up toward the lip of the arroyo. "Sarge would do it for me."

He heard a sound and glanced back to see the captain crawling after him, protesting. "I didn't give you an order. This is mutiny, Lieutenant. I'll have you busted for this."

"Bust me and be damned!" Colt swore and kept crawling.

"Don't leave me here, I don't know what to do," the captain sobbed behind him.

"Shut your goddamned mouth!" Colt hissed, "before some warrior hears you." He began to crawl again through the rocks toward the jagged rim of the arroyo. It occurred to him there might be tarantulas, scorpions, and big diamondback rattlers among these rocks, but he'd have to take that chance.

Behind him, the captain made enough noise crawling to make Colt uneasy. Only Sarge's shrieks drowned out every possible sound.

Colt crawled carefully, the rifle in his left hand making progress slow. Now he was up over the rim of the arroyo and there didn't look to be enough vegetation to hide a lizard. He lay on his belly a long moment, getting his bearings. Ahead of him were three big boulders and in the distance, he saw the faint glow of the Comanche campfire. Behind any one of those giant rocks might be a Comanche warrior. He'd have to take that chance. As he put his hand gingerly atop a stone and pulled himself forward, he thought again about rattlesnakes and poisonous insects.

Maybe worse than dying from Comanche torture was the thought of dying slowly by snake bite, the venom making your arm swell and turn black while your pulse pounded like a drum in your head and your arm split open and you writhed in agony. He'd seen a man stung by a scorpion once who was in such pain, he tried to cut off his own hand before anyone could stop him.

Colt's mouth felt so dry, he was unable to swallow. Okay, so there was a chance he was going to crawl right into a snake or deadly spider and get bit. In a few minutes, he'd be so feverish, he wouldn't know the difference, maybe. *Stop it, Prescott*, he scolded himself. *None of that can happen to you—you can't leave this patrol leaderless.*

Sarge screamed again and the sound drifted on the hot night air.

Behind him, he could hear the captain crawling and he made as much noise as a horse rolling in the dust. The captain commanded in a hoarse whisper, "Lieutenant, come back here! Come back here, that's an order."

"I've suddenly gone deaf from the gunfire," Colt flung over his shoulder. "Now if you're goin' with me, Captain, you'd better shut your mouth. These warriors have ears that can pick up a sigh, much less shoutin'."

The captain quieted immediately to a soft moan. "Please, I don't want to go out there."

"You think I do? Goddamn it, then stay here and show your men you're as big a coward as they think you are." Colt kept crawling forward. Now he reached the three boulders and tensed, listening for the slightest sound of a moccasin crackling on dry brush or the soft gritty sound of sand.

Nothing. Nothing but the rising wind, Sarge's screams, and the drumming and chanting. Most of the sentries must have gone to camp to enjoy the torture of the captured prisoner. If what he planned wasn't a success, they'd have two more soldiers to torture soon.

The captain crawled up beside him and took a deep breath. "I guess if you're going, I need to come with you."

Colt grinned back at him. "You've suddenly got more guts than I gave you credit for, Captain."

"I guess I'm crazy or too scared to care anymore or maybe I figure if there's anyone in this patrol who's got a chance of getting out alive, it'll be you."

"I wouldn't count on that," Colt said. "If they get us, the torture will be twice as bad because you're a big chief and I used to be one of them. One of their main leaders, Spider, is dead because of me."

"Oh hell, now you tell me."

"Watch those clouds." Colt pointed upward. "When they scud across in front of the moon so it gets darker, I'm gonna start crawlin' through the buffalo grass toward their camp. With any luck, I can get a ways before the moon comes out again."

"And then what?" The other man's voice shook.

"I'm not sure." Colt shrugged. "They might spot us, but I figure they're too interested in their captive."

"I had a chance at a desk job in Washington, but no, I wanted to win some medals." The captain moaned.

"It's a little late for regrets. By the way, Captain, look out for rattlesnakes and scorpions."

"What? Sonovabitch, why do you mention that now?" He scrambled like he intended to jump up.

Colt grabbed him by the shoulder and yanked him down hard. "Goddamn it! Stay down. You'll get us both killed. Now watch the moon." Colt signaled for silence as the few clouds drifted across the face of the moon, throwing the flat landscape into darkness. "Get up and move!" he commanded, and the two of them scurried in a low squat across the landscape and into a bunch of claret cup cacti. Their blooms were as scarlet as fresh blood. Very appropriate, Colt thought.

The captain whimpered and cursed, and Colt beckoned him to silence. "Damn it, you're a liability to me, you crybaby! Shut up. If the Injuns get you, they'll make a little cactus seem like a bed of roses."

Ahead of Colt, he saw a distant campfire and warriors silhouetted against the flames as they drummed and danced.

Sarge screamed again and Colt cursed under his breath. The captain crept up close to him. "If you fire a shot, won't that alert the Indians and they'll come after us?"

"Of course."

"Damn it, man, you're putting both of us in danger!"

Colt took a deep, shuddering breath to keep from slugging the other man as hard as he could. "Captain, go back to the arroyo, if you're yellow. This is something I've got to do for a friend."

The captain, lying on his belly, looked behind him. "It's a long way back to the arroyo."

"Well, goddamn it, make up your mind! I'm movin' ahead. Sir, you do what you want to."

The captain looked uncertain in the moonlight. Then the moon slid behind clouds again and Colt began to crawl forward.

"Wait, don't leave me here alone!"

Colt kept crawling. To be honest, he didn't think he had much of a chance of making it back to the arroyo after his mercy mission, but that didn't matter. He had to bring peace to Sarge. The Comanche could keep a prisoner alive for days before he got the mercy of death. He didn't intend that should be the old Irishman's fate. Colt kept crawling, the captain at his heels, and then the moon came out again and he stopped behind the body of a dead white horse. God, it stunk.

He lay there catching his breath and thinking. Maybe if the soldiers in the arroyo could hold out long enough, it might occur to the major that they'd run into trouble and he'd send out reinforcements. However by the time the major decided that, the trapped men would probably already be dead. Come dawn, the warriors would be shooting down into the arroyo again, picking off the soldiers one at a time.

Colt cursed the captain again for getting them into this mess. He didn't give a damn if the captain put him up for court-martial; Colt didn't expect to live to see the fort again.

The captain lay close to him. He was so scared Colt could smell his sweat and his voice quavered. "How— how close do you intend to get?"

"Close enough to get a clean shot," Colt said and started crawling across the dead horse.

When he looked back, the captain was retching and Colt sighed, wondering why it had been his luck to be saddled with this green officer?

"Stay here!" he ordered. "You're a burden to me."

He left the captain cowering behind the dead horse and crawled forward through sticker burrs and sparse buffalo grass. He could smell the smoke from the big campfire now and see the outline of warriors dancing around the flames and the drummers over on the side. There was a picket line of horses and Rascal was tied there. If he could reach his horse, Rascal, he might have a chance of escaping, but that would mean deserting the soldiers who depended on him.

Oh, God. He saw Sergeant Mulvaney tied down out on the sand, his hands and feet staked out. Mulvaney screamed again, and Colt closed his eyes, sickened at the sight of what the Comanches were doing to the brave old soldier. For a moment, he almost retched, and then he scolded himself, knowing he had to stay strong. If he didn't do something to help Sarge, the old man could last for days in terrible agony.

And yet, if he were captured, they would do the same to Colt or even worse since he had once been one of them. He was tempted to turn and crawl back to the relative safety of the arroyo because he knew that the minute he fired his rifle, the warriors would be after him. Plus he had the burden of the green captain to look after.

Colt crawled closer, feeling every sticker and pebble underneath him as he moved. The Comanche were all intent on torturing their prisoner, so no one seemed to be looking his way. Could he force himself to do this? He brought his rifle up and aimed and his hands began to shake. He cursed himself under his breath. "You chicken-livered bastard, this is no time to get weak. You owe this last favor to Sarge."

He aimed his rifle, took a deep breath, and tried to say a prayer, but it had been a long time since Colt had been in church. It was terrible for the old man to die without a priest or any friends comforting him, but this was what he would want. It was difficult to get a clear shot with the warriors dancing around the fire. He watched the soldier writhing in pain as he aimed and said a final prayer for his faithful sergeant, blinked back tears, and asked God to steady his shaking hand.

"I only hope you'd do this for me if the tables were turned, old buddy," he whispered, and then he fired.

It was a direct shot and the writhing man stopped moving, at peace at last. The warriors abruptly ceased dancing, puzzled at what had happened. Then they seemed to realize their victim was dead and they began to shout and look around, trying to figure out from where the shot had come. However, Colt was already on his feet and running back toward the arroyo. He could hear the outraged Indians behind him setting up a cry and pursuit. They had been done out of their pleasure and they would have their revenge.

Colt dived across the dead horse and almost landed on the cowering captain. "Let's get the hell out!" he shouted, grabbed the other by the sleeve, and, half dragging him, started back toward the safety of the canyon.

The Comanche were now in hot pursuit, shouting and shrieking as they grabbed up rifles and spears, chasing the two through the moonlit night. Colt could hear them as he and the captain ran, stumbling over rocks and cactus.

It seemed a long, long way back across the prairie with the Indians hot on their trail and bullets flying around them as they ran. The wind came up strong, blowing toward them and blowing the scent of the sage and the broken weeds as they raced for their lives.

Bullets zipped around them and one of them took off Colt's hat, but he was only glad it was a near miss. Then the captain cried out, stumbled, and went down.

"Goddamn it, get on your feet!" Colt tried to keep him from falling, but the captain had bright red blood running down his side as he hesitated and put his hand up to keep it in.

"I—I can't! Don't let them get me!" Scarlet blood streamed between his pale fingers and down the blue uniform.

The Indians were gaining on them. Colt hesitated. He didn't intend to be captured alive, but he didn't want the captain captured either. It would be so easy to run on and leave the green officer out here at the Comanches' mercy, but he was hanging onto Colt's sleeve now.

"Please!" he begged. "Please!"

Colt half carried, half dragged the wounded man across the prairie with him. It was slowing him down and he might not make it, but he wasn't going to leave a wounded man for the Comanche to torture. "Don't shoot! Comin' in!" he yelled, "Comin' in!"

The alerted soldiers set off a barrage of rifle fire around him, and Colt fell and rolled down the ravine, dragging the captain with him. They went all the way to the bottom, scratched and bruised by stones and brush. Colt thought he might've broken some bones, but at least they were back in the arroyo with the soldiers setting a defending barrage of rifle fire behind them. He dragged the half-conscious captain over behind a rock.

"Cease fire, men!" he ordered. "You're wastin' your ammo!"

The soldiers stopped shooting although the Comanches had gathered around the rim and were firing down in among the rocks. Here and there Colt heard a bullet strike home. "Keep under cover!" he yelled.

His heart pounded so hard, it felt like a Comanche drum and his breath came in harsh, ragged gasps, but he decided he wasn't hurt. The captain was another story. Colt reached for his canteen and held it up to the captain's lips.

The captain's handsome face was pale and his blue uniform was dark with blood.

"Did—did we make it?"

"Yeah, we made it," Colt assured him. "You're braver than I gave you credit for, Captain."

The captain drank deep, his hands trembling. "Thank you," he gasped. "Thank you for not leaving me behind."

"Don't thank me yet," Colt snapped. "We still got a long night to go. But you can count on gettin' that medal." He leaned back against the rocks and reached for his makins', then cursed as he realized he couldn't light a cigarette, it would make too good a target.

Now he had time to think about Sarge, and his eyes blurred and he swallowed hard. He'd done the best he could for his old buddy.

"Sorry I couldn't do more, Sarge," he whispered. "I would have rescued you if I could." Then he bowed his head and buried his face in his hands for a long minute. He had to stay strong because he was the officer in charge now with the captain not likely to make it to dawn. That's about when they would run out of ammo and be overrun. He'd better give the men instructions to save the last bullet, so they wouldn't be taken alive. However he wouldn't tell them that yet. As long as they had some hope, he wasn't going to dash it.

The Indians had tired of wasting their bullets shooting into the dark canyon and had retreated back to their fire and dancing. They knew better than anyone, Colt thought, that their time would come right after dawn.

Corporal Wilson crawled over to Colt. "How's the captain, sir?"

Colt examined the officer again. He was barely conscious. "He'll be all right," he lied in a more positive tone than he felt.

"You got any ideas, sir?" The corporal looked barely old enough to shave and his eyes were wide with fear.

"Let me think a minute," Colt said. "This isn't the first time I've been in a tight spot."

"The men have a lot of confidence in you, Lieutenant. What—what happened to Sarge? He's stopped screaming."

"He died," Colt said softly.

"The men want to know—?"

"Corporal, just tell them I've got everything under control and to ration their water, okay?"

"Yes, sir." The young corporal saluted and crawled away.

Colt leaned back and watched him go. In truth, Colt was only buying time. They were outnumbered and low on water and ammunition without the supply wagon. They hadn't a ghost of a chance of winning the battle tomorrow morning and no reinforcements were on the way. He thought about sending out another messenger, decided against it. The Comanches would be watching for that now.

He checked the captain again, sighed, and closed his eyes, feeling the wind blowing the sweat and cooling his face. In this almost desert, it would be bone-chilling before morning. The wind. It had picked up considerably. An idea came to him. It was a wild idea, but it was the only one he had except to sit here and wait for daylight to be shot like ducks in a barrel.

"Corporal?" he yelled.

"Yes, sir?" The young man crawled back.

"I've got an idea, but it may be useless."

"The men are up for anything, sir." The young soldier looked at him eagerly.

"The wind has shifted and is now blowin' toward the Comanche camp."

"Yes, sir, but what—?"

"If we could get a prairie fire goin', in this wind, those Comanche would be on the run ahead of it and maybe we could get away in the confusion."

"What about our wounded, sir?"

"Well, we sure as hell aren't gonna leave them for the Comanche," Colt promised. "We'll have to take them with us."

"They'll slow us down."

Colt looked over at the almost unconscious captain.

If Van Smyth made it back alive, he would have Colt court-martialed for disobeying orders. "Damn it to hell, Corporal, don't you think I know that? But I'm not leavin' them for the Comanche to torture."

"Yes, sir." Colt caught the respect in the young man's voice. "May I say, sir, it's been an honor to serve with you? You're a soldier's soldier."

"Wait 'til we get back to the fort before you say that," Colt grinned. "None of us may make it back alive."

"The men trust you, sir, more than they trust the captain. They'll do anything you say."

Colt chewed his lip, thinking. He had the rest of the patrol's lives in his hands and it was a heavy burden. To think, if he hadn't run away to return to his own people, he would be one of those warriors right now dancing around the fire.

"Corporal, I'm gonna try to light the fires myself."

"Sir, there's a couple of warriors stationed at the opening of the arroyo to keep us from escaping."

"I know that. I was raised by the Comanche—I can deal with them."

"You want I should go with you, sir?"

Colt shook his head. "If I'm successful, you'll see the brush along the rim of the arroyo blazin' soon. Alert the men. When they see that fire movin' toward the Indian camp, they're to be ready to move out as fast as they can and don't look back."

"What about you, sir?"

"Damn it, don't worry about me. Just get these men out of here and headed back to the fort."

The young corporal looked down at the groaning, half-conscious captain. "What about him?"

"Tie him on his horse if you have to, but don't leave him for the Indians."

"Yes, sir."

"Now watch for the fire," Colt cautioned, checked the bowie knife in his belt, and began to creep up the length of the arroyo. There was a sentry all right. He could see the silhouette of the man leaning on his spear and gazing toward the camp in the distance. As Colt watched, the warrior tipped back a bottle and took a long drink. Colt could smell the whiskey from here. So that was what the war party was about, some renegade trader had sold the Comanche some firewater. Colt hoped fervently the outlaw roasted in hell for the misery he'd caused.

He crawled up the side of the arroyo and watched the warrior lean on his spear and drink. He seemed a little wobbly. Colt tossed a small rock up over the rim, where it bounced across the grass. The warrior turned to look that direction and Colt eased himself up over the rim, lying flat on the ground. He could feel his heart pounding inside his sweat-soaked blue uniform as he reached for his knife. Then he stood up and crept up behind the warrior, knife in hand.

Oh, hell. He could see another warrior walking this direction, maybe to relieve this sentry. What was he to do?

The moon went behind clouds again as Colt stepped up behind the drunken warrior and grabbed him from behind. The Comanche only had a moment to fight, but he never had a chance as Colt cut his throat and the man gurgled on his own hot blood and went down.

The warrior in the distance was still sauntering this direction. Colt could shoot him, but that would alert the whole camp. If he could just get a fire going, this prairie wind would whip it fast as a deadly red sea across the dry grass. He pulled out his little match safe and tried to light one. Damn, they were old and weren't going to light. He only had two left. Now what?

The other warrior was still walking toward him and called out in Comanche, "Strong Bull, you have been missing the party. I will take your spot now."

Colt grabbed the slain warrior's spear and stood up, leaned against it, knowing in the darkness, the warrior could only make out the outline of a man. He called back in Comanche, "I am enjoying standing guard on these white dogs. You go back to the war dance."

The other seemed only too happy to turn and leave. Colt leaned on the spear, shaking. He waited until the man was only a distant silhouette in the distance before he crouched over the edge of the arroyo. In a coarse whisper, Colt called, "Corporal, are your men ready to ride?"

"Yes, sir, we've got the wounded mounted, too."

"If you believe in prayer, say one for all of us."

"Sir, I'm a preacher's son; I'll say a special one for you."

That comforted Colt somehow, although he had never thought of himself as a religious man. Colt said, "My matches may not work in this wind. In that case, I'll have to use a pistol and that will alert the Comanche."

"We're ready, sir!"

Colt walked down the length of the arroyo so that he was nearest the Indians and their campfire. Behind him, he heard the soldiers riding out the other end of the arroyo.

He knelt and struck another match, shielding it with his hands from the wind. It blew out immediately. Colt cursed. He had one match left. "Please, God," he prayed and lit the last match. It flickered, seem to catch the dry grass while Colt held his breath, and then it went out, leaving only a glowing bit of grass and smoke.

Now what? He had only one more idea and it would make noise. Maybe the Comanches' drums and chanting would muffle the sound. Colt flipped open the barrel of his Colt, took out a cartridge. His hands shook as he broke open the cartridge and poured the gunpowder out on the ground in a tiny pile. Then he put the cartridge back together and slipped it back into the barrel.

Behind him, he heard the soldiers riding out the other end of the arroyo. If this worked, he'd have to run like hell and try to catch a Cavalry horse because there was no way he could get Rascal out of that Indian camp.

The empty cartridge would spark the gunpowder as it fired and not make as much noise. *Here goes.* He bit his lip and made ready to run as he fired the blank cartridge into the tiny pile of gunpowder. It sparked and caught the dry grass. For a moment, he did not think the Indians had heard the shot over their drums, but now a few heads were turning even as the gunpowder caught the dry grass and it glowed into a tiny flame. His hands shook as he delayed retreating to blow on the tiny flame that now blazed larger.

Behind him, he heard the Cavalry riding out of the arroyo and saw the Indians pausing in their dancing as the strong wind caught the flicker of fire and in seconds turned it into a roaring blaze. Now the warriors were shrieking and running toward him as the Cavalry rode their horses out of the arroyo, heading toward the fort.

Colt turned and ran as hard as he could after the fleeing soldiers. A gray Cavalry horse galloped past Colt, and using his Indian training, he reached out, caught it by the mane, and hung on. The ground was passing underneath him and he knew if he couldn't get to the saddle, he'd be trampled by the running horse. He hung on, gritting his teeth as the fire built in the strong wind behind him. He glanced back and saw the Indians who were in pursuit suddenly stop, realize a huge prairie fire was heading straight for them and their camp. They turned and ran ahead of the flames, confusion and panic all around.

Colt used his last bit of strength to pull himself up into the saddle and now he hung onto the horse's neck, urging it on. How he wished he had Rascal under him. He had no faith in these fancy thoroughbreds, but he knew if Rascal got a chance to get loose from the Indians' picket line, the little mustang would head back to the fort.

The escaping Cavalry rode away from the roaring flames that had the Comanche temporarily confused. Colt joined them. They moved more slowly than Colt would have wished, but they had wounded men and limping horses and he knew they could not ride much faster. He reined in next to the half-conscious captain, who was reeling in his saddle. Colt only hoped they could make it back to the fort before the officer bled to death. They were expected back at the fort by mid-morning, but when they didn't arrive, the major might send out a search party.

As dawn came over the horizon with great paint splashes of pink and gold, Colt kept looking behind him. If the Comanches were to give pursuit, the tattered Cavalry patrol would be sitting ducks out here on the bald prairie. Every muscle in his body ached and the men riding with him weren't much better off. Some of them were barely conscious and hanging onto their saddles. If one fell, Colt wasn't sure any of them had enough strength to get the man back in his saddle.

He licked his cracked lips and thought of water, cool water, enough to splash and drink and drink and drink. He must not think of that, he thought, keeping his stumbling horse moving forward. It was getting much more difficult to keep the captain in the saddle, and the exhausted horse might go down anytime. Then they would be in worse trouble than before.

A morning breeze came up, but it was not cool. It felt more like a fire against his blistered skin. That made him think of Sarge, and he shook his head to cut off the sound he heard in his brain of screaming. Would he never stop hearing that sound?

The captain groaned again, and Colt patted his shoulder, smelling the blood-soaked shirt the officer wore. "It's okay, sir. We're almost home. We'll be there soon."

He was lying and he knew it. As slow as they were moving and as thirsty as men and horses all were, none of them might make it back, even if the Comanches didn't come after them.

All he could do was keep riding and praying and maybe—maybe—some miracle might happen. It wasn't too likely, but maybe God would be merciful.

Chapter 16

It was just a little after dawn when Hannah fed her little son, and they walked over to open the sutler's store. She had made the tea cakes and cookies for Miss Olivia's tea, and last night, the captain's aunt, under a Cavalry escort, had taken the stage to Galveston to catch a ship back to Boston.

She had barely opened the store and was dusting shelves and putting out new stock when a big, red-faced man in overalls came in the front door and took off his straw hat awkwardly.

"Excuse me, miss, is the owner around?"

She smiled at him. "No, I'm working here now. May I help you?"

"My sons usually bring our stuff in and deal with Mr. Hutton, but you're a heap purtier." He grinned and she noted he was missing a front tooth.

"Well, thank you. You've got something to trade or sell?"

He nodded. "Fresh eggs. I got a purty good-sized farm east of here. My boys and I farm it."

"I'm sure Mr. Hutton will be happy to get fresh

eggs." She came out from behind the counter, wiping her hands on her apron. "You've got sons?"

"Yes, ma'am. Five all growed up. My wife died four years ago."

She took the basket of eggs from him. "I've got a son, too."

Travis came out from behind the counter then, holding his wooden horse and smiling up at the big man.

The big man frowned. "Oh, yeah. We heard about you, ma'am. Everyone has. How are you doin' here at the fort?"

She put the eggs on the counter, went over to scoop up Travis. "All right, I reckon." She wasn't about to admit how hostile the atmosphere had been. "I'll give you a credit for the eggs, Mr.—?"

"Holbrinker. And you are?"

"Mrs. Brownley."

"That'll be good, ma'am, and I'll pick up some stuff I'm about out of, like coffee and tobacco."

She took out the ledger book and checked to see what the owner usually paid for eggs and wrote in a credit for the farmer.

"Don't seem to be many soldiers out this morning." He paused and looked out the front window.

"Most are out on patrol," Hannah answered as he brought his purchases over and she wrote them down. "They're supposed to be in sometime this morning, I hear." She tried not to worry as she wrapped the package.

"Ma'am, you got a husband or a sweetheart with that patrol?"

She shook her head. "No." She couldn't call Colt a sweetheart, not when he was engaged to another woman.

He brightened and gave her a big, shy smile. "I reckon I didn't know what I was missin', sendin' the boys in for supplies. Thank you kindly, ma'am." He took the package and nodded to her, turned toward the door.

"You're welcome," she sighed, her gaze on the big clock hanging over the cash register. "Come back anytime."

"I surely will do that." He nodded to her again and put on his straw hat as he went out the door.

She watched him drive away. He had a good-quality wagon, pulled by two fat horses. His farm must be prospering.

She let Travis play on the floor while she cleaned and dusted shelves, put up new merchandise.

Two women came in, gave her cold looks although she tried to be friendly. They left without buying anything.

Hannah watched the hands of the clock move toward noon. Then she went and looked out the window. The street was empty, save for two soldiers on horseback riding toward the stable. The patrol should be back soon unless they had run into trouble. She didn't even want to think about that.

Hannah put up her CLOSED FOR LUNCH sign, took her little son home, and fixed him a sandwich. She tried to eat a little herself, but she was getting too worried to eat.

She needed to get back to the store. Taking Travis by the hand, they walked toward the store.

"Soldier Colt?" he said.

"Not yet home." She smiled down at him with a cheeriness she didn't feel. Inside the store, she put him down on a pallet behind the counter to nap and decided to clean the big window. It was covered with fingerprints and fly specks. She got a rag and some soapy water and set to work. Olivia rode by in her fine buggy, saw her, scowled, and quickly turned her face away. Hannah sighed. She needed to get away from this place, Olivia had made that very clear, and it was painful being in love with a man who was engaged. Even though he claimed he wasn't, she knew Olivia was determined to have him and her father could decide whether Colt was promoted or not. That was a pretty powerful weapon.

In early afternoon, a soldier came in to buy some tobacco.

"Afternoon, ma'am." He took off his hat.

"Afternoon, soldier. Anyone heard anything of the patrol yet?"

He shook his head. "They're overdue."

How well she knew that. She sold the man the tobacco. "You think they'll be sending out a patrol looking for them?"

"Hard to tell, ma'am. Gossip is if they don't turn up by late afternoon, the major will send out a patrol. Can't afford to send too many and leave the fort open to attack."

"Yes, I know."

Travis woke up as the soldier left, and she played with him a little and let him help her stack boxes of dried apples and dry goods on the lower shelves. The day seemed intolerably long.

She kept looking up at the clock. Something had to be wrong or the patrol would have been back by now. She tried not to picture Colt dead or wounded, or even worse, a captive of the Comanches. That thought made her shudder.

Finally, it was five o'clock. She put up the CLOSED

sign, picked up her child, and started out into the street. A soldier ran down the street yelling, "They're comin'! They're comin'! Somebody find Doc."

Oh my God, something must be terribly wrong. Clutching her little son, Hannah joined the crowd coming out of buildings and gathering near the major's office. She saw Doc come out of the infirmary, his bald head shining, and he was clutching a medical bag.

Holding her breath, she looked toward the gate. A shocked sigh went up around her as the patrol limped in, and a sorry sight it was. Men were reeling in their saddles, covered with dust and blood. Horses looked lathered and exhausted. Hannah did a silent count, realized some were missing. However she only had eyes for one man. Her gaze traveled quickly from one bloody, disheveled man to the next until she saw Colt dismount and drag the unconscious captain from his horse. She cried out with relief and started to run toward him, but then Olivia came out of her father's office and raced to Colt, threw her arms around him.

"Oh, my darling Colton! What happened?"

She couldn't hear any more as people crowded around, helping the soldiers and asking questions. The major strode out of his office, looking grim.

Doc shouldered his way through the crowd. "Get back! Dag nab it, get back! Some of you soldiers, get me some stretchers!"

Hannah stood watching the bloodied Colt help put the captain on a stretcher, and then he went into the major's office with Olivia still hanging onto him and crying uncontrollably.

Doc spotted her in the crowd then. "You, Hannah, I'm going to need all the help I can get."

"Yes, Doc." She handed little Travis over to the Indian servant, Maria, and ran over to help. The captain looked pale and breathed shallowly. Other men were dismounting and limping toward the infirmary.

She forgot about Colt then. These wounded men needed her help, and she followed Doc into the infirmary and helped men into bunks, began to wash the blood and the dirt from strained faces.

"It's all right, soldier. We'll take care of you now."

"Comanches," one whispered as she put a cold rag on his fevered forehead. "Comanches ambushed us, lost a lot of men."

"It's okay. Don't think about that. Here, let me get you some water."

Someone in another bed was calling for water.

Hannah got up and filled a pitcher, went from man to man, giving them water. Most of them drank and drank and drank. One of them called faintly for water and Hannah started toward him, but Doc frowned and shook his head. Then she saw why: belly wound. There was nothing to be done for this soldier; he was barely alive.

Still Hannah wet a cloth and wiped his cracked lips and dirty face, singing softly to him until he closed his eyes and smiled.

"My mama used to sing that song," he whispered, and then he died.

She must not break down; there wasn't time for that luxury. She pulled the sheet up over the boy's tired face and went to help Doc, who was bandaging the captain. She knelt by him and took his hand. His handsome face was almost unrecognizable with dirt and blood.

"My fault," he whispered. "Too green. Led them into an ambush. . . ."

"Don't talk," Doc admonished. "You can give a report later, Captain."

The officer continued to mumble incoherently as Hannah bathed his face and looked over at Doc.

He frowned. "I don't know," he whispered. "He's lost a lot of blood and I don't have much in the way of medical supplies. See to the others, Hannah."

She checked on the ones less hurt, bandaging heads, putting arms in slings. Then she started a pot of hot broth because men were crying out for food.

It took her over an hour before she got the soup around to everyone, and Doc sat down in a chair near her and sighed. "I've done everything I can do. Now it's up to God."

It was turning dark outside. Hannah thought about her child, but there were so many needs here.

The captain moaned again, and seemed to be having a nightmare or delirium. She knelt by his bed and took his hand. "It's all right, Captain. You're safe now."

His curly light hair was plastered to his head with sweat and he quieted. "Sarge," he whispered. "Poor Sarge."

"What about Sarge?" she whispered and wiped his pale face with a cold cloth.

"My fault, mine. Led them into an ambush."

"Take it easy, Captain." She held his hand and stroked his fevered brow.

". . . Lieutenant killed him," he muttered.

She didn't know what he was talking about, but if it were about Colt, it might be important. "Killed who?" she whispered.

"Sarge. He killed Sarge. . . . Indians had him."

She winced. *Oh, my God.* "Just rest, Captain. Think

about Boston; think about going back there where it's cool and there's civilization and codfish dinners and lobsters."

Doc walked over just then, and Hannah looked up at him, a question in her eyes.

Doc sighed and shook his head.

Captain Van Smyth smiled in his sleep and then drifted off again, still holding onto Hannah's hand. Gradually he relaxed and she tucked his hand under the covers. Right now, he looked like a sad, dying little boy with light ringlets of hair plastered against his sweating forehead, and she couldn't hate him.

Just then, the major, Colt, and Olivia came in, Olivia still clutching Colt's arm possessively. Hannah tried not to look at them as they went from bed to bed. She turned to Doc. "Can I go now? My little boy—?"

"Sure, you've worked hard and there's nothing else you can do. I can use some help in the morning, though."

"I'll be here," Hannah promised. She thought she felt Colt's gaze on her, but she didn't look at him as she turned and left the infirmary, went back to her cabin and her child.

She fed Travis and put him to bed, went to bed herself, but she could not sleep. She kept seeing the exhausted, haunted eyes of Colt as he helped lift the captain down from the horse. Something terrible had happened out there on the plains, something too horrible to imagine, but she had lived among the Comanches for almost four years and she knew their savage ways. The captain had told her enough to guess.

It was a hot night and all her windows were open, but there wasn't much breeze. What there was felt like the breath of the devil, hot as a branding iron across her skin and sheer nightdress. In her mind, she saw Colt in Olivia's arms and cursed herself because she could not forget him. He did not belong to her and never had, but she could not forget his smoldering kiss that one night.

It must be almost midnight or even later. The post was quiet. She got up to go into the kitchen and get a dipperful of water. From her window, she saw the lights in the infirmary on. Maybe she should go help Doc. Then she remembered that her child was asleep and she could not leave him alone. She might get a little more air through the house if she opened the front door. She opened it, then realized there was a man sitting in the shadows on her front step. Hannah started to slam the door, but then he turned and the moonlight half lit his strained face.

"Hannah?"

"Colt? What are you doing here?"

He stumbled to his feet, and from here, she could smell the whiskey. "I don't know," he mumbled. "Couldn't sleep. Sarge keeps screamin' in my ears."

She walked out onto the porch and looked at him as he swayed on his feet. He was not only drunk; his green eyes had the glazed look of someone who had survived something too horrible to speak of. "You ought to go to bed," she said gently.

"Can't. Can't sleep. Comanches."

"I know." She took his hand. "Maybe Doc can give you something to help."

He shook his head, swaying on his feet. "Nothin' can help. I killed him. I killed Sarge. They had him."

She realized what was haunting this big man and her heart went out to him. She put her finger to his lips to silence him and nodded that she understood. "It's all right," she whispered. "You're a hero, you got most of the men home."

"We lost a bunch," he muttered and staggered, reaching for the bottle in his pocket. "No hero." He could be in trouble if the guards found him drunk and wandering the post.

"Come in," she whispered. "Come in and I'll make you some coffee."

He shook his head and tipped up his bottle again. "No coffee. Don't want to get sober."

Oh, God, what was she going to do? "Come inside, Lieutenant," she said. "There's not enough whiskey in the whole world to wipe out those memories."

He looked at her again gravely. "You understand." He nodded. "Maybe the only one who understands."

She had to do something. How could she explain to a guard or an outraged Olivia what she was doing out here on the porch in her nightgown with a very drunken Lieutenant Prescott?

"Come inside, Colt," she whispered. "Come inside and we'll talk." She took his arm and maneuvered him through her front door with him leaning on her. He was a big man, and it was all she could do to keep her balance under his weight.

Now that she had him inside, what was she to do with him? Maybe she could fill him with coffee and send him back to his quarters. Maybe she could lay him across her bed and let him sleep it off and get him on his feet and out of here before dawn. She led him toward her bedroom and helped him fall into bed.

He fell heavily and put his hand across his face while she took the bottle from his hand and set it on the dresser. "Sarge," he mumbled. "Sarge. I killed him. They were torturin' him—"

"You didn't mean to." She reached to pull off his dusty boots and her lips trembled at his plight. She lay down next to him, kissed his cheek. "Go to sleep, Colt. Everything will be all right."

"No, never be all right," he mumbled. In the moonlight, she saw tears on his cheeks, and she had never felt such pity and such love before.

She put her arms around him and pulled his face against her breasts, ran her hands through his ebony hair very gently. "It will be all right," she promised, although she had no idea how to comfort a man in such terrible mental anguish. "Sarge would have done the same for you. It takes a brave man to do what you did."

He turned on his side and took her in his arms, crushing her to him, burying his face against her breasts. "Keep me from hearing screams," he begged. "I keep hearin' Comanche drums and screams."

She cuddled his face against her breast and kissed the side of his face and his ear. "All you hear is my heart beating. You're safe, Colt. You're safe now."

He seemed to gradually relax in her arms and drifted off to sleep, but he didn't relax his grip on her. She lay holding him, stroking his hair and murmuring to him, wishing he was hers, knowing they would both be in big trouble if he was found here in her bed. But for tonight, she didn't care. She could pretend he was her man, and she kissed his face and whispered to him as he dropped off into a heavy sleep.

After an hour or so, she grew cramped, but she couldn't move because he had such a death grip on her with his face against her breasts. She could feel the heat of his breath through her thin nightdress, and she had yearnings that she had never had before and it surprised her. She lay holding him, thinking nothing good could ever come of her attraction to the lieutenant. In fact, she stood in the way of his advancement and society marriage. But for now, whatever comfort she could give him, he was welcome to.

Sometime in the middle of the night, he awakened and he was sober. He reached up and touched her face. "Have I been here long?"

"Yes," she whispered and kissed his forehead.

He said nothing else, only turned up his face and kissed her in a slow, gentle way that made her want to pat his cheek and return his kiss and comfort him. He tasted of whiskey, but his mouth was warm and gentle. His big hand went to cover her breast, and she did not object as he pulled her nightdress off her shoulder and kissed there.

Tomorrow, he would again be Olivia's fiancé, but tonight, he was in Hannah's bed and if she could give him comfort, she would because she loved him so.

Colt kissed her breast and she threw her head back and let him do with her as he would. Perhaps a whore would have filled his need, but she did not care to think about that. She only wanted to hold him close and bring him whatever peace she could.

Now his kisses became more intense as he pulled her nightdress low and kissed and caressed both her breasts, fondling them gently while her breath quickened. Two men had bedded her in the past, but all had been hurried, vicious matings, with no tenderness and no love from either of the two. She knew she was getting only a glimpse of what love could be like with the right man, but of course, she would get only this small taste tonight, and tomorrow, he would return to the major's beautiful daughter.

Hannah did not care. She had tonight and maybe only tonight to last her the rest of her life, and maybe, just maybe, years from now when he was celebrating a golden anniversary, he might sip his wine, smile a little, and remember her and this night fondly.

She kissed his ear and breathed into it so that his breath deepened and he kissed and caressed her breasts and stroked her belly until her thighs felt hot and trembling.

He kissed her then again, deep and hot and possessive and she opened her lips and took his tongue and sucked it deep into her mouth while his hands roamed her as if she belonged to him.

"I—I have no right—" he gasped.

"I give you that right," she whispered against his lips and pressed her body against him.

He groaned aloud and then his hand went between her thighs, touching her boldly and she let her thighs fall apart so that his fingers stroked her deeply and made her gasp and arch her back.

Then he was in her embrace, and he hesitated. "Hannah, I can't promise—"

"I don't give a damn," she whispered fiercely. "Give me this night and I'll not ask for more!"

He put himself into her, and she knew at that moment what it meant when it was said two become one, for it seemed like they were one entity with them locked in each other's arms as he rode her very, very gently.

Hannah had never known desire. With both Luther and Spider, she had lain there stoically, gritting her teeth and waiting for them to finish humping and gasping on her, then roll off and turn their backs to sleep. But now she wanted Colt with every fiber of her being, and she felt her sudden wetness as her straining body welcomed his. They were locked in the rhythm of love until she reached a pinnacle she had never known before and began to stiffen and buck wildly under him.

As if he had been awaiting that signal, his rhythm became faster and more intense until almost at the same moment, they were gasping and straining together as if they could not get enough of each other.

And afterward, he pushed her blond curls from her damp forehead and kissed her long and deep. "I'm sorry, Hannah," he murmured. "I had no right—no right."

She embraced him and realized he had dropped off to sleep again, lying on her and in her, and she held him close and kissed his face. Tomorrow he would return to the major's daughter, but Hannah had had one brief glimpse of what love could be like and it would have to be enough to last her the rest of her life.

Sometime toward dawn, she dropped off to sleep, and when she awakened, Colt was gone. Maybe she had only dreamed she had spent the night in his arms, but then she saw the whiskey bottle on the dresser and knew he had been here.

She got up and looked around. There was no note, nothing to show that he cared or that she had been anything more than an eager vessel for his lust. Well, what had she expected? And how could she face him if she met him from now on?

Last night had made her situation even worse. She needed to get away from this fort because now that she knew what it was like to be in Colt's embrace, she couldn't bear to keep seeing him with Olivia on his arm. She'd have to make plans to leave, but how?

Little Travis came toddling in from his room and she leaned over and picked him up and hugged him. Her son needed her, the store needed her, and this morning, Doc's patients needed her. After that, she'd think about how she was going to leave and where she might go. She had to leave Colt while she could still force herself to do it.

Chapter 17

After she fixed breakfast for Travis, she took him with her and walked down to the infirmary to see how the wounded soldiers were faring.

A weary Doc met her as she came in. "The captain died during the night," he said, "but the others seem to be better."

She bit her lip, hoping he had died thinking he was back in Boston with the cool breezes of the Atlantic Ocean blowing on his fevered face. Even now, his aunt was on her way back to Massachusetts, not knowing her darling nephew lay dead in Texas.

"What can I do to help?" She put her son down on the floor to play.

"See if you can get some breakfast in them while I begin to change bandages."

"Sure." She left the door open to Doc's kitchen so she could watch her child playing as she made scrambled eggs and bacon. The eggs made her think about the farmer again. No doubt he could use a cook . . . or a wife. That thought made her shudder. After being in Colt's arms, the thought of sleeping with any other man made her frown.

She took the food around to the grateful soldiers, and then she gathered up Travis and went to unlock and open the store.

Colt woke up with a bad headache that felt like someone pounding a hammer on an iron anvil in a blacksmith's shop. He groaned and tried to remember yesterday. A flood of memories came back, most of which he'd just as soon forget. Some of them he knew he never could. He swung his legs off his bunk and sat up, his head pounding. He'd been so drunk that he couldn't remember a lot of what had happened.

Hannah. Abruptly he remembered being in her bed and in her arms, drunken and remorseful, haunted by what had happen on the patrol. Yet the one thing that he didn't want to forget was how tender she had been to him, how comforted he had felt in her arms. How could he face her today? What could he promise her? He'd behaved like a villain.

There was a knock at the door. He didn't answer it, but the knock was insistent. Cursing, he stumbled over and opened it to a short, thin private who saluted.

Colt returned the salute halfheartedly. "Yes?"

"Begging your pardon, sir, but Miss Murphy requests that you join her and her father for breakfast this morning."

Colt almost moaned aloud. He didn't feel like eating anything, much less making small talk with the senior officer and Olivia. "Tell them I'm indisposed."

"Sir, I've been told not to take no for an answer. The major insists."

He'd have to go. Colt waved the boy away. "Tell them I'll be there in a few minutes."

He slammed the door and went to the washbowl, poured a pitcher of cold water over his head, then plunged his face in the bowl. It only helped a little. Then he stumbled over and looked in the cracked mirror over the dresser. He looked like death warmed over. His head pounded hard, but he had to get himself presentable and show up. What the hell could this be about?

A few minutes later, looking as presentable as he could, he walked to the major's office. The bright sun made his head hurt worse. He squinted against the light and thought he saw Hannah crossing from her cabin to the store, but she either didn't see him or didn't acknowledge him. Well, he couldn't blame her. He had taken advantage of her kindness and warmth last night without offering her any promises in return. He was a bit angry with her for the obligation he now felt.

Colt knocked on the door and took off his hat as Olivia opened it.

She wore a fine lavender dressing gown. "Come in, Colton, dear, we've readied a fine breakfast for the hero."

He came inside. She had set up a dainty table in the office and there was everything imaginable to eat, steak and fried potatoes, a Mexican omelet, a plate of rare strawberries. The sight of all that food made his stomach roil. He saluted the major and swallowed hard.

"Oh, come now, my boy, let's not be formal. This is a friendly breakfast, not army business."

Olivia directed him toward a chair. "Dear, would you like some coffee?"

"Yes, coffee sounds good."

The major looked at him critically "I think like me, you might like a bit of picker-up in your coffee?"

Colt gave him a grateful smile. "That sounds even better."

"Oh, you men and your liquor." Olivia pouted prettily and sat down while waving to her maid, who came forward and poured cups of strong coffee, to which the major added some brandy.

Colt tasted it and sighed. It was strong and hot, and immediately, he felt better. "I'm sorry our patrol was such a defeat, sir."

"Nonsense." The major sipped his own coffee. "You ran into superior forces and got trapped."

Colt didn't say anything and looked into his coffee cup instead. He didn't want to place blame on the badly wounded captain.

"I talked to Captain Van Smyth last night," the major said. "He gave me a full report about how he erred by leading the patrol into the arroyo and that you had protested."

Colt shrugged and sipped his coffee. "He was the superior officer and in charge."

"He died early this morning," the major said, "but not before he told me everything that happened. He said you were a hero and asked that you be given a battlefield promotion to captain."

The captain was dead. Colt felt like he'd been hit hard in the stomach. The whole patrol had been useless and gotten some good men killed.

"Isn't that exciting?" Olivia clapped her hands in glee. "I can already imagine how handsome you'll look in a captain's uniform."

"That was very generous of the captain." Colt put his coffee down and took a deep breath. He hadn't liked

the captain, but the man had behaved bravely the last
few hours of his life. He didn't want to think about the
battle; that made him think of Sarge. "I—I don't think
I deserve praise, sir. All the men acted admirably. I'd
like to request that the captain be awarded a medal for
bravery."

"That will be lovely." Olivia smiled. "His aunt will be
proud."

Colt frowned at her. "The man is dead, Olivia. The
army isn't about promotions and medals."

Her eyebrows went up in shock. "Are you scolding
little old me?"

Oh, God, he hoped she didn't cry. He shook his
head. "Merely pointin' out the truth."

"I know about the sergeant," the major murmured
and gave Colt a sympathetic look.

"What?" Olivia glanced up, but her father shook his
head at her.

"It's nothing that would interest you, my dear."

Colt played with the eggs on his plate to keep from
looking at either one of them. "I don't know that I
want or deserve the promotion," he said.

"But of course you do!" Olivia exclaimed. "I can already see my brave soldier boy moving on up to major,
and colonel and maybe even general. That uniform
would look so impressive in Philadelphia."

"Olivia," Colt began, then stopped. His breakup
with the major's daughter was a sensitive subject and
the major might not know about it yet.

The major glanced at his daughter. "Olivia, dear, it
looks like you've finished your breakfast. Why don't
you and your maid run along so we men can talk?"

Olivia's pretty face broke into a pout. "But, Daddy—"

"I think this is army business from here on out," the major said.

Olivia got up from the table and left in an indignant swish of lavender satin. She slammed the door behind her as she went into their living quarters.

"Now," said the major, "would you like more coffee?"

"Thank you, sir," Colt said and the major poured him more and put another slug of liquor in it.

"You don't seem pleased over the promotion." The major cut up his steak and began to eat.

"To be honest, sir, I haven't quite decided what I want to do. You know my enlistment is almost up."

"Well, Olivia seemed to be sure you were planning on making the army a career."

He couldn't call the major's daughter a liar, nor did he feel comfortable telling him the pair had broken up. It might be impossible to serve on this post and see her every day because it would be so awkward. His mind went to Hannah. Last night had complicated everything. "I haven't decided yet what I'm gonna do, Major."

"Still?" The major smiled at him and leaned over to pat him on the shoulder. "I'll plan on the promotion ceremony for after you reenlist, and you give me your answer day after tomorrow, okay?"

He didn't answer, sensing the silent pressure. He felt suddenly hungry and attacked the steak and potatoes. "Might I ask if Miss Olivia is planning on stayin' at this fort?"

"I think she's bored here, but then my spoiled daughter is easily bored." The major sighed. "If she wangles you a good position in Washington, D.C., being a captain will open a lot of doors for you, especially if we go to war."

"Hmm." Colt gave his attention to his food. Now he

didn't know how he felt about anything. His good sense told him he was lucky the major's beautiful daughter wanted to marry him and take him far away from this hostile country where a man had to kill a friend as a mercy. He thought about Sarge and abruptly stopped eating.

"What's the matter?" the major asked.

"I—I'm not very hungry," Colt said. "And I think I want to go see my men and how they are doin'."

"Sure. That's just what I would expect from you." The major smiled and patted Colt on the shoulder again.

Colt walked out into the blinding sunlight and down to the infirmary. His head still pounded and the light hurt his eyes as he entered. "Hello, Doc. How are the patients?"

"Good, although we lost Captain Van Smyth last night. It was amazing that you managed to get him back here alive, but he was too badly shot-up." He wiped his bald head.

"I heard. I reckon we'll have a funeral today or to-morrow for him, poor devil." Colt sighed.

"Oh, Hannah just came down and fixed the men some breakfast. She's such a thoughtful girl."

"Isn't she though?" Colt remembered last night and how a warm, sympathetic woman had opened her arms and her bed to him. No doubt she had felt terribly sorry for him, that was all. He had acted like such a drunken fool. "I came to see the men."

"Sure." He led the way, and Colt went from bed to bed, shaking hands and thanking them for their service.

In turn, they thanked him for getting them out of the trap alive.

Colt felt awkward accepting their gratitude. He didn't feel like a hero, and he didn't tell them about the promised promotion. Afterward he went outside and sat down on the step, his hands shaking as he rolled a cigarette. He ought to say something to Hannah, but he wasn't sure what to say. Simply "I was a drunken, grief-stricken fool last night and thank you for taking me into your arms and your bed" didn't seem like the proper thing to say. He sat and smoked, unsure what to do.

It was almost noon now and he saw Hannah come out of the store, leading her little boy by the hand. She hesitated when she saw him as if waiting for him to make the first move, and he wasn't sure how. Instead, he nodded to her, and she returned the nod and went on. He wanted to get up and run after her, but he wasn't sure what he would say when he got there. She probably felt used and disappointed.

Anyway he had duties to perform and he went over to the stable to see what kind of shape the horses were in. Too bad he'd lost Rascal. He and the wiry mustang had been partners for many years.

However, even as he stood in the barn talking to a private, he heard a whinny and a bay mustang stuck its head around the door.

"Rascal?" He could hardly believe it as the small horse trotted up to him. It was Rascal all right because the horse nuzzled him affectionately and started sniffing him all over for apples and sugar cubes. Colt threw his arms around the mustang's neck and hugged him. "You little devil, how did you make it all the way back?"

The private grinned. "He sure looks glad to see you, sir."

Colt examined the horse. He was thin and looked exhausted, but otherwise, in good shape. "Private, let's get him some oats and hay and some cool water. He'll be all right in a day or two."

For the first time in days, Colt was actually smiling as he fed and brushed Rascal and left him in the care of the private. Then he went about his other duties.

That night, he decided he must go down and see Hannah and talk this out. However, just as he started out of his quarters in the cool dusk of evening, he was suddenly joined by Olivia. She wore a fine lavender dress and carried a matching parasol.

"There you are, Colton. I've been waiting for you to come out. Want to accompany me on a stroll?"

"As a matter of fact, I was really just goin' over to the stable to see my horse," he lied, hoping against hope the dainty Olivia would think that walk too far.

"Fine, I'd love to walk over to the stable." She smiled up at him.

There was nothing he could do but offer his arm and start walking. As luck would have it, they passed in front of the store about the time Hannah and her little boy came out, walking toward their cabin.

The child gave a glad cry and ran to Colt, throwing his arms around Colt's legs. Without thinking, Colt stooped and scooped him up. "How are you, my little man?"

"Go with us," Travis begged.

Olivia looked annoyed and Colt felt awkward, not sure what to do, but Hannah came over and took the child from his arms. "I'm so sorry. He only wanted to play."

"That's all right," Colt said.

However, Olivia gave her an angry look as the two walked away. "I guess she told you about the tea?"

"Tea? What tea?" Colt was less than interested.

"Never mind. It was a going-away tea for Captain Van Smyth's aunt."

"I reckon the major can send her the captain's medal."

"I thought Mrs. Brownley might have told you—"

"I haven't talked to her," he blurted in confusion, afraid Olivia might have found out he'd been in Hannah's bed.

"It's not important then. I do hope that woman and her son, will be leaving this post soon."

Colt felt his anger rise. "Olivia, they aren't hurting' anyone. You ought to feel sorry for her after what she's been through."

"Oh, that's what I meant, darling." She smiled up at him. "I just thought for her own good—"

"Usually when people say something is 'for your own good,' they are really thinkin' something else."

Are you defending her?" Olivia bristled.

"Yes, maybe I am."

"Well, goodness gracious, I never!" Olivia stuck her nose in the air and strode away.

He should have done that long ago. He watched Olivia turn back toward her quarters, and after a long moment, he went up on the porch of Hannah's cabin and knocked softly.

"Who is it?"

"It's me, Colt."

"Go away. We have nothing to say to each other."

"Not even if I want to apologize?"

"You don't owe me any explanation."

"I'd like to explain anyway."

No answer.

"Hannah?"

"Go back to the major's daughter."

Then the lights went out inside. Colt rapped again, but there was no answer. He went around to her window, but it had been closed. Well, what the hell? He must look like a perfect fool, banging on doors and lurking around windows. A sentry might shoot him as a prowler. Maybe Hannah was right. There was nothing to discuss and anyway, what could he offer her? His good sense told him he should pursue the beautiful and rich Olivia. And yet, he yearned for the arms of the slender Texas girl.

In disgust, he returned to his quarters and spent a sleepless night.

The next morning, there was a somber funeral for Captain Van Smyth that everyone attended. Both Hannah and Olivia acted as if Colt didn't exist, and the major was so busy conducting the ceremony that he didn't seem to notice the situation as they put the plain wooden box in a prairie grave and Hannah scattered a few wildflowers on it. The bugle played a long, mournful dirge, and six soldiers fired rifles over the grave, the shots echoing over the desolate prairie.

After everyone else had left, Colt stood there a few minutes, regretting the senseless loss of life and the fact that the inexperienced officer who hated Texas would spend eternity out here on the lonely vast plains with coyotes howling over his grave. He hadn't loved Texas like Colt did. The captain had been a man of civilization, not a frontiersman who loved a challenge.

As for Sarge, he would get no burial at all. By now the aging son of Ireland's bones were being scattered by animals and the howling winds would blow his ashes to mix with the west Texas sand. They had left two other good men back in that arroyo, too, and there would be no official burial for them, either. Such was the fate of good soldiers.

Colt returned to his quarters to concentrate on writing a report about the battle. Since he was the surviving superior officer, he also added a note to the one the major would write. He didn't tell the aunt all the

terrible details, only that her nephew had died bravely
in the line of duty, and that the Second Cav was proud
of him and would be sending a medal.

It was past noon when Colt heard a horse galloping
madly and rose to go to the door. A small boy raced
onto the post, his bay horse lathered and the boy
bleeding. He fell off the exhausted horse right in front
of Colt's quarters.

Colt ran up and gathered the boy into his arms.
"What's wrong? Who are you?"

The little boy looked up at him, bloody and terrified. ". . . Texas Rangers sent me for help. Comanche
have everyone surrounded at my folks' ranch."

Men were running now from every direction.

"You're okay now, boy. Who are you? Where's the
ranch?"

The boy broke into sobs. "I'm—I'm Jed Schultz.
Our spread is about twenty miles west of here."

Colt handed the injured boy to Doc, who had just
come out of the infirmary. "Someone get the major
and have the bugler sound boots and saddles."

Doc took the child in his arms and grinned. "Come
on, young man. After I bandage you up some, we'll
have some dinner."

The major came out just then, accompanied by
Olivia. Colt ran over to him, saluted. "Sir, Comanches
have attacked the Schultz ranch about twenty miles
west of here. The Texas Rangers are holdin' them off,
but they need help."

In the background, the bugle rang out and others
came running from their quarters.

"Sir," Colt said, "I'd like to mount a patrol."

"Not you," Olivia wailed. "You just got back from a
patrol. Daddy, send someone else."

"Be quiet, Olivia!" the major barked. "Yes, Lieutenant Prescott, get all the men you need and make sure you have plenty of ammo."

Men were pushing up in front of Colt. "Sir, I'd like to volunteer. Take me with you."

"And me, sir!"

"Me too, sir!"

It felt good to know the soldiers had such confidence in him. He picked out a dozen of his best men, and in minutes, the horses were saddled up. Colt ordered Rascal to be left in the stable to recover and took a blood bay thoroughbred.

Now he turned to his new, young sergeant. Someday, he might be as good a soldier as old Sarge. Colt must not think about that now. "Sergeant Clancy, are the troops ready?"

The man saluted. "Yes, sir."

"Then mount the troops."

The order went down the line, echoing in the tense silence as the Cavalry mounted up. Colt stood by his horse, looking around at the gathered crowd. In the background, he saw Hannah's worried face, but she didn't approach. Just before he swung into his saddle, Olivia threw herself into his arms. "Oh, my darling, come home safely to me!"

He managed to pull away from her, but Hannah was already gathering up her little boy and heading for her cabin. Well, there was nothing he could do about that now. She'd have to think what she liked. He had Indians to fight.

He mounted and swung into the lead next to his Tonk scout and Sergeant Clancy.

The air was both hot and tense as the Cavalry trotted out from the fort. Colt turned in his saddle and looked back. A tearful Olivia waved a lace hankie at him. He pretended he didn't see her.

He spoke to his sergeant. "Let's ride as fast as we can without exhaustin' our horses."

"Yes, sir." The young, red-haired man saluted and wheeled his mount to ride back to the ranks.

Yes, the Cavalry tradition continues, Colt thought with a smile. The army would always be there; Sergeant Clancy replacing Sergeant Mulvaney, and soon, a new captain and a new lieutenant, too.

Helluva thing, Colt thought, a dangerous patrol on the very day he had to decide whether to reenlist. He must be a fool to have volunteered. Maybe he should have played it safe and let the major send someone else, but that wasn't the way with Texans. If there was fighting to be done, they only felt comfortable in the middle of it.

Right now, he couldn't think about women or danger. There was a fight ahead and he and his patrol would soon be in the thick of it. He might get killed and not have to make his monumental decision. But right now, the Second Cav was raring for a fight and he only hoped the patrol reached the ranch in time.

Chapter 18

Back at the fort, Hannah had stood in her cabin door and watched with regret as the troops rode out. Suppose Colt didn't come back? She was sorry she hadn't said good-bye to him, but with Olivia making such a melodramatic scene, Hannah knew she had no chance to even approach him. What would she have said anyway? It would be best if Hannah got herself out of the picture completely. She didn't want to ruin Colt's rosy future and promotion. What to do? She hadn't earned enough money for stagecoach fare and had no place to go anyway.

There was nothing left of the view of the Cavalry now but a small cloud of red dust on the distant horizon. Hannah sighed, picked up Travis, and returned to the store.

Olivia came in an hour later, wearing a fine yellow dress.

Hannah took a deep breath. "May I help you?"

The major's daughter looked her up and down, cold scorn in her dark eyes. "The ladies liked the tea cakes." Her voice was grudging.

"Thank you."

Olivia looked around the little store. "I don't suppose you have any French imported soap or scented English talcum?"

"I'm afraid not." Hannah tried to be polite.

"Goodness gracious, it's terrible to have to do without nice things out here on the frontier." The beauty came toward the counter, and before Hannah could stop him, little Travis ran out and smiled up at Olivia, grabbed at the folds of her dress.

Olivia backed away in horror.

Hannah hurried around the counter to pick up the chubby toddler. "I'm sorry."

"Well, you should be." Olivia drew herself up proudly. "Just look, that little half-breed brat has gotten smears on this expensive yellow silk."

"He didn't mean to," Hannah defended her child hotly, "and I'd appreciate it if you'd not call him names."

"Well, that's what he is, everyone says so."

Hannah was facing the shorter girl now, her temper blazing, and without thinking, she slapped Olivia.

Olivia set up a howl and a flood of tears. "You—you harlot, you! I really came in here to tell you to stop chasing after Lieutenant Prescott. Everyone says you're making a spectacle of yourself."

"How dare you!" Hannah advanced on her. "Now get out of here before I show you just how mad a real Texas gal can get!"

Olivia turned and ran out of the store, her sobs echoing all the way down the road.

"Well, Travis, I reckon that finishes it." She set the child on the floor and went behind the counter to get him a cookie. "She'll have us both thrown off the post now. Where are we to go?"

The child merely giggled and accepted the cookie while Hannah leaned against the counter and tried to think. The situation was dire. She should have held her temper, but she would not allow anyone to call her precious child a "half-breed brat."

In less than half an hour, as Hannah was restocking shelves, Mr. Hutton came through the door. He cleared his throat. "Mrs. Brownley, we need to talk."

Her spirits sank. "About what?"

"Uh, I've had some complaints that some customers think you might be stealing." He stared at the floor and stubbed his toe.

"Stealing? That's outrageous. I would never do such a thing."

He looked at her a long moment, and she knew he didn't believe it, either. "I—I've had some complaints—" he began.

"Never mind, Mr. Hutton. I know the major's daughter is behind this. I'll save you the trouble of firing me. I quit." She took off her apron and came out from behind the counter. "You owe me three dollars for my past work."

He came around to the cash register and looked shame-faced. "I'm really sorry."

She felt sudden sympathy for him. "I know. A sutler is sort of beholden to the commanding officer. It's okay."

He handed her some money and she looked at it. He had given her an extra dollar.

"You didn't need to do that." She tried to hand it back, but he shook his head.

"Please take it. It makes me feel better about this."

She stuffed the money in the pocket of her worn dress, picked up her chubby toddler, and started out the door. What in the hell was she going to do now with only a few dollars and Olivia scheming to get her thrown out of the fort? Colt might have been able to help her, but he was gone for the next several days and anyway the young officer surely realized which side his bread was buttered on. She started to walk away from the store just as farmer Holbrinker drove up and reined in with his wagon.

He tipped his hat. "Afternoon, Mrs. Brownley." He smiled, reddened.

Abruptly Hannah knew what to do; she could take care of her little boy in only one way she could think of at the moment: by marrying the big farmer.

Leaving the fort, Colt took his patrol and headed out to the Schultz ranch. He could only hope they were not too late as they galloped west. However, after they had ridden hard and fast for a good part of the afternoon, and their horses were lathered and blowing, he heard shots and shrieks in the distance. Were the Rangers and the family still holding out, or were those victory shouts and even now, the warriors were dancing around tortured bodies?

He signaled his sergeant to halt the patrol, and he and his Tonk scout rode ahead. It would soon be dark, and in the distance, he saw a burning ranch house and silhouetted against the firelight, mounted warriors rode circles around the flaming buildings. Shots rang out and he saw one warrior drop from a paint horse.

He leaned over to the scout. "I make out about twenty warriors. What do you think?"

The scout nodded. "Lieutenant, even with our men, we'll be outnumbered."

"We can't help that." Colt shrugged and wheeled his blowing horse. The two rode back to the patrol. "Sergeant, we make out about twenty warriors. There's whites inside the corral still firing, but we don't know how many are wounded or dead."

"Yes, sir." Sergeant Clancy snapped a salute.

Colt mused a long moment. "If we ride in at a full gallop, with guns blazing, they may think we've got a hundred soldiers and take off."

"Yes, sir. You think we can take 'em by surprise?"

Colt sighed and wiped his sweating face. "We'll have to try. We'll ride through their circle and into the corral. Pass the word."

"Yes, sir." The sergeant saluted and wheeled his sweating horse to ride back along the line of Cavalry.

Colt leaned on his saddle horn, thinking about the attack. They were outnumbered and depending on surprise. His enlistment was up at midnight tonight, and he might not live to make that decision he'd been so concerned with. He chuckled aloud.

The Tonk scout looked startled. "What's so funny?"

"Nothin'," Colt said and nodded to his sergeant as the man returned. "We ready?"

The man saluted. "Yes, sir."

"Then let's go give 'em hell and save those Rangers!" Colt said and nudged his horse into a canter. He was saving his horse's strength. When he got almost within sight of the enemy, he would spur the thoroughbred on and they would come in at a full gallop, guns firing. Automatically he reached for his Colt pistol.

He could see the warriors shrieking and galloping around the corral now, the barn aflame and the house already a blazing pile of glowing embers. The acrid smell of smoke made him choke as he leaned over his mount's neck and galloped forward.

"Now!" he shouted to his men.

Behind him, he heard galloping horses and pistols roared as they rode toward the Comanches. The warriors seemed to hesitate in mid-stride, confused about what was happening. Colt had counted on that pause. As the Comanche milled about, trying to judge the strength and firepower of this new enemy, the Cavalry rode hard directly toward them.

Colt kept shooting, taking a warrior off his horse as the Cavalry broke through the Comanche line of fire and made for the corral. He glanced back over his shoulder and saw his men hugging their horses' necks as they fired, and here and there, a mounted brave fell and the horse took off running.

"The corral!" he shouted back over his shoulder. "The corral!"

The Indians seemed frozen in surprise for maybe a full minute, and the Cavalry charged through their line and made for the corral. If only his horse still had strength enough to clear the wooden fence, Colt thought as he tensed for the jump. He felt the big, blood bay thoroughbred leave the ground, and for only a second, it seemed they hung in midair. As they cleared the corral fence, he got a quick glimpse of tense, white faces of men and one woman crouched behind hay bales and water troughs. Then his horse hit the ground inside the corral and Colt reined in and cleared his saddle, grabbing for his rifle as he landed behind a water trough. He looked up to see his patrol jumping the corral fence, dismounting and taking refuge behind any big object they could find.

The Ranger captain next to him grinned with a

smudged and weary face. "Lieutenant, we sure are glad to see you!"

"Likewise." Colt watched the braves recovering from their surprise and now shouting angrily and circling the barn and corral again.

Colt aimed and took a warrior from his saddle. The Indian hit the ground and rolled over and over. Then he turned his head and said to the Ranger. "Don't be so happy. All I've got is the men you see here."

"No more out there?"

Colt shook his head and grinned. "I thought Rangers always bragged they didn't need any help?"

"In this case, maybe a little," the Ranger admitted as he aimed his rifle at the charging Indians.

A white woman crawled across the dirt to Colt. Her brown hair was loose and blew around her dirty and bloodied face. "My boy? What about my boy?"

"Stay down, ma'am." Colt jerked her behind the water trough. "He's fine. I left him with Doc at the fort."

She sighed and then began to cry. "Then at least he's safe if we don't make it. My older son is lyin' over there."

"I'm sure sorry, ma'am." Colt looked at the lanky youth, probably not sixteen years old, lying crumpled and bloody by the fence.

"Give me a gun," the woman said fiercely. "I'm a pretty good shot."

Colt handed her his extra pistol. "Ma'am, if we get overrun, remember—"

"I know." And now her face was strong and determined. "Save the last bullet just in case."

"We don't aim to lose," said the Ranger captain, and they all commenced firing again.

He heard one of his soldiers shout in pain and looked over to see a private holding his arm.

"How bad is it?" Colt shouted at him.

The sergeant was already tearing away the boy's sleeve. "Sir, I can tie it up and he'll be all right."

It was dark now and it seemed to Colt they had been here a million years, but he knew that couldn't have been. He was bone tired and hot on this summer night. He reached up into the horse trough and got a handful of water, wiped it all over his sweating, dirty face. The loud gunfire seemed to almost deafen him as soldiers and Rangers fired at charging warriors. The bloodied pioneer woman was over by her son's body, firing with grim determination.

Colt wondered if this was a suicide mission. Was he going to be remembered as the officer responsible for leading a whole patrol to its death? His mind went to Hannah, and he smiled, wishing he were in the refuge of her tender embrace. He made a decision then about what he was going to do if he got out of this alive.

Now they were being showered with flaming arrows, men dipping grain sacks into the horse troughs to beat the fires out. The water wouldn't last much longer, Colt knew, and what's worse, he was sure the warriors knew that also.

If only he could take down a Comanche leader, the Indians would think it was bad medicine and retreat. He studied the line of braves galloping around the corral. Yes, that big one with the painted face was the war party leader. If he could only take him out.

A call came down the line of soldiers and Rangers. "Low on ammo. Anyone got extra?"

Of course nobody did. At least the war party hadn't figured that out yet. He didn't have a handful of shells left himself. He had to get that leader. Even as he and the fierce Comanches' gazes locked, the warrior came riding right toward him, and Colt recognized the man even as the brave rode straight for the corral fence. It was Bloody Hand, one of the cruelest and most skilled of the warriors.

He had evidently recognized Colt, too, because he grinned without humor, showing white teeth in a dark, scarlet painted face as his white horse cleared the fence. Bloody Hand jumped from his horse, dagger in hand, and landed on Colt.

"Ha! Young Stallion!" he shouted in Comanche. "I come to cut your heart out!"

"Not yet!" Colt yelled back as the two men grappled. He grabbed the man's knife hand to keep from being stabbed, and now they rolled over and over in the dust of the corral. Colt knew the soldiers and Rangers were watching helplessly, afraid to fire for fear of hitting Colt.

He knew that Bloody Hand was a strong and ruthless fighter and would give his life to take Colt's. If only he could get that knife away from the warrior, but it was all he could do to hang onto the man's wrist as they scuffled and fought.

Now Bloody Hand came up on top, and he grinned down at Colt as he struggled to bring the knife lower. Colt could see the blade reflecting light from the burning barn. He fought with all his strength to get out from under the Comanche, but the man was so big and strong.

"Now you die!" Bloody Hand shrieked in Comanche as he brought the blade down toward Colt's throat.

There was the sudden bark of a pistol and for a split second, Bloody Hand froze in midair, wavering and looking astounded, and then the knife tumbled from his dead fingers and he fell across Colt's body. Colt shoved him aside and staggered to his knees, looking around.

The dusty, determined ranch wife nodded as she lowered her smoking pistol. "That's for my dead boy," she said.

Colt noticed that word began spreading through the warriors that their leader had been killed. They broke their circle and hesitated uncertainly and then began to move away in twos and threes, riding away from the ranch, chanting a mourning cry. It seemed almost unbelievable.

"Cease fire!" Colt ordered and the word went down the line of Cavalry.

The Ranger captain pushed his Stetson back, leaned against the bale of hay, and grinned. "Well, I'll be damned. Boys, we'll get to see the dawn after all."

A cheer went up from the troops and the handful of Rangers as the Comanche rode away. Colt stood up and looked around. There was nothing left of the house or the barn except the corral.

Mrs. Schultz and her husband had gone over to their dead son. The woman held the boy close and sobbed, rocking back and forth. The grizzled rancher had tears in his eyes as he tried to comfort her.

Colt said to his sergeant, "Sergeant, I think a big pot of coffee and some grub is in order, and at dawn, we've got to do a funeral. Have some troopers start dousin' these fires and see if anything can be saved."

The sergeant saluted. "Yes, sir. We'll see to it."

Colt stood up and walked over to the grieving ranch family. "Ma'am, we'll have some coffee and food in a minute, and then we'll do a service for your son at dawn."

She wiped her eyes on her apron. "Yes, we'll bury him right here on the ranch. Nate loved this place."

The Ranger captain had joined them and looked around. "You folks don't have much left. You gonna stay?"

The rancher looked up at him, anger on his weary face. "You're damned right. This is our home. We've shed blood on this dirt. We ain't gonna turn tail and run. No, sirree. We'll start over. Some of the other settlers will help us."

Colt said, "It's the Comanches' home, too." For a long moment, he felt sorry for the Indians. They were being pushed off the land they had held forever and were fighting to hold on to it. It was all they knew.

The Ranger nodded as he and Colt walked back to their men. "In a way, I almost pity the Indians. They can't win, but they won't stop fightin'."

Colt paused and rolled a cigarette. "You got to admire them for that. They probably know they can't win, but they want to live free, like every other human bein'. How would you like to live penned up on a reservation?"

"I'm a Texan, born and bred." The Ranger captain leaned on the fence. "True Texans live free or die tryin'."

Colt reached over, picked up a burning piece of wood from the barn, and lit his smoke. "Ain't that the truth?"

It was a long night as the men treated their wounded and fought the fires.

The summer sky was giving birth to the first bloody rays of dawn in the east as the troopers finished putting the fires out and ate their grub. Colt looked out across the endless prairie and then at his men and the brave ranch couple waiting to bury their son. He was suddenly both weary and sad. His sergeant handed him and the Ranger captain tin cups of coffee.

Colt took his gratefully. "Damn, that's good. The men find anything worth savin'?"

"Not much. Part of the barn, is all."

Colt looked at the couple laying out their son and wiping his smudged and bloody face. "Give those folks a clean shirt. It ain't right to bury that boy in dirty clothes. And make sure those people get some food and any of our extra supplies."

"Yes, sir."

"And catch some of those stray Indian ponies. This family will need livestock and especially ammunition to start over."

"They gonna stay?" The young sergeant looked surprised. "They don't have a thing left—it's all burned up."

Colt nodded and sipped his coffee. "They're Texans, they'll stay and rebuild. People in the Lone Star State have grit. They don't give up land they've spilled sweat and blood into."

"Yes, sir." The sergeant saluted and walked away.

Colt watched the coming sunrise as he smoked, and then he laughed.

The Ranger captain asked, "What's so funny?"

"My enlistment ran out at midnight last night. I'm not a U.S. Cavalry lieutenant anymore."

"We could use some men in the Rangers," the captain said.

"I know." Colt sipped his coffee. "But the Cavalry needs men, too, and there's a woman back at the post."

The captain leaned against the fence and nodded. "The major's daughter? I hear she's the most beautiful girl in Texas and rich besides. Good catch."

"I reckon," Colt said, picturing the lovely, genteel Olivia in his mind. The captain was right. Any man in his right mind would be lucky to marry her and share her bed and her fortune.

"Even if I'm not a Cavalry officer, I reckon I am until I get these soldiers back to the fort and reenlist."

"They say once a soldier, always a soldier," the captain said.

Colt thought a moment, and then he knew what he was going to do. Maybe he had known all along and just hadn't admitted it to himself. He tossed away his smoke and called out to the sergeant. "Sergeant Clancy, let's get gathered up and then help these people bury their son before we leave."

"Yes, sir."

Colt smiled and watched the sunrise. It was going to be a typical Texas summer day, a light breeze, a little heat, and then a dusty ride back to the fort to report to the major.

It was a sad, makeshift funeral. There was no wood left that hadn't been burned, so they couldn't build a coffin. Instead they washed the boy's body, put a clean shirt on him and combed his hair before they wrapped him in an army blanket. His mother leaned over and kissed his cheek before the troopers lowered him into a hole they had dug.

The parents stepped forward and threw a handful of soil into the hole, and then the soldiers filled in the rest. Now the Ranger captain gestured for everyone to surround the grave and they all took their hats off and bowed their heads.

He began to speak in a soft Texas drawl. "God, do look down upon us this hot June mornin' and see that we are buryin' young Nate Schultz. He had hardly begun to live afore his life was took as he helped his folks defend their ranch. He was a brave son of Texas and we hope you've saved a special place for him where the grass and the wildflowers are always tall and the wind blows free, and there's no pain or sweat or worry anymore. Havin' always lived in Texas, heaven will have to be extra nice to live up to the Lone Star State. Don't disappoint Nate, please. Then look after the rest of us as we try to make it through life and tame this wild country. We're only men, after all, and sinful, but we are Texans, so that should count for something in your Big Book. Amen."

A chorus of amens from the others echoed across the silent landscape.

A hawk flew over just then and soared upward, calling in a sound that echoed across the plains.

"It's a sign," said the old rancher somberly. "Nate is flyin' free and out of pain forever now."

The mother tried to hold back her tears as a Ranger stepped forward and began to play "Amazing Grace" on his harmonica.

When the last haunting notes died away, a soldier held out a small, ragged Texas flag he had pulled from the burning house. He hung it from a burnt stick of barn wood and placed it on the grave where it flapped in the wind.

"It don't seem right not to have flowers," Colt said and looked around. "Sergeant, I see a claret cup cactus over on that rise. Dig it up and replant it here on the young man's grave, will you?"

"Yes, sir."

The woman took a deep breath and approached Colt. "Thank you for comin', Lieutenant. Thank you, too, Captain." She held out trembling hands to Colt and the Ranger.

Colt took her hand and squeezed it. It was work-worn and callused, just like Hannah's.

"We're just sorry we couldn't do more, ma'am. We'll have some soldiers bring your younger boy back to you when we reach the fort." He couldn't help but think of a small boy that he had grown to love over the past few weeks.

Colt heard a bark and a whining sound and a non-descript brown dog sniffed the fresh grave and then laid down upon it.

The old rancher said, "That's Shep, Nate's dog."

"Poor Shep." Colt nodded. "He don't understand."

The woman put her chin in the air, and her voice, when she spoke, was as stubborn as her lined face. "We'll be all right, Lieutenant. Every time I think about givin' up, I'll look out and see that grave and remember we're here to stay. We're Texans."

Colt sighed and nodded to the Ranger captain, then turned to the sergeant. "Sergeant Clancy, let's see if the men can salvage anything else from the fire for these folks and do whatever you can to help them. After that, we'll go. I got things to do back at the fort."

Chapter 19

Hannah was up with the sunrise, looking out the window and hoping the troops were all right. With any luck, they'd be back at the fort maybe around noon. She sighed, thinking she intended to be gone by then, one way or another. Olivia was right; Colt had a great future ahead of him if he married the high-class beauty. What could Hannah offer him?

Nothing but her love, and she wasn't even certain he wanted that. She smiled ruefully. Maybe she had only been convenient for him the other night.

Travis woke up just then, and she went into the kitchen and fixed her child some scrambled eggs. She had counted her money over and over, but the amount didn't change. She had eleven dollars and thirty-two cents. That wouldn't go very far or even buy a stage ticket.

She went to the front door and opened it. The day was going to be a typical Texas summer morning, hot and fair. Across and down at the sutler's store, she saw the farmer pulling up in his wagon. Taking a deep breath, she took Travis by the hand and walked over, intercepting him. Maybe she could get a ride to the next town.

"Hello, there."

He grinned. "I was hopin' to see you."

She shrugged. "I don't work here anymore."

"Oh?" He looked disappointed.

"I'm thinking of leaving the fort, maybe going to a town." She smiled up at him as Travis played in the dirt at her feet.

He pushed his hat back. "Long way to the next town, Mrs. Brownley, maybe twenty miles to the east."

"Maybe I can hitch a ride with you?"

"What are you gonna do when you get there?" He leaned against his wagon.

"Whatever I can to support my child," she said. "Scrub spittoons at a saloon, clean houses, I'm not sure."

He took off his straw hat and fumbled with the brim. She noticed his hair was thinning and his bald head was freckled. "Ma'am," he began awkwardly, "I know this ain't the proper way to go about this, but since I'm needin' a wife and you're on your own, maybe, well, maybe we might get hitched."

"What? I don't know, Mr. Holbrinker. I barely know you."

"I know, but we could get to know each other." He grinned down at her. "I need someone who can cook and clean and you need a home. Maybe we could make it work, and maybe you could grow to at least like me."

"It wouldn't be fair to you. If you must know, I'm in love with someone else." She half turned away, think-ing about spending the rest of her life sleeping with a man who wanted sex from her, a man she did not love.

She'd had a loveless marriage, and then there had been the cruel Spider. There had only been one man in her life who she loved with all her heart and for his own good, she needed to put Colt out of her mind and let him go his own way.

"Well, ma'am, that hombre don't seem to be lookin' after you, and I sure would. I got a big farm."

She looked down at Travis playing in the dirt. She had to put her own desires aside and think about her child and his future. "My little boy—" she began.

"Why, shucks, ma'am, I'd treat him like my own. I got five grown sons, you know. What do you say?"

She had to be truthful with him. "It doesn't bother you that I don't love you?"

"That's fine, ma'am. Maybe you can learn to. You'd share my bed, wouldn't you? Give me a husband's rights?"

Hannah winced at the thought, but if she married him, he would have a legal right to her body. She looked up at the sun. Colt would be back at the fort in a few hours and if she saw him again, she knew she would weaken and not be able to leave him. "Maybe you are right. Maybe we can make this work. Can you find a preacher and let's get this done?"

He grinned, showing his snaggled teeth. "What's the hurry, ma'am?"

She dare not tell him. "I just make quick decisions," she said. "You get a preacher and I'll gather up my things. We can be out of here before one o'clock."

"You betcha!" He grabbed her and gave her a quick smack on the lips. He tasted of chewing tobacco and smelled like sweat.

She tried not to recoil. She had to think of Travis.

"Where do you want to have the ceremony?"

"How about down by the river?" she said and fought not to tear up. "I'll invite Doc and a few people so we'll have witnesses. I'll meet you down there about noon."

"Yes, ma'am." He seemed to forget about the delivery he had come for, jumped in his wagon, and took off at a fast trot.

Hannah stared after him. She regretted her decision almost immediately, but what else was she to do? The farmer was rich and he had promised to take care of her little boy, and that was most important to her—more important than her own happiness. She would be married and gone before Colt ever got back to the fort.

She grabbed Travis's hand and started to her small cabin. She didn't have much stuff to collect; she could wrap it up in a knapsack. Olivia's maid would help her get herself dressed for the wedding. Doc might try to talk her out of it, but she was determined to leave Colt behind forever. She knew she could not say no to him if he came to her bed again, and it was morally not right to sleep with another woman's man. She went into her cabin and began to get her things together.

Back at the Schultz's burned-out ranch, Colt's troopers and the Texas Rangers were almost ready to ride out.

Mrs. Schultz nodded and smiled at the bright red cactus now planted on her son's grave. "When we rebuild the ranch house, I'll be able to look out and see it bloom," she said and wiped tears away with her apron.

The Texas Ranger pushed his hat back. "I sure am sorry we didn't get here in time to save him. Maybe you ought to think about movin' into town?"

The old father shook his head. "We're like other Texans. We've shed blood to hold this land, and we ain't leavin'. The Injuns will just have to give way."

Colt nodded sympathetically. "I understand. It is their land, too, and they'll fight for it."

The old man set his jaw. "But we will not be moved. Even if they kill us, there'll be more of us. This is good land for ranching and there's more of us comin' all the time. We intend to stay, even if we have to live in a soddie for a while."

Colt and the Ranger captain walked away. The Ranger got his makin's from his shirt pocket. "Them's tough people, they got grit. They'll stay all right."

Colt paused and reached to roll a cigarette. "You're right about that. Kinda sad, really, but there's no way Comanches and farmers can live side by side peacefully."

He was bone tired as he lit his cigarette and a private brought him and the captain tin cups of strong coffee.

"Come to think of it"—he grinned as he sipped the coffee—"I shouldn't even be givin' them orders. I'm a civilian as of last midnight."

The Ranger leaned on the fence and sipped his coffee. "You gonna reenlist?"

"That's the plan," Colt said. "The major's beautiful daughter wants to marry me. She's got a rich, influential family, too."

The captain nodded knowingly. "Looks like you got your future made. You could end up as a general."

"I reckon." Colt took off his hat and watched the rising sun as he smoked. "You think there's a Civil War comin'?"

The captain nodded. "Everyone says so."

"Then the Cavalry will be pullin' out of Texas, and

the Rangers will have to hold off the Comanches alone."

"I thought about that; ain't lookin' forward to it." The captain smoked and stared off into the distance. "We're stretched purty thin already. We could use some good men like you. Of course, you'd be a fool to turn down the opportunity you got back at the fort."

"Wouldn't I though?" Colt watched his men cleaning up the last fires, burying the dead warriors. "Well, I got to get back. The major and Olivia will be wonderin' where I am."

The captain extended a hand and they shook. "You ever change your mind, I'm in Austin. Otherwise, maybe we'll meet again after the war we both know is comin'."

"You're a good man, Captain. I'm glad my troops were able to help."

The two separated and Colt watched the Rangers mount up and ride out; then he called to his sergeant. "Sergeant, assemble the troops. Our job here is done. If we hurry, we might be back at the fort before noon."

The sergeant saluted. "Beggin' your pardon, sir. The men and the horses are both bone tired. I think they'd appreciate a slow ride back."

Colt shrugged. There was no reason to rush, he had finally made his decision and he wasn't going to change it now. "You're right, Sergeant Clancy. If we've done whatever we can to assist the Schultzes, we'll leave."

He strode over to the campfire and poured himself another cup of coffee, watched the troopers helping the family gather up whatever was not burned or destroyed; then he walked over and shook the old man's hand. "You sure you folks don't want to move back to the fort for a while?"

The old man shook his head. "No, we'll start rebuilding this morning. We'll come to the fort with a wagon in the next couple of days for supplies and to pick up our son. We'll build this ranch so he'll have a future."

"I understand." Colt touched his fingers against the brim of his hat by way of farewell and walked to his horse. "Sergeant, mount the troops."

The sergeant saluted. "Yes, sir." He turned to the soldiers. "Prepare to mount. Mount."

The Cavalry soldiers swung into their saddles and the patrol started away from the ranch. The sergeant was right, Colt thought as they turned back toward the fort. There was no reason to hurry; the horses and the men were tired. They'd get there a little before noon. As he rode, he thought about the decisions facing him and the two women who loved him. Then he smiled, knowing what he was going to do.

Colt led his weary Cavalry troop back through the fort gates a little before noon, dismounted, handed his horse over to a trooper, and went inside to report to the major.

"Sir, Lieutenant Prescott reporting in," he saluted.

"At last, Colt. Sit down, have a drink and report." The major grinned and poured two tumblers of whiskey. Colt took the drink and settled down in the opposite chair, slapping at the dust on his blue uniform. Quickly, he told about the fight with the Comanches.

"Good job." The major grinned and lit his pipe.

Colt took a deep breath. "Sir, you know my enlistment was up at midnight last night."

"I thought we had that settled. You're going to reenlist and be promoted to captain. With a war coming—"

"Beggin' your pardon, sir, I don't think I am."

"What? Saint Mary's blood." The major sat bolt upright. "But you've been in the army for years—"

"Yes, sir, but I know if a war starts, the Cavalry will be pullin' out of Texas and the Rangers can't handle the Comanches alone. They'll be desperate for men."

The major shook his gray head. "So you'd pass up all the promotions and better pay to stay here in Texas and fight Indians?"

"Texas will need me, sir, and I'm first and foremost a son of Texas."

The major sighed and sipped his drink. "All right, I don't like your decision, but I admire you for it. In the meantime, what is Olivia going to say? You know she doesn't like Texas."

Colt chewed his lip. "I'm going to go see her next. She's a beautiful girl, sir. Any man would be proud and pleased to marry her, but I'm not sure we could make a go of it. Anyway, another woman has taken my heart."

The major nodded knowingly. "You know, Colt, we're more alike than you realize. I was in the same spot more than twenty years ago. I was a poor Irish immigrant lad, but a handsome one, driving a coal wagon to the De Ville family mansion. There was a beautiful daughter and she fell in love with me. I turned my back on a poor Irish lass and married the rich beauty and I've regretted it ever since."

"Olivia's mother?" Colt asked.

The other nodded. "Any man who marries money earns it." He shrugged. "So we stay in different parts of the country. Unfortunately, my daughter is just like her mother, vain, spoiled, and shallow, but she'll get by on her beauty."

"I'm sorry I don't want to marry her." Colt leaned back in his chair.

"I don't blame you," the major sighed. "You've got more gumption than I had." He leaned across the desk and offered his hand and the two shook. "Best of luck to you in the future. I'll take care of the paperwork and you send me word where to send your last pay."

Colt shook his hand and stood up, put down his glass. "Thank you, sir. And now I'll go tell Olivia."

"There'll be a scene," the major warned. "My daughter is used to getting what she wants."

"But not this time," Colt promised and went out.

First he walked to his quarters and changed into jeans, a denim shirt, and cowboy boots; then he walked to the barn and saddled up Rascal. Now the part he dreaded. He didn't really want to hurt the girl, but he was following his heart, not his brain, with this decision.

He rode over and tied up Rascal at the hitching post, knocked on the door at the major's quarters.

Olivia answered. "Oh, Colton." She threw her arms around him. "I've been so worried about you." Then she stepped back and stared. "Why are you out of uniform?"

Colt took a deep breath and looked down at her. "Olivia, I've decided not to reenlist. I've already talked to your father. He'll do the necessary paperwork."

She shook her head. "No, you can't do this. Why, I've got our lives all planned out, the big wedding in Philadelphia, the posh post in Washington, the—"

"I'm sorry, Olivia. I'm not gonna marry you. I apologize for behavin' like a cad, but I just don't think we could make a marriage work. My plans and your plans don't seem to mesh."

Now her beautiful face went livid. "How dare you?

You can't just break our engagement like this, not when I had such plans for us—"

"I'm sorry if I've hurt you, Olivia, but I'd like to make my own plans and mine include stayin' in Texas. I couldn't be happy anyplace else."

"I'll be the laughingstock of the fort—"

"Tell everyone you broke the engagement. I won't dispute it."

About that time, he heard a door open in the back and Olivia's maid called, "Ma'am, I'm returned from the wedding, but—"

"Weddin'? What weddin'?" Colt asked.

Olivia smiled most evilly. "Oh, didn't you know? Mrs. Brownley got married down by the river about noon and—"

Colt didn't hear the rest. He turned and ran out the door, swung up on Rascal's back, and took off at a gallop for the river. He could only hope he wasn't too late. He intended to marry Hannah himself.

He galloped up to see a handful of people including a big fat farmer in an ill-fitting suit standing talking to what must be a preacher, judging from his somber black suit. Doc stood nearby, visiting with a trooper.

Colt reined in and dismounted, ran up to Doc. "Where is she? Did she get married?"

The farmer turned toward him, his face red and angry. "That slutty bitch! She changed her mind, and here I was ready to overlook her sleepin' with an Injun buck and take in her half-breed kid, too."

Colt hit him then, knocking him backward into the dirt.

Doc grabbed his arm. "Easy there, Colt. Say, what happened to your uniform?"

"Never mind." Colt shook his hand off, rubbing his knuckles. "I decided not to reenlist. Where's Hannah?"

Doc grinned at him and shrugged. "You heard the man. She decided not to marry him, even though he has a big farm. She said the only man she'd ever love was marrying the major's daughter, so she's on her own and headed east to the nearest town."

Colt looked around. "On foot?"

Doc nodded. "She's a stubborn one, a real Texas gal. It's about twenty miles, but she says she and Travis will walk all night if she has to."

"Now just what the hell will she do there?" Colt griped.

"Oh, clean houses, work as a cook in a café, whatever she has to." Doc winked at him. "If you hurry, you might catch up with her. She's only been gone about fifteen minutes."

Colt needed no more urging. He shook Doc's hand. "Good-bye, Doc. Maybe we'll meet again sometime. I'm aimin' to get a little ranch, maybe join the Rangers."

"Quit jawing and get riding," Doc said.

Nodding, Colt swung up in the saddle; then he turned and headed for the road that led away from the fort. After riding about ten minutes, he saw a woman's figure walking ahead of him. She was tall and slender, and her yellow hair shone in the sun. She carried her head high and proud, and she walked with a stubborn stride. In one hand she carried a small bundle. With the other, she held onto the hand of a small, dark boy, and he in turn, carried a small wooden horse dangling from chubby fingers.

Colt's heart swelled and his eyes misted. Hannah's life had not been easy, but her spirit would never be broken because she had courage and grit like every Texas girl.

He rode up beside her. "Where do you think you're goin'?"

She glanced up at him and kept walking, straight and proud. "If it's any of your business, Lieutenant, I'm going to the next town and see if I can find a job."

He kept riding next to her. "You passed up a good offer back there. I understand that farmer has a big place, plenty of money."

"I didn't love him so it wouldn't be fair to him. Besides I had a feeling he wouldn't be good to Travis."

He dismounted and walked alongside her, leading Rascal. "You and Travis can't walk twenty miles to the next town."

"I'm a Texas girl, born and bred. Just watch me."

"Damn it, will you stop walkin'?" He confronted her and for the first time, she seemed to notice he was dressed like an ordinary cowboy.

"What—?"

"I didn't reenlist." He shrugged. "I've got some money saved so I thought I'd buy a little spread of my own, and then if war comes, I'll join the Rangers. They're gonna need all the help they can get."

"Congratulations, but I don't think the major's daughter will like ranching."

"I don't give a damn what she likes." Colt leaned over and picked up Travis.

The little boy hugged his neck with glee. "Colt," he laughed. "Colt."

Colt kissed the child on the forehead and put him on Rascal's back, then turned to Hannah. "At least let me give you a ride to the next town."

She frowned. "We don't need your help. Your fiancée isn't going to be happy to find you out here."

"Hannah, I told you I broke up with Olivia. She wouldn't accept it, but this time she'll have to because I'm in love with somebody else."

Her pale blue eyes grew wide. "You're turning your back on an easy life." `

He shrugged. "You just did the same thing. Would you settle for a small ranch with a Texan who hasn't got much to offer?"

For a moment, it appeared she could not speak. "Are you asking me—?"

"I'm not good at this, because I never did it before, but I want to marry you and look after you and Travis. There's bound to be a preacher in the next town. What do you say?"

She looked up at him and she couldn't help it, the tears began to build. She had not let herself be vulnerable in all these years, but she loved this man so.

"Did I make you unhappy?" His tanned face grew anxious. "Hannah, I love you, I wouldn't do anything to make you cry."

"You just did," she sobbed and, abruptly, he held out his arms. She went into them and he held her tightly and kissed her hair while she wept against his broad shoulder. All these years and now she had finally found a man she could depend on, who would always love and defend her and she let herself be vulnerable. Slipping her arms around his neck, she held him tightly as she unleashed a flood of tears.

She heard Travis say. "Why is Mama crying?"

And Colt said gently. "I reckon she's happy, Travis. Women are funny that way. You want to be my son from now on?"

"Yes, daddy Colt."

Hannah pulled away from Colt and looked up at him through a blur of tears. "You sure you want to do this?"

"Damned sure!" And he pulled her to him again and kissed her like she had never been kissed before, his mouth warm and possessive on hers, his big frame protecting her from anything that might ever harm her. She was no longer on her own, a slender woman fighting the whole world. She now had a protector and a partner, and his embracc held all the promises of a warm, wonderful life ahead.

Colt lifted her up on Rascal's back. "Honey, I'll buy us another horse at the next ranch we pass and once we get to town, we'll get married. I aim to buy a nice spread somewhere."

"In Texas?" she asked, smiling down at him as they started off with Rascal plodding along.

"Of course in Texas." He winked up at her as he led Rascal down the road. "We're Texans and always will be! Isn't that true, Travis?" He looked back at his new son.

"True," lisped the little boy, who grinned, holding tightly to his mother and the precious toy horse as the trio crossed over the ridge and into the bright future ahead.

Fans of Western historical romances won't want to miss any books in Georgina Gentry's exciting new series, THE TEXANS. Read on for samples of:

DIABLO
and
RIO,

DIABLO

On a northbound train to Wyoming, early April 1892

Diablo paused between the swaying cars, looking through the door to see who was inside before he entered. No gunfighter worth his bullets would enter an area without checking out the lay of the land, especially since this car was full of Texas gunfighters, all hired killers like himself.

He had come a long way since Trace Durango had found him fifteen years ago when he was a Santee slave known as He Not Worthy of a Name. Well, he had earned a name now, and when men heard it, they turned pale and backed down from the big, half-breed gunfighter with the scarred face. He dressed all in black, from his Stetson down to his soft, knee-high moccasins. The superstitious peasants along the Rio Grande had given him the name: Diablo, the devil. It suited him just fine.

Now finally he was headed north to take care of unfinished business. He had waited a long, long time for this, and all these years he had been planning and perfecting his aim. Though the Wyoming Stock Growers Association was paying exorbitant money to bring this trainload of killers north, the money did not interest Diablo. What interested him was vengeance, and now, finally, he would have it. He was no longer the small and weak half-breed slave. No, now he had a name and was respected and feared throughout the West. Diablo had gained a reputation as a fast, deadly gunman.

Trace Durango had done well in teaching him to use a Colt, and he had used it time and time again in range wars and saloon showdowns. His gun was for hire, and he had fought side by side with men like Billy the Kid. Billy had been dead more than ten years now. Many of the others were dead too, before they reached middle age. In the end, that would probably be his fate, but for now, all that mattered was finishing his business with four men. His biggest fear was that they might now be dead and no longer able to face a showdown.

Diablo swung open the door and stood there watching the others inside. The shades had been ordered drawn, and the light in the swaying car was dim. Most of the men turned to stare at him, unsmiling, cigar smoke swirling above their heads. They did not nod a welcome, and he had expected none. These were hired pistoleros like himself, Texas gunfighters, on a special train to Wyoming where a range war was about to start. An hombre named Frank Canton had come down to hire twenty-five of the best, offering great pay and bonuses for every rustler and nester killed.

The train swayed, and the tracks made a rhythmic click-clack as conversation in the car ceased. All the men were looking at him, but he stared only at the men in the first row of seats. Diablo liked to have his back against the wall. The two men withered under his frown and hurriedly got up and retreated down the car. Diablo took the space they had vacated as if it were his right.

"Who in the hell is that half-breed?" The growling voice drifted toward him.

"Shh! Be quiet, Buck; that's Diablo. You don't want to make him mad."

"The Diablo?" Now he sounded impressed.

"There's only one," said the other.

"He don't look like so much."

"You challenge him, you'll find out."

"Maybe I'll just do that when we hit Wyoming."

Diablo sighed, pulled his black Stetson down over his eyes, and leaned back against the scarlet horsehair cushions, then opened the shade, stared out the window at the passing landscape. Quickly he averted his eyes, not wanting to see the reflection of his scarred face, and closed the shade again.

He probably didn't look like much to the others, who sported noisy, big spurs, fancy silver conchos and pistols, and boots of the best leathers in bright colors. Diablo dressed in the color of the night, and he wore moccasins, the better to move silently against an enemy without them knowing he was coming. Silver conchos and pistols had a way of reflecting light that an enemy could see for a long way. He not only moved silently, but his appearance was as black as a thunderstorm, with no bit of reflected light to give him away.

Now he stuck a slender cigarillo between his lips, but he did not light it. He never lit them. The flash of a match or the slightest scent of tobacco smoke would also give a man away, and he had learned from the Santee Sioux that he must move as silently as a spirit—kill and be gone. No wonder the Mexicans averted their eyes and crossed themselves as he rode past.

* * *

Hours later, Diablo decided he would have a drink and moved toward the club car. Balancing lightly in his moccasins as the train rumbled and click-clacked along the rails, he was acutely aware of each man he passed, sensing whether each was a threat or not. One or two eyed him, hands fidgeting nervously, as if thinking of being the one who killed the infamous Diablo, but each seemed to think twice and let him pass unchallenged.

In the club car, five men hunched over a table playing cards. Diablo paused in the doorway, looking them over. Then slowly the conversation ceased as each turned to look at him.

"Good God, look at his face!" the big, unshaven one muttered. He had red hair, and freckles showed through the balding spots.

"Be quiet, Buck," warned a pudgy one with missing teeth, and a greasy ponytail of brown hair. "You want to die before you ever get to Wyoming?"

"But he looks like a monster."

Nobody else said anything, waiting to see if the newcomer would take offense, but Diablo pretended he had not heard the remark. If he killed or challenged everyone who commented on his scarred face, his six gun would never be in its holster. Instead, he walked softly to the small bar and addressed the black waiter. "Beer."

He felt the gaze of the others on his back, but he ignored them.

"Hey," the one called Buck asked, "you got a big rattlesnake hatband and rattles on that Stetson. You kill it yourself?"

Diablo nodded as he took his beer and moved

across the scarlet carpet to a comfortable chair with its back against a wall and sat down. Play at the poker table seemed suspended.

"Hell," snorted a short man in a derby hat, "it ain't no big thing to kill a giant rattler. Anyone can shoot them."

Diablo drilled him with his hard stare. "I didn't shoot it. When it struck at me, I put my foot on its head and killed it with my knife."

The man with the ponytail raised his bushy eyebrows, and the light reflected off the silver conchos on his leather vest. "Man has to be fast as greased lightnin' to kill a snake that way."

Diablo didn't answer, and he knew they all stared at his rattler hatband with the dozen rattles still attached. Now he took out a fresh cigarillo, stuck it in his mouth, and gazed out the window.

"Hey, half-breed, you need a light?" The one called Buck half rose from his chair, his voice challenging. He wore big spurs, and when he moved, they rattled like the tin pans on a peddler's cart.

The others tried to shush him.

Diablo was in no mood to kill someone today. He merely looked at the challenger, dark eyes glowering, and the man sat down suddenly.

"Well, boys," Buck huffed, his dirty, freckled hands as nervous as his unshaven face, "let's get this game goin', shall we?"

Diablo watched the country gliding past the train windows for a long moment. They were only hours from Wyoming, and he was weary of the long trip. He reached for a newspaper on the nearby table. Cimarron Durango had taught him to read, and that made up for his loneliness. The others raised their heads and watched him as if astounded that a gunfighter was reading, then returned to their poker game.

Sunny sat between her father and Hurd Kruger as Hurd drove the buggy along the dusty road toward the train station in the town of Casper. Early spring flowers now bloomed along the way and in the fields where hundreds of cattle grazed.

"Thank you, Mr. Kruger, for inviting me along," she said politely, looking up at him. He was a big, beefy man with yellow teeth that he sucked constantly. His hair and mustache were coal black, and when he sweated, little drops of dye ran down the sides of his ruddy face.

"Now, Sunny, dear, you ought to at least call me Hurd. I'm not really your uncle."

The way he looked at her made her feel uneasy. He'd been looking at her that way ever since she'd gone into her teens, and now that she was eighteen, he looked at her that way more and more often. She brushed a blond wisp back under her pale blue bonnet. "All right," she agreed and looked over at her father. Swen Sorrenson did not look pleased.

"Hurd, I still don't think much of this idea," he said, his Danish accent still strong after all these years.

"Now, Swen, we've been through this before, and anyway, we shouldn't discuss this in front of our Sunny, should we?"

It upset her that her father seemed uneasy. Her mother had died giving birth to her, and Sunny felt obliged and guilty about Dad's loss. If it hadn't been for his obligations in raising a daughter in this rough land, he might have remarried or even returned to

Denmark. He had always seemed frail and ill suited to this wild wilderness.

"Uncle Hurd, I mean Hurd, why are we going to town?" she asked.

"Business. The Stock Growers Association business. You know I am the president. But don't you worry your pretty little head about that, Sunny—you can go shoppin' while your dad and I tend to it."

That didn't account for the unhappy look in Swen's pale blue eyes, but she decided not to ask any more questions. A trip to a big town was a rare treat for a ranch girl.

They were approaching the town, and her excitement built. In the distance, she heard the distinctive wail of a train whistle. "Oh, a train! Who do you suppose is coming in?"

Her father started to say something, then closed his mouth.

"Some men," Hurd said, sucking his teeth, "part of the cattlemen's business."

They came into town on the main road and headed toward the train station. Others were gathering, too. The arrival of a train in this small, isolated town was big news.

They pulled into the station, and Hurd got down and tied the horse to the hitching rail. Then he came around to help Sunny out of the buggy, but her father got there first.

Hurd frowned. "Now, Sunny, dear, you go along and shop. Your dad and I and some of the other members will meet the train."

"But it's so exciting!" she protested, shaking the dust from her pale blue cotton dress and readjusting her skewed bonnet, "I want to see who's getting off."

"Next year," Swen said to her with a smile, "maybe you will ride the train to Boston and go to college."

Hurd frowned. "Aw, don't put such highfalutin ideas in her head, Swen. Maybe she'll want to get married instead. There ain't much need for a ranch wife to get an education."

Swen looked like he might disagree, but instead, pulled his Stetson down over his sparse hair as pale as Sunny's and turned toward the station.

The crowd of curious onlookers was growing on the platform as the trio joined them. In the distance, Sunny could see the smoke from the engine and hear the whistle as it chugged toward the town.

"Casper! Coming into Casper!" The conductor walked up and down the aisle and into the next car, "Casper next stop!"

On the sidewalk near the station, Sunny Sorrenson smiled at her father. "Oh, Dad, I never saw a train up close!"

"Yes, dear." Swen smiled back at her with eyes as blue as hers. "Hurd's been expecting it."

"Yep, this is a special train." Hurd walked toward them, smiling. "Now we'll get some action."

"What's going on?" Sunny smiled up at him. She was petite next to the big man.

"Now, sweetheart, never mind." Hurd paused in sucking his yellow teeth and nodded. "It's just cattle business—nothing to worry your pretty little head about."

"All right, Uncle Hurd." She saw a slight look of worry pass over her father's tanned face. He didn't often disagree with Hurd Kruger, their neighbor from the big

K Bar ranch, especially since Hurd held the mortgage on their small spread and had been extra nice to them.

The train pulled into the station, puffing and blowing acrid smoke. People started gathering on the platform. The train arrival was always a big event in town. The three of them walked to the station in time to see the conductor step down and begin unloading baggage. After a moment, the passengers began to disembark. They were all men—tough-looking, weathered men, all wearing gun belts. The newcomers looked over the crowd, not smiling, then strode to the stock car, started unloading horses.

Sunny shielded her pale eyes from the sun. "Look at all those cowboys. Do you think they'll be able to find work here? I thought there were plenty in the area."

"Uh," her father cleared his throat, "Hurd brought them in."

"Be quiet, Swen," the other man snapped; then he smiled at her and said, "Now, Sunny, dear, why don't you run along and do some shopping? We men have things to discuss."

There was something wrong here, but she wasn't quite sure what it was. There must be almost twenty-five or thirty of these tough-looking cowboys milling about on the platform, gathering up their carpetbags and unloading their horses.

A tall, straight man with a mustache got off the train and strode over to them, smiling. "Well, Mr. Kruger, I brought them. Handpicked them, too, twenty-five or so of the best from Texas."

"Shut up, Canton," Hurd said, glancing at her. "We'll talk later."

She felt the men were withholding something because of her, but she was always obedient, as was expected of a young lady, so she walked away down the platform as Canton, Dad, and Hurd went to meet some of those men. They gathered and began to talk as she looked up at the train.

Then one final man stepped into the doorway of the railcar, looking about as if checking out the landscape. He caught her attention because he was so different from the others—taller and darker. He was dressed all in black, his Stetson pulled low over his dark face, and he wore moccasins instead of boots. From here, she could see the left side of his face, and he was handsome, with dark eyes and just wisps of very black hair showing beneath his hat. *A half-breed,* she thought. Unlike the others, he wore no silver conchos or spurs, and his pistol and gun belt were very plain and worn low and tied down. This was no ordinary cowboy, she realized with a sudden interest.

At that point, he turned his face toward her, and she took a deep breath and stepped backward in shock. While the left side of his face was handsome, the right side was scarred and twisted. "Oh, dear Lord," she whispered, trying not to stare but unable to take her eyes off the stranger.

He seemed to sense her horror, and he winced and turned quickly away so that his right side was hidden again.

Diablo watched her from the car step. He was almost hypnotized by the girl. She was certainly not yet twenty, and small. Her blue dress accentuated her eyes, which were as pale as a Texas sky, and her hair was lighter than corn silk. The tight waist accentuated her tiny body, and she was fragile and delicate, almost too delicate to be in this cold, harsh country. He had never seen anything like her before. He found himself staring at her full, pink lips, and without thinking, he turned his head to get a better look.

Too late he saw her hand go to her mouth and the way she stepped backward in dismay. Diablo turned his face away, too aware that his scarred face had frightened her, and the old anger arose in him. He would always have this effect on women, always. The fact made him angry with the beautiful, petite girl, although he knew it was not her fault.

Two men walked up to join the girl, not looking at Diablo. The older one had wispy hair, almost snow blond, and eyes as pale as the girl's. The other was middle-aged, perhaps in his forties with a small potbelly, and hair and mustache dyed too black to hide the gray.

Diablo's hand went to his pistol as the old memories flooded back. Then he forced himself to concentrate and not think of that long-ago day. He would pick the day and time, and this was not it. He grabbed his carpetbag and stepped back into the shadows of the car door so the men would not see him. He stared at the girl again, thinking he had never seen anything so fragile and beautiful. He wanted her as a man wants a woman, but was angry because she had recoiled from him. What could he expect? Didn't women always shrink back from his ugly face? And yet, he always hoped there would be one who wouldn't. Sunny, yes, that was what they had called her, and that was a good name for her. This girl was a magnificent princess; she could have any man she wanted, and she would not want him. He sighed and turned his attention again to the men congregating on the platform.

The man called Canton had joined the other two,

and everyone's attention was on the crowd of gunfighters as they gathered around.

Diablo heard the big man say something to the girl about going shopping. She nodded, but Diablo saw that she was still staring back at him in a sort of horrid fascination.

"But Uncle Hurd, what about you and Dad?" the girl asked.

"We've got Stock Growers Association business to tend to. Now don't worry your pretty little head—you just run on, and we'll meet up with you later in the day. Here"—the big man reached into his pocket—"here's some extra money to spend."

The older man objected. "But Hurd, I give her money already."

"So I give her some more. I've got plenty to spoil her."

The girl tried not to accept it. "Oh, Uncle Hurd, it's too much—"

"Nonsense. Now you run along and buy yourself something nice to wear at the party I might give soon."

The girl took the money, hugged both the two men, and left. Diablo's gaze followed her until she disappeared down the brick sidewalk and past the station. Then he watched the two men she had accompanied, and a terrible rage built in him as he remembered something too horrible to be voiced.

After fifteen years, he had returned as he had always promised himself he would. He cared nothing for the cattlemen's war. Diablo had come to Wyoming for one reason and for one reason only: he had come to torture and kill certain men, and one of them was one of the two men the girl had embraced.

RIO

Padraic Kelly looked around at the cactus and barren land, then chafed at the hemp rope around his neck that also tied his hands behind him. The oxcart he stood in creaked under his feet as the animal stamped its hooves in impatience at the smell of blood and gunpowder.

In the gray light of dawn, the roar of cannons and the screams of dying men echoed across the desert battleground.

Ah, but by Saint Mary's blood, the delay would not be long enough for the thirty condemned soldiers. Padraic turned his head and looked down the line of other men standing in oxcarts, ropes around their necks. Some of them seemed in shock, some had their eyes closed, praying to the saints for a miracle.

There'd be no miracles this morning, Padraic thought bitterly and wished he could reach his rosary, but it was tucked in the breast pocket of his uniform. It was ironic somehow that he had fled the starvation of Ireland to come to America and now his new country was going to execute him.

The colonel walked up and down the line of oxcarts, the early sun glinting off his brass buttons.

"Beggin' your pardon, sir," Padraic called, "for the love of mercy, could ye hand me my holy beads?"

The colonel sneered, his tiny mustache wiggling on his ruddy face. "Aw, you papist traitor! You'll not need your silly beads when the flag falls. We're sending all you Irish traitors to hell, where you belong."

He should have known better than to ask the Protestant officer for help. Hadn't he and most of the other officers treated all the new immigrants with disdain and bullying, which was the very reason some of the St. Patrick's battalion had gone over to the Mexican side? It hadn't seemed right, fighting fellow Catholics just because America had declared war on Mexico.

A curious crowd of peasants gathered, most with sympathetic faces, but the American soldiers held them back. There was nothing the unarmed peasants could do to rescue all these condemned men.

Padraic mouthed a silent prayer as he stared at the distant castle on the horizon. The early sun reflected off steel and gun barrels as the soldiers of both sides battled for control of the landmark. Smoke rose and men screamed and Padraic held his breath, watching the Mexican flag flying from the parapet.

"Yes, watch it!" The colonel glared up at him. "For when it falls and is replaced by the stars and stripes, you cowardly traitors will die!"

The Mexicans seemed determined to hold the castle as the hours passed, and the sun moved across the sky with relentless heat, throwing shadows of the condemned men in long, distorted figures across the sand.

Padraic's legs ached from hours of standing in the cart and his mouth was so dry, he could hardly mouth prayers anymore. Behind him he heard others in the oxcarts begging for water. Padraic was proud; he would not beg, though he was faint from the heat and the sweat that drenched his blue uniform. He knew they would not give the condemned water anyway. Their guards did bring water to the oxen and Padraic tried not to watch the beasts drinking it.

In one of the carts, a man fainted and the colonel yelled for a soldier to throw water on him. "I don't want him to miss that flag coming down!" he yelled.

Padraic could only guess how many hours had passed from the way the sun slanted now in the west. The castle itself was cloaked in smoke and flames. He began to wish it would soon be over. Better to be dead than to stand here waiting all day in the hot sun for the hanging.

Sweat ran from his black hair and down the collar of his wool Mexican uniform. God, he would give his spot in Paradise for one sip of cool water. Well, his discomfort would soon be over. He didn't regret that he had fled the U.S. Army; he had done it because of his love for a Mexican girl. That love had transcended everything else. He did regret so many had followed him, some of them so young and barely off the boat. They had been escaping from the potato famine, but now they would die anyway.

The heat made dizzying waves across the barren landscape and he staggered a little and regained his footing. If he must die, he would go out like a man.

The crowd of sympathetic peasants was growing as word must have spread that the Americans were hanging their deserters. Padraic looked around for Conchita, hoping yet dreading to see her. He did not want his love to see him die this way.

Hail Mary, Mother of God . . . he murmured the prayer automatically and he was once again a small boy at his mother's knee as they said their beads together. Now she would never know what happened to her son who had set off for the promise of America. It was just as well. He'd rather her think he was happy and successful than know he had been hanged like a common thief.

The riches of the new country had not been good, with so many Irish flooding in and everyone hating and sneering at the immigrants. If he could have found a job, he wouldn't have joined the army, but no one wanted to hire the Irish.

The fighting in the distance seemed to be slowing, though he choked on the acrid smell of cannon smoke and watched the castle burning in the distance. The Mexican flag flew bravely on the parapet, but he could see the bright blue of the American uniforms like tiny ants as the invaders attacked the castle. It wouldn't be long now. The ropes bit into his wrists and he would give his soul for a sip of cold water, but he knew better than to ask. He closed his eyes and thought about the clear streams and the green pastures of County Kerry. He was a little boy again in ragged clothes, chasing the sheep toward the pens with no cares in the world save hoping for a brisk cup of tea and a big kettle of steaming potatoes as he ran toward the tumbledown stone cottage.

If only he could see Conchita once more. He smiled despite his misery and remembered the joy of the past three months. The pretty girl had been the one bright spot in his short, miserable life. He closed his eyes and imagined her in his arms again: her kisses, the warmth of her skin. He hoped she had not heard about the court-martial and the public hangings. He did not want her to see him die, swinging and choking at the end of a rope like a common criminal.

The rope rasped against his throat, the ox stamped its feet, and the cart creaked while Padraic struggled to maintain his balance. The colonel had stood them here all afternoon, and now he almost wished the cart would pull ahead because he was so miserable, with his throat dry as the barren sand around him and his arms aching from being tied behind while his legs threatened to buckle under him. *No,* he reminded himself, *you are going to die like a man, and a soldier. You just happen to be on the losing side.*

In the distance, he could see the blue uniforms climbing ladders up the sides of the castle as the fighting grew more intense. Screams of dying men mixed with the thunder of cannons and the victorious shrieks as the Americans charged forward, overrunning the castle now as the sun became a bloody ball of fire to the west.

The ruddy colonel grinned and nodded up at Padraic. "It won't be long now, you Mick trash. I knew I could never turn you Irish into soldiers."

"If ye'd treated us better, we wouldn't have gone over to the other side, maybe," Padraic murmured.

The colonel sneered. "And look what you get! We're hanging more than the thirty I've got here. General Scott asked President Polk to make an example of the Saint Patrick's battalion. If it'd been up to me, I'd have hung the whole lot, especially that John Riley that led you."

"Some of them would rather have been hung than to have been lashed and branded," Padraic snarled.

"It's better than being dead," the colonel said. Then he turned and yelled at the soldiers holding back the

Mexican peasants. "Keep those brown bastards back. We don't want them close enough to interfere with the hanging."

Padraic watched the peasants. Some of them were on their knees, saying their rosaries, others looking up at them gratefully with tears making trails down their dusty brown faces.

"Paddy, dearest!" He turned his head to see Conchita attempting to fight her way past the soldiers.

"Hold that bitch back!" the colonel bellowed. "Don't let her through the lines."

"Get your filthy hands off her!" Padraic yelled and struggled to break free, although he knew it was useless. Conchita was so slim and small and her black hair had come loose and blew about her lovely face as she looked toward him and called his name.

There was too much roar of battle now as the Yankees overran the castle for her to hear him, but he mouthed the words, *I love you. You are the best thing that has happened to me since I crossed the Rio Grande.*

She nodded that she understood and her face was so sad that he looked away, knowing that to see her cry would make him cry, too, and he intended to die like a man.

A victorious roar went up from the American troops as they finally fought their way to the top of the distant tower. It would only be a few moments now.

"Take her away," Padraic begged his guards. "I don't want her to see this!"

The colonel only laughed. "No, we want all these Mexicans to see what happens to traitors. Why don't you beg, Kelly? Don't you want your little greasy sweetheart to see you beg for your life?"

In the distance, the American soldiers were taking

down the ragged Mexican flag, but even as it came down, one of the young Mexican cadets grabbed it from the victors' hands and as they tried to retrieve it, he ran to the edge of the parapet and flung himself over the edge to the blood-soaked ground so far below. The Mexican peasants sent up a cheer, which the colonel could not silence with all his shouting. The cadet had died rather than surrender his country's flag to the enemy.

Now the American flag was going up, silhouetted against the setting sun. The peasants shouted a protest as soldiers climbed up on the oxcarts and checked the nooses.

"No! No! Do not hang them!"

Conchita screamed again and tried to break through the line of solders holding back the crowd. "Paddy! My dear one!" She couldn't get to him, although she clawed and fought.

Padraic smiled at her and gave her an encouraging nod. If only things were different. He would have built a mud hut on this side of the Rio Grande and lived his life happily with this woman. If only he could hold her in his arms and kiss those lips once more.

Conchita looked up at him, her brave, tall man with his fair skin and wide shoulders. She made one more attempt to break through the guards, but they held her back. A roar of protests went up around her from the other peasants. He was her man and they were going to execute him and there was nothing she could do to stop it. She screamed his name and tried to tell him the secret, shouting that she carried his child, but in the noise of distant gunfire and the peasants yelling, she wasn't sure he understood, although he smiled and nodded at her and mouthed *I love you, too.*

"Your child!" she shrieked again. "I carry your child!"

At that precise moment, she heard the officer bark an order and all the oxcarts creaked forward. For just a split second, the condemned men swayed, struggling to keep their balance, and then the carts pulled out from under the long line of soldiers and their feet danced on air as they swung at the end of their ropes.

Conchita watched in frozen horror and tried to get to her Paddy as he fought for air, but the soldiers held her back. Her eyes filled with tears and the sight of the men hanging grew dim as they ceased to struggle.

"This is what the U.S. Army does to traitors and deserters!" the colonel announced to the crowd with satisfaction.

Conchita burst into sobs. She was in great pain as if her heart had just been torn from her breast. She did not want to live without her love, but she must, for his child's sake. She was not even sure he had heard her as she tried to tell him he would be a father. If it was a boy, she would raise that son and call him Rio Kelly for his father and the river that made a boundary between the two civilizations. And then she would go into a cloistered order and spend her life praying for the souls of her love and the other condemned men.

The soldiers were cutting the thirty bodies down now, and she broke through the line of guards and ran to her Paddy as he lay like a tattered bundle of rags on the sand. She threw herself on the body, weeping and kissing his face, but his soul had fled to his God and he could no longer feel her kisses and caresses.

Only now did she realize he had died smiling and so she knew he had heard her and knew he would have a child.

To My Readers:

As I have told you in this story, the Second Cavalry was the army's crack unit and the equivalent of today's Special Forces. Each soldier was handpicked and specially equipped with all the best in weapons and supplies, including new uniforms, the first to have the yellow stripes down the pants; the new five-shot Colt pistol; and fine, color-matched thoroughbred horses that did poorly on the Texas plains. The Second Cav was the darling of U.S. secretary of war Jefferson Davis (the future president of the Confederacy), and was conceived in 1855 as the answer to the dangerous Comanches wreaking havoc in the Lone Star State.

Sixteen of the officers who accepted positions in the Second Cav went on to become generals in the Civil War. Half of the Confederate generals had served with the Second Cav. Some of the famous men who served in Texas with the Second Cavalry were: Robert E. Lee, John Bell Hood, George Thomas, Fitzhugh Lee, and Albert Sidney Johnston. These officers served together in Texas and then went home to fight each other in the Civil War. An excellent research book on the subject is *Jeff Davis's Own: Cavalry, Comanches, and the Battle for the Texas Frontier* by James R. Arnold, Castle Books, John Wiley & Sons, Hoboken, New Jersey.

The Comanches were the deadly scourge of Texas as they defended territory they had held for hundreds of years, first against the Spanish, the Mexicans, and then against the white pioneers who wanted the land for ranches and farms. For more about this tribe, I suggest these excellent resource books: *Comanche: The Destruction of a People* by T.R. Fehrenbach, and *The Comanche: Lords of the South Plains,* by Ernest Wallace & E. Adamson

Hoebel, University of Oklahoma Press, Norman, Oklahoma.

The well-known Cynthia Ann Parker was carried off at the age of nine by the Comanche in the year 1836. She was recovered by the Texas Rangers and returned to her family in 1860. With her was her baby, Prairie Flower. Cynthia Ann left behind two half-Comanche sons. One of them died and the other would become the last chief of the Comanche, Quanah Parker. Cynthia did not adjust well to white society and tried to escape back to the Comanche. Her baby girl died and Cynthia Ann died soon after in 1870. Today, she is buried next to her son, the great Chief Quanah in the Fort Sill cemetery in Lawton, Oklahoma. The John Wayne movie *The Searchers* is based on the abduction of Cynthia Ann.

As my imaginary hero Colt predicted, when the Civil War began in 1861 and all the United States troops left Texas, the Comanches took full advantage of their absence to wreak havoc on outlying settlements and ranches. Their war against the white invaders would not cease until 1874 when Colonel Ranald MacKenzie defeated them and forced them all to move to a reservation at Fort Sill. The Indians had fought fiercely, but they were no match for the power and military might of the U.S. Army. A good reference book on this is: *The Buffalo War* by James L. Haley, Oklahoma University Press, Norman, Oklahoma.

Texas was a nation from 1836 until she joined the Union in 1845. Sam Houston, who had struggled to get Texas into the Union, did his best to keep her there, but hotheads prevailed and Texas seceded and joined the Confederacy in 1860. Two excellent books on Texas are: *Lone Star: A History of Texas and the Texans* by T.R. Fehrenbach, American Legacy Press, Crown

Publishers, New York. Also: *Passionate Nation: The Epic History of Texas* by James L. Haley, Free Press, a division of Simon & Schuster, New York.

Remember that our heroine, Hannah, mentions that her father was killed in the Fannin Massacre, also known as the Goliad Massacre. A few days after the Alamo fell, Colonel Fannin and hundreds of his troops, surrounded and out of supplies, surrendered to the Mexicans on an agreement that the soldiers would be well treated as prisoners of war. Instead, General Santa Anna ordered that they all be executed and they were slaughtered on Palm Sunday, March 27, 1836. Only a handful escaped to tell the story. A few of the prisoners were spared because of the pleas of a girl known as "The Angel of Goliad," and she is herself one of Texas's most beloved legends.

I know someone is going to write and ask why I don't have the soldiers playing taps at the funeral services in this story. It might interest you to know the bugle call we know as "taps" didn't exist in 1856. It won't be written until 1862, during the Civil War.

For some of you who don't live in the Southwest, the Osage Orange tree, also known as "horse-apple, "Bodark," or "Bois D'Arc" —that's the wood Colt carves into a wooden horse for little Travis—was the principal wood used by plains tribes to make bows. It bears a hard, green seed ball about the size of an orange. I own a beautiful belt buckle made from this wood.

My faithful readers know that all my stories connect in some manner, so Colt Prescott, as a small boy, was with the wagon train from which Texanna was kidnapped by War Bonnet in my very first book: *Cheyenne Captive*.

Also, when he and Sergeant Mulvaney are discussing hanging the Irish soldiers who had revolted during the

Mexican American War, that event connects to my last book: *Rio.* Rio's father was one of the men hanged.

In this series, *The Texans,* I've had a gunfighter, Diablo; a vaquero, Rio; a Cavalry officer, Colt; and next, a Texas Ranger, Travis. This next story will be about Travis Prescott, who grows up to become a Texas Ranger.

Half-Comanche Travis, a confirmed bachelor, and his old dog are only looking for a peaceful and early retirement since Travis was injured in a shootout with outlaws. Of course that's not what he's going to get. He's about to meet a saloon tart named Violet, disguised as an innocent schoolgirl, and four children she's rescued from an orphan train. The kids are on the run from the mean supervisor of the orphanage and Violet's escaping from the deadly gambler who owns the saloon and wants her back.

Unwittingly, Travis is about to get involved with all five of the runaways, plus some very indignant upright citizens who want to help find him a respectable wife and mother for all those children. Of course, there'll be a showdown with the tough gambler and his hired gunfighter. Maybe Travis is not going to find the peaceful bachelor life he is hankering for, but he just might find love and a ready-made family. Look for *Travis: The Texans*, coming probably in 2013.

You can order some of my past books at most bookstores or from kensingtonbooks.com. Also a number of them are now out in the new e-books for electronic readers. I realize some of my earliest books are difficult to find. Perhaps someday Kensington will reprint them.

I have a website: georginagentrybooks.com. Or you may write me at: Box 162, Edmond, OK 73083.

Wishing you romance and happiness,
Georgina Gentry